Sophia's Secret

SUSANNA KEARSLEY

Allison & Busby Limited
13 Charlotte Mews
London W1T 4EJ
www.allisonandbusby.com

Hardback and trade paperback editions published
in Great Britain as *The Winter Sea* in 2008.
This mass market paperback edition first published in 2008.

'On the Shore' by EJ Pratt, from *Complete Poems*
edited by Sandra Djwa and RG Moyles,
University of Toronto Press © 1989.
Reprinted with permission of the publisher.

A CIP catalogue record for this book is available from
the British Library.

10 9 8 7 6 5 4

ISBN 978-0-7490-8078-5

Typeset in Sabon by
Terry Shannon.

The paper used for this Allison & Busby publication
has been produced from trees that have been legally sourced
from well-managed and credibly certified forests.

Printed and bound by
CPI Group (UK) Ltd, Croydon, CR0 4YY

To My Father:

You asked me once to write for you a story
you could love as much as you loved Mariana, so...

For all that you have given me,
and all that you have helped me be,
this book is yours,
with love.

Come home! The year has left you old;
Leave those grey stones; wrap close this shawl
Around you for the night is cold;
Come home! He will not hear you call;

No sign awaits you here but the beat
Of tides upon the strand,
The crag's gaunt shadow with gull's feet
Imprinted on the sand,
And spars and sea-weed strewn
Under a pale moon.

Come home! He will not hear you call;
Only the night winds answer as they fall
Along the shore,
And evermore
Only the sea-shells
On the grey stones singing,
And the white foam-bells
Of the North Sea ringing.

E. J. Pratt, 'On the Shore'

Chapter One

It wasn't chance. There wasn't any part of it that happened just by chance.

I learnt this later; though the realisation, when it came, was hard for me to grasp because I'd always had a firm belief in self-determination. My life so far had seemed to bear this out – I'd chosen certain paths and they had led to certain ends, all good, and any minor bumps that I had met along the way I could accept as not bad luck, but simply products of my own imperfect judgement. If I'd had to choose a creed, it would have been the poet William Henley's bravely ringing lines: *I am the master of my fate; I am the captain of my soul.*

So on that winter morning when it all began, when I first took my rental car and headed north from Aberdeen, it never once occurred to me that someone else's hand was at the helm.

I honestly believed it was my own decision, turning off the main road for the smaller one that ran along the coastline. Not the wisest of decisions, maybe, seeing as the roads were edged with what I'd been assured was Scotland's deepest snow in forty years, and I'd been warned I might run into drifting and delays. Caution and the knowledge I was running on a schedule should have kept me to the more well-travelled highway, but the small sign that said 'Coastal Route' diverted me.

My father always told me that the sea was in my blood. I had been born and raised beside it on the shores of Nova Scotia, and I never could resist its siren pull. So when the main road out of Aberdeen turned inland I turned right instead, and took the way along the coast.

I couldn't say how far away I was when I first saw the ruined castle on the cliffs, a line of jagged darkness set against a cloud-filled sky, but from the moment I first saw it I was captivated, driving slightly faster in the hope I'd reach it sooner, paying no attention to the clustered houses I was driving past, and feeling disappointment when the road curved sharply off again, away from it. But then, beyond the tangle of a wood, the road curved back again, and there it was: a long dark ruin, sharp against the snowbound fields that stretched forbiddingly between the cliff's edge and the road.

I saw a car park up ahead, a little level place with logs to mark the spaces for the cars, and on an impulse I pulled in and stopped.

It was empty. Not surprising, since it wasn't even noon yet, and the day was cold and windy, and there wasn't any reason anyone would stop out here unless they wanted to walk out to see the ruin. And from looking at the only path that I could see that led to it – a frozen farm lane drifted deep with snow that would have risen past my knees – I guessed there wouldn't be too many people stopping here today.

I knew I shouldn't stop, myself. There wasn't time. I had to be in Peterhead by one o'clock. But something in me felt a sudden need to know exactly where I was, and so I reached to check my map.

I'd spent the past five months in France; I'd bought my map there, and it had its limitations, being more concerned with roads and highways than with towns and ruins. I was looking so hard at the squiggle of coastline and trying to make out the names in fine print that I didn't see the man till he'd gone past me, walking slowly, hands in pockets, with a muddy-footed spaniel at his heels.

It seemed a strange place for a man on foot to be, out here. The road was busy and the snow along the banks left little room to walk beside it, but I didn't question his appearance. Any time I had a choice between a living, breathing person and a map, I chose the person. So I scrambled, map in hand, and got my car door open, but the salt wind blowing off the sea across the fields was stronger than I'd thought it would be. It stole my voice. I had to try again. 'Excuse me…'

I believe the spaniel heard me first. It turned, and then the man turned too, and seeing me, retraced his steps. He was a younger man than I'd expected, not much older than myself – mid-thirties, maybe, with dark hair whipped roughly by the wind and a close-trimmed dark beard that made him look a little like a pirate. His walk, too, had a swagger to it, confident. He asked me, 'Can I help you?'

'Can you show me where I am?' I held the map towards him.

Coming round to block the wind, he stood beside me, head bent to the printed coastline. 'Here,' he said, and pointed to a nameless headland. 'Cruden Bay. Where are ye meant to be?' His head turned very slightly as he asked that, and I saw his eyes were not a pirate's eyes. They were clear grey, and friendly, and his voice was friendly too, with all the pleasant, rolling cadence of the northern Scot.

I said, 'I'm going north, to Peterhead.'

'Well, that's not a problem.' He pointed it out on the map. 'It's not far. You just keep on this road, it'll take you right up into Peterhead.' Close by his knee the dog yawned a complaint, and he sighed and looked down. 'Half a minute. You see that I'm talking?'

I smiled. 'What's his name?'

'Angus.'

Bending, I scratched the dog's hanging ears, spattered with mud. 'Hello, Angus. You've been for a run.'

'Aye, he'd run all the day if I'd let him. He's not one for standing still.'

Neither, I thought, was his master. The man had an aura of energy, restlessness, and I'd delayed him enough. 'Then I'll let you get going,' I said as I straightened. 'Thank you for your help.'

'Nae bother,' he assured me, and he turned and started off again, the spaniel trotting happily ahead.

The hardened footpath stretched ahead of them, towards the sea, and at its end I saw the castle ruin standing stark and square and roofless to the swiftly running clouds, and as I looked at it I felt a sudden pulling urge to stay – to leave the car parked where it was and follow man and dog where they had gone, and hear the roaring of the sea around those crumbled walls.

But I had promises to keep.

So with reluctance, I got back into my rental car, turned the key and started off again towards the north.

* * *

'You're somewhere else.' Jane's voice, accusing me but gently, broke my thoughts.

We were sitting in the upstairs bedroom of her house in Peterhead, the bedroom with the little chains of rosebuds on the wallpaper, away from the commotion of the gathering downstairs. I gave myself a mental shake, and smiled. 'I'm not, I—'

'Carolyn McClelland,' she said, using my full first name in the way she always did when catching me about to tell a lie, 'I've been your agent for nearly seven years, I can't be fooled. Is it the book?' Her eyes were keen. 'I shouldn't have dragged you over here like this, should I? Not when you were writing.'

'Don't be silly. There are more important things,' I said, 'than writing.' And to show how much I meant that, I leant forward for another close look at the sleeping baby wrapped in blankets on her lap. 'He's really beautiful.'

'He is, rather, isn't he?' Proudly, she followed my gaze. 'Alan's mum says he looks just like Alan did.'

I couldn't see it. 'He's got more of you in him, I think. Just look at that hair.'

'Oh, the hair, God, yes, poor little chap,' she said, touching the bright copper-gold softness of the small head. 'I did hope he'd be spared that. He'll freckle, you know.'

'But freckles look so cute on little boys.'

'Yes, well, be sure you come and tell him that, when he's sixteen and cursing me.'

'At least,' I said, 'he won't begrudge the name you gave him. Jack's a nice, good, manly name.'

'The choice of desperation. I was hoping for something that sounded more Scottish, but Alan was so bloody-minded. Every time I came up with a name he'd say, "No, we had a dog called that", and that would be the end of it. Honestly, Carrie, I thought for a while we'd be having him christened as "Baby boy Ramsay".'

But of course they hadn't. Jane and Alan always found a way around their differences, and little Jack Ramsay had made it to church today, with me arriving in time to stand up as his godmother. That I'd managed to do it only by breaking every speed limit between my stop in Cruden Bay and here had left the baby so supremely unimpressed that, when he'd first laid eyes on me, he'd yawned and fallen fast asleep, not even waking when the minister had doused his head with water.

'Is he always so calm?' I asked now, as I looked at him.

'What, didn't you think I could have a calm baby?' Jane's eyes teased me, because she knew her own nature. She wasn't what I would have called a calm person. She had a strong will; she was driven, and vibrant, so very alive that she made me feel colourless, somehow, beside her. And tired. I couldn't keep up.

It didn't help that I'd been struck by some virus last month that had kept me in bed over Christmas and taken the fun out of New Year's and now, a week later, I still wasn't back to full speed. But even when I was in good health, Jane's energy level was miles above mine.

That was why we worked so well together; why I'd chosen her. I wasn't any good myself with publishers – I gave in far too easily. I couldn't stomach conflict, so I'd learnt to leave it all to Jane, and she had fought my battles for me, which was why I found myself, at thirty-one, with four bestselling novels to my credit and the freedom to live anywhere, and anyhow, I chose.

'How is the house in France?' she asked me, coming back, as she inevitably would do, to my work. 'You're still at Saint-Germain-en-Laye?'

'It's fine, thanks. And I'm still there, yes. It helps me get my details right. The palace there is central to the plot, it's where the action mostly happens.' Saint-Germain had been the French king's gift of refuge to the Stewart kings of Scotland for the first years of their exile, where old King James and young King James by turns had held court with their loyal supporters, who'd plotted and schemed with the nobles of Scotland through three luckless Jacobite uprisings. My story was intended to revolve around Nathaniel Hooke, an Irishman at Saint-Germain, who seemed to me to be the perfect hero for a novel.

He'd been born in 1664, a year before the Plague, and only four years after the restoration of King Charles II to the battered throne of England. When King Charles had died and his Catholic brother, James, came to the throne, Hooke had taken up arms in rebellion, but then had changed sides and abandoned his Protestant faith for the Catholic Church, becoming one of James's stout defenders. But it wasn't any use. England was a nation full of Protestants, and any king who called himself a Catholic couldn't hope to keep the throne. James's claim had been challenged by that of his own daughter, Mary, and William of Orange, her husband. And that had meant war.

Nathaniel Hooke had been right in the thick of it. He'd fought for James in Scotland and been captured as a spy, and held a prisoner in the fearsome Tower of London. After his release he'd promptly taken up his sword again and gone to fight for James, and when the battles all were over, and

William and Mary ruled firm on their throne, and James fled into exile, Hooke had gone with him to France.

But he did not accept defeat. Instead, he'd turned his many talents to convincing those around him that a well-planned joint invasion by the French king and the Scots could set things right again, restore the exiled Stewarts to their rightful throne.

They nearly had succeeded.

History remembered the tragic romance of Culloden and Bonnie Prince Charlie, years after Hooke's time. But it was not in that cold winter at Culloden that the Jacobites – quite literally, the 'followers of James', and of the Stewarts – came closest to a realisation of their purpose. No, that happened in the spring of 1708, when an invasion fleet of French and Scottish soldiers, Hooke's idea, anchored off the coast of Scotland in the Firth of Forth. On board the flagship was the tall, twenty-year-old James Stewart – not the James who had fled England, but his son, whom many, not only in Scotland but in England, accepted as their true king. On shore, assembled armies of the highlanders and loyal Scottish nobles waited eagerly to welcome him and turn their might against the weakened armies to the south.

Long months of careful preparations and clandestine plans had come to their fruition, and the golden moment seemed at hand, when once again a Stewart king would claim the throne of England.

How this great adventure failed, and why, was one of the most fascinating stories of the period, a story of intrigue and treachery that all sides had tried hard to cover up and bury, seizing documents, destroying correspondence, spreading rumours and misinformation that had been believed as fact down to the present day.

Most of the details that survived had been recorded by Nathaniel Hooke.

I liked the man. I'd read his letters, and I'd walked the halls of Saint-Germain-en-Laye, where he had walked. I knew the details of his marriage and his children and his relatively long life and his death. So it was frustrating to me that, after five long months of writing, I still struggled with the pages of my novel, and Hooke's character refused to come alive.

I knew Jane sensed that I was having trouble – as she said, she'd known me far too long and far too well to overlook my moods. But she knew, too, I didn't like to talk about my problems, so she took care not to come at me directly. 'Do you know, last weekend I read through those chapters that you sent me—'

'When on earth do you have time to read?'

'There's always time to read. I read those chapters, and I wondered if you'd ever thought of telling things from someone else's point of view…a narrator, you know, the way Fitzgerald does with Nick in *The Great Gatsby*. It occurred to me that someone on the outside could perhaps move round more freely, and link all the scenes together for you. Just a thought.' She left it there, and no doubt knowing that my first response to anyone's advice was staunch resistance, changed the subject.

Nearly twenty minutes later, I was laughing at her dry descriptions of the joys of caring for a newborn, when her husband, Alan, thrust his head around the doorway of the bedroom.

'You do know there's a party going on downstairs?' he asked us, with a scowl I would have taken much more seriously if I hadn't known it was all bluff. He was a softie, on the inside. 'I can't entertain this lot all on my own.'

'Darling,' Jane replied, 'they *are* your relatives.'

'All the more reason not to leave me alone with them.' But he winked at me. 'She's not got you talking shop, I hope? I told her she's to let you be. She's too concerned with contracts.'

Jane reminded him, 'Well, that's my job. And for your information, I am never in the least concerned that Carrie's going to break a contract. She has another seven months before the first draft's due.'

She'd meant for that to cheer me, but I think that Alan must have seen my shoulders sag, because he held his hand to me and said, 'Come on, then. Come downstairs and have a drink, and tell me how the trip was. I'm amazed you made it all that way in time.'

There were enough jokes floating round about my tendency to get distracted when I travelled, so I opted not to tell them anything about my detour up the coast. But it reminded me, 'Alan,' I asked, 'are you flying tomorrow?'

'I am. Why?'

Alan's little fleet of helicopters helped to serve the off-shore oil rigs dotted through the North Sea off the rugged coast of Peterhead. He was a fearless pilot, as I'd learnt the one and only time I'd let him take me up. I'd barely had the legs to stand when he'd returned me to the ground. But now I said, 'I wondered if you'd fly me up the coast a bit. Nathaniel Hooke came over twice from France, to intrigue with the Scottish nobles, and both times he landed at the Earl of Erroll's castle, Slains, which, from the map I've got, the old one, looks to be somewhere just north of here. I'd like to see the castle, or what's left of it, from out at sea, the way it would have looked to Hooke when he first saw it, coming over.'

'Slains? Aye, I can take you over that. But it's not up the coast, it's down. At Cruden Bay.'

I stared. 'Where?'

'Cruden Bay. You would have missed it, coming up the way you did.'

Jane, sharp as ever, noticed something in my face, in my expression. 'What?' she asked.

I never ceased to be surprised by serendipity – the way chance happenings collided with my life. Of all the places that I could have stopped, I thought. Aloud I only said, 'It's nothing. Could we go tomorrow, Alan?'

'Aye. Tell you what – I'll take you early so that you can have your look from out at sea, and if you want when we get back I'll watch wee Jack awhile and Jane can drive you down to have a wander round. It'll do you both good, get a breath of sea air.'

And so that's what we did.

What I saw from the air looked much larger than what I had seen from the ground – a roofless, sprawling ruin that seemed to sit right at the edge of the cliffs, with the sea boiling white far below. It sent one small cold thrill down my spine, and I knew that familiar sensation enough to be frankly impatient to get on the ground, so that Jane could take over and drive me back down.

There were two other cars in the car park this time, and the snow of the footpath showed deep, sliding prints. I ploughed ahead of Jane, and raised my face towards the salt blasts of the wind that left a taste upon my lips and set me shivering again within the warm folds of my jacket.

I confess I couldn't, afterwards, remember any other people

being there, although I knew there had been. Nor could I recall too many details of the ruin itself – just images, of pointed walls and hard pink granite flecked with grey that glittered in the light...the one high square-walled tower standing solid near the cliff's edge...the silence of the inner chambers, where the wind stopped raging and began to moan and weep, and where the bare roof timbers overhead cast shadows on the drifted snow. In one large room a massive gaping window faced the sea, and when I stood and leant my hands against the sunwarmed sill I noticed, looking down, the imprints of a small dog's paws, perhaps a spaniel's, and beside them deeper footprints showing where a man had stood and looked, as I was looking, out towards the limitless horizon.

I could almost feel him standing at my shoulder now, but in my mind he'd changed so that he wasn't any more the modern stranger I had talked to in the car park yesterday, but someone of an older time, a man with boots and cloak and sword. The thought of him became so real I turned...and found Jane watching me.

She smiled at the expression on my face. She knew it well, from all the times that she'd been present when my characters began to stir, and talk, and take on life. Her voice was casual. 'You know that you can always come and stay with us, and work. We have the room.'

I shook my head. 'You have a baby. You don't need a house guest, too.'

She looked at me again, and what she saw made her decide. 'Then come on. Let's go down and find a place for you to let in Cruden Bay.'

Chapter Two

Cruden Bay's Main Street sloped gently downhill and bent round to the right and then left again, curving away out of sight to the harbour. It was narrow, a line of joined cottages and a few shops on the one side, and on the other a swiftly running stream that surged between its frozen banks and passed a single shop, a newsagent's, before it ran to meet the wide and empty sweep of beach that stretched away beyond the high snow-covered dunes.

The Post Office was marked by its red sign against the grey stone walls, and by the varied notices displayed in its front window announcing items for sale and upcoming events, including an enticingly named 'Buttery Morning' to be held at the local hall. Inside the shop were postcards, books, some souvenirs for tourists, and a very helpful woman. Yes, she knew of one place in the village that might suit me. A little cottage, basic, nothing fancy on the inside. 'It was old Miss Keith's before she passed away,' she said. 'Her brother has it now, but since he has a house himself down by the harbour, he's no use for it. He lets it out to tourists in the summer.

Winters, there'll be no one there except his sons from time to time, and they're not often home. The younger lad, he likes to travel, and his brother's at the university in Aberdeen, so Jimmy Keith would probably be glad to let you have the place these next few months. I can give him a phone, if you like.'

And so it came to pass that, with a newly purchased pack of postcards stuffed into the pocket of my coat, I walked with Jane along the sidewalk by the rushing stream and down to where the road bent round and changed its name to Harbour Street. The houses here were like the ones along Main Street higher up – still low and joined to one another, and across from them a series of small gardens, some with sheds, sprang up between us and the wide pink beach.

From down here I could see the beach itself was huge, a curve at least two miles long with dunes that rose like hills behind it, casting shadows on the shore. A narrow white wood footbridge spanned the shallow gully of the stream to where those dunes began, but even as I paused and looked at it and wondered if I might have time to go across, Jane said with satisfaction, 'There's the path,' and shepherded me past the bridge and round to where a wide and slushy pathway veered up from the street to climb a good-sized hill. Ward Hill, the woman at the Post Office had called it.

It was a headland, high and rounded, thrusting out above the sea, and as I came up to the top I looked behind and saw I'd climbed above the level of the dunes and had a view not only of the beach, but of the distant houses and the hills beyond. And turning back again I saw, towards the north, the blood-red ruin of Slains castle clear against cliffs of the next headland.

I felt a small thrill. 'Oh, how perfect.'

'I don't know,' Jane said, slowly. 'It looks rather dismal.' She was looking at the cottage, standing all alone here on the hill. It had been rubble-built, with plain square whitewashed walls beneath a roof of old grey slates that dripped with dampness from the melting snow. The windows were small, with their frames peeling paint and the worn blinds inside were pulled down like closed eyelids, as if the small cottage had wearied of watching the endless approach and retreat of the sea.

I reached out to knock at the door. 'It's just lonely.'

'So will you be, if you live up here. Perhaps this wasn't such a good idea.'

'It was your idea.'

'Yes, but what I had in mind was more a cosy little place right in the village, near the shops...'

'This suits me fine.' I knocked again. 'I guess he isn't here yet.'

'Try the bell.'

I hadn't seen the doorbell, buried deep within the tangle of a stubborn climbing vine with tiny leaves that shivered every time the wind blew from the sea. I stretched my hand to press it, but a man's voice from the path behind me warned, 'It winna dee ye ony good, it disna ring. The salt fae the sea ruins the wiring, fast as I fix it. Besides,' said the man, as he came up to join us, 'I'm nae in the hoose tae be hearin ye, am I?' His smile made his rough, almost ugly face instantly likeable. He'd have been well into his sixties, with whitening hair and the fit build and ruddy complexion of someone who'd worked hard outdoors all his life. The woman at the Post Office had seemed sure I'd like him, although she had warned me I might have some trouble understanding him.

'He speaks the Doric,' she had said. 'The language of this area. You'll likely find it difficult to follow what he says.'

I didn't, actually. His speech was broad and quick, and if I'd had to translate every word I might have had a problem, but it wasn't hard to catch the general sense of what he meant when he was talking.

Holding my hand out, I said, 'Mr Keith? Thanks for coming. I'm Carrie McClelland.'

'A pleasure tae meet ye.' His handshake was sure. 'But I'm nae Mr Keith. Ma dad was Mr Keith, and he's been deid and beeried twenty years. Ye ca' me Jimmy.'

'Jimmy, then.'

Jane introduced herself, never content to be out of the action for long. She didn't exactly nudge me to one side, but she was an agent, after all, and though she likely didn't even notice it herself, she liked to take control whenever somebody was bargaining.

She wasn't pushy, really, but she led the conversation, and I hid my smile and let her lead, content to follow after them as Jimmy Keith fitted his key in the lock of the low cottage door, and then with a jiggle and thump of the latch made it swing inwards, scraping the tiles of the floor.

My first impression was one of general dimness, but when the blinds were raised with a rattle and the faded curtains pushed back, I could see the place, although not large, was comfortable – a sitting room, with thinning Persian carpets on the floor, two cushioned armchairs and a sofa, and a long scrubbed wooden table pushed against the farther wall, with wooden kitchen chairs around it. The kitchen had been fitted at the one end of the cottage with the snugness of a galley on a ship. Not many cupboards, nor much countertop, but everything was in its place and useful, from the one sink with its built-in stainless draining board to the small-sized electric stove that had, I guessed, been meant to take the place of the old coal-fired Aga standing solid in its chimney alcove on the back wall.

The Aga, so Jimmy assured me, still worked. 'It's a bit contermacious – that's difficult, like – but it aye heats the room, and ye'll save on the electric.'

Jane, standing by the front door looking up, made a pointed remark about that being handy. 'Do you know,' she said, 'I haven't seen one of these since I rented my first flat.'

I came to gaze up, with Jane, at the little black metal box fixed to the top of the door jamb, with the glassed-in meter and assorted gauges set above it. I had heard of such contraptions, but I'd never seen or used one.

Jimmy Keith looked up as well. 'Michty aye,' he agreed. 'Ye dinna see those ony mair.'

It took 50p coins, he explained, and was fed like a parking meter – run out of coins and the power went off. 'But nae bother,' he promised. He'd sell me a roll of the coins and, when I'd used them all, he'd come open the meter and take them back out and just sell me the coins back again.

Jane gave the box one final doubtful look and turned to carry on with her inspection. There wasn't much left, just a bedroom, not large, at the back, and an unexpectedly roomy bathoom across from it, complete with footed tub and what the British called an 'airing cupboard', open shelves set round a yellow water heater, good for storing towels and drying clothes.

Jane moved to stand beside me. 'Well?'

'I like it.'

'Not much to it.'

'I don't need much when I'm working.'

She considered this, then turned to Jimmy Keith. 'What sort of rent would you be asking?'

Which was my cue, I knew, to leave them to it. Jane had often told me how inept I was at making deals, and she was right. The cost of things had never much concerned me. Someone told me the price, and if I could afford it, I paid it, and didn't waste time wondering if I could have had the thing for less. I had other things to occupy my mind.

I wandered through again into the sitting room, and stood a moment looking out the window at the headland reaching out into the sea, and dark along its length the ruined castle walls of Slains.

Watching, I could feel again the stirrings of my characters – the faint, as yet inaudible, suggestion of their voices, and their movements close around me, in the way someone can sense another's presence in a darkened room. I didn't need to shut my eyes. They were already fixed, not truly seeing, on the window glass, in that strange writer's trance that stole upon me when my characters began to speak, and I tried hard to listen.

I'd expected that Nathaniel Hooke would have the most to say, and that his voice would be the strongest and the first that I would hear, but in the end the words I heard came not from him, but from a woman, and the words themselves were unexpected.

'So, you see, my heart is held forever by this place,' she said. 'I cannot leave.'

I cannot leave.

That's all she said, the voice was gone, but still that phrase stayed with me and repeated like a litany, so urgently that when the deal was done and Jane and Jimmy Keith had settled things and I was asked when I would like to take possession, I said, 'Could I have it now? Tonight?'

They looked at me, the two of them, as though I'd lost my mind.

'Tonight?' Jane echoed. 'But your things are still at our house, and you're flying back to France tomorrow, aren't you?'

'Onywye,' said Jimmy Keith, 'it's nae been cleaned.'

They were right, I knew, and really, one or two days more would hardly make a difference. So we set the date for Wednesday, just the day after tomorrow. But that didn't stop me feeling, as we locked the cottage door behind us, that I was committing a betrayal.

I felt that way all through the drive back to Peterhead, and through my last night visiting with Jane and little Jack and Alan. And next morning on my way back down to Aberdeen I drove deliberately along the coast, through Cruden Bay, to let the castle ruins know that I had not abandoned them.

It didn't take me long to settle things in France. I'd rented the house for the season, but the money didn't matter, and the things that I'd had with me there didn't fill two suitcases. My landlady, who wasn't losing anything because I had already paid up front in full, still looked a bit put out until I told her I would probably be back before the winter's end, to do more research up at the chateau. But I knew, as I was saying it, that I would not be back. There was no need.

My characters had chosen not to come to life at Saint-Germain-en-Laye because their story wasn't meant to happen there. They were supposed to be at Slains. And so was I.

I'd never been so sure of anything as I was sure of that.

On Tuesday night, the last night that I spent in France, I dreamt of Slains. I woke, still in my dream, to hear the roaring of the sea beneath my windows and the wind that raged against the walls until the air within the room bit cold against my skin. The fire was failing on the hearth, small licks of dying flame that cast half-hearted shadows on the floorboards and gave little light to see by.

'Let it be,' a man's voice mumbled, low, against my neck. 'We will have warmth enough.' And then his arm came round me, solid, safe, and drew me firmly back against the shelter of his chest, and I felt peace, and turned my face against the pillow, and I slept...

It was so real. *So* real, in fact, that I was half-surprised to find myself alone in bed when I woke up on Wednesday morning. I lay blinking for a moment in the soft grey light, and then without waiting to switch on the lamp I reached out for the paper and pen that I kept at my bedside for moments like this, and I wrote down the scene. I wrote quickly, untidily, scratching out the dialogue before the voices of the dream began to fade. I'd learnt from hard experience that bits of plot that came to me this way, from my subconscious, often disappeared before they could be registered within my waking mind. I knew I couldn't trust to memory.

When I finally put the pen down, I sat still a moment, reading what I'd written. Here, again, it was a woman I was seeing, like the woman's voice I'd heard when I was standing in the cottage. So far, all my major characters were men, but here this woman was, demanding to be part of things. Characters sometimes came into my books that way, unplanned and unannounced, often unwanted. But maybe, I thought, I should let this one stay. Maybe Jane had been right to suggest that my story would be better told by someone other than Nathaniel Hooke, someone I created from my own imagination, who could link the scenes together by her presence.

Besides, I found it easier to write about a woman. I knew what women did when they were on their own, and how they thought. Perhaps this dream last night was my subconscious telling me that what my novel really needed was a woman's point of view.

The character, I thought, would form herself; I only had to name her.

Which was easier, as always, said than done.

The names of characters defined them, and like clothing, either fitted them or not. I'd tried and tossed out several by the time I reached the Paris airport.

On the plane to Aberdeen, I tried a more methodical approach, by taking out my notebook and dividing one page into two neat columns, and then listing every Scottish name I knew – for I'd decided she would have to be a Scot – and trying different combinations of the first names and the surnames in my search for one that worked.

I'd gone a good way down the list before I noticed I'd become a source of interest to my seatmate. He'd been sleeping when I'd boarded, or at least he had been sitting with his head back and his eyes closed, and since I hadn't really been in a mood to strike up a conversation on the plane anyway, I'd happily left him in peace. But now he was awake and sitting forward, with his dark head angled slightly so that he could see what I was writing. He was doing it discreetly enough, but when I glanced over he met my gaze cheerfully, not at all embarrassed he'd been caught, and with a nod at the paper said, 'Choosing an alias, are ye?'

Which settled the question of his nationality. I'd been thinking he might have been French, with his nearly black hair and good looks, but there was no mistaking the burr of his accent. He looked to be close to my age, and his smile was friendly, not flirting, so I smiled back. 'Nothing so exciting. I'm naming a character.'

'Oh, aye? So you're a writer? Should I know you?'

'Do you read historical fiction?'

'Not since I left school, no.'

'Then you likely wouldn't know me.' Holding out my hand, I told him, 'Carolyn McClelland.'

'That's a good, fine Scottish name, MacLellan.'

'Well yes, except we spell it wrong. My family are Ulster Scots,' I said, 'from Northern Ireland. But my ancestors did come from Scotland, way back. From Kirkcudbright.' I pronounced it 'Kir-COO-Bree', the way I'd been taught. My father was an avid genealogist who spent his spare hours buried in the history of our family, and I'd learnt from a young age the varied details of my pedigree, and how the first McClelland of our line had crossed from southwest Scotland into Ulster. That had happened, now I thought of it, about the same time as the story I was writing now, in the first years of the eighteenth century. A David John McClelland, it had been, who'd up and moved to Ireland, and...who had been his wife? Sophia something.

With an idle frown, I wrote that first name down beneath the others on my page.

My seatmate, watching, said, 'I like Sophia, for a name. I had a great aunt named Sophia. Remarkable woman.'

I found myself liking the name, too. It had a nice ring to it. If only I could remember the surname…no matter, my father would know it. And he'd be pleased beyond measure if I used our ancestor's name in a novel. So what if she'd lived on the wrong side of Scotland and likely had never seen Edinburgh, let alone Slains? She'd lived at the right time – her name would be right for the period, and I'd be making her life up, not writing biography, so I could put her wherever I wanted.

'Sophia,' I said. 'Yes, I think that's the one.'

Satisfied, I folded the page and settled back to watch the window, where the coastline was just coming into view.

The man beside me settled back as well, and asked, 'You're writing something set in Scotland, are you? Whereabouts?'

'Just up the coast from Aberdeen. A place called Cruden Bay.'

'Oh, aye? Why there?'

I didn't usually talk work with total strangers, and I wasn't sure what made me do it now, except maybe that I hadn't had enough sleep, and his eyes were engagingly warm when he smiled.

Whether he actually found it all interesting, what I told him about Slains and the failed Jacobite invasion and Nathaniel Hooke, or whether he was just a practised listener, and polite, I couldn't tell. Either way, he let me go on talking till we'd landed, and still chatting, he walked out with me, waiting while I got my bags, and helping with the heavy ones.

'It's a good place for a writer, Cruden Bay,' he said. 'You know Bram Stoker wrote the better part of *Dracula* while staying there?'

'I didn't, no.'

'Aye, it was your castle, Slains, and not the one in Whitby, that inspired him. You'll hear the whole story, I'm sure, from the locals. You'll be there a while, did you say?'

'Yes, I've rented a cottage.'

'In the wintertime? That's brave of you.' We'd reached the rental car counter, and he rested his arms as he let down my suitcases, frowning a bit at the length of the queue in front of us. 'You're sure that you won't let me give you a lift?'

It was tempting, but my parents had long ago taught me that taking rides with strange men, even friendly ones, was not a good idea, so I said, 'No, that's all right, I'll manage. Thanks.'

He didn't push the point. Instead, he took his wallet out and shuffled through its contents for a scrap of paper. Finding one, he clicked a ballpoint pen. 'Here, write your name on that, I'll look for your books next time I'm in a shop.' And while I wrote, he added, smiling, 'If you write your number down, as well, I'll come and take you out to lunch.'

Which I found tempting, too, though I was forced to say, 'I don't know what my number is, I'm sorry. I don't even know if there's a phone.' And then, because his face was *so* good-looking, 'But my landlord's name is Jimmy Keith. He'll know how to get hold of me.'

'Jimmy Keith?'

'That's right.'

He gave a smile so broad it fell just short of laughter, as he bent to pick up both my suitcases. 'You'd best let me give you that lift, after all. I'm not so big my father wouldn't skelp me if he knew I'd left you here to hire a car when I was heading north myself.'

'Your father?'

'Aye. Did I not say my name, before? I'm Stuart Keith.' He

grinned. 'And since it appears that you've taken the cottage where I like to stay, so you're making me sleep on my father's spare bed – and a very uncomfortable bed it is, too – then the least you can give me is company during the drive,' he concluded. 'Come on.'

And having no argument, really, for that, I had little choice left but to follow.

Chapter Three

He drove a silver Lotus, sleek and fast, and drove it recklessly. I found it hard to focus on the things that he was pointing out as we went whizzing past.

'Of course it's all changed since the big offshore oil rigs went in, in the seventies,' he said. 'Not that I remember what it was like before then, I'm not so old as all that, but the area's been built up, with the people coming north to work in Aberdeen and Peterhead. And we've got the golf course, and the beach. The golf course is a good one, it draws a fair number of tourists. Do you play?'

'Golf? No, not really. You?'

'It all depends what you call playing. I can knock the ball around, no problem. Putting it anywhere close to the hole, well…' He shrugged. 'It's too slow a sport for my liking.'

From the way he was driving, I guessed that he didn't like anything slow. We covered the twenty-five miles in about half the time it had taken me on Sunday. The thick snow that had been here then had melted so the green of grass showed through the white in places, and as we turned down Main

Street to the harbour I could see the golden grasses blowing wild along the dunes above the wide pink curve of beach. Already the place had a welcoming feel, half-familiar. As we parked the car on Harbour Street, I felt a settling of my spirit that reminded me a little of the feeling that I got whenever I flew back to Canada and knew that I was home.

It was a nice way to feel, after spending the past year in transit, bouncing from author appearances to writers' conferences, one hotel to another, and then the months of fruitless work in France. Something told me that spending this winter in Scotland would be good for me, as well as for the book.

'Come on,' said Stuart Keith. 'You'll want to get your key, I'm sure, and Dad will want to walk you up the hill and see that you've got everything you need. In fact, if I know him,' he said, and checked his watch, 'he'll likely have you stay to lunch.'

Jimmy Keith lived in a grey, stone-built cottage wedged tightly between its two neighbours and set at the edge of the street. His sitting room was at the front. I knew this because he had the window partly open, and I could hear a television announcer giving a play-by-play of something that sounded like soccer.

Stuart didn't ring the bell or knock, but simply used his own key to walk in, with me behind him. The narrow front hall, with its mirror and mat, and the cheerfully yellowing wallpaper, wrapped me with warmth and the faintly lingering smells of a fried-egg-and-sausage breakfast.

From the front room, Jimmy called, 'Aye-aye. Which one o ye is that?'

'It's me, Dad.'

'Stuie! I didna expect ye till Friday. Come in, loon, drap yer things and come and watch the match wi' me. It's on video – I'll wind it back.'

'In a minute. I just need the key to the cottage.'

'The cottage, aye.' Jimmy's voice took on a note of apology. 'Listen, there's been a wee change o plan...'

'I gathered that.' And taking two more steps so that he stood within the open doorway of the sitting room, Stuart motioned me to come stand at his side. 'I've brought your tenant with me.'

Jimmy Keith rose from his chair with that chivalric reflex that some men of his generation hadn't lost, and most men of my own had never learnt. 'Miss McClelland,' he said, sounding pleased. 'How on earth did ye manage tae meet up wi' this sorry loon?' He used that last word the way people from elsewhere in Scotland used 'lad', so I guessed that it meant the same thing.

Stuart said, 'We were on the same plane. We—'

'Ye micht let the quine spik a word fer hersel.' Which was harder to fathom, but my ear was retuning itself to the sound of the Doric, the language that Jimmy Keith spoke, and I translated that to 'You might let the girl speak a word for herself', which I figured was right because Jimmy's mild eyes held the warning of a parent to a child to mind its manners. Then he thought of something else, and turned to me. 'Ye nivver let ma Stuie drive ye fae the airport? Michty, come in,' he said, as I nodded. 'Sit down, quine. Ye must have been feart fer yer life.'

Stuart shifted to let me go by him. 'You know, Dad, you're meant to be telling her all of my good points, not all of my faults. And *you* might want to try speaking English.'

'What way?' Jimmy asked, which I knew from my past trips to Scotland meant 'Why?' But when Jimmy pronounced it in Doric the first word came out more like 'fit' – which I later would learn was a feature of Doric, the way that some 'w's sounded like 'f's – and the second word came out as 'wye'. So, 'Fit wye?' Jimmy asked. 'She can folly me fine.'

He was right, I could follow him easily, though Stuart seemed unconvinced. Jimmy saw me settled in an armchair by the window, with my feet warmed by an old electric heater in the fireplace, and a clear view of the television. 'Stuie, awa up tae the St Olaf wi' ye, and bring us back three plates o huddock and chips.'

'They don't do take-away at the St Olaf.'

'Na, na,' his father said, knowing, 'they'll dee it fer me. Ye'll stay tae lunch,' he told me, but he made it sound an invitation rather than an order. 'Efter drivin wi' ma Stuie ye'll be needin tae recover. We can take yer things up tae the cottage later.'

Stuart didn't argue, only smiled as though he'd long since learnt there was no point resisting. 'You do *like* fish and chips?' was the only thing he wanted to make sure, before he left. 'Right then, I won't be long.'

His footsteps echoed on the road outside as he went past the window, and his father drily said, 'Dinna believe it. Ma Stuie's nivver gone past the St Olaf Hotel athoot tasting a pint. Mind, he's nae sic a bad loon,' he added, as he caught my eye, 'but dinna tell him I telt ye that. He thinks a great deal o hisself as it is.'

I smiled. 'You have two sons, somebody said.'

'Aye. There's Stuie, he's the younger, and his brother Graham's doon in Aiberdeen.'

'He's a student, isn't he, at the university?' I was trying to remember what the woman at the Post Office had told me.

'Ach no, quine. He's nae a student, he's a lecturer. In History.' His eyes crinkled at the corners with good humour. 'They're naething alike, ma twa sons.'

I tried to imagine Stuart Keith attending classes, much less teaching them, and failed.

'Graham taks efter his mither, God rest her sweet soul. She loved her history, loved tae read.'

Which would have been the perfect opening for me to tell him what I did, and why I'd come to Cruden Bay, but at the moment, with the warm fire at my feet and in the comfort of the armchair, I felt no sense of urgency to talk about my work. He'd find out soon enough, I reasoned, from his son. And anyway, I doubted that a man like Jimmy Keith would take an interest in the sort of books I wrote.

We sat companionably in silence as we watched the game on television – Scotland playing France. And after several minutes Jimmy asked, 'Ye were coming fae France, weren't ye?' and when I told him yes, he said, 'I've nivver been. But Stuie's aye ower there these days on business.'

'And what's his business?'

'Geein me grey hairs,' said Jimmy, straight-faced. 'He disna stick at onything fer lang. It's computers the noo, but I cwidna say just fit he does wi' them.'

Whatever he did, I decided, he must do it well, to be able to afford the Lotus. And his clothes had an expensive cut, for all that they looked casual. But when he came back several minutes later with our fish and chips in paper, the salt wind – no doubt with the help of a pint from the Hotel's bar – had rumpled him enough to make him lose the city slickness, and he looked at home, relaxed, as we three sat and watched what they would have called 'football'.

Not that I actually saw much of the game. My lack of sleep the night before was catching up with me, and with the warmth and heavy food and Jimmy Keith and Stuart talking on to one another in their deeply lilting voices, it was all that I could do to keep my eyes from drifting closed. I fought the urge as best I could, but I was nearly gone when Jimmy said, 'Stuie, we'd best get the quine tae her cottage afore it gets too dark tae see.'

I forced my eyes full open. It *was* darkening outside, the daylight giving way to that grey, colder gloom that marked the start of evening, in the winter.

Stuart stood. 'I'll take her, Dad. You sit.'

'Na, na.' The older man stood, too. 'I widna send ony quine oot on her ain wi' ye, at nicht.'

Stuart looked down. 'I'm not really that bad,' he assured me, and reached a hand to help me up.

But I was glad to have the two of them for company, as we walked through the swiftly falling darkness up the hill along the rutted path that was in places inches deep with melted snow. Not just because they gallantly carried all my luggage and the heavy briefcase holding my computer, but because I felt an unexpected twisting of unease deep in my chest, there on the path – a sense of something at my back that made me scared to look behind.

If I had been alone, I would have run the whole way to the cottage, suitcases or no, but as it was I simply shook the feeling off and looked instead toward the sea, where I could just make out the running lines of white that were the waves, advancing in their rhythm to the shore. The sky was thick with cloud, and veiled the moon, so that the dark line where the sea met the horizon was not easy to make out. And yet I looked for it, and searched it without knowing what, exactly, I was searching for, or what I hoped to see.

'Mind yersel,' said Jimmy's voice. His hand came out to steer me, fatherly, back to the path. 'Ye dinna wish tae fa, yer first nicht here.'

We'd reached the cottage. It was dark as well, but not for long. A scrape of the door on the floor tiles, a flip of a switch, and we stood in the bright, shabby cheer of the main front room, with its worn Persian rugs and the armchairs and long, scrubbed wood table pushed up to the wall, and the coal-fired Aga snugged tight in its small kitchen alcove.

Jimmy swung the door shut behind us, checked to see the latch was working properly, then handed me the key. 'That's yers, quine. Ye've got coal in the back fer the Aga. Ye've usit coal afore? Weel, dinna worry, I'll show ye.'

I watched him very carefully, then tried my hand at doing it, arranging the coals in the way he instructed and swinging the Aga's cast iron door shut with a competent clang.

'Aye, that's richt, ye're deein gran,' said Jimmy. 'Ye'll hae this room fairly warm in nae time ata.'

Stuart, not so encouraging, said, 'There are electric fires, too. One in here, and one in the bedroom, if you need to switch them on. Just don't forget to feed the meter.'

'Aye, ye'll need yer siller.' Jimmy put a hand in one pocket and pulled out a fat roll of coins in brown paper. 'There's ten pound, tae start wi'.'

I traded him a ten pound note for the coins, and he thanked me.

Stuart watched me tilt my head back to examine the black

box above the door, with all its spinning dials and knobs, and with a grin he reached above me to explain. 'This shows how much time you've got left, you see? And there's the meter – that's how much electricity you're using. If I turn another light on…there, see how it's going faster? So you have to keep an eye on it, and make sure when the needle on the gauge gets down to here you plunk another coin in, or you'll find yourself sitting in the dark. Let me fill it for you, then you'll have a little while before you have to worry.'

He was tall enough to simply reach and pop the coins into the slot. I'd need to stand on a stool when my turn came.

Jimmy said, 'I've gotten some food in fer ye. Bread and eggs and milk, like, so ye winna need tae bother wi' the shops the morn.'

'Thanks,' I told him, touched that he'd have taken so much trouble. He'd cleaned the place as well, I noticed. Not that it had been dirty before, but now it was decidedly dust-free, and smelt of soap and polish. Once again I felt that sense of something settling round me like a shawl around my shoulders, as though I'd found a place where I could rest, and be at home. 'It's really lovely, all you've done.'

'Na, na,' Jimmy shrugged, but his voice was pleased. 'If ye need onything ata, just speir. I'm nae far awa.' He glanced around, and seeming satisfied with everything, announced, 'We'll leave ye tae yersel, quine. Let ye get a bit o rest.'

I thanked them both a final time, and said good night, and saw them out. I was about to close the door when Stuart stuck his head back round, and told me,

'Incidentally, there *is* a phone, just over there.' He pointed, making sure I saw. 'And I already know the number.'

And with one last charming smile he withdrew again,

and left me on my own to latch the door.

I heard their footsteps and their voices on the path as they retreated, and then silence. Just the rattle of the windows as the night wind struck the glass, and in the space between the gusts the measured crashing of the waves along the shore below the hill.

It didn't bother me to be alone. I'd gotten so I liked it. Still, when I'd unpacked my suitcases, and made myself a cup of instant coffee in the kitchen, something drew me to the armchair in the corner, by the table with the telephone, and made me dial the number that I always dialled when I was wanting somebody to talk to.

'Daddy, hi,' I said, when he picked up. 'It's me.'

'Carrie! Good to hear from you.' My father's warm voice jumped the miles between us, sounding close against my ear. 'Hang on, I'll get your mother.'

'No, wait, it's you I called to talk to.'

'Me?' My father, love me as he might, was never very comfortable with talking on the phone. A few minutes' small talk, and he was ready to pass me off to my more chatty mother. Unless, of course, I had a...

'Family history question,' I said. 'David John McClelland's wife. The one who moved with him to Ireland, from Scotland. What was her last name? Her first name was Sophia, right?'

'Sophia.' He absorbed the name, and paused a moment, thinking. 'Yes, Sophia. They were married about 1710, I think. Just let me check my notes. It's been a while since I did anything with the McClellands, honey. I've been working on your mother's family.' But he was well organised. It didn't take him long. 'Oh, here it is. Sophia Paterson. With one "T".'

'Paterson. That's it. Thanks.'

'What got you wondering about her, all of a sudden?'

'I'm making her a character,' I said, 'in my new book. It's set in Scotland, and I thought that, since she comes from the right period—'

'I thought your book was set in France.'

'I've changed it. It's in Scotland, now, and so am I. In Cruden Bay, not far from where Jane and her husband live. Here, let me give you the address and number.'

He noted it down. 'And how long will you be there?'

'I don't know. The rest of the winter, maybe. What else do we know,' I asked, 'about Sophia Paterson?'

'Not a lot. I haven't found her birthdate, or her parents, or her birthplace. Let's see...according to the family Bible, she married David John in June of 1710, at Kirkcudbright, Scotland. I've got the births of three of their children – John, James, and Robert, in Belfast. And her burial in 1743, the same year that her husband died. I'm lucky to have that much. It's not easy to find details of a woman's life, you know that.'

I *did* know, from long experience of helping him track down our family's records. Once you got back past the mid-1800s, women seldom rated more than an occasional notation. Even churches often didn't bother listing what the mother's name was, in their registers of births. And newspapers would only state 'The wife of Mr So-and-So' had died. Unless there was money in the family, which there rarely was in ours, a woman's life left scarcely any mark upon the pages of the history books. We were fortunate we had the family Bible.

'That's all right,' I said. 'I'm just making up her life for my book anyway, so I can make her any age I like. Let's just imagine she was twenty-one when she got married, that would make her birthdate...1689.' I did the math. It also made her eighteen in the year my story started, which seemed just about the right age for my heroine.

A muffled voice said something in the background, and my father said, 'Your mother wants a word. Did you need anything else on the McClellands, while I've got the files out?'

'No, thanks. I just wanted Sophia's last name.'

'Make her nice,' was his only advice, lightly given. 'We don't want any villains in the family.'

'She's the heroine.'

'That's fine, then. Here's your mother.'

My mother was, predictably, less concerned with family history and the book that I was working on than why I'd moved so suddenly from France, and why on earth I'd picked a cottage on the Scottish coast in *winter*, and whether there were cliffs. 'On second thought,' she said, 'don't tell me.'

'There are no cliffs where my cottage is,' I promised her, but she was far too sharp to fool.

She said, 'Just don't go near the edge.'

That made me smile when I remembered it a little while later, when I made myself another cup of coffee. You couldn't get much closer to the cliff's edge than the ruins of Slains castle, and my mother would have had a minor heart attack if she had seen me climbing round them Monday. Better that she didn't see the things I did, sometimes, for research.

The fire had died down a bit in the stove, and I threw on a shovel of coals from the big metal coal hod that Jimmy had left for me, not really knowing how many to put on to last through the night. I poked at them inexpertly, and watched the new coals catch and hiss to life with clear blue flames that seemed to dance above their darkness. And while I watched the fire I felt the writer's trance take hold of me. I seemed to see, again, the dying fire within that castle chamber, and to hear the man's voice saying, at my back, 'We will have warmth enough.'

I needed nothing more. I firmly closed the Aga's door, and taking up my coffee went to set up my computer. If my characters were in a mood to speak to me, the least that I could do was find out what they had to say.

I

She fought the need to sleep. It caught her up in rolling waves, in rhythm with the motion of her horse, and lulled her weary body till she felt herself relaxing, giving in. The blackness flooded round her and she drifted in it, slipping in the saddle, and the loss of balance jerked her into wakefulness. She clutched the reins. The horse, who must have surely been as tired as she was, answered with an irritated movement of its head, and turned a dark reproachful eye towards her before swinging its nose round again to the north.

The eyes of the priest who was riding beside her were more understanding. 'Do you grow too tired? We have not far to go, and I would wish to see our journey end tonight, but if you feel that you can ride no further…'

'I can ride, Mr Hall.' And she straightened, to prove it. She had no desire to stop so near the goal. It had been two weeks since she had set out from the Western Shires, and every bone within her ached from travelling. There had, of course, been Edinburgh – one night upon a proper bed, and water hot for bathing – but that memory seemed distant, four long days since.

She closed her eyes and tried to conjure it: the bed with its crimson and gold hangings, the fresh-ironed linens that smelt sweetly scorched against her face, the smiling maid who brought the jug of water and the basin, and the unexpected kindness of her host, the Duke of Hamilton. She'd heard of him, of course. There were few people in these times who didn't have a firm opinion of the great James Douglas, Duke of Hamilton, who'd all but led the Parliament in Edinburgh and had been long considered one of Scotland's fiercest patriots.

His sympathies towards the exiled Stewart king in France were widely whispered, if not openly expressed. He'd been arrested in his youth, so she'd been told, for his connection to a Jacobite conspiracy, and held prisoner in the Tower of London, a fault which could do nothing but endear him to his fellow Scots, who had no love for England or its laws – and even less since this past winter's Act of Union, which in one swift, bloodless strike had stripped the Scottish people of what shreds of independence they had clutched as their inheritance from Wallace and the Bruce. There was to be no government in Scotland now; no parliament in Edinburgh. Its members would disperse to their estates, some made the richer by the lands they had been granted in return for their approval of the Union, others bitter and rebellious, talking openly of taking arms.

Alliances were forming where they never had before. She'd heard the rumours that her own kin from the Western Shires, all staunchly Presbyterian and reared to loathe the Jacobites, were seeking now to join them in conspiring to restore the Catholic king James Stewart to the throne of Scotland. Better a Catholic Scot to rule them, so they reasoned, than Queen

Anne of England or, worse still, the German prince the queen had named as her successor.

She had wondered, when she'd met the Duke of Hamilton, just where he'd stood upon the matter. Surely there could be no restoration of the Stewarts without his knowledge of it – he was far too well-connected, too powerful in his own right. There were voices still, she knew, that called him Jacobite, and yet he had an English wife, and English lands in Lancashire, and seemed to make himself at home as well at Queen Anne's court as here in Scotland. It was difficult to judge which side he'd choose if it should come to war.

He hadn't talked of politics while he had been her host, but then she hadn't thought he would. She had been thrust upon him suddenly, and, for her part, unwillingly, when the kinsman who had ridden with her from the west, as chaperone and guide, had fallen ill upon their entry into Edinburgh. Her kinsman claimed some slim acquaintanceship with the duke, having once served the dowager duchess his mother, and from that had gained for his young charge a bed for the night at the duke's grand apartments at Holyroodhouse.

She had been accepted kindly, and been fed such food as she'd forgotten in the long days of her journey – meat, and fish, and steaming vegetables, and wine in crystal goblets that reflected back the candlelight like jewels. The room she'd been shown to had been the chamber of the duke's wife, who was visiting relations in the north of England at the time, and it had been a gloriously rich room, with its gold and crimson bedcurtains, and the Indian screen, and the paintings and tapestries, and on the one wall, a looking-glass larger than any she'd seen.

She'd looked at herself with a sigh, having hoped her reflection would show something more than the road-weary waif who sighed back at her, bright curls dishevelled and darkened by dust, pale eyes reddened and circled by shadows of sleeplessness. Turning, she'd washed in the basin, though it had been no use. Her reflection, while cleaner, had looked no less pitiful.

She had sought solace in sleep.

In the morning she had breakfasted, and after that the Duke of Hamilton himself had come to see her. She had found him very charming, as his reputation promised. In his youth, so it was said, he'd cut a dashing, gallant figure at the Court. In middle age, he had grown slacker in the contours of his face, perhaps, and less firm round his middle, but he had not lost the gallantry. He'd bowed, his dark wig spilling past his shoulders in its fashionable curls, and he had kissed her hand as though she had been equal to his rank.

'So you are stranded in my care, it seems,' he'd said. 'I am afraid your kinsman is quite seriously ill, with fits of fever. I have seen him lodged as comfortably as possible, and found a nurse to tend him, but he will not be able to ride for some time.'

'Oh, I see.' She had lowered her head, disappointed.

'You find these apartments so lacking in comfort that you wish to be gone?' He'd been teasing, of course, but his voice had held true curiosity at her reaction.

'Oh, no, it is not that, Your Grace. 'Tis only...' But she could not name the cause herself, except that she wanted to be at the end of her journey, and not in its middle. She did not know the woman she was going to, the woman who was not her own relation, but that of her uncle's by marriage. A woman of power and property, who had been somehow moved by Providence, upon that uncle's recent death, to write and say that she would take Sophia in and offer her a home.

A home. The word had beckoned to her then, as it did now.

''Tis only,' she said, faltering, 'that I will be expected in the north.'

The duke examined her a moment, then he said, 'Pray, sit.'

She sat, uncomfortably, on the narrow settee by the window, while he took the velvet chair opposite, watching her still with a curious look. 'You go to the Countess of Erroll, I'm told. To Slains castle.'

'I do, sir.'

'And what is your connection to that remarkable lady?'

'She was kin to my uncle, John Drummond.'

A nod. 'But you are not a Drummond.'

'No, sir. My own name is Paterson. It was my aunt who married to the Drummonds. I have lived with them these eight years, since my parents died.'

'Died how?'

'They were both taken by the flux, Your Grace, while voyaging to Darien.'

'To Darien!' He spoke it like a hammer's blow. He had, she knew, been one of the most ardent of supporters of the Scottish dream to found a New World colony poised on the spit of land between the North and South Americas. So many had put faith in it, and poured their wealth into the venture, trusting it would give the Scots control of both the seas – a route to India that none could rival, cargoes being carried overland across the isthmus from the one sea to the other, bringing riches that would see the country rise to untold power.

Her father had believed the dream, had sold all he possessed to buy a passage on the first brave voyage. But the golden dream had turned a nightmare. Both the English and the Spanish had opposed the Scottish settlement at Darien, and nothing there remained except the natives and the empty huts of those who would have built themselves an empire.

The Duke of Hamilton had been outspoken in condemning those who'd played a hand in Darien's undoing, and he looked at her with newfound kindness as he said, 'It was by God's grace that you did not travel with them, else you, too, had lost your life.' He thought a moment. 'Would you then be kin to William Paterson?'

The merchant and adventurer who first had dreamt of Darien, and who had set its fateful wheel in motion.

She said, 'I believe he is a distant cousin, but we have not met.'

'That is, perhaps, as well for you.' He smiled, and settled back to think. 'So you would travel north to Slains?'

She had glanced at him, not daring yet to hope...

'You will have need of one to guide you, and protect you from the perils of the road,' he had continued, still in thought. 'I have a man in mind who might be like to suit your purpose, if you are content to trust my judgement.'

She had asked, 'Who is the man, Your Grace?'

'A priest, named Mr Hall. He knows the way to Slains, he has been there on my behalf before. And you would have no cause for fear,' he'd told her, 'in his company.'

No cause for fear. No cause for fear.

She slipped again upon the horse, and Mr Hall stretched out a hand to right her in the saddle. 'We are here,' he said, encouraging. 'I see the lights of Slains ahead.'

She shook herself awake and looked, eyes strained against the evening mists that swirled upon the barren lands around them. She could see the lights as well – small dots of yellow burning in the blackened spears of turrets, and unyielding walls. Below, unseen, she heard the North Sea raging on the rocks, and closer by, a dog began to bark a sharp alarm, unwelcoming.

But when she would have held her horse back, hesitant, a door swung wide and light spilt warm across the roughened turf. A woman came towards them, in a widow's gown of mourning. She was not young, but she was handsome, and she walked towards them hatless, without shawl or cloak, and heedless of the damp.

'Your arrival is most fortunate,' she told them. 'We shall presently be sitting down to supper. Bed your horses in the stable, you will find my groom to help you,' she instructed Mr Hall. 'The lass can come with me. She will be wishing to refresh herself, no doubt, and dress.' She held a hand to help the girl dismount, introducing herself. 'I am Anne,' she said, 'Countess of Erroll, and, till my son's marriage, the mistress of Slains. I do fear I've forgotten your name.'

The girl's voice was hoarse from disuse, and she had to clear her throat before she spoke. 'Sophia Paterson.'

'Well, then,' said the countess, with a smile that seemed at odds with the bleak landscape at her back, 'I bid you welcome home, Sophia.'

Chapter Four

Somebody was knocking at the cottage door.

It took a while to register. Still half-asleep, I raised my head a little stiffly from where it had lain the past few hours across my arm, outstretched along the hard wood table. My laptop computer had grown tired of waiting for me to go on, and had switched to the screen-saver, infinite stars rushing at me and past me as though I were hurtling through space.

I blinked, and then remembering, I tapped a key and watched the words scroll past. I hadn't really believed they would be there. Hadn't really believed that I'd written them. I'd never been a fast writer, and five hundred words in one day was, to me, a good effort. A thousand words left me ecstatic. Last night, in one sitting, I'd written twice that, with such ease I felt sure it had all been a dream.

But it hadn't been. Here was the evidence, plain black and white on the screen, and I couldn't help feeling the way I might feel if I'd opened my eyes to discover a dinosaur in my front garden. With disbelieving hands, I saved the document again and hit the key to print.

The knocking came a second time. I scraped back in my chair, and stood, and went across to answer it.

'I didna mean tae waken ye.' Jimmy Keith was all apology, although he had no reason to be, given that it was, as near as I could tell, the middle of the day.

I lied. 'You didn't, that's all right.' I clenched my cheeks to hold the yawn back that would have betrayed me. 'Please, come in.'

'I thought ye micht be wanting help, like, wi' the stove.' He brought the cold in with him, clinging to his jacket like the briskness of the salt wind off the sea. I couldn't see too far behind him for the fog that hung above the waves was like some great cloud that was too heavy to get airborne. Leaving his mud-bottomed boots at the doormat, he went past and into the kitchen and opened the stove door to peer at my coal fire. 'Ach, it's gone and deed on ye, it's fairly oot. Ye should've ca'd me.'

Sweeping the dead ashes out, he relaid the coals, his rough hands so quick and neat in their movements that I wondered again what he did for a living, or what he had done. So I asked him.

He glanced up again. 'I was a slater.'

A maker of slate roofs. So that would explain why he looked like he'd lived his whole life in the open air, I thought.

He asked what *I* did, and there was the 'f' sound again, in the place of a 'w' – making the word 'what' in Jimmy's speech come out as 'fit': 'Fit aboot yersel?' He gave a nod to my laptop computer, its printer still humming away on the long wooden table against the far wall. 'Fit d'ye dee wi' that?'

'I write,' I told him. 'Books.'

'Oh, aye? Fit kind o books?'

'Novels. Set in the past.'

He clanged the door shut on the Aga and stood, looking fairly impressed. 'Oh, aye?'

'Yes. The one that I'm working on now is set here,' I said. 'That's why I wanted this cottage. My story takes place at Slains Castle.'

'Oh, aye?' Jimmy repeated, as though he'd discovered a thing of great interest. I had the feeling that he would have asked me more if someone hadn't, at that moment, knocked again at the front door.

'Yer in demand the day,' said Jimmy as I went to open it, and found, as I had half-expected, Stuart on the doorstep.

'Morning. Thought I'd come and see how you were getting on,' he said.

'I'm fine, thanks. Come on in, your father's here.'

'My father?'

'Aye,' said Jimmy, from the kitchen, his eyes crinkling at their corners. 'I've nivver seen ye up sae early, loon. Are ye a'richt?'

Stuart parried the jab with a smile. 'It's after eleven.'

'Aye, I ken fine fit time it is.'

He finished restoking the fire in my stove and stood when I thanked him. But he didn't look as though he were in any hurry to go anywhere, and neither did Stuart, so I asked, 'Does anyone want coffee? I was just about to make a cup.'

To both Keith men, apparently, a cup of coffee sounded fine. They didn't sit while waiting. Jimmy wandered out into the main room, whistling faintly through his teeth, while Stuart came after me into the kitchen and leant with his back to the wall, his arms folded. 'So, how did you like your first night in the cottage? I should have warned you that the bedroom window rattles like the devil when the wind blows off the sea. It didn't keep you up, I hope?'

'I didn't actually make it to the bedroom last night. I was working,' I said, with a nod to the long wooden table.

Jimmy, who'd been having a look at my computer, added, 'She's a writer.'

'Aye, I know she is,' said Stuart.

'She'll be writin,' Jimmy said, 'aboot oor castle.'

Stuart looked at me with what might have been pity. 'It's a big mistake, to tell my Dad a thing like that.'

I set the kettle on to boil. 'Why's that?'

'He'll be up to the St Olaf for his lunch, that's why, and by this afternoon the whole of Cruden Bay will know exactly why you're here, and what you're doing. You won't have a moment's peace.'

'Ach, the loon disna ken fit he's on aboot,' Jimmy said. 'I've nae time fer claikin.'

'That's "gossiping",' Stuart translated the word for my benefit. 'And don't believe him. He loves telling stories.'

His father put in, 'Aye, and lucky fer me I've yersel tae keep geein me somethin tae tell aboot. Is that the kettle?'

It was. I made the coffee, and we sat around companionably and drank it, and then Jimmy checked his watch and said, 'Weel, I'm awa hame.' He jabbed a finger at his son. 'And dinna ye stop here lang, either.' And he thanked me for the coffee, and went out.

The fog was lifting, but the damp sea air surged in behind him, and I felt it even after I had closed the door. It made me restless.

'Tell you what,' I said to Stuart. 'Why don't I go get my coat, and you can give me the Cook's tour of Cruden Bay?'

He cast an eye towards the window. 'What, in this?'

'Why not?'

'Why not, she says.' But he gave in, unfolding himself from the chair. 'Well, the weather's as good as you're likely to get at this time of the year, I suppose, so all right.'

It was good to walk out in the wind, with my hair blowing loose and the spray from the sea carried up from the breakers that crashed on the empty pink beach. The path down the hill was still slippery with water and mud, but whatever misgivings I'd felt here last night in the dark were forgotten by day, and the harbour below looked quite friendly and welcoming.

It wasn't a large harbour, just a small square of calm water behind a protective wall fronting the sea, and there were no boats actually moored there – the few I could see had been pulled up and out of the water completely to lie on the land, and I gathered that no one went fishing from here in the wintertime.

Stuart led me up the other way and past his father's cottage and the others huddled tight beside it, with their roughened plaster walls and roofs of dripping slate. We passed the long, white-painted footbridge that crossed over to the high dunes and the beach, and while I would have liked to detour off in that direction, Stuart had another place in mind.

We'd turned the 'S' curve where Harbour Street changed into Main Street, with its row of houses and its few shops climbing up the one side, and the lively stream cascading down the other, overhung by leafless trees. At the top of the hill, Main Street ended by running straight into the side of another main road – the same road I'd been driving on when I'd come through here last weekend, only I hadn't stopped then till I'd followed it further and round through the woods. I'd been so focused that day on chasing my view of the ruins that I hadn't taken much notice of anything else. Like the beautiful building that held court just over the road at the top of Main Street.

It had red granite walls and white dormers and several bow-fronted two-storey projections that gave it a look of Victorian elegance. We were approaching it now from the side, but its long front looked over a lawn that sloped down to the stream which appeared to behave itself better up here, running quietly under a bridge on the main road as though it, too, felt that the building was owed some respect.

'And this,' said Stuart grandly, 'is the "Killie" – the Kilmarnock Arms Hotel. It's where your friend Bram Stoker stayed when he first came to Cruden Bay, before he moved to Finnyfall, the south end of the beach.'

'To where?'

'To Finnyfall. Spelt "Whinnyfold", but everybody says it like you'd say it in the Doric. It's not a large place, just a handful of cottages.'

Somehow I couldn't imagine Bram Stoker at home in a cottage. The Kilmarnock Arms would have suited him better. I could easily imagine the creator of the world's most famous vampire sitting at his writing table in an upstairs window bay, and gazing out across the stormy coast.

'We could go in,' said Stuart, 'if you like. They've got a Lounge Bar, and they serve a decent lunch.'

I didn't need a second nudge. I'd always taken pleasure in exploring places other writers had been to before me. My favourite small hotel in London had once been a haunt of Graham Greene, and in its breakfast room I always sat in the same chair he'd sat in, hoping that some of his genius might rub off on me. Having lunch at the Kilmarnock Arms, I decided, would give me a similar chance to commune with the ghost of Bram Stoker.

'All right,' I said. 'Lead on.'

The Lounge Bar had red upholstered banquet seats with brass and glass globe lamps set at their corners, and dark wood chairs and tables on a carpet of deep blue, but all the woodwork had been painted white, and all the walls, except the stone one at the far end, had been papered in a softly patterned yellow that, together with the windows and the daylight, gave the place a cheerful ambiance, not dark at all. No vampires here.

I ordered soup and salad and a glass of dry white wine. Wine with lunch was a habit I'd picked up in France, and one I'd likely have to break myself of now that I was here in Scotland. I'd have to be totally sober to face the coast paths, I reminded myself. Even without my mother's warning, I knew from experience it wouldn't do to go tottering close to the cliffs. But for now, since I wasn't intending to go very far from a sidewalk, I judged myself safe.

Stuart, true to his father's prediction of yesterday, ordered a pint and sat back in the booth with me, settling his shoulders against the red leather. He was, I thought, a very handsome man, with that nearly black hair falling carelessly over his forehead, and his eyes that were so quick to laugh. His eyes were blue, I noticed, like his father's, but he didn't look like Jimmy. Still, in this light, something in his features struck me as familiar, as though I had seen his face, or one quite like it, somewhere else before.

'Why the frown?' he asked.

'What? Oh, no reason,' I said. 'I was thinking, that's all. Occupational hazard.'

'I see. I've never had lunch with a writer before. Should I watch my behaviour, in case I end up as a character in your new book?'

I assured him he wasn't in danger. 'You won't be a character.'

He feigned a wounded ego. 'Oh? And why is that?'

'It's just that I don't base my characters on people I know. Not a whole person, anyway. Bits and pieces, sometimes – someone's habits, someone's way of moving, things they might have said. But everything gets mixed up with the person I imagine,' I explained. 'You wouldn't recognise yourself, if I did use you.'

'Would you cast me as the hero, or the villain?'

That surprised me. Not the question, but the tone in which he asked it. For the first time since I'd met him, he was flirting. Not that I minded, but it did catch me off guard, and it took me a moment to shift my own footing, adjust to the change. 'I don't know, I've just met you.'

'First impressions.'

'Villain,' I said, lightly. 'But you'd have to grow a beard, or something.'

'Done,' he promised. 'Could I have a cape?'

'Of course.'

'A man can't be a villain,' Stuart said, 'without a cape.' He grinned, and once again I had that feeling, strange and new, unsettling, that I had seen his face before.

I asked, 'Were you in France on business, or on holiday?'

'On business. Always working, I am.' His sigh was so long-suffering as he sat back and raised his pint that I couldn't help challenging.

'Always?'

'Well, maybe not *now*,' he admitted. 'But in a few days I'll be back at it, away down to London.'

'You work with computers, your dad said?'

'In a way. I do pre-sales support for an enterprise resource planning system.' He named the firm he worked for, but it meant nothing to me. 'Their product is good, so I'm in high demand.'

And with a smile like that, I knew, he likely had a girl in every port. But still, he made me laugh, and it had been at least a year since I'd been on a date. I'd been too caught up in my work – no time for meeting men, no time to do much with one even if I'd met one. Writing got like that for me, sometimes. It could be all-consuming. When I got deep in a story I forgot the need for food, for sleep, for everything. The world that I'd created seemed more real, then, than the world outside my window, and I wanted nothing more than to escape to my computer, to be lost within that other place and time.

It was probably just as well Stuart Keith's work kept him moving. He'd find me poor company, were he to stay.

The Kilmarnock Arms was the start and the end of my first tour of Cruden Bay. Stuart seemed happy to sit there in comfort and warmth and displayed no great interest in taking me anywhere else. He was back to being friendly when he walked me home. No flirting, just a smile on the doorstep and a promise he'd look in on me tomorrow.

I checked the kitchen fire and found it burning low, and so I stoked it in the way that Jimmy'd shown me, feeling almost expert. 'There,' I said and stood, raising a hand to catch the sudden yawn that was intended to remind me I had barely slept at all last night, and had just drunk a glass of wine and needed to lie down.

My little bedroom in the back had just a wardrobe and an iron bed, complete with sagging mattress on old-fashioned springs that squeaked when I sat down. There was a window here that looked towards the north, and I could see the jagged outcropping of rock with ruined Slains high on it, rising red against the sky. But I was far too tired, just now, to take much notice of the view.

The bed squeaked loudly when I lay on it, but to my weary face the pillowcase felt soft and cool, and when I slipped beneath the freshly laundered warmth of sheets and blankets I could feel my state of consciousness slip, too.

I should have slept.

But what I saw when my eyes closed was neither darkness nor a dream.

I saw a river, and green hills with trees below a sky of summer blue. Although I didn't recognise the place, the image would not leave. It went on playing like a private film within my mind until I lost all sense of being tired.

I rose, and went to write.

II

She dreamt of the woods, and the soft western hills, and the River Dee dancing in sunlight beyond the green fields, and the soft waving touch of the high grasses bowing before her wherever she walked. She could feel the clean air of the morning, the cool gentle breeze, and the happiness carried upon it, while nearby her mother sat singing a tune that

Sophia could only remember in dreams...

It was gone, words and all, when she opened her eyes. And the sun was gone, too. Here, the light was a harder flat grey, and it couldn't reach into the bedchamber's corners, so they stayed in darkness, although she knew well from what she'd seen last night by the candle that there would be little to hide in the shadows. The room was a plain one, with only one tapestry trying to soften the stark grey stone walls, and one painting – a portrait of some unknown woman with sad-looking eyes – hanging over the mantel. Below both of those lay a hearth that was too small to be any match for the wail of the wind at the rain-spattered glass of the window.

She clutched a blanket to her for protection from the cold, and rose, and crossed to see what view she had. She hoped for hills, or trees...though she could not remember seeing trees upon the landscape when they had approached the house last night. In fact, this part of Scotland seemed quite bare of vegetation save the gorse and rougher grasses that grew close beside the sea. The salt, perhaps, made it impossible for anything more delicate to grow.

Another angry blast of rain assailed the window as she reached it. For a moment she saw nothing, then the wind chased off the water in thin, sideways-running rivulets, and let her see beyond the glass.

The sight was unexpected, and it stole her breath. She saw the sea, and nothing else. She might have been aboard a ship, with days of journeying between herself and land, and nothing round her but the grey sky and the storm-grey waves that stretched forever to the grey horizon. She'd been warned by the Countess of Erroll at supper last night that the walls of Slains Castle had been, at some places, set close to the cliffs, but it seemed to Sophia the walls must rise straight from the rock for her chamber to have such a view, and that there could be nothing below but a sheer drop of stone wall and precipice, down to the boiling foam of the sea round the rocks of the shore.

The wind hurled a fierce blast of rain at her window and turning, she drew near the small fire and took her best gown from the clothes-press, doing what she could to make herself presentable. It had been her mother's gown, and was not nearly as in fashion as the one that the countess had been wearing last night, but the soft blue colour suited her, and with her hair combed carefully and pinned into its style she felt more capable of facing what might come.

She did not know, yet, her position in this house. It had not been discussed at supper, the countess seeming quite content to feed her guests and see their needs attended to with gracious hospitality that asked for nothing in return, and gave Sophia hope that here indeed might be the kind and happy home whose promise she had followed all these days and nights since she had first begun her eastward journey.

But life, if nothing else, had taught her promises weren't always to be counted on, and what appeared at first a shining chance might end in bitter disappointment.

Drawing in a calming breath, she squared her shoulders, smoothed her hands along the bodice of her dress, and went downstairs. It was yet early, and it seemed she was the only one awake. She moved from empty room to empty room, and since the house was large, with many doorways, she soon found herself quite turned around, and might have gone on wandering if she had not become aware of sounds of life from one rear hallway – voices, and a clanking that she took to be a kettle, and a snatch of cheerful singing drew her steps toward the kitchen door. She had no doubt it was the kitchen. Even through the panelled oak, the warmth and comfortable smells of cooking reached to make her welcome, and the door itself swung open to her touch.

It was a long and well-scrubbed kitchen, with a massive hearth at one end, and a flagstone floor, and one long table, very plain, at which a young man, roughly dressed, was sitting with a pipe between his teeth, chair tilted back, his booted feet crossed at the ankles. He hadn't seen Sophia yet, because his eyes were for the girl who had been singing and who, having perhaps reached a place in her song where the words were forgotten, had happily changed to a hum while she laid out a tray with clean dishes.

And at the hearth, a woman, middle-aged, stood with her broad back turned to both of them, and stirred at something in an open kettle. That something, to Sophia, smelt like barley, and her stomach gave a hungry twist, and so she said, 'Good morning.'

The humming stopped. The young man's chair thumped down, and all three heads came round in mild surprise.

The girl spoke first. She cleared her throat. 'Good morning, mistress. Were ye wishing something?'

'Is that broth?'

'Aye. But ye'll be having more than that, the day, for breakfast. I'll be serving in the dining room in half an hour's time.'

'I...could I please just have a bowl of that, in here? Would that be possible?'

The mild surprise grew more pronounced. Sophia stood uncomfortably and sought the words to tell them she was not accustomed to a great house such as this, that hers had always been a simple life – not poor, exactly, but not far above their own place in the order of society – and that, to her, this clean and cheery kitchen had an air of home about it that the dining room did not.

The older woman, who till now had stood in silence at the hearth, looked Sophia up and down and said, 'Come have a seat, then, mistress, if it pleases ye. Rory, shift your great and useless self and let the lady sit.'

'Oh, please,' Sophia said, 'I didn't mean—'

The young man, Rory, stood without a protest, and with no change of expression to betray what he might think of this intrusion. 'Time I got on with my work,' was all he said before he left by the back corridor. Sophia heard the swing of hinges followed by the slamming of a door that sent a wave of chill air swirling through the kitchen's warmth.

'I didn't mean that anyone should leave,' Sophia said.

''Tis nae your doing,' said the older woman firmly. ''Tis my own. The loon would sit there half the morning if he thought I'd let him do it. Kirsty, bring a bowl and spoon, so I can serve our guest her morning draught.'

Kirsty looked to be about Sophia's age, if not a little younger, with black curling hair and wide eyes. She moved, as Rory had, with the kind of swift obedience that came not out of fear, but from respect. 'Aye, Mrs Grant.'

Sophia sat and ate the hot broth, saying nothing lest she might disrupt these women more than she already had. She felt their eyes upon her as they moved about their work, and she was glad when she had finished and could push away the bowl, and thank them.

Mrs Grant assured her it had been no trouble. 'But,' she

added, carefully, 'I dinna think that it would please the countess if ye were to make a habit of it.'

Sophia glanced up, hopeful that the servants might already know what place she was to have within the household. 'Am I then to take meals with the family?'

'Aye, of course, and where else?' Mrs Grant asked, 'with ye being kin to the countess?'

Sophia said, slowly, 'There are many levels of kinship.'

The older woman looked at her a moment, long, as though she sought to read behind those words, and then she hoisted another kettle onto its hook and said, 'Nae to the Countess of Erroll, there aren't.'

'She seems a good woman.'

'The best of all women. I've workit in this kitchen thirty years, since I was ages with Kirsty, and I ken the countess's ways mair than most, and I'll tell ye ye'll nae find her equal on God's earth.' Her sideways glance smiled. 'Did ye think ye'd be put into service?'

'I did not know what to expect,' said Sophia, not wanting to bare all her longings and fears to a stranger. The past was the past, after all, and what cared these two women for how she had struggled since losing her parents? She showed them a smile of her own. 'But I see I have come to a good place.'

Again Mrs Grant's eyes searched hard for a heartbeat before she said, 'Aye, that ye have. Kirsty.'

Kirsty turned round.

'They'll be missing our guest in the dining room, presently. Best ye should show her the way.'

'Aye,' said Kirsty. 'I'll do that.'

Sophia stood, gratefully. 'Thank you.'

The creases on Mrs Grant's face that had looked stern

beforehand now seemed to have been carved by smiles. 'Ach, 'tis nae bother, mistress. Just mind now that ye eat your meal at table, else they'll ken that I've been feedin ye in secret.'

In the end, Sophia found she had no trouble eating everything that Kirsty served. The four days' ride from Edinburgh had left her feeling ravenous, and Mrs Grant's good cooking rivalled anything she'd eaten at the Duke of Hamilton's own table.

If the Countess of Erroll had wondered at Sophia's late arrival to the dining room, she made no comment on it, only asked her in a friendly way if she had found the chamber to her liking.

'Thank you, yes. I rested well.'

'It is a plain room,' said the countess, 'and the fire must work to warm it, but the view is quite unequalled. On those days when the weather is fine, you must look to the sunrise, and tell me if it's not the prettiest one you have seen.'

Mr Hall, reaching for bread, gave Sophia a confiding wink. 'That would be only one day of each month, my dear. The Lord has favoured Slains in many ways, not least by providing this castle with such an amiable mistress, but He prefers, for reasons of His own, to leave those favours wrapped in fog and foul winds. If you should see the sunrise twice before the summer comes, then you may count yourself most fortunate.'

The countess laughed. 'Good Mr Hall, you'll make the poor lass melancholy. I grant that you yourself have never seen Slains in fair weather, but the sun shines even here, from time to time.'

She looked a younger woman when she laughed. She would have been approaching sixty, so Sophia judged, and yet her face was firm and well-complexioned, and her eyes were clear and knowing, lively with intelligence. They noticed when Sophia's own gaze travelled to the portraits hung to each side of the window.

'They are both handsome men,' the countess told her, 'are they not? That is my husband, the late earl. The artist gave him a stern countenance, but he was a most kindly man, in life. The other is my son, Charles, who is now the Earl of Erroll and, by birthright of that title, Lord High Constable of Scotland. Or what may be left of Scotland,' she said, drily, 'now that parliament has ratified the Union.'

Mr Hall said, 'Yes, it is a troubling thing.'

'An injury,' the countess said, 'which I do hope will not go long unanswered.'

Mr Hall glanced at Sophia in the way her uncle had when a discussion touched on something he had not thought fit for her to hear. He asked, 'How does your son? I do regret I have not seen him much of late, in Edinburgh. Is he well?'

'Quite well, I thank you, Mr Hall.'

'His Grace the Duke of Hamilton remarked to me the other day he feared the Earl of Erroll did think ill of him, because the earl no longer keeps his company.'

The countess sat back to let Kirsty clear the empty plate away, and smiled a careful smile that had an edge of warning to it. 'I do not know my son's opinions, nor yet his affairs.'

'Of course not, no. I did not think that you should do so. I was only saying that the duke—'

'Is surely man enough to ask directly of my son that which he wishes to be told, and not rely upon my word in such a matter.'

It was a soft rebuke, but Mr Hall accepted it. 'My lady, I apologise. I did not mean to give offence.'

'And none is taken, Mr Hall.' She deftly brought the conversation back to firmer ground. 'You are not pressed to carry on your travels just at present, are you?'

'No, my lady.'

'I am pleased to hear it. We could do with a man's company at Slains. There has been little entertainment here this winter, and our neighbours have kept closely to their own estates. I do confess that I have found the days here very dull, of late.'

'Perhaps,' said Mr Hall, 'these next few weeks will bring a change.'

The countess smiled. 'I do depend upon it.' Turning to include Sophia, she said, 'And I shall have no great fear of boredom now, with such a lively young companion. It is you, my dear, whom I suspect will find this house so dull that you will wish yourself away from it.'

Sophia said, 'I can assure you I will not.' She said that with more certainty than she had first intended, and she added in a lighter voice, 'I am not used to towns or cities. I do much prefer a quiet life.'

'That I can give you,' said the countess. 'For a time, at least. Until the families round us learn that I have now a pretty, unwed kinswoman who bides with me, for then I fear that we may be lain siege to by the curious.' Her eyes danced warmly, welcoming the sport.

Sophia took it in good part, and made no comment. She had no expectations of local young men clamouring for her attentions, for she knew that she was no rare beauty – just an ordinary girl of common parentage, without an income or a dowry that could make a man of good birth think she was desirable.

Mr Hall remarked, 'Then it is just as well that I should stay, to help you fight them off.' He pushed his chair back on the floor. 'But now, with your indulgence, I must go and write a letter to His Grace, so to acquaint him with my plans. You have the means, my lady, do you not, to see that such a message reaches Edinburgh?'

The countess answered that she did, and with a formal bow he left them, wishing them good morning. The little maid, Kirsty, moved to clear his plate as well, and the countess said, 'Kirsty, I do owe you thanks for showing Mistress Paterson the way to us this morning. It was fortunate that she did find you.'

Kirsty glanced up in surprise, and seemed to pause a moment as if seeking how to twist the truth, before she said, 'My lady, ye've no need to thank me. All I did was meet her in the passageway. She would have found ye here without my help.'

The countess smiled. 'That may be so, but I confess I did forget my duties as a hostess, and how simple it can be to lose one's way, at Slains. If you have finished now, Sophia, come and let me show you round the castle, so you will not need to fear becoming lost.'

The tour was long, and thorough.

At its end the countess showed her to a small room on the ground floor at the corner of the castle. 'Do you sew?' she asked.

'I do, my lady. Is there something you wish mended?'

The answer seemed to strike the countess strangely, for she paused, and turned her gaze upon Sophia for a moment, and then told her, 'No, I only meant to tell you that this room is good for sewing, as it has the southern light. I am, I fear, an indifferent seamstress myself. My mind does not compose itself to detailed work, but is inclined to drift most shamefully to other thoughts.' She smiled, but her eyes held to Sophia's face.

The little room felt warmer than the others, being smaller and more cosy, and with greater light which flooded through the windows and did not permit the gathering of shadows.

The countess asked, 'How long, Sophia, were you in the household of John Drummond?'

'Eight years, my lady.'

'Eight years.' There was a measured pause. 'I did not know my kinsman well. We played some time as children long ago, in Perth. He was a most unpleasant child, as I recall. And very fond,' she said, 'of breaking things.' She raised a hand, and with a mother's touch, smoothed one bright curl back from Sophia's face. 'I rather would repair them.'

That was all she said, and all she was to say, about John Drummond.

As the days went on, Sophia came to realise that the countess rarely ventured to speak ill of anyone, for all she was a woman of opinions. And she treated all the servants of her household, from the lowest maid who laboured in the scullery to the solemn-faced chaplain himself, with an equal grace and courtesy. But an impression grew upon Sophia, based on nothing greater than a certain guarded tone of voice, a flash of something deeper in the eyes when the countess and Mr Hall were speaking, that the countess did not share his admiration of the Duke of Hamilton.

But she plainly did like Mr Hall, and when three weeks had come and gone the priest was still a guest at Slains, and no one talked of his departure.

Every day he kept the same routine: his morning draught,

and then a private hour in which Sophia thought he might have prayed or tended to his business, then in fair or foul weather he would walk along the cliffs above the sea. Sophia envied him those walks. She was herself, by virtue of her sex, expected to keep closer to the castle's walls, and venture not much further than the kitchen garden, where she felt the ever-watchful eyes of Mrs Grant. But on this day the sky was clearing, and the sun hung like a beacon in it, and there was in every one a restlessness, such as all creatures felt in those first days when dying winter started giving way to spring, and so when Mr Hall announced that he would take his walk, Sophia begged to be allowed to go with him, although he made a protest that the path would be too difficult.

'It is too far, and over ground too rough. Your slippers would be ruined.'

'Then I shall wear my old ones. And I do not fear the walk with you to guide me.'

The countess glanced towards her with a blend of understanding and amusement, and then shared that look with Mr Hall. 'She is most uncommonly healthy. I have no objection to letting her go, if you will see she does take care, when on the cliffs, that she goes not too near the edge.'

He did not take her near the cliffs, but inland, past hard fallow fields and tenant farms, where soft-eyed cows came out to stare, and red-cheeked children peered around the cottage doors and wondered at their passing. To Sophia, this was more familiar than the wilder landscape of the North Sea coast, although a part of her this morning seemed to want to feel that wildness, and she did not mind when Mr Hall suggested they start back to Slains.

The sky above the sea was almost free of cloud, and bright

as far as she could see, and while the wind blew strongly it had come around and blew now from the southwest, and it did not seem as cold against her face. The water, too, although still ridged with white, had lost its angry roll and came to shore with better manners, not exploding on the rocks but merely curling foam around them and receding, in an almost soothing rhythm.

It was not the sea itself, though, that Sophia's gaze was drawn to, but the ship that rode upon it, rode to anchor with its sails tight-folded underneath the white cross of Saint Andrew blazoned on a field of Scottish blue.

She hadn't expected to see a ship so close to land, and so far to the north, and the sight of it took her entirely by surprise. 'What ship is that?' she asked.

The sight of the ship appeared to have affected Mr Hall even more strongly than it had herself, for it took him a moment before he replied, and his voice held a curious quality that might have been disappointment, she thought, or displeasure. ''Tis the *Royal William*. Captain Gordon's ship.' He looked at it a minute longer, then he said, 'I wonder if he simply pays the countess his respects, or if he means to come ashore?'

The answer waited for them in the drawing room.

The man who rose for introduction cut a gallant figure. Sophia judged him to be about forty, and good-looking in his naval captain's uniform, with gold braid on his long blue coat and every button polished, and a white cravat wound elegantly round his throat and knotted, and a curled wig of the latest fashion. But his stance was firm and not the least affected, and his blue eyes were straightforward. 'Your servant,' he assured Sophia, when she was presented to him.

'Captain Gordon,' said the countess, 'is an old and valued friend, and does us honour with his company.' She turned to him. 'We've missed you, Thomas, this past winter. Have you been laid up, or were you on another voyage to the Indies?'

'The *Royal William* has been these months in the road of Leith, my lady. This is our first journey north.'

'And where, now, are you bound?'

'I am commissioned to keep up the old patrol, between the Orkney Isles and Tynemouth, though I do not doubt but that will alter when the Union takes effect.'

Mr Hall said to Sophia, 'Captain Gordon is the commodore of our Scots navy frigates on the eastern coast, which soon will be absorbed into the navy of Great Britain.'

'And who then,' asked the countess, 'will protect our shores from privateers?' But she was smiling when she said it, and Sophia had again the sense of being on the outside of a private understanding. 'Please,' the countess said, 'be at your ease, and let us have a proper visit.' And with that she sat, and called Sophia over to the easy chair beside her, while the gentlemen took rush chairs with red leather cushions nearer to the window.

Sophia was aware of Captain Gordon's gaze upon her, and because it made her feel a bit uncomfortable, she sought to break the silence. 'Are there many privateers, sir, who would prey upon our coast?'

'Aye, that there are,' the captain said. 'The French and Spanish have an eye for our Scots shipping.'

Mr Hall's good-natured comment was, 'I would suspect their interest profits you far more than it does them. Do you not keep the spoils of any ship you capture?'

'Aye,' said Captain Gordon, comfortably. 'And few ships

can outrun the *Royal William*. Even French ones.'

Mr Hall asked, 'Have you come across a French ship lately?'

'I've not seen one. But I'm told Queen Anne does take a special interest in ships setting out from France this spring. And I am warned, by those above me, to be particularly watchful.'

'Is that so?'

'It is.' The captain's answer hung in silence for a moment, as though needing thought. And then he shrugged a shoulder and said, 'Still, it is not easy to be everywhere at once. I dare say anyone determined to slip by me could accomplish it.'

The countess cast a glance towards Sophia, and then lightly changed the subject to the news that Captain Gordon brought from Edinburgh, and gossip of the Union.

When the captain took his leave an hour later, he said fondly to the countess, 'I remain, my lady Erroll, your most steadfast friend and servant. Trust in that.'

'I know it, Thomas. Do take care.'

'There's none can harm me.' With a smile, he bent to kiss her hand, and turned the remnants of his smile upon Sophia, though he still addressed the countess. 'You may well,' he said, 'be seeing even more of me this year than you have done. I have a weakness for good company, and God knows my own crew does ill supply it.' Then he kissed Sophia's hand as well, and bid farewell to Mr Hall, and left to make his way down to the boat that would return him to his ship.

'A dashing man, would you not say so?' asked the countess of Sophia, as they stood and watched him from the window.

'He is very handsome, yes.'

'And very loyal, which in these days makes him rare.'

Behind them, Mr Hall spoke up. 'My lady, if you will

excuse me, I have correspondence to attend to.'

'Yes, of course.' The countess, turning from the window, nodded, and the priest, too, took his leave, departing with a bow. The countess smiled and sat, and motioned for Sophia to resume her seat. 'He's gone, you know, to write the Duke of Hamilton a letter, for he is obliged to tell his master all.' A pause, and then, 'What did you think of him?'

'Of whom, my lady?'

'The Duke of Hamilton.'

Sophia did not know how to respond. 'He was quite kind to me.'

'That is not what I asked, my dear. I asked for your opinion of his character.' And then, because she saw the consternation on Sophia's face, 'Or do you not believe that the opinion of a woman is of value? For I tell you, I would rather have a woman's thoughts on character than those of any man, because a woman's thoughts are truer, and less likely to be turned by outward charm.'

'Then I'm afraid I'll disappoint you, for I found the duke to be most charming, though we did not speak at length.'

'What did you speak about?'

'He asked me my relation to you.'

'Did he?' asked the countess in that tone of guarded interest that Sophia was beginning to associate with any conversation that involved the Duke of Hamilton. 'What else?'

'We spoke of Darien. He said it was a blessing I had not gone with my parents.'

'And it was.'

'And that was all. The interview took but a quarter of an hour, perhaps. No longer.'

'And you thought him charming.'

'Yes, my lady.'

'Well,' the countess said, 'I can forgive you that.' She gave no further explanation of that statement, nor did she reveal her own opinion of the man, although Sophia reasonably guessed that, in the judgement of the countess, she had been herself deceived.

But nothing else was said about it.

Two more weeks passed, and the days began to lengthen, and the restlessness that held those in the castle in its grasp grew ever stronger.

'I would ride today,' the countess said, one morning after breakfast. 'Will you come with me, Sophia?'

In surprise, Sophia said, 'Of course.'

'We need not trouble Mr Hall, I think. He is yet occupied.' The countess smiled, and added, 'I believe I have a riding habit that would well become you.'

The countess's chamber was larger by half than Sophia's and looked to the sea, too, although it was not as impressive a view, as one wall of the castle intruded upon it. The bed, richly carved, had silk hangings of blue, and the chairs in the room all had backs of the same blue silk, artfully reflected in the gilt-edged looking glass that caught the daylight from the narrow windows. Blue was clearly a favourite colour of the countess, because the velvet riding habit that she spread upon the clothes-press in the ante-chamber was blue as well, a lovely deep blue like a clear loch in autumn.

'My hair was the same shade as yours once,' the countess said, 'and I did always believe that this habit looked well on me. My husband brought it back from France. He chose it, so he said, to match the colour of my eyes.'

'I could not wear a thing so precious to you.'

'Nonsense, child. I had rather that you would make use of it than it should lie in a corner, unworn. Besides,' she added, 'even were I not in mourning, there is no known magic that could make this fit my waist. Come, take it, wear it, that I might have a companion on my ride.'

The groom who brought the horses round to them was Rory, the same young man whom Sophia had seen rocking on his chair and watching Kirsty in the kitchen that first morning, when she'd lost her way. She'd seen him several times since then, but always he had passed her with a downturned glance, and only nodded briefly to her greeting. 'He's nae one for talk,' was Kirsty's explanation, when Sophia asked if she had somehow given him offence. 'He told me once there were so many folk lived in his house when he was just a bairn, that now he likes a bit of peace.'

Sophia said good morning to him anyway, and Rory nodded, silent, as he helped her to the saddle. He had given her the same horse she had ridden north from Edinburgh, a quiet mare with one white stocking and a way of twitching back her ears to catch the slightest sound or word.

The mare seemed faintly agitated and impatient, as though she, too, felt the changing of the season and the warming of the wind, and wanted only to be off. Sophia had to take a firm hold on the reins, once they were on the road, to keep her to a walk. When the mare danced lightly sideways in a step that nearly knocked them into the countess and her mount, Sophia said, as an apology, 'My horse has a mind to go faster.'

The countess smiled. 'Mine also.' Looking at Sophia, she said, 'Shall we let them have their way?'

It was so glorious a feeling, that free run along the road, with the wind at her back and the sun on her face and the sense of adventure before her, that Sophia half wished it could go on forever, but at length the countess reined her horse and turned it back again, and with regret, Sophia did the same.

Her horse, though, did not wish to slow the pace, and before Sophia could guess the mare's mind, she had bolted. There was no response to the reins, though Sophia pulled strongly, and all she could do was to hold on as best she could, watching with fear as the mare left the road, running overland straight for the sea. For the cliffs.

When it seemed she must let go the reins and the stirrups and throw herself down from the saddle to save her own life, the mare suddenly wheeled and changed course, running not at the sea but alongside it. The great walls of Slains, soaring out of the shoreline, grew nearer with each pounding volley of steps.

She *must* stop, thought Sophia, or else the mare might go the wrong way around those walls, into the precipice. Pulling the taut reins with all of her strength, she called out to the mare, and the brown ears twitched round, and the mare unexpectedly came to a sliding halt, flinging Sophia clear out of the saddle.

She had a vague awareness of the sky being in the wrong position before the ground came up with bruising force, and stole her breath.

A sea bird floated overhead, its eye turned, curious, toward her. She was gazing upwards at it, with a roaring in her ears, when a man's voice asked her, 'Are you hurt?'

She wasn't sure. She tried her limbs and found them working, so she answered, 'No.'

Strong hands came under her, and helped her sit. She turned to better view the man, and found he was no stranger.

'Captain Gordon,' she said, wondering if she perhaps had suffered greater damage to her senses than she'd realised.

But he seemed real enough, and his smile seemed pleased she'd remembered his name. 'Aye,' he said. 'I've the devil's own habit of turning up anywhere, and it's a good thing for you that I did.'

Running hoofbeats interrupted them as, breathlessly, the countess caught them up. 'Sophia—' she began. Then, 'Thomas! How in God's name do you come here?'

'By His grace, my lady,' said the captain, kneeling still beside Sophia. 'Sent, it would appear, to keep your young charge here from being sorely injured, though I must confess I've done no more than set her upright.' With a grin, he asked, 'Do you indulge in racing now, your Ladyship? I should point out that, at your time of life, it is not wise.'

Her look of worry cleared. She said, 'Impertinence,' and smiled, and asked Sophia, 'Are you truly unharmed?'

Sophia answered that she was, and stood to prove it. She was shaky on her feet, though, and glad of Captain Gordon's firm hand holding to her elbow.

He looked to the mare, quiet now, standing several feet off. 'She does not appear such a dangerous mount. Will you try her again, if I stand at her head?'

He did not say as much, but Sophia well knew he was urging her back on the horse for a reason. She'd only had such a great fall once before, as a child, and she yet could remember her father, in helping her back on the pony that had thrown her, saying, 'Never waste a moment getting back into the saddle, else your confidence be lost.'

So she went bravely to the standing mare and let Captain Gordon help her up into her seat, and saw his eyes warm with approval. 'There,' he said, and took hold of the bridle. 'If you will permit me, we shall set a slower pace, on our return.'

The countess rode beside them on her own well-mannered gelding. 'Truthfully, Thomas,' she asked him, 'how came you to Slains? We have had no account of your coming.'

'I sent none. I did not know if my landing would be possible. We are on our return from the Orkneys and must keep to our patrol, but as the winds have been most favourable I find myself quite able to drop anchor here some few hours without causing us delay.'

The countess said, 'You have not then been troubled much by privateers?'

'I have not, my lady. It has been a voyage fraught with boredom – much to the frustration, I might add, of my young colleague, Captain Hamilton, who travels in my wake. He is most keen to fight a Frenchman, and can scarcely be contained from running out to open sea,' he said, 'in search of one.'

The countess smiled faintly at the joke, but she looked thoughtful. 'I confess I did forget your Captain Hamilton.'

'I know. But I did not.' His sideways look held reassurance. 'Do not worry. I have everything in hand.'

It was a function of his character, Sophia thought. He did, indeed, appear to have a flair for taking charge. Within a minute of their getting back to Slains, he had dispatched the mare to Rory to be groomed and searched for injuries, and Kirsty had been summoned to attend Sophia, much to the same purpose, while the captain and the countess waited downstairs in the drawing room.

'I am not hurt,' Sophia promised, watching Kirsty fuss round with the washing-bowl and linens, 'and you do not need to wait upon me.'

'Captain Gordon's orders,' Kirsty said, and cheerfully absolved herself of all responsibility. 'Och, just look at this mud!'

'I do fear I have ruined the countess's beautiful habit.'

'Well, ye've done it nae good. Nor yourself, either. See your back – ye'll have great bruises. Disna that hurt?'

'Only a little.' Sophia winced, though, at the touch.

'Ye'll be stiff come the morning. I'll ask Mrs Grant if she'll make up a poultice to draw out the swelling. Although I would not be surprised if Captain Gordon has not ordered one for ye already.' Kirsty paused, as though considering, which made Sophia think that, like herself, the girl felt unsure where the boundaries of their new acquaintance lay, for all she wanted to be friends. At long last Kirsty said, 'Ye must be pleased, to have so great a man as Captain Gordon take an interest in ye.'

'Take an interest...? Oh, no, I am certain he is only being kind,' Sophia said. Then, to Kirsty's glance, she added, 'He is in his forties, and must surely have a wife.'

'A wife does rarely keep a man like that from looking where he likes.'

Sophia felt her face begin to flush. 'But you are wrong.'

'If ye would so believe,' said Kirsty, gathering the muddied clothes. But she was smiling, and her smile broadened when Sophia chose her plainest, least becoming gown to wear downstairs.

It was not that Sophia did not think the captain an attractive man, but only that she did not wish to have his admiration in that way, and it relieved her that he took but little notice of her when she joined the others in the drawing room.

He was already standing, and he said to Mr Hall, 'Are you so sure you wish to leave? The winds are blowing fair, these days.'

'I cannot stay. His Grace the Duke of Hamilton has sent me word that I am sorely needed back in Edinburgh.'

'Then I shall be pleased to convey you to Leith. But we sail on the hour. Can you make yourself ready?'

'I can, Captain.' Turning, he said to the countess, 'My lady Erroll, I do thank you for your kindness in allowing me to linger here. Were it not for the strong tone of His Grace's recent message I do fear that you might never have been rid of me.'

'Good Mr Hall, you are welcome at Slains, now and always. I wish you a safe journey home.'

He nodded his acceptance of her blessing. 'Is there any message you would send the duke?'

'None, except I wish him health, and recommend him to the Lord High Constable, my son, if he should wish to send me word.'

The priest gave one more nod, and to Sophia said, 'I wish you well, my dear. I shall remember you in prayer.' He left them then, presumably to gather to his belongings.

Captain Gordon stayed some minutes more, and sat and talked of idle things, but it was clear that he, too, wanted to be off. At length he stood, and took his leave. 'I'm bound for Tynemouth, after Leith,' he told the countess. 'It will be no less than fourteen days before I once again come north, and I will be certain to send you a proper account of my coming.'

'Thank you, Thomas. That would be most helpful.'

'Mistress Paterson.' He touched his smiling lips against her hand, and then he straightened, and with mild dismay Sophia realised Kirsty had been right, for there was more than friendly interest in his eyes. 'I trust,' he said, 'that, in my absence, you'll endeavour to have no more misadventures. Though I'll warrant you may find that rather difficult, before too long.'

She murmured a polite reply, not wanting to detain him. It was not till some time afterwards, when she could no more see the *Royal William*'s sails upon the wide horizon, that she wished she'd asked him to explain the meaning of those final words. Because, to her ears now, they sounded rather like a warning.

Chapter Five

Jane, my agent, set the final page aside and curled her legs up underneath her in the armchair, in the front room of my cottage. 'And you've written all of this in just two days? It must be thirty pages.'

'Thirty-one,' I told her, as I dragged a wooden chair across to the front door so I could stand on it to feed more coins into the black electric meter.

'I don't remember you writing this quickly, before.'

'That's because I haven't. It feels great, it really does. It's like I'm channelling. The words just come in through the top of my head and run right out my fingers, the voice is so easy. I'm glad you suggested a woman.'

'Yes, well,' she said drily, 'I do have my uses.' She ruffled the pages again, as though, like me, she hardly believed they could be there. 'At this rate, you'll have the book done in a month.'

'Oh, I doubt it.' I wobbled a little on top of the chair, and caught at the door jamb to steady myself. 'I'm bound to slow down when I get to the middle. I usually do. And besides, this new angle is taking me straight into plot lines that I haven't researched. I've spent most of my time reading up on the French side of things, and Nathaniel Hooke's viewpoint, and what he got up to in Paris. I know some of what was going on in Edinburgh, of course, among the Jacobites, but apart from what Hooke wrote I don't know that much about Slains, and the things that went on there. I'll have to do some digging.'

'I do like your Captain Gordon,' Jane decided. 'He's a good complicating character. Is he real?'

'Yes. I was lucky to remember him.' The coins dropped one by one into the meter, and the slender needle, which had started drifting to the 'empty' mark, rebounded with reluctance. 'It's funny, the stray things that stick in your mind. Captain Gordon gets mentioned a couple of times in Nathaniel Hooke's papers. Not in detail, and Hooke never says his first name, but I guess he made an impression, because I remembered him.'

She was looking at me, curious. 'Why did you name him Thomas, then? I thought you had opinions on the naming of historical characters, and how they shouldn't be guessed at.'

I did. Ordinarily, I would have left the first name blank until I'd had a chance to look it up. This time, 'He wanted to be Thomas,' was the only way I could explain it, 'so I let him. I can always change it later, when I find out what his first name really was.'

His ship's name, too, the *Royal William* – I had made that up as well, but I knew that would be a simple thing to fix. The British navy kept good records, it would all be written down somewhere.

Jane said, 'You'll have to change the name of his "young colleague" while you're at it. Captain Hamilton. You've got a

Duke of Hamilton already, you can't have another Hamilton. Your readers will be too confused.'

'Oh. I didn't even notice that.' It was a bad habit of mine, playing favourites with names. In one of my first books I'd nearly had two men named Jack running round, mixing everyone up. Jane had caught that one, too, at the very last moment. 'Thanks,' I told her now, and started looking for my workbook, to remind myself.

My workbook was the only way that I could keep things organised. Before, I'd carried pocketfuls of notes and scribbled scraps of paper. Now, I wrote down all my thoughts on characters and plotting in the pages of a weathered three-ring binder, where I also kept the photocopied pages from the books I'd used for research, and the maps and timelines that I would refer to as my story took its shape. I'd got the inspiration for my workbook from my father's family history binders, neatly kept and sectioned in a way that satisfied his sense of order. He had worked his whole life as an engineer, in charge of building things, and second only to his love of making every surface level, was his need to battle chaos with pure logic.

I did try. I flipped my workbook to the section labelled 'To Be Checked' and jotted down the names of Captain Gordon and his ship and Captain Hamilton.

'So you think it's all right?' I asked.

'I love it. It's fantastic. But you don't need me to tell you that,' Jane said, and smiled at me, a parent indulging a child. 'You writers and your insecurities. Honestly. You said yourself you felt you were creating something wonderful.'

'I said the feeling of *writing* it was wonderful. That doesn't mean the story's any good.'

'Come on. You know it is.'

'OK,' I said. 'I think that it's fantastic, too. But it's still nice to hear it from somebody else.'

'Insecurities,' she said again.

'I can't help it.' It came with the job – all the time that I spent on my own, with that blank stack of paper I had to turn into a book. Sometimes I felt like the girl in the fairy tale Rumplestiltskin, locked up and told to spin straw into gold. 'I'm never sure,' I said, 'if I can pull it off.'

'But you always do,' Jane pointed out. 'And brilliantly.'

'Well, thank you.'

'All you need is a break. I could take you to lunch.'

'That's all right, we don't have to go out. I can make you a sandwich.'

She looked round. 'With what?'

I hadn't realised, till I looked around myself, that I had nearly used up the supplies that Jimmy Keith had stocked my kitchen with. I was down to three slices of bread and an egg. 'Oh,' I said. 'I guess I need to do some shopping.'

'We can do that,' said Jane, 'on our way back from lunch.'

After lunch, though, I managed to talk her into walking up to Slains with me, again. We went from the village this time, by the footpath that led from Main Street. It took us through a wood of tangled trees behind Ward Hill, where a small and quiet stream ran through a gully to the sea. The footpath crossed the stream by way of a flat bridge, then climbed the further hill that changed from coarse, shrub-covered ground into a proper cliff as we came up above the level of the trees. Another steep turn and we stood at the top, with the sea far below us and Slains in our sights. The walk here wasn't difficult, as coast paths went, but it was slippery in spots, and twice Jane nearly lost her footing near the edge.

'You are *not*,' she said, emphatically, 'to come up here alone.'

'You sound exactly like my mother.'

'She's a sensible woman, your mother. I mean, look at this, will you? What kind of a madman builds his home right at the edge of a cliff?'

'The kind of a madman who likes good defences.'

'But they're not such good defences, really, are they? If your enemies came overland, they'd have you trapped. There'd be nowhere to go.' She glanced down again at the foaming sea striking the rocks far below, and I could see that it affected her. I hadn't expected that she would be bothered by heights. After all, she'd flown with Alan, and the two of them were known to do some crazy things on holidays, like climbing into caves and parasailing in the Amazon.

'Are you OK?' I asked.

'I'm fine.' But she did not look down again.

I felt completely in my element, myself. I liked the sea sounds and the crisp wind in my face, and my feet placed themselves with confidence upon the path, as though they felt quite certain of the way.

There were no other footprints ahead of our own, and no tracks of a dog in the soft, muddy places. Which wasn't too surprising, since it stood to reason that the man I'd run into that first day in the parking lot, the man I'd asked directions of, could hardly spend his whole day, every day, up here. He might not even be a local man. I hadn't seen him round the town – and, for no reason other than the fact I'd liked his smile, I had been looking.

I was looking for him now, but when he wasn't at the top,

I took care not to show my disappointment. Jane didn't miss much, and she always had been quick to take an interest any time *I* took an interest in a man. I didn't want her asking questions. After all, there wasn't anything for me to say, I'd only met him once. I didn't even know his name.

Jane asked me, 'What's the sigh for?'

'Did I sigh?'

'With feeling.'

'Well, just look at this,' I said, and spread my hands wide to the view. 'It's all so beautiful.'

The ruins felt much lonelier this afternoon, with us the only visitors. The wind wept round the high pink granite walls and followed when we walked along the grassy floors of what had once been corridors. I had wanted to see if, from what still remained, I could make out the floor plan, and Jane, her equilibrium restored now that we'd stepped a little further from the edge, was keen to join me in the game.

'I think,' she said, 'this might have been the kitchen. Here's a bit of chimney stack, and look at the size of that hearth.'

'I don't know.' I walked further along. 'I think maybe the kitchen was somewhere down here, near the stables.'

'And what makes you think those are stables?'

She wasn't convinced, and I knew I was letting the house I'd imagined last night, when I'd written the scenes of Sophia at Slains, shape my judgement of where things should be. There was nothing at all at this end of the house to suggest what the rooms might have been – only roofless rectangular spaces with crumbling walls, nothing more. But I still spent a happy few minutes meandering round, playing at fitting my made-up rooms onto the real ones.

Sophia's bedchamber, I thought, could be within that tall

square tower standing proudly at the corner of the castle's front, against the cliffs. I couldn't see a way to get inside it, but my mind could fill the details in, and guess at what the views might be. And down there, at the end of this long corridor with all the doors, could be the castle's dining room, and this, I thought as I stepped through a narrow arching door into the soaring room I'd liked so much my first time here, the one where I had seen the tracks of man and dog and where the gaping window gave a wide view of the sea, this surely must have been the drawing room. Well, *under* the drawing room, actually, since I was standing in what would have been the lower level of the house, the floorless main rooms being all above me, but the view would be the same from the great window I saw higher up the wall. A person could have stood there and looked out towards the east along the glinting path of sunlight on the waves to the horizon.

I was gazing out that way myself, when Jane came up to join me.

'What?' she asked.

I turned, uncomprehending. 'Pardon?'

'What's so interesting?'

'Oh. Nothing. I'm just looking.' But I brought my head back round again and stared a moment longer at the line where sea met sky, as though I needed to be sure, now that she mentioned it, that there was nothing there.

Jane left just after two o'clock, and I went into Cruden Bay to get some food for supper. I'd never much liked shopping in the larger modern grocery stores, it took too much time to find anything, so I was delighted when I found a little corner shop on Main Street. I didn't need much – just some apples and a pork chop and another loaf of bread. The man who kept the shop was friendly, and because my face was new to him, he asked me where I came from. We were deep in a discussion about Canada and hockey when the shop's door jangled open and the wind blew Jimmy Keith in.

'Aye-aye.' He looked happy. 'I've been lookin fer ye.'

I said, 'You have?'

'Oh, aye. I was up tae the St Olaf Hotel yestereen, and I found some folk tae help ye wi' yer book. I've made a wee list.'

His 'wee list' appeared to have at least a half a dozen names. He read them off and told me who they were, although I couldn't keep them straight. I wasn't sure whether the schoolteacher or the plumber had offered to give me a driving tour of the district. But I did take note of one name.

'Dr Weir,' said Jimmy, last of all, 'taks a rare interest in the local history. He's a gran man. He's aye fightin tae save Slains. He'll be at hame the nicht, if ye've a mind tae wander ower there and spik wi' him.'

'I'd like that very much. Thanks.'

'He's got hissel a bungalow up by the Castle Wood. I'll tell ye the wye, it's nae bother tae find.'

I walked out after supper. The dark had settled in, and on the path down from my cottage to the road the strange, uneasy feeling gripped me once again, although there was no one and nothing there that could have threatened me. I shook it off and made my legs move faster, but it followed, like an unseen force that chased me to the road, and then retreated into darkness, waiting...knowing it would have another chance at me, tonight, when I came home.

Chapter Six

The Castle Wood stood not far up past the Kilmarnock Arms. I'd gone through it that first day when I had been driving to Jane's, and by daylight had thought it a peaceful place, but in the dark it was different, and I was grateful that I could pass by it tonight on the far side of the road. There were masses of rooks wheeling noisily over the treetops, their harsh cries unnerving. And the tall trees themselves with their strange gnarled branches looked twisted and weird, like the wolf- and witch-concealing forests in the illustrations of my old book of *Grimm's Fairy Tales*.

Dr Weir's house was a welcome sight – a neat, low bungalow, with wind chimes hung beside the door and a family of small painted gnomes peering up from the tidy front garden.

I was clearly expected. I barely had to knock before the door was opened to me. Dr Weir looked like a gnome himself: not tall, moon-faced, with round, old-fashioned spectacles. I couldn't judge his age. His hair was white, but his complexion had a healthy, ruddy smoothness, and the eyes behind the spectacles were clear and sharp. He'd been a surgeon, Jimmy had explained, and had just recently retired.

'Come in,' he said, 'come in.' He took my coat and shook the dampness from it, hanging it with care upon the antique mirrored hall tree. I could see, in every corner of the entryway, the evidence of good taste and a love of timeworn things. There was no clutter, but the fading prints hung on the wall, the Persian carpet runner on the floor, and the soft light from old glass sconces on the walls, all lent the space an atmosphere of permanence and comfort.

And that atmosphere was stronger in the narrow, lamplit study that he showed me to. One wall was lined from floor to ceiling with glass-fronted bookcases, their shelves packed tight with volumes old and new, hardback and paperback. And where he had run out of room to stand a book up properly on edge, he'd laid it horizontally across the top of its companions and stacked others over that, so there were books wedged in wherever there was space. It had the same effect on me as the sight of a toy shop would have on a six-year-old.

But because I didn't want to *seem* like a six-year-old, I held in my enthusiasm and let him introduce me to his wife, who had been sitting in a chintz-upholstered chair, one of a pair that flanked a small round table at the narrow end wall. Behind these, a fall of striped, pinch-pleated curtains had been drawn across the room's one window, shutting darkness out and keeping in the warm glow of the reading lamps. A leather wing chair with a smoking table at its side completed the room's furnishings, and on the wall that didn't have the bookcases, a handful of seascapes and nautical prints caught the light in the glass of their frames.

The doctor's wife, Elsie, was compact like him, and white-haired, but not round in the slightest. More a fairy than a gnome, I thought. Her blue eyes seemed to dance. 'We were about to have our evening whisky,' she informed me. 'Will you join us? Or perhaps you'd like some tea?'

I told her whisky would be fine.

Because the wing chair was so obviously the doctor's, I took the other chintz-covered chair, angled with the bookcases to my one shoulder and the curtains of the window to my other, and the small round table set between myself and Elsie Weir.

Dr Weir stepped out a moment, and returned with three large tumblers of heavy cut glass, each a third of the way filled with rich amber whisky. He handed mine to me. 'So, Jimmy said you were a writer. Historical fiction, is that right?'

'That's right.'

'I'm that ashamed to say I didn't recognise your name.'

Elsie smiled. 'He's a typical man. Never picks up a book if the writer's a woman. He always expects it to end with a kiss.'

'Well, mine usually do,' I admitted. I tasted my whisky, and let the sharp warmth sear a path to my stomach. I loved the pure taste of a single malt Scotch, but I had to consume it in small, measured sips, or it did me in quickly. 'The book that I'm working on now has to do with the French and the Jacobites trying to bring James VIII back to Scotland, in 1708.'

'Does it, now?' He had lifted his eyebrows. 'That's a lesser-known skirmish. What made you choose that one?'

I wasn't sure myself. The main ideas for my novels never struck me like a lightning bolt. They formed themselves in stages, like a snowball packed in layers, with clumps padded on here and lumps scraped away there, till the whole thing was rounded and perfect. But by then, I could no longer see the shape of that first handful I'd scooped up, that first small thought that had begun the process.

I tried to think of what had started this one.

I'd been working on my last book, which was set in Spain, and, needing to find out some minor detail about eighteenth-century hospitals, I'd come across the memoirs of a doctor who had lived in France about the time I needed. That doctor had done surgery on Louis XIV – the Sun King – and had been so proud of it that he'd written several detailed pages on the incident. And that had got me interested in Louis XIV.

I'd started reading up on him, and on his court and all its goings-on. For pleasure, nothing more. And then one night I'd turned my television on to catch the news and got the channel wrong and tuned in an old movie – Errol Flynn in 'Captain Blood' – and because I'd always had a thing for Errol Flynn I'd watched him instead, enjoying the swordfights and the romance and the swashbuckling, and at the end he'd leapt onto the foredeck of his ship and told his fellow pirates they could all return to England, now that bad King James had fled to France and good King William ruled the country.

And *that* had set me thinking, idly, of what rotten luck the Stewart kings had suffered, King James in particular, and how it must have felt for him to lose the crown, give up his throne, and have to live in exile.

And, still thinking this, I'd turned the television off and opened up the book that I'd been reading, a biography of Louis XIV, and on the page where I'd left off there'd been a mention of the palace, Saint-Germain, that Louis had loaned to the Stewart kings in exile, so they still could keep a royal court. Intrigued, I'd started reading up on *that* – on all the Scottish nobles coming in and out of Saint-Germain, and all the plotting that went on. I'd found it all so fascinating.

Shortly after that, I'd found the papers by Nathaniel Hooke, and learnt about his dream of a rebellion, and...

It was, I knew, a convoluted explanation, and most people who asked where I got my ideas were looking for a shorter answer, so I said to Dr Weir that I had picked the 1708 rebellion just because, 'I liked Nathaniel Hooke.'

'Ah, Hooke.' The doctor nodded. 'He's an interesting character. An Irishman, though, not a Scot. You knew that? Yes, he came to Slains on two occasions, I believe. The first in 1705, to gauge support among the nobles for his plan to bring the young king back, and then again in 1707, to set everything in motion.'

'I'm just dealing with the second visit, really. And the actual attempt at the invasion, the next winter.' I settled back and took another careful sip of whisky, and explained how, since I'd started writing my book from the French side of things, I needed to fill in some gaps on my knowledge of Slains. 'Jimmy said you knew a lot about the castle.'

'That I do.'

'It's his pet subject,' Elsie told me, with a fond, indulgent smile. 'I hope you've nothing else to do, this evening.'

Dr Weir, ignoring her, said, 'What, specifically, were you wanting to know?'

'Whatever you can tell me.' I had learnt from years of doing research not to put restrictions on the things that people told me and although he'd likely touch on things I'd read about already, I'd learn more from him if I just let him talk, and kept my own mouth shut.

He started with the history of the Hays, the Earls of Erroll, who had built Slains. 'It's an old and noble family. There's a legend told about the Hays, you know, that in the ancient days an ancestor of theirs was ploughing a field with his two sons, in sight of a battlefield on which the Danes were destroying the Scots forces. And, says the legend, when one of the Scots lines began to break up and retreat, well, this farmer – a large man, with powerful arms – snatched the yoke from his oxen to use as a weapon, and called to his sons, and together the three of them herded the Scots soldiers back into battle and reformed the line, and the Danes, in the end, were defeated. The king then took the farmer and his sons to Perth, and let a falcon off from Kinnoull Hill, and said that all the land the falcon flew over was to be theirs. And the bird flew to a stone, still called the Hawk's Stone, in St Madoes Parish, so then the farmer was master of some of the finest lands north of the Tay, and a man of great wealth.

'It's no more than a tale, mind, and there's nothing written down to give it proof, but to this day the Chiefs of Hay still carry as their coat of arms the king's falcon, and the ox-yoke, and three bloodstained shields, one each for that brave farmer and his sons. And the family's motto, translated, means "Keep the Yoke". So they believe it, anyway.'

He paused, because he'd noticed that I'd taken out my notebook and was writing down the legend, and he gave me time to finish.

'Do you have all that?' he asked me. 'Good. I'll try to go more slowly for you. Now, about the Hays. They came from Normandy, according to the history books. They were raised to the title of earls in the mid-fifteenth century, and fully a hundred years before that, they'd been made Lord High Constables of Scotland by Robert the Bruce himself. That's an influential office, Lord High Constable, and a hereditary one, passed down the family through the generations, along with a fierce devotion to the Catholic cause.

'They supported Mary, Queen of Scots' son, James VI, till James decided to turn Protestant. That was too much for the 9th Earl of Erroll, and he led a mounted attack on the king's forces. Got himself an arrow wound for his efforts, as I recall. And he made King James so angry that the king marched north personally to sack the Earl of Erroll's castles at Delgatie and Old Slains, just south of here. Destroyed them both with gunpowder and cannon. The Earl of Erroll spent a few years biding time in exile, then came back to Scotland, and, instead of trying to rebuild Old Slains, decided to build anew, around a tower house the Hays kept here. So then he called this New Slains.

'*New* Slains is the one you want to know about. The other was long gone when Colonel Hooke came over. In 1708...now, let me think...the Earl of Erroll who'd have been here would have been the 13th earl, Charles Hay, the last male of the line. And his mother, the Countess of Erroll, Anne Hay, was a driving force in the conspiracy. But then,' he said, 'she would have been. She was a Drummond, and her brother was the Duke of Perth, a powerful man at the court of the Stewarts, in France. She was committed to trying to bring back the king. A remarkable woman. The Countesses of Erroll have, through history, been more interesting,' he told me, 'than their men.'

He drank his whisky, and the warm light in the little room reflected on the thousand points of intricately cut glass on his tumbler, and his round, old-fashioned glasses, behind which his eyes turned thoughtful. 'Mind you, her son, the 13th earl, did have some fire in his belly. He hated the Union, and fought it till his dying breath, in any way he could. And then, of course, he was a Hay, and a supporter of the Stewart kings, and that was not a choice a man made lightly. Dangerous times, so they were.' He mused on this a moment, then went on, 'He didn't think to marry and produce an heir before he died, and so he passed the title to his sister. Another interesting Countess of Erroll, she was, but that's a different story altogether. Anyway, she had no heir either, so from her the title went sideways, into her nieces and nephews, and out of the old family. Slains, though, stayed with the Earls of Erroll until 1916, when the 20th earl had to sell it for death duties. The new owner eventually gave up on it, and had the roof taken off in the 1920s – for safety, they say, though more likely it was so he wouldn't have to pay the taxes. After that, well, with no roof, the place just fell to ruin.'

Elsie said, 'A shame, it was, a grand old house like that, with such a history. Samuel Johnson stayed there once, you know, with Mr Boswell, his biographer. Douglas, you used to have copies of what they both wrote about Slains. It was fair interesting.'

'Aye,' he said. 'I forgot about those.' Rising from his leather chair, he left the room a moment and returned with a file folder full of papers. 'You can keep these, if you like. I've other copies. Boswell's account is by far the more colourful. Johnson's is drier, but still good to read. There are one or two other bits in the folder that might be of help to you, having to do with the history of Slains. And somewhere,' he said, looking round, at a loss, 'I did have the old plans for the castle, that showed where the rooms were. I can't think what I've done with it.'

Elsie said, 'You may have loaned it out.'

'Oh, very likely.' He sat down again and smiled at me. 'The curse of age. I can't remember anything. I'll see if I can't find them for you though, those plans. You'd like to have a look at them, I'm sure.'

'I would, yes. Very much.'

Elsie smiled. 'It must be fun to write about the past. What made you interested in history?'

There was no short answer to that question either, but I did my best, and so we talked about my father's love of genealogy, and the trips we had taken to places our ancestors came from, and all of the hours that I'd spent as a child walking with him in graveyards to search out the headstones of great-great-great grandfathers. All of those people were real to me. Their faces in the framed and yellowed photographs that hung around our house were as familiar as my own, and when I stopped to look at them their eyes looked back at me, and pulled me with them to the past.

The doctor nodded understanding. 'Aye, my father had no great love of history, but he'd inherited a portrait, quite a good painted portrait, of a Weir who had been a sea captain. It hung in the study, when I was a lad. A fair bit of imagining, I did around that portrait. I don't doubt it's why I'm so fond of the sea.'

That reminded me. 'Do you, by any chance, know where I could find out about Scottish naval history in the early eighteenth century?'

He smiled, and setting down his glass, looked over to his bookcases. 'Well, now, I might have a few odd volumes on the subject.'

Elsie said, 'He has a shelf full. Were you wanting information on the ships?'

'The people, mostly. I need to do research on one of the captains Nathaniel Hooke writes about.'

'Ah, Captain Gordon, is it?' Dr Weir glanced at me to make sure it was, then stood to search the shelves. 'There's quite a lot on Gordon in *The Old Scots Navy*. I did have a copy here...aye, here it is. You can take that with you, if you like, and read it over, see if what you want is in there. If not, I have other books that you can—'

Someone knocking at the front door interrupted.

'Do excuse me,' said the doctor, and he went out to the entry hall. I heard the door swing open, and the muffled voices of the doctor and another man, a burst of laughter, and the stamp of feet as someone crossed the threshold.

Dr Weir returned, all smiles. 'Your driver's here.'

'My driver?'

Stuart Keith came close behind him, handsome in his leather jacket, with his near-black hair. 'I was just on my way home, and I thought you might need a lift down to the harbour. The wind's picking up something fierce.'

I hadn't noticed it earlier, while we'd been talking, but now I could hear the wind raging against the front window behind me. And I thought of walking back in that, alone, past Castle Wood, and of that dark and lonely stretch of path that led from Harbour Street up to my cottage on the hill, and having Stuart take me home seemed suddenly a very good idea.

So I thanked the Weirs for what had been a really useful evening, and I finished off my whisky in a rather too-large swallow, and with borrowed book and files in hand, I said good night.

Outside, the wind rocked Stuart's low-slung car as I slid into it. 'How did you know where I'd be?' I asked.

'Someone mentioned it tonight in the pub.' When he saw my expression he said, 'Well, I told you, now, didn't I? One hour at the St Olaf Hotel and my dad can spread any news round half the village. Has he got you on a schedule, yet?'

'Not quite. He just gave me a list of people he thought could help.'

'Oh, aye? Who were they?'

'I can't remember their names, honestly. But I think I'm supposed to be getting a driving tour this weekend, from either a plumber or a schoolteacher.'

He smiled. 'That would be the plumber. You don't have to go – I can give you a driving tour.' He turned the wheel smartly as he said that, and the back tires swung out as we made the turn down into Main Street.

I gripped my armrest. 'I think that my odds of survival are better,' I said, 'with the plumber.'

He laughed, and I went on, 'Besides, you're off again this weekend, aren't you? Down to London.'

'Aye, but not for long.' I felt his glance, although I couldn't see him clearly in the dimness of the sports car's warm interior. 'I will be back.'

I knew he liked me. And I liked him, too, but not that way. Despite his looks, there wasn't any spark, and although it had been some time since I'd felt a spark with anyone, I knew enough to know when it was missing. So I felt a little guilty when I let him park the car and walk me up the muddy footpath to my cottage. I didn't want to lead him on, or give him false encouragement, but neither did I want to be alone. Not here. Not in the dark, when every hair along my neck was rising with the sense of something wicked on its way.

'Mind how you go,' said Stuart, reaching out to grab my

arm. 'That's the second time you've done that, nearly stepped clean off the path.' He stopped. Looked down at me. 'What's wrong?'

I couldn't answer him. The moment that he'd grabbed me, I'd been gripped by panic, sudden and unreasoning. My heart was beating so hard in my chest that I could hear it, and I didn't have the least idea why. I took a breath, and forced a smile. 'You just...surprised me,' was the only explanation I could offer.

'I can see that. Sorry.'

'Not your fault. I hate this path at night, to tell the truth,' I said, as we fell back in step. 'It's all right in the daytime, but at night it always spooks me.'

'Really? Why?'

'I don't know. Curse of my profession, I suppose. I have a wild imagination.'

'Well, you can call me any time you like, I'll come and walk you home.'

'You won't be here,' I pointed out.

'Aye. I'm away tomorrow morning, early. But I've told you, I'll be back.'

We'd reached the cottage. Stuart watched me fit my key into the lock, and asked, 'D'ye want me to come in and see you don't have any monsters in your cupboards?'

From his smile I thought it far more likely that he had a mind to look for monsters underneath my bed, and I was not about to fall for that. I took his offer lightly. 'No, you don't have to do that, I'm OK.'

'You're sure?'

'I'm sure.'

I saw how he was watching me, and knew he was

considering attempting a good night kiss, but before he followed through with it, I reached instead to hug him – just a friendly hug that made no promises and wouldn't be misunderstood. 'Thanks again for bringing me home,' I said. 'Have a safe trip down to London.'

The hug seemed to surprise him, but he took it all in stride. 'I will,' he said, and let me go, and took a backwards step onto the path. 'And I'll be seeing you,' he promised, 'very soon.'

For all the complications that I knew I'd just avoided, I was sorry to see him go. The cottage felt lonely when I went inside. And cold. The coal fire in my Aga had burnt so low that it took an hour of concentrated effort to revive it, and by then I was so chilled and tired I wanted just to fall into my bed, and go to sleep.

I took the book with me – the one that Dr Weir had loaned me, on the Scottish navy, because, tired or not, I felt I should do *some* work, since I clearly wasn't going to write tonight. It was an older book with blue board covers, and the title page read helpfully: 'The Old Scots Navy, From 1689 to 1710, Edited by James Grant, L.L.B.' The frontispiece was black and white, a portrait of a white-wigged naval officer in an authoritative stance, his finger pointing to a sailing vessel in the background. There was something in his eyes, his face, that struck me as familiar, so I peered more closely at the light italic script beneath the portrait, looking for his name. I found it.

Thomas Gordon.

Admiral Thomas Gordon, to be sure, but every Admiral was a captain, once.

I sat upright. Cold rushed in beneath the blankets, crept around me, but I hardly felt it. Flipping to the index, I began a careful reading of the references to Thomas Gordon.

'Thomas Gordon had,' the book informed me, 'a remarkable career...His voyages embraced such distant places as Shetland, Stockholm, Norway, and Holland. On 17th July, 1703, he received a regular commission in the Scots Navy as captain of the *Royal Mary*.'

Well, I thought, I'd almost got it right. The *Royal Mary*. William and Mary had reigned as a couple – I'd just picked the wrong half, when I'd named my fictional ship.

I kept reading. And here was the transcript of part of a letter Nathaniel Hooke wrote, of his first visit over to Scotland, two years before my story started:

'While I stayed with my Lady Erroll, our frigate [the Audacious] was within musket shot of the castle. The day after my arrival Mr Gordon, captain of a Scotch frigate commissioned to guard the coast, appeared in the southward. My Lady Erroll bid me be under no apprehensions, and sent a gentleman in a cutter to desire the captain to take another course, with which he complied. The lady has gained him over, and as often as he passes and repasses that way he takes care to give her notice...'

I knew I'd read that bit before, because I'd remembered his role in avoiding the French ship that carried Hooke over.

And after that came other varied documents: Sailing orders to Captain Gordon, and more sailing orders; a warrant to Captain Gordon to sail to Scarborough; a commission to Captain Thomas Gordon in 1705 to be commander of the ship the *Royal William*...

I read that last one over, to be certain I'd made no mistake. But there it was, as plain as plain. And right below it on the page, a similar commission to James Hamilton of Orbieston, to be commander of the ship the *Royal Mary*.

In my mind, I played the scene that I'd just written, with the countess saying, 'I confess I did forget your Captain Hamilton.'

And Captain Gordon – Captain *Thomas* Gordon, yet – replying, confident, 'I know. But I did not.'

No more, it seemed, had I. But how on earth had I remembered such a tiny, minor detail as the name of Captain Hamilton? I must have read it somewhere, though I couldn't for the life of me think where. I kept a written record of each document I used in my research, in case I missed a fact and needed to go back again to check it, and I knew I hadn't read one single thing about the Scottish navy apart from what Nathaniel Hooke had written, and that hadn't been much. Still, you couldn't just remember something if you hadn't had it in your memory to begin with.

Could you?

At my back, the window rattled fiercely from a gust of wind that sent me sliding underneath my covers, seeking warmth. I closed the book and set it safely on the table at my bedside, but it didn't leave my thoughts, and by the time sleep finally claimed me I'd have paid a lot for one more glass of Dr Weir's good whisky.

Chapter Seven

I was my father's daughter in more ways than one. When something made no sense, I tried attacking it with logic. When that failed – when I'd read through all my notes, and all Hooke's papers, and could find no mention there of either Captain Gordon's first name or his ship's name, or of any Captain Hamilton – I moved on to my second coping tactic: putting something in order.

What I chose to do was take my observations of the castle ruins, and the pages I had written, and attempt to draw a floor plan of the castle I'd imagined. Until I got the proper one from Dr Weir, it would at least help keep the daily movements of my characters consistent, so I wouldn't have them turning left into the drawing room one day, and right the next.

My father would have called what I was doing 'colouring maps'. That was what he called it when I filled in time and wasted effort, in his view, by taking lots of trouble to do something wholly unessential, as when I had coloured maps in high school for geography, feathering blue round the shorelines and shading in valleys and hills. But he always said it fondly, as though he also knew and understood that there were times when what the brain most needed was to simply colour maps.

It did, in fact, bring me a certain sense of satisfied accomplishment to draw my castle floor plan, all those neatly ruled lines on the page, and the room names spelt out in block capital letters. I didn't have crayons, or else I'd have coloured it, too, for good measure. But when it was done, I felt better.

I set it to the side of my computer, where I'd see it while I worked, and went to make myself a sandwich. I was standing at my window, eating lunch and looking out to sea, as I so often did, my mind on nothing in particular, when I first saw the dog.

A small dog, running down the beach, ears flapping happily as it splashed through the foam-edged tracks of waves as though it scarcely felt the cold, pursuing something round and bright that rolled along the sand. A tennis ball, I guessed, and watched the dog catch up the ball in triumph, wheeling back to run the way that it had come. A spaniel, spotted brown and white.

Even before I saw the man the dog was running to, the man who stood with hands deep in his pockets, shoulders braced against the wind, I'd set my plate down and was looking for my toothbrush. And my coat.

I didn't know exactly why. I could have, if I'd wanted to, explained it in a few ways. He'd been friendly to me that first day, and after spending all this morning cooped up in the cottage, I was keen to get outside and talk to someone, and I liked his dog. That's what I told myself the whole way down the hill and up the road, across the narrow wooden footbridge and around the looming dunes. But when I'd reached the beach myself, and when he turned his head at my approach and smiled a welcome, I knew then that none of those was actually the reason.

He looked more like a pirate this morning, a cheerful one, with his dark hair cut roughly in collar-length layers and blown by the wind, and the flash of his teeth white against the clipped beard. 'Were my directions no help to you, then?' he asked.

'I'm sorry?'

'You were on your way to Peterhead, the last we met. Did ye not find the way?'

'Oh. Yes, I did, thanks. I came back.'

'Aye, I see that.'

'I've rented a cottage,' I said, 'for the winter.'

His grey eyes moved with interest to the place where I was pointing. 'What, the old one on Ward Hill?'

'Yes.'

'The word is, it's been taken by a writer.'

'Right. That's me.'

He looked me up and down, with humour. 'You don't look much like a writer.'

My eyebrows lifted. 'Should I take that as a compliment?'

'You should, aye. It was meant as one.'

The dog was back, all muddied feet and wagging tail and wet nose snuffling at my knees. I scratched his floppy ears and said, 'Hi, Angus,' and the spaniel dropped the tennis ball, expectantly, beside my shoe. I picked it up and threw it out again for him as far as I could throw.

The man beside me looked impressed. 'You've a good arm.'

'Well, thank you. My father played baseball,' I said, as though that would explain it. And then, because I realised that we'd never introduced ourselves, I said, 'I'm Carrie, by the way.'

He took the hand I offered him, and in that swift, brief contact something warm, electric, jolted up my arm. He said, 'I'm Graham.'

'Hi.'

He really did have the best smile, I thought. It was sudden and genuine, perfect teeth gleaming an instant against the neat beard, closely trimmed to the line of his jaw. I missed it when he turned his head to watch the progress of the dog. 'So, Carrie, tell me, what is it you're writing?'

I knew that everyone I met in Cruden Bay would ask that question, and eventually I'd have to come up with a tidy, single-sentence answer, something that satisfied their polite interest without boring them to sleep. I tried it now, and told him, 'It's a novel set at Slains, back in the early eighteenth century.'

I'd thought that he might nod, or maybe say that sounded interesting, and that would be the end of it. Instead, he turned his head again, face angled so the strong wind kept the hair out of his eyes. 'Oh, aye? What year?'

I told him, and he gave a nod.

'The Franco-Scots invasion, is it? Attempted invasion, I guess I should call it. It wasn't exactly a raging success.' He bent briefly to wrestle the ball out of Angus's teeth and then tossed it back out, several yards past the point where my own throw had landed. 'An interesting choice,' Graham said, 'for a novel. I don't ken that anyone's written about it, that way. It barely makes the history books.'

I tried to hide my own surprise that he would be aware of what was written in the history books. Not because I'd made any assumptions about his intelligence, but because, based on the way he looked, the way he moved, I would have expected he'd be more at home on a football field than in a library. Showed what I knew, I thought.

I hadn't noticed that the dog was overdue in coming back, but Graham had. He looked along the shore, eyes narrowed to the wind, and whistled sharply through his teeth to call the spaniel back. 'I think he's hurt himself,' he said, and sure enough, Angus came limping towards us, the ball in his mouth, but one front paw held painfully.

'Stepped on something,' Graham guessed, and crouched down to investigate. 'Broken glass, it looks like. Not a bad cut, but I'll need to get that sand out.'

'You can use my kitchen sink,' I offered.

He carried Angus easily against his chest, the way a man might hold an injured child, and as I led them across the white footbridge and up the steep side of Ward Hill I was thinking of little else but the dog's welfare. But with both of them inside, the cottage felt a little smaller, and I found myself becoming more self-conscious.

'Sorry for the mess,' I said, and tried to clear a space for him to lay the dog down on the narrow counter.

'That's all right. I've seen it worse. Is there a towel in the airing cupboard? One of those old yellow ones will do, don't use a good one.'

I stopped, in the middle of moving a teacup, and stared at him. And then the gears of memory clicked a notch, and I remembered Jimmy Keith describing his two sons to me. He'd said, 'There's Stuie, he's the younger, and his brother Graham's doon in Aberdeen.'

'Your last name isn't Keith, by any chance?' I asked.

'It is.'

So that was why he seemed at home in here, and why he knew his local history. He should do, I thought. He lectured in it at the university.

He glanced at me, still holding the dog's paw beneath the running water. 'What's the matter?'

Looking to the side, I smiled. 'Nothing. I'll go get that towel.' I found the ones he wanted, the yellow ones, tucked in the back of the cupboard, and chose one that was worn, but clean.

He thanked me for it without looking up, and went on working at the wound. He had nice hands, I noticed. Neat and capable and strong, and yet their touch upon the spaniel's paw was gentle. He asked, 'Has Dad been telling tales about me, then? Is that it?'

'No. It's just that I keep tripping over members of your family. First your brother, and now you. There aren't any other Keiths running around here in Cruden Bay, are there?'

'Not counting cousins, there's only the two of us.' Still looking down and concentrating, he asked, 'How did ye come to meet my brother?'

'He was on my plane. He drove me up here from the airport.'

That brought his head around. 'The airport?'

'Yes, in Aberdeen.'

'I ken fine where it is,' he said. 'But when I saw you last week, you were on your way to Peterhead, and driving by yourself. How did ye get from there,' he asked me, 'to the airport?'

I explained. It sounded decidedly odd to my own ears, the story of how I had looked at Slains castle and known that I needed to be here, and flown back to Paris to clear out my things and come over again, in the space of a couple of days. But if Graham thought anything of it, he didn't say. When I had finished, he tore a long strip from one end of the towel and wrapped it with care around Angus's paw.

'So, you're finished with France, then,' he said, summing up.

'Yes, it seems so. The book's coming along well, now I'm here.'

'Well, that's good. There,' he said, to the dog, 'how is that, now? Feel better?'

Angus stretched his neck to lick at Graham's face, who laughed and gave the floppy ears a tousle. 'There now, we'll clear off and let the lady get to work.'

I didn't want them to clear off. I wanted them to stay. I wanted to tell him I did my writing mostly in the evenings, that my afternoons were free, that I could make some tea, and maybe we could talk... But I couldn't think of a way I could say that without sounding forward, and he hadn't given me any real reason to think he'd say yes, or to think that he found me one tenth as attractive as I found him.

So I just stood to the side as he thanked me again for my help, and he picked Angus up and I opened the door for them. That's when he stopped and looked down at me, thinking.

He asked, 'Have ye been to the Bullers o' Buchan?'

'The what?'

He repeated the name, taking care to speak slowly. 'A sort of a sea cave, not far to the north.'

'No, I haven't.'

'Because I was thinking, if you're feeling up to a bit of a walk, I could take you tomorrow.'

Surprised, I said, 'That would be nice.'

I was kicking myself for my bland choice of words, but he didn't appear to have noticed.

'Right, then. How does ten o'clock suit you? You've no problem walking the coast path?'

'No problem at all,' I assured him.

'I'll see you tomorrow.'

Again I was hit with that flash of a smile, and as I looked at it I realised why I'd had that niggling feeling I'd seen Stuart's face before. The brothers weren't that much alike, but there was still a slight resemblance, although Graham's features, to my mind, revealed a force of character, a strength, that had no echo in the face of his more handsome brother.

Stuart might be nice to look at. Graham was the kind of man I couldn't look away from.

Maybe that was why, when he had gone, the first thing that I did was make a beeline for my workbook. In the section bookmarked 'Characters', I wrote three pages, longhand – the descriptive details of a man with eyes the colour of the winter sea.

I didn't know exactly how I'd use him yet, but I had a suspicion that when I began to write tonight he'd turn up somewhere, entering the story with that easy, rolling stride that said he had a right to be there.

It was nearly time for supper when the knock came at my door.

I knew it was unlikely to be Graham, but my face must still have shown at least a trace of disappointment when I saw that it was Dr Weir, because he said, apologetically, 'I didn't interrupt your work, I hope?'

Recovering, I said, 'Oh, no, of course not. Please, come in.'

'I'll not stay long.' He wiped his feet, and stepped inside. 'I promised Elsie I'd be home by dark. I've found those plans that I was telling you about, the plans that show Slains as it was in the old days, before the Victorian earls made it over. And I found a few old photographs I thought might be of interest to you. Where did I put them, now?' Feeling inside his coat pocket, he found the small envelope holding the photos. The plans he'd brought rolled in a brown cardboard tube that he'd put, in its turn, in a clear plastic bag so it wouldn't get wet. A wise precaution, I decided, since the strong wind off the sea had spattered water on his eyeglasses.

He took them off and wiped them while I put the plans and photos on my work table. 'I don't have any Scotch,' I said, 'but I could make you tea or coffee.'

'No, my dear, I'm fine.' He looked around with open interest and approval. 'Jimmy's made this very cosy.'

'He's been wonderful.'

'Aye, all the Keiths are fairly that,' he told me. 'Even Stuart, for his faults. He got you back home in the one piece, I see.'

'Yes, he did.'

'He's a good lad, Stuart is, but...' The doctor appeared to be choosing his words. 'He's still a lad, in many ways.' Which, so I gathered, was meant as a fatherly warning.

I smiled, to show him there wasn't a need. 'Yes, I've noticed.' And then, pretending ignorance, I asked him, 'What's the other brother like? The one who teaches?'

'Graham? Well now, Graham is a very different animal from Stuart. Very different.' He turned thoughtful. 'He's a person you should talk to, now I think of it. His memory's remarkably good, and he has the resources to look things up for you. Besides,' he said, 'he's something of a Jacobite himself, young Graham. Anything to do with the '08, he'll likely know it. He lives down in Aberdeen now, but he comes up nearly every weekend. You might see him sometimes on the beach – he has a dog with him, a little spaniel dog.' He tapped his watch. 'Is that the time? I must be going. Keep those photographs as long as you've a use for them. The plans, as well. I hope they'll be some help.'

I knew they would be, and I told him so.

Mind you, I thought, when he had gone and I was left alone again, they'd also serve to make my morning's work a waste of effort. Crossing to my work table, I pushed my made-up floor plan to one side so I could make room for the real one.

It slid smoothly from its tube, and I unrolled it on the table, pinning down the upcurled edges with a ruler and the long edge of my workbook. There it was – the proper layout of Slains castle, drawn to scale and neatly labelled.

I examined it, then frowned, and with a disbelieving hand reached for the plan I'd drawn this morning. I laid it carefully alongside, for comparison.

There was no way, I thought, this could have happened. But it had.

They were the same.

Not just a little bit alike. They were identical. The kitchen, and the drawing room, the chamber where Sophia slept, the little corner room with light for sewing, they were all here, in the places where I'd put them in my writing, where I'd seen them in my mind.

But how? How did a person draw a thing so perfectly they'd never seen before?

I felt a stirring in the depths of my subconscious, and again the woman's voice within my mind said softly, 'So, you see, my heart is held forever by this place...'

Except the voice I heard this time was not Sophia's.

It was mine.

Jane was calming, on the telephone. 'All right, it's weird, I'll grant you that.'

I told her, 'Weird is not the word. It's freaky.'

'Carrie, darling, you've got a photographic memory. You can quote entire conversations that we had three years ago. I'm telling you, you've seen the castle plans somewhere before, that's all. You've just forgotten.'

'If my memory's so terrific, why would I forget?'

She sighed. 'Don't argue with your agent. Just accept the fact I'm right.'

I had to smile at that. I'd never even tried to have an argument with Jane, because I'd known I wouldn't win. When she was certain she was right, I stood a better chance of moving mountains than of changing her opinion. 'You don't think I'm turning psychic?'

'When you start to win the lottery,' she promised me, 'I'll think you're turning psychic. If you want to know the truth, I think you're simply so absorbed in this new book that you're letting yourself get exhausted. You need a night off. Put your feet up, do nothing.'

I pointed out that there was nothing *to* do, if I didn't write. The cottage had no television.

'So find a pub, have a few drinks.'

'No, that's no good, either. I'm going walking in the morning, up the coast path. I can't be hung over.'

Her voice grew accusing. 'You promised me you wouldn't walk that coast path on your own.'

'I won't be on my own.' The minute I'd said that I wished that I hadn't. Jane had a ferret's own instinct for sniffing things out, and I hadn't a hope of running something like Graham Keith under her radar.

'Oh, yes?' Her tone was a study in nonchalance. 'Who's going with you?'

'Just someone my landlord knows.' Trying to muddy the scent, I told her how Jimmy had come back from his favourite haunt with his list of people I was supposed to meet. 'He's got me on a schedule.'

'Very helpful of him.' But she came right back to, 'What's his friend like? Young? Old? Good-looking?'

I said, 'He lectures in history, at the university in Aberdeen.'

'That isn't what I asked.'

'Well, what do most history professors look like, in your experience?'

She let me leave it there, but I had known her long enough to know she wasn't finished asking questions. This was only the beginning. 'Anyhow,' she said, 'don't write tonight. Your poor brain obviously needs a rest.'

'You may be right.'

'Of course I'm right. Ring me tomorrow, will you, after your walk, so I'll know that you didn't go over the cliffs?'

'Yes, Mom.'

But I did take her advice about not working. I didn't even read for research, though the pages Dr Weir had given me the night before – the articles having to do with Slains castle, along with the copies of Samuel Johnson's and Boswell's account of their visit there – sat in their folder, enticingly close to my armchair. Deliberately, I took no notice of them. Instead, I made a cup of tea and switched on the electric fire and sat there doing absolutely nothing till I fell asleep.

III

She didn't like the gardener. He wasn't like Kirsty, or Rory, or Mrs Grant the cook; or the slow-moving maltman who kept to the dark, fragrant brewing house and whom Sophia had actually seen only once; or the dairy and byre maids who did little more than go giggling past her whenever she ventured outdoors. No, the gardener was different.

He was not a very old man, but he looked it sometimes, bending over his hard-scraping tools, with his sharp-featured face and the mirthless dark eyes that seemed always, whenever Sophia looked round, to be fixed upon her.

Now that spring had come, he seemed to be around Slains all the day, although he didn't live there.

'Oh, aye,' Kirsty said, with understanding. 'Billy Wick. I canna bide the man, myself. He makes me feel I'm standing in my shift, like, when he looks at me. The late earl had a fondness for his father, who was gardener here afore. 'Tis why her ladyship, the countess, keeps him on.' She had been laying fires, and now was walking back along the corridor towards the kitchen, with Sophia following. There wasn't anyone around to raise an eyebrow at the two girls keeping company. A message had come that morning from the present Earl of Erroll, who had been expected these days past, and on receiving it, the countess had retreated to her chamber to reply.

So when they reached the kitchen door, Sophia walked right through in Kirsty's wake, and even Mrs Grant did not look disapproving, having long since given up her attempts to persuade Sophia of the impropriety of mixing with the servants. It was clear to all that Kirsty and Sophia, being ages with each other and of friendly dispositions, would be difficult to keep apart. Here in Scotland, it was common for the sons of lairds and sons of farmers to sit side by side in school, and play at games together in their youth, a custom which produced a friendly feeling in the greater houses between those who served and those who sat at table. And as long as Kirsty showed Sophia all the deference and respect that was befitting to their roles when they were in the main rooms of the castle, Mrs Grant appeared to care but little these days what they did when they were on the servants' side.

She, too, had nothing good to say about the gardener. 'Allus lookin tae hisself, is Billy Wick. He couldna fairly wait tae see his father deid sae he could get his fingers on the siller that was left. There wisna much. Tis why he keeps on here. But Billy thinks hisself above the likes of us. Ye keep well clear of him,' she warned Sophia, motherly. 'He's nae the sort o man ye need tae ken.'

Rory, coming through the back door, caught the last bit and his eyebrows lifted just a bit, enquiring.

Mrs Grant said, 'We're nae spikkin aboot ye. Tis Billy Wick I meant.'

He simply gave a nod and said, 'Oh, aye,' which meant he either was acknowledging her comment or agreeing with it. Guessing Rory's mind was never easy. He took an oatcake from a nearby plate and ate it, and when Mrs Grant prepared to scold him for it, he answered it was likely all the food he'd have that afternoon. 'I'm away within the hour with her ladyship. We ride to Dunottar.'

Another clifftop castle to the south of Aberdeen – the home, so Kirsty told Sophia now, of the countess's nephew by marriage, the Earl Marischal. It was not uncommon for there to be visits between Slains and Dunottar, but not within an hour's notice. Kirsty frowned. 'Would there be trouble, then?'

'I dinna ken.' Rory shrugged. 'Her ladyship telt me to get the horses ready and prepare to ride with her, and that much I can do.'

'And you, Kirsty,' said Mrs Grant, 'should nae worry aboot what the countess does, or why. Things happen in this house that none of us need question.'

Kirsty bore the reprimand in silence, but she pulled a face when Mrs Grant had turned her back.

The cook, not turning, said, 'And if ye carry on wi that, I may forget I have a mind tae let ye have a holiday the morn.'

Kirsty stopped, amazed. 'A holiday?'

'A wee one, aye. I'd need ye back again by supper, but with her ladyship away to Dunottar, and Mistress Paterson the only one about, there widna be sae much tae do I couldna spare ye for the day.'

The prospect of a day to spend whatever way she wished left Kirsty without speech a moment, something none of them had seen.

But she knew what she would do with such a gift. 'I'll go to my sister.'

'Ye'll have a long walk,' Rory said.

''Tis but an hour up the coast, and I've nae seen her since the birth of her last bairn.' Inspired, she asked Sophia, 'Will ye come with me? She'll give us dinner, that I'm sure of. Even Mrs Grant's fine broth is nae match for my sister's kail and cakes. And she would be that glad to meet ye.'

Mrs Grant was not so sure it would be fitting for two girls to walk so far, and on their own.

'Och, we'll have the castle in our view the whole way,' Kirsty argued. 'And her ladyship is highly thought of in these parts, so none will think to harm us when they ken we come from Slains.'

'The countess,' Mrs Grant said, looking squarely at Sophia, 'widna like it.'

To which Kirsty's pert reply was, 'Will ye tell her?'

Mrs Grant considered silently. 'No,' she said, and turned back to her cooking. 'I'll say naethin. But ye'd do well tae mind that, even here, the devil turns men's thochts when it amuses him.'

'Is that what ails ye, Rory?' Kirsty smiled at the groom. His stoic features didn't change, but his eyes warmed a trifle.

'Aye,' he said, 'but I'm long past redemption. Take the dog,' was his advice on leaving, as he tucked a final oatcake in his jacket. 'Devil's thoughts or no, there's none will lay a hand on ye with Hugo at your heels.'

Sophia thought it sound advice, and the next morning after breakfast when she started out with Kirsty, she held Hugo, the huge mastiff, by his lead. Hugo's bed was in the stables, and by day he roamed the castle grounds with Rory, as a child might keep close by his father's knee. He was a gentle beast, for all he barked at strangers and at any sound he took to be a threat. But when they passed the garden wall where Billy Wick was hoeing over stony earth to make a plot for planting physick herbs, the mastiff curled his lip and laid his ears back, growling low.

The gardener took no notice. Straightening his back, he leant upon the hoe and looked them over. 'Comin tae see me, my quines?' His hard eyes speculated in a way Sophia found discomforting.

She knew that Kirsty felt it, too, because the younger girl lied bravely, 'We're away to run an errand for her ladyship.' And without further explanation, she urged Sophia to quicken her pace and the two of them passed by and out of the castle's great shadow. Ahead lay the broad, grassy sweep of the land curving clean to the edge of the black cliffs, the sea stretching wide to the sunwashed horizon.

Kirsty paused, in full appreciation. 'There,' she said. 'The day is ours.'

And though Sophia hadn't felt at all confined within Slains castle, nor had she been treated any way but with great kindness by the countess, she too found that she was glad, in that one moment, that the countess was away from home, that she and Kirsty might enjoy such freedom.

There were countless sights to wonder at.

They passed above a large rock at the sea's edge that was coloured with the stainings of a multitude of seabirds, flapping wings of all varieties, returning to their roosts. The rock, said Kirsty, was called locally 'Dun Buy', which meant the yellow rock, and was to many visitors a pleasing curiosity.

The mastiff found it curious as well, and it was plain from Hugo's interest and the way he eyed the birds that he would happily have lingered for a closer look, but Kirsty gripped his lead more tightly and persuaded him to move along.

A little further on, they came to a great circular shaft, like a giant's well, cut at the edge of the cliff, where the sea had eroded the walls of a mammoth cave till the cave's roof had collapsed, leaving only a strip of stone bridging the cleft at its entrance, through which the waves sprayed with such force that the water appeared to be boiling below when Sophia dared stand at the edge to look down.

Kirsty came, too, though she stayed one step back. 'Tis the Bullers o' Buchan,' she named the strange, open-roofed cavern. 'We call it "The Pot". Many times a ship chased on this coast by a privateer makes for the Pot, and slips in here to hide.'

It would not, thought Sophia, as she watched those waves beating wild on the rocks, have been her choice of where to seek shelter. But surely no privateer would have attempted to follow.

'Come,' said Kirsty, tugging at Sophia's cloak. 'I'll nae be forgiven if I lose ye into the Pot.'

So Sophia came away reluctantly, and in a quarter of an hour they had arrived at Kirsty's sister's cottage and were seated by the fire, admiring Kirsty's newest nephew, ten months old, with ready mischief in his eyes and dimpled cheeks to rival those of his two sisters and his elder brother, none of whom was yet six years of age. But Kirsty's sister seemed to take the challenge of so many children cheerfully. Like Kirsty, she was fair of face and quick to speak and quicker still to smile, and as Sophia had been promised, her kail – the dinner broth – was richer and more flavourful than any she had tasted.

The children were delighted by the presence of the mastiff, Hugo, and tumbled anyhow about him, fearless of the jaws that could have crushed a man, and he, in turn, lay lordly on the hearthrug and accepted their affections and their play with stoic patience.

Time passed happily, and when Sophia finally left with Kirsty in mid-afternoon, she counted those few hours well spent. 'Your sister seems to have a pleasant life,' she said, and Kirsty answered, 'Aye, she chose her husband well. He is a good man, with a world nae wider than his home and family. He disna seek adventure.'

With an eyebrow raised, Sophia asked, 'And Rory does?'

'Why would ye think I'd be speaking of Rory?'

'Kirsty, I have eyes.'

The housemaid blushed. 'Aye, well, twill come to naethin. I wish for bairns, a hearth and home, but Rory dreams of things beyond that. When he sees the open road, he wonders only how far it will carry him. There is nae future in a man like that.'

'My father was a man like that,' Sophia said. 'But he craved not the open road. For him, it was the sea. He always marvelled at the sea, and how its waves appeared to have no ending, and he longed to follow on with them, and touch a foreign shore.'

'And did he?'

'No.' The mastiff dragged a little at his lead, head bent to sniff a clump of grass, and so she slowed her steps to let him. Her cloak dragged heavily behind her, and she lifted it a little from the ground. 'He died on board the ship that would have carried him to Darien. They put his body overboard.'

The mention of the Darien disaster sobered Kirsty, as it did all Scots. She would have been still younger than Sophia when it happened, but the sad details of Darien were scribed into the memory of the nation that had pinned its hopes of future wealth and independence on those few ships of settlers who had sailed to found a colony intended to control the route of trade through the Americas to India.

'It must have been a hard blow for your mother,' Kirsty said.

'She never learnt of it.' Long months had passed before the news had found its way to Scotland, with the rumours that the colony itself had failed, and been abandoned. By that time, a second eager wave of colonists had sailed. Sophia's mother, bright and fair, had been among them. 'She was fortunate,' Sophia said, when she'd told this to Kirsty, 'she did not survive the voyage.' Those who had survived found only bitter disappointment, for the settlement in truth was left defenceless and deserted, and the land that had been promised to bear riches offered nothing more than pestilence and death.

And James and Mary Paterson were now but names amid the countless others broken by the dream that had been Darien.

'How could ye bear so great a loss?' asked Kirsty.

'I was young.' Sophia did not say that she had borne much more in the unhappy years that followed. Kirsty looked too sad already, and this day was not a day for sadness. 'And I did hear a minister who preached once that there never was a tragedy except the Lord had some great plan for turning it to good. And here I am,' she said, 'so it is true. Had both my parents lived, I never would have come to Slains, and we should not have met.'

Kirsty, presented with this, answered, 'Aye, that would have been a tragedy indeed.' And taking up Sophia's hand, she swung it while they walked and chattered on about less dismal things.

They passed the Bullers by this time and did not stop to look, but when they reached Dun Buy, and Hugo tried again to make them pause and let him chase a seabird supper, Kirsty stopped, pointed down the coast and said, 'There is a ship off Slains.'

Sophia looked, and saw it, too – the furled sails and the rocking hull that rode upon its anchor, some fair distance from the shore. 'Is that the *Royal William*?'

Kirsty raised one hand to shade her eyes, and slowly shook her head. 'No. That ship is nae Scottish.'

Sophia's hand was tugged more firmly, not by Hugo this time but by Kirsty. 'Come, we canna tarry here. We must get back.'

Sophia did not fully understand the urgency, but she could feel it surging through her own self as she ran along the clifftop, keeping breathless pace with Kirsty while the mastiff strained against the lead and pulled her onward ever faster.

She could see the ship's hands lowering the jolly boat with several men aboard it, and her run, without her knowing why, became a race to reach the castle first, before the jolly boat's strong oars could land its men upon the shore.

Near the garden wall the mastiff tore his lead free of her hand and made a dash towards the stables with a single woof of welcome. Rory stood within the stable doorway, wiping down his horse with hay to dry its sweat-stained flanks. He said, 'We saw the sails from Dunottar. Her ladyship is in the house already.'

'And the ship?' asked Kirsty, breathless. 'Is it—?'

'Aye. Now get inside, afore the twa of ye are missed.' He said no more, but turned back quickly to his work, and Kirsty tugged Sophia's hand again and told her, 'Come,' and so

Sophia hurried with her to the kitchen door, not knowing what awaited her inside, nor why the ship was so important, nor indeed if those men rowing to the shore below the castle, who might even now have landed, carried with them something pleasurable, or something to be feared.

Chapter Eight

I woke, still in the armchair, to the hard grey light of morning, and a numbing sense of cold. In the confusion of new consciousness, I looked around and noticed that the lamp I'd left switched on last night was off, as was the little electric fire plugged into the wall at my feet. And then, becoming more awake, I realised what had happened, and a quick look at the black box fastened to the wall above the door confirmed that the meter was no longer spinning. The needles rested in the red. I'd used up all my coins, and now my power had gone off.

Worse, I had gone to sleep before I'd stoked the stove up for the evening, and the kitchen fire was out, as well. The stove, when I got up to touch it, wasn't even warm.

I swore, with feeling, since my mother wasn't in the room to hear me, and dropping to my knees began to rake the old dead coals and ashes over, hoping there would be enough left in the hod to start a new fire.

I was still at it when Graham came to fetch me for our walk. I must have looked a sight when I opened the door to him, with my face smudged and my clothes in hopeless wrinkles from my sleeping in them, but he was nice enough not to comment on it, and only the deepening creases at the corners of his eyes as I explained the situation to him showed that he found anything amusing.

'And I can't get the stove to start again,' I finished in frustration. 'And because it's hooked up to the water heater, that means I have no hot water for washing, and—'

Graham cut in. 'You look fine,' he said, calmingly. 'Why don't you go and find something warm to put on over that shirt, and I'll take care of this out here, all right?'

I looked at him with gratitude. 'All right.'

I did a little more than simply put a sweater on. I scrubbed my face, uncaring of the freezing water, and used a wet comb to bring my hair back into order. When I'd finished, my reflection in the mirror was a bit more recognizable. It wasn't quite the face I'd hoped to show him when he came, but it was one that I could live with.

In the kitchen, I found Graham boiling water on the small electric stove. The air already felt a little warmer from the fire he'd started in the Aga, and the lamp that I'd left burning in the front room by my chair was on again. I crossed to switch it off, and, bending, pulled the plug on the electric fire.

'Thanks,' I said.

'No problem. I take it you haven't had breakfast? You'll need to eat something, before we head out. It's a fair walk. What is it you drink, tea or coffee?'

He was reaching in the cupboards with the confidence of somebody who knew where things would be, and I wondered whether he, like Stuart, had ever stayed here on his own. The thought of Stuart having lived here, on and off, had not affected me, but knowing Graham might have once slept in that small back bedroom, in my bed, was something different. I chased the stray thought from my mind, and asked instead, 'How did you get the meter running?' People these days, after all, weren't likely to be going round with pockets full of 50p coins.

'That,' he told me, smiling, 'is a trick that Stuie taught me, and I swore I'd never tell. It wouldn't do to let Dad's tenants learn the way of it.' The kettle had boiled, and he took it off, asking again, 'D'ye take tea, or coffee?'

'Oh. Coffee, please.'

He took a pan and cooked me eggs, as well, and made me toast, and served it all up with a slab of cheese. 'To weigh you down,' he said, 'so that the wind won't knock you off the path.'

I took the plate, and looked towards the windows. 'It's not windy.'

'Eat your breakfast.' Having made a cup of coffee for himself, he poured the rest of the hot water in the frying pan and washed it, while I watched and tried to think of the last time a man had cooked for me *and* washed my dishes afterwards. I drew a total blank.

I asked, 'Where's Angus? How's his paw?'

'It's not so sore, but if he tried to walk the way up to the Bullers, it would be. I left him with my father for the day. He'll be all right. Dad always stuffs him full of sausages.' He rinsed the pan and set it on the draining board to dry.

His mention of the Bullers made me stop dead in the middle of my toast. *Oh, damn*, I thought. I hadn't written down my dream. I'd had that marvellous, long dream last night, with all that perfect action, and I'd gone and let it go to waste, because I hadn't thought to write it down. It would be lost, now. If I concentrated, maybe I could reconstruct some bits of it, but dialogue just disappeared unless I got it down on paper moments after it had formed.

I sighed, and told myself to never mind, that these things happened. There was nothing to be done for it. I'd just been too distracted, when I'd woken, by the cold, and the more pressing need to see I didn't freeze to death in my front room.

The room had grown much warmer now, but whether that was wholly from the stove or from the fact that Graham Keith was standing a few feet away from me, I didn't know. He had crossed to examine the plans of Slains castle, spread out on my work table. 'Where did you get these?'

'From Dr Weir. He loaned them to me.'

'Douglas Weir? How did you meet with him?'

'Your father set it up.'

'Oh, aye.' His brief smile held a son's indulgence. 'Dad does have connections. Give him time, he'll have you meeting half the village. What did you think of Dr Weir?'

'I liked him. And his wife. They gave me whisky.' Which, I realised, made it sound as though the two facts were related, so I stumbled on, 'The doctor told me quite a lot about the history of the castle, and the Earls of Erroll.'

'Aye, there isn't much he doesn't ken about the castle.'

'He said the same thing about you,' I told him, 'and the Jacobites.'

'Did he, now?' His eyebrows lifted, interested. 'What else did he say about me?'

'Only that he thinks that you're a Jacobite yourself.'

He didn't exactly smile at that, but the corners of his eyes did crinkle. 'Aye, there's truth in that. Had I been born into another time,' he said, 'I might have been.' He traced a corner of the Slains plan with his fingers, lightly, then he asked, 'Who else has my dad got you meeting?'

I told him, as best I could remember, ending with the plumber's driving tour. 'Your brother said he'd drive me round instead.'

'You've seen him drive?'

'I said I'd take my chances with the plumber.'

Graham *did* smile, then. 'I'll take you for a driving tour some weekend, if you like.'

'And you're a safer driver, are you?'

'Aye,' he told me. 'Naturally. I'm all the time driving old ladies to Kirk on a Sunday. You've nothing to fear.'

I'd have gone with him anywhere, actually. My mother, had she known that I was walking on the coast path with a man I barely knew, would have been close to apoplectic. But instinctively, I knew that Graham told the truth – I didn't have to fear when I was with him. He would keep me safe.

It was a newfound feeling, and it settled on me strangely, but I liked the way it felt. I liked the way he walked beside me, close but not too crowding, and the way he let me go ahead of him along the path, so I could set the pace.

We went the back way down Ward Hill and found ourselves in the same gully with its quiet tangled trees and running stream that I'd gone through with Jane, two days ago, when she and I had headed from the village up to Slains. It was a drier day today. My boots were not so slippery as we crossed the little bridge and made our way up and around until we'd climbed again up to the level of the clifftop.

Ahead, I could see the long ruins of Slains with the one tall square tower that stood at the end overlooking the sea, and I looked at the windows and tried to decide which ones should be Sophia's. I would have liked to spend a few minutes in the castle, but there was another couple walking round the walls this morning, loud and laughing, tourists, and the atmosphere was not the same. And Graham must have felt it, too, because he didn't slow his steps, but followed as I set my back to Slains and started off again along the coast.

I found this new part of the path disturbing. Not the walk itself – it wasn't really all that difficult, for someone used to walking rough – but just the sense that everything around me, all the scenery, was familiar. I'd had flashes, in my life, of déjà-vu. Most people had. I'd felt, from time to time, a moment's fleeting sense that I'd performed some action once before, or had some conversation twice. But only for a moment. I had never felt this long, sustained sensation, more a certainty, that I'd already come this way. That just up here, if I looked to my right, I'd see—

'Dunbuy,' said Graham, who'd come up to stand behind me on the path, where I had stopped. 'It means the—'

'Yellow rock,' I finished for him, slowly.

'Aye. What turns it yellow is the dung of all the seabirds nesting there. Come springtime, Dunbuy is fair covered with them, and the noise is deafening.'

The rock was near abandoned now, in winter, but for several gulls that stood upon it sullenly, ignoring us. But I could hear, within my mind, the seabirds that he spoke of. I could see them. I remembered them…

I frowned and turned away and carried on, still with that sense of knowing just where I was going. I might have been walking the streets of the town where I'd grown up, it was that sure a feeling.

I knew, without Graham's announcement, when we were

approaching the Bullers of Buchan. There wasn't anything remarkable to see at first, only a tight-clustered grouping of cottages built at the edge of a perilous drop down another deep gully, and in front of them a steep path winding upwards to what looked to be an ordinary rise of land. Except I knew, before we'd even started up that path, what waited at the top. I knew what it looked like before I had seen it – a circular shaft, like a giant's well, cut at the edge of the cliff, where the sea had eroded the walls of a mammoth cave till the cave's roof had collapsed, leaving only a strip of stone bridging the cleft at its entrance, through which the waves sprayed with such force that the water appeared to be boiling below when I stood at the edge to look down.

Graham stood at my side with his hands in his pockets, and standing there he, too, seemed part of a memory, and I wondered if this was what people felt like when they started going insane.

He was talking. I could hear him, vaguely, telling me the history of the Bullers, and how its name had likely come from the French word for 'kettle', *bouilloire*, or perhaps more simply from the English, 'boiler', and how in the past small ships had hidden there from privateers, or if they were smugglers themselves, from the Scottish coast patrols.

On one level, I took this in quite calmly, and yet on the other my thoughts swirled as fiercely as the waves below me. I didn't think Graham had noticed, but in the middle of telling me how he and his brother had ridden their bikes the whole way round the rim of the Bullers once, when they were younger and more daring, and how he'd almost lost control going over the thin bridge of sunken earth not far from where we were standing, he stopped talking and gave me a penetrating look.

'You all right?' he asked.

I lied. I said, 'I'm not so good with heights.'

He didn't move an inch, or take his hands out of his pockets, but he looked at me and gave his pirate's smile and said, 'Well, not to worry. I won't let you fall.'

I knew it was too late. I had already fallen. But I couldn't tell him, any more than I could tell him what I'd felt today on our walk here, and what I was still feeling. It was craziness. He would have run a mile.

The sense of déjà-vu stayed with me on the long walk back, and worsened when I saw the jagged walls of Slains, and I was glad when we'd gone past and down into the wooded gully. On the little bridge that crossed the stream I thought that Graham hesitated, and I hoped he might suggest we take the pathway to the right and stop in at a pub for lunch, but in the end he only walked me back up onto Ward Hill and across the tufted grass until we stood before the cottage.

He said nothing to begin with, so I filled the pause by lamely saying that I'd had a lovely time.

'I'm glad,' he said. 'I did, as well.'

I cleared my throat. 'Would you like to come in for a coffee, or something?'

Stuart, I knew, would have picked up on the 'or something', but Graham only took it at face value, and replied, 'I can't, the day. I have to get back down to Aberdeen. I have a stack of papers sitting waiting to be marked.'

'Oh.'

'But I'll take you for that driving tour next weekend, if you'd like.'

My answer came a bit too fast. 'Yes, please.'

'Which would be better for you, Saturday or Sunday?'

'Either.'

'Then let's make it Saturday. We'll call for you at ten, again, if that won't be too early.'

'We?' I asked him.

'Angus and myself. He loves a drive, does Angus, and I'd never hear the end of it if I left him behind.'

I smiled, and told him ten o'clock would be just fine, and having thanked him once again and said goodbye, I went inside the cottage.

But my nonchalant attitude vanished the minute I stepped through the door, and I grinned like a schoolgirl just back from a date. Standing in my kitchen, well back from the window so he wouldn't catch me watching him, I saw him take a pebble from the path and skip it deftly out to sea, and then he kicked one booted foot into a tuft of grass and, looking pleased himself, strolled down the hill towards the road.

I wasn't holding out much hope, when I sat down to write.

It would be gone, I knew. The dream I'd had last night would be long gone. It was no use.

But when I turned on the computer and my fingers touched the keyboard, I surprised myself. I hadn't lost it after all. It was all there, the whole of it, and as I wrote each detail I remembered having dreamt it. I could not recall this happening in all the years that I'd been writing. It felt...well, like I'd said to Jane, it felt the way a medium must feel, when they were channelling the dead.

The story flowed from my subconscious in an easy, rapid

stream. I saw the leering face of Billy Wick, the gardener, and the smile of Kirsty's sister in her cottage, with the children playing round the gentle mastiff, and I felt Sophia's sadness as she spoke about her parents, and her thrill of expectation as she saw the ship at anchor near the castle, and the mad confusion of her run with Kirsty to the house, and Rory's warning they should get inside, before the countess missed them.

And tonight, my writing went beyond the dream. And there was more.

IV

She had no time to change her gown before the countess called for her. She had just reached her chamber and had seen with her own eyes, within the looking-glass, the rare disorder of her hair, the wild colour that her run along the clifftop had raised in her cheeks.

And there was Kirsty, breathless too, and knocking at her door to say the countess had requested that Sophia join her downstairs in the drawing room.

'I cannot go like this,' Sophia said.

'Och, ye look fine. Tis but your hair that needs attention.' And with reassuring hands, the housemaid helped Sophia smooth her windblown curls and pin them back into their proper style. 'Now, go. Ye canna keep her waiting.'

'But my gown is muddied.'

'She will never see it,' Kirsty promised. 'Go.'

Sophia went. Downstairs, she found the countess in an outward state of calm, but standing close beside the windows of the drawing room as though she were anticipating something and did not wish to be sitting when it came. She held her hands toward Sophia with a smile. 'Come stand with me, my child. We will this day have visitors, who may be in this household for a month or more. I wish you to be at my side, when I do bid them welcome.'

Sophia was amazed, and touched. 'You do me an honour.'

'You are,' the countess told her, plain, 'a member of this family. It is fitting you should stand where my own daughters would be standing, were they not already married and departed from me.' She paused, as though what she meant next to say took thought, and needed to be weighed. 'Sophia, in the coming months, there will be much that you will see and hear within these walls. I pray that you will understand, and find the means to let it rest with ease upon your conscience.'

There were heavy steps within the hall, and voices, and then Kirsty came ahead and at the open door announced the guests: 'My lady, here are Colonel Hooke and Mr Moray.'

For Sophia, that small moment which came afterwards would evermore be burnt within her memory. She never would forget.

Two men stepped through the doorway of the drawing room, but she saw only one. The man who entered first, with hat in hand, and crossed to greet the countess, might have been a shade, for all Sophia paid him notice. She was looking at the man who'd come behind, and who now stood two paces back and waited, at a soldier's ease.

He was a handsome man, not over tall, but with the broadened shoulders and well-muscled legs of one who did not live a soft and privileged life, but earned his pay with work. He wore a wig, as fashion did demand of any gentleman, but while the wigs of most men were yet long about the shoulders, his was short at top and sides, drawn back and tied with ribbon in a queue that neatly hung behind. He wore a leather buffcoat, with no collar and no sleeves, split at the sides for riding, with a long row of ball buttons up the front, and at the back a black cloak fastened to the coat below the shoulders, hanging full so that it covered half the sword hung from the broad belt passing over his right shoulder. His sleeves were plain, as was the neckcloth knotted at his throat, and his close-fitting breeches ended at the knees in stiff dragoon boots, not in buckled shoes and stockings.

To Sophia's mind, he cut a proud, uncompromising figure, yet his grey eyes, in that handsome and impassive face, were not unkind. They swung to hers in silence, and she could not look away.

Could scarcely breathe, in fact. And so she was relieved to hear the countess speak her name in introduction to the first man, who now stood quite close beside her. 'Colonel Hooke, may I present Sophia Paterson, the niece of my late cousin, come to live with me at Slains and bring some brightness to my days.'

Colonel Hooke was taller than his soldierly companion, and his clothes were of a finer cut, with holland sleeves and edgings of expensive lace. He wore the high-arched periwig she was more used to seeing, and his manners were the manners of a gentleman. 'Your servant,' he said, bending to her hand. He had an Irish voice, she noted, pleasant in its tone. He told the countess, 'And in turn, I would present to you my travelling companion, Mr Moray, who is brother to the Laird of Abercairney.'

'We are already acquainted.' The countess smiled, and to the silent Mr Moray said, 'It was not quite four years ago, I do believe, in Edinburgh. You travelled with your uncle, and were kind enough to bring me certain letters for my husband, I recall.'

He gave a nod, and crossed the room to greet the countess with respect. Sophia waited, eyes cast down, and then his deep Scots voice said, 'Mistress Paterson, your servant,' and her hand was taken firmly in his own, and in that swift, brief contact something warm, electric, jolted up her arm. She mumbled something incoherent in reply.

Colonel Hooke said to the countess, 'Do I understand your son is not, at present, with you here at Slains?'

'He is not. But he is soon expected, and I do have several letters of his which he does desire that I should put into your hands.' Her tone turned serious. 'You do know that the Union has been ratified by parliament?'

Hooke seemed to find the news not unexpected. 'I did fear it.'

'It has happened to the discontent and hearty dislike of our people, and the peers and other lords, together with the members of the parliament, are all returned now to their residences in the country. Only my son, and the Earl Marischal, and His Grace the Duke of Hamilton do yet remain at Edinburgh. The last two of these men, so I have been informed, are dangerously ill, and are not fit to travel.'

'I am sad to hear it,' Hooke said, frowning. 'I did write the Duke of Hamilton before our ship set sail. I asked that he might send some person, well-instructed, who could wait upon me here.'

The countess nodded. 'He did send a Mr Hall, a priest, who

kindly served as guide for Mistress Paterson when they came north from Edinburgh. Mr Hall consented to stay with us, and did wait for you a month, but he could wait no longer.'

Hooke looked disappointed. 'We have been delayed at Dunkirk these past weeks. The winds were contrary.'

Dunkirk, Sophia thought. So they had come from France. And from the pallor of Hooke's face, their journey had not been a gentle one.

The countess, who missed little, must have drawn the same conclusion, for she said to Colonel Hooke that their delay was of no consequence. 'But surely you must both be very weary from your voyage. Colonel, please do read your letters, and refresh yourself. There will be time for talk when you have rested.'

'You are kind. 'Tis sure that travelling by ship does never much improve my health. I should prefer the most ill-tempered horse beneath me to the calmest sea.'

Sophia bravely glanced toward the place where Mr Moray stood in patient silence, noting that the sea did not appear to have in any way affected *his* health. He looked to be fit enough to stand all day, as he was standing, letting others make the conversation. She recalled her father saying, 'Men who watch, and say but little, very often are much wiser than the men they serve.' She had a feeling that, in this man's case, it might be true.

Aware of her appraisal, Moray's grey eyes shifted quietly to hers, and once again she found she had no will to break the contact.

'Come, Sophia,' said the countess, 'we shall give our visitors some peace.' And with a smile the countess took her gracious leave of both the gentlemen, and in her wake, Sophia did the same, not daring this time to look back.

She found a refuge in the little corner sewing room, where for a mindless hour or so she struggled with her needlework and tried to think of nothing else. Her fingertips were painful from the needle-pricks when she at last gave up and went to look for Kirsty, hoping that companionship might have success where solitude had failed.

At this hour of day, and with guests in the house, Kirsty should have been setting the dining room table for supper, but she was not there. Sophia was still standing in that room, in faint confusion, when the rustling of a woman's gown, in concert with more manly, measured steps, approaching down the corridor, intruded on her thinking.

The voice of the Countess of Erroll was serious. 'So, Colonel, I should advise you to not be in haste. You will find his affairs greatly altered, within these past months. All the world has abandoned him, and all the well-affected have come to an open rupture with him. He is suspected of holding a correspondence with the court of London, therefore it would serve you well to be upon your guard before you trusted much to him.'

They were near the open doorway of the dining room. Sophia smoothed her gown and linked her fingers and prepared an explanation of her presence there, for it seemed sure to her they would come in. But they did not. The footsteps and the rustling passed her by, and when Hooke spoke next he had moved too far away for her to know his words.

She felt relieved. She had not meant to listen to a private conversation, and it would have pained her had the countess known she'd done it, even if it were by accident. Eyes briefly closed, she waited one more minute before stepping out herself into the corridor to carry on her search for Kirsty.

She could not have said from which direction Mr Moray had been coming, nor how boots like his upon the floorboards could have made no sound. She only knew that when she stepped out through the doorway he was there, and had it not been for his swift reflexive grabbing of her shoulders, their collision would have surely damaged more than her composure.

He had clearly not expected her to be there either, for his first reaction was to swear, then to retract the oath and ask for her forgiveness. 'Did I hurt ye?'

'Not at all.' She drew back quickly – just a little bit too quickly – from his grasp. 'The fault is mine. I did not look where I was going.'

He seemed taller here, at such close quarters. If she kept her eyes fixed to the front, they looked directly on a level with his throat, above the knotted neckcloth. He had taken off the buffcoat and replaced it with a jacket of a woven dark green fabric set with silver buttons. She did not look higher.

He seemed interested by her voice. 'Your accent,' he said, 'does not come from Edinburgh.'

She could not think why that would matter, until she remembered that the countess, just that afternoon, had told the men that Mr Hall had journeyed with Sophia up from Edinburgh. Surprised that Mr Moray would have taken note of such a trifle, she said, 'No. I did but break my journey there.'

'Where do ye come from, then?'

'The Western Shires. You would not know the town.'

'I might surprise ye with my knowledge.'

So she told him, and he nodded. 'Aye, 'tis near Kirkcudbright, is it not?' She felt him looking down at her. 'Are ye then Presbyterian?'

She couldn't tell him that she was not anything; that living in her uncle's house, she'd long since lost her faith. Instead she said, 'My parents were, and I was so baptised, but I was brought up by my aunt and uncle as Episcopalian.'

'That does explain it.'

Curiosity compelled her to look up at last, and see that he was smiling. 'What does it explain?'

'Ye do not have the long and disapproving face,' he told her, 'of a Presbyterian. Nor would a lass who goes God-fearing to the Kirk be like to run so free and wanton on the hills above the shore, for God and all the world to see. Unless it was not you I saw this afternoon, when we were being rowed to land?'

She stared at him and made no answer, for it was quite clear he did not need one.

'Faith, lass,' he said, 'there's no need to look like that. Ye'd not be beaten for it, even if I had a mind to tell. But in the future, if ye wish to keep your pleasures secret, ye'd do well to wash the mudstains from your gown before ye come to greet your company.'

And with that small bit of advice, he took his solemn leave of her and left her in the corridor, and she—

The phone rang loudly, for the second time. Like scissors rending fabric, it effectively destroyed the flow of words, the mood, and with a sigh I stood and went to answer it.

'Bad timing?' guessed my father, at the other end.

I lied. 'Of course not. No, I was just finishing a scene.' I was out of my writer's trance, now, and more fully aware of who

I was, and where I was, and who was on the phone. And then I started worrying, because my father almost never called me, so I asked, 'Is something wrong?'

'No, we're fine. But you've got me back onto the trail of the McClellands. I haven't done much on them lately, but I thought I'd take minute on the internet, and see if there was anything new on the IGI.'

The IGI, or International Genealogical Index, was one of the most useful tools for family history searchers. It was created and maintained by the Church of Latter Day Saints, whose members went worldwide to search out every single register of marriages and births in every church that they could find. They put the pages of those registers on microfilm, transcribed them, and then indexed them. And now, with the arrival of the internet, the indexes were easier to access, to my father's great delight.

The index was constantly being updated. When my father had last done a search for McClellands, he hadn't been able to find any entries that matched *our* McClellands, the ones in the old family Bible. But this time…

'I found him,' my father announced, with that satisfied tone of discovery that he knew I'd understand fully, and share. 'They've done a few more churches since the last update, and when I went online tonight, there it was – David John McClelland's marriage to Sophia Paterson, on the 13th of June, in Kirkcudbright, in 1710. That's our man. So I'll order the actual film, to look at. I likely won't find out much more. If Scottish records are anything like the ones in Northern Ireland, they won't mention the parents of either the bride or the groom, but you never do know. We can hope.'

'That's great, Daddy.' Though somehow, with what I'd just

written, I didn't like being reminded that Sophia Paterson had, in real life, married into what probably had been a dull, Presbyterian family.

'There's more, though,' my father assured me. 'And that's why I'm calling.'

'Oh, yes?'

'Yes. Remember you said that you'd give your Sophia, the one in your new book, a birthdate of...what was it, 1689?'

'That's right.'

'Well, on the IGI, I also found the baptism of a Sophia Paterson in Kirkcudbright in December, 1689. How's that for coincidence? There's no way, at the moment, we can tell if this is *our* Sophia. We don't have anything to cross-reference it with. If we knew the name of our Sophia's father, we could at least see if it matched the name of the father on the baptism...'

'James Paterson,' I murmured automatically.

'It *is* James, actually,' my father said, but he was too amused to think that I'd been serious. It was a running joke between us that whenever we discovered a male ancestor, his name was either John or James, or, very rarely, David – common names that made it difficult to trace them in the records. There might be countless James McClellands listed living in a town, and we would have to check details of every one of them before we found the one that we were after. 'What we need,' my father always used to say, 'is an Octavius, or maybe a Horatio.'

He told me, now, 'I had a quick look on that Scottish will site, but of course there are so many James Patersons listed there's no way to narrow them down. I don't know when he died. And even if I did know, and I managed to download the right will, he would still have to have actually left something to David John McClelland, or to have mentioned a daughter Sophia McClelland, for us to be able to make a connection between them.'

'You wouldn't remember if one of those wills had been proved around 1699?' I asked, almost not wanting to know what the answer might be.

He paused. 'Why 1699?'

I thought about my character Sophia telling Kirsty of the kind of man her father was, and how he'd died on board the ship to Darien. And the first Scots expeditions into Darien, if I remembered rightly, had begun in 1699.

Aloud I said, 'It doesn't matter. Just forget I asked,' and steered our talk to other things.

He wasn't on the phone for too much longer, and when we'd said goodbye I went to make a cup of coffee, thinking maybe, with the help of some caffeine, I could pick up again where I'd been interrupted in my writing.

But it didn't work.

I was just sitting there and staring at the cursor blinking on the screen, when my father called back later on.

'What do you know,' he asked, 'that I don't know?'

'I'm sorry?'

'Well, I went back on the Scottish will site, and I found a will there for James Paterson, in 1699, in which he leaves a third of his estate to his wife, Mary, and another third to be divided between his two daughters, Anna and Sophia.' His small silence was accusing. 'That doesn't mean, of course, that he's in any way connected to us, or that his Sophia is the one who later married David John McClelland, but still...how did you hit on that year, in particular?'

I cleared my throat. 'Who did he leave the final third to?'

'What?'

'The final third of his estate. Who did he leave it to?'

'A friend of his. I don't recall...oh, here it is. John Drummond.'

It was my turn to be silent.

'Carrie?' asked my father. 'Are you still there?'

'I'm still here.' But that was not exactly true, because a part of me, I knew, was slipping backward through the darkness, to a young girl named Sophia, living in the stern, unloving household of her Uncle John – John Drummond – while she dreamt of fields of grass that once had bowed before her when she walked, and of the morning air that carried happiness upon it, and the mother who lived only in her memory.

Chapter Nine

The Castle Wood was silent at this hour of the morning. No rooks were wheeling round the treetops, though I saw a few hunched high up in the bare and twisted branches, looking down on me in silence as I passed.

The garden gnomes, more welcoming, laughed up at me from their close huddled spot beside the front walk of the neat, white-painted bungalow. And Dr Weir seemed pleased I'd come to visit.

'How's the book coming?' he asked me, ushering me into the front entry, with its atmosphere of comfort and tradition.

'Fine, thank you.'

He hung my jacket on the hall tree. 'Come into the study. Elsie's just gone with a friend up to Peterhead to have a wander round the shops. She'll be sorry she missed you.'

He'd clearly been all set to enjoy his day of solitude – beside his leather wing chair in the study lay a tidy stack of books, and on the smoking table one of the great cut-glass tumblers that we'd used the other night was sitting with a generous dash of whisky in it, waiting. Dr Weir explained it as, 'My

morning draught. I always thought the ancient ways of
starting off the day were more appealing. An improvement
over soggy breakfast flakes.'

I smiled. 'I thought the morning draught was meant to be
strong ale, with toast.'

'I've had the toast already. And in Scotland, we did things a
little differently,' he said. 'A man might have his ale and toast,
but he'd not be a man unless he finished with a dram of good
Scots spirits.'

'Ah.'

He smiled back. 'But I could make you tea.'

'I wouldn't mind a morning draught myself, if that's all
right.'

'Of course.' His eyebrows raised a fraction, but he didn't
look at all shocked as he saw me settled into the chintz
armchair by the window, as before, with my own glass of
whisky beside me.

'So,' he said. 'What brings you by this morning?'

'Actually, I had a question.'

'Something about Slains?'

'No. Something medical.'

That took him by surprise. 'Oh, aye?'

'I wondered...' This was not as easy as I'd hoped. I took a
drink. 'It has to do with memory.'

'What, specifically?'

I couldn't answer that until I'd laid the background
properly, and so I started with the book itself, and how the
writing of it was so unlike anything I'd experienced before,
and how sometimes it felt that I wasn't putting it down on
paper so much as trying to keep up with it. And I told him
how I'd picked Sophia Paterson, my ancestor, to be my

viewpoint character. 'She didn't come from here,' I said. 'She came from near Kirkcudbright, in the west. I only put her in the story because I needed somebody, a woman, who could bind all the historical characters together.'

Dr Weir, like all good doctors, had sat back to let me talk, not interrupting. But he nodded now to show he understood.

I carried on, 'The problem is that some of what I'm writing seems to be more fact than fiction.' And I gave him, as examples, my correctly guessing Captain Gordon's first name, and his ship's name, and the name of Captain Hamilton; and how my own invented floor plan of the castle rooms had so exactly matched the one he'd given me. I told him, too, about my walk along the coast path yesterday – although I didn't tell him that I hadn't been alone, I only told him of my sense that I had made that walk before.

'And that's OK,' I said, 'because I know there's probably a simple explanation for it all. I've done a lot of research for this book. I've likely read those details somewhere, and seen photographs, and now I'm just recalling things that I forgot I knew. But...' How did I say this, I wondered, without sounding crazy? 'But some of the things that I've written are details I couldn't have possibly read somewhere else. Things I couldn't have known.' I explained about Sophia's birthdate, the death of her father, his will that had given the name of her uncle. 'My father only found those dates, those documents, because I told him where to look. Except I don't know how I knew to look there. It's as if...' I stopped again, and searched for words, and then, because there wasn't anything to do but take a breath and dive right in, I said, 'My father always says I like the sea so much because it's in my blood, because our ancestors were shipbuilders from Belfast, Northern Ireland.

He doesn't mean it literally, but given what's been happening to me I wondered if you knew if there was such a thing,' I asked him, 'as genetic memory?' His eyes, behind the spectacles, grew thoughtful.

'Could you have Sophia's memories, do you mean?'

'Yes. Is it possible?'

'It's interesting.' He gave it that, and for a moment he was silent, thinking. Then he told me, 'Memory is a thing that science doesn't fully understand, at present. We don't even properly know how a memory is formed, or when our memories start – at birth, or in the womb, or if, as you suggest, we humans carry memory in our genes. Jungian psychologists would argue, in a broader sense, that such a thing exists; that some of us share knowledge that is based, not on experience, but on the learnings of our common ancestors. A sort of deep instinct,' he said, 'or what Jung liked to call the "collective unconscious".'

'I've heard the term.'

'It's still a controversial theory, though it might, to some degree, explain the actions of some primates, chimpanzees, who, even after being raised in isolation from their families so they couldn't have learnt anything directly, still showed knowledge that the researchers could not explain – the way to use a rock to open nuts for food, and such like. But then, a good part of Jung's theories can't be tested. His idea that our common human wariness of heights, for instance, might have been passed down to us from some poor, luckless prehistoric man who took a tumble off a cliff and lived to learn the lesson of it. Pure conjecture,' he pronounced. 'And besides, the "collective unconscious" idea is not about people recalling specific events.'

'These are pretty specific,' I said.

'So I gather.' He gave me another look, closely assessing, as though I were one of his patients. 'If it were only déjà-vu, I'd have you in to see a specialist tomorrow. Déjà-vu can be a side effect of certain kinds of epilepsy, or more rarely of a lesion on the brain. But this, from what you've said, is something more. When did this start?'

I considered the question. 'I think when I first saw the castle.'

'That's interesting.'

'Why?'

'Well, you said that your ancestor came from the west coast of Scotland.'

'That's right.'

'So it's unlikely she ever saw Slains.'

'Well, we know she was born near Kirkcudbright. We know she was married there. People in those days just didn't go traipsing all over the country.'

'Aye, true enough. So it may not be memory, after all. How could you have her memories of Slains,' he said, 'if she was never here?'

I had no answer to that question, and I'd come no closer to one by the time I left, a little dazed, less from our talk than from the fact that I'd drunk whisky before noon.

I nearly walked past Jimmy Keith, just coming out of his front door, no doubt on his way to his daily lunch at the St Olaf Hotel.

'Aye-aye,' was his cheerful greeting. 'Foo are ye the day?'

I didn't know exactly how I was, but I told him, 'Fine, thank you,' and we passed a bit of small talk back and forth about the weather, which was grey and dismal.

'Ye'll be needing yer electric meter emptied. I've nae done it yet this week.'

I had forgotten. 'Yes, I'm nearly out of coins.'

'I'll come along and dee it noo. Ye dinna wish tae find yerself on such a day as this, athoot the lichts.'

I glanced at him from time to time as we walked up Ward Hill, and tried to think which of his sons was most like him. Stuart, I thought, had his straight nose and effortless charm, whereas Graham had more of the roughness, the strength of his build and the roll of his walk. Strange, I thought, how genetics worked – how one man could pass on such diverse traits to his children.

It was clear, though, that neither one of *them* had taught their father how to make the meter over my door run without the key. Inside, he emptied out the coins and gave them back to me, and I in turn fished out a ten pound note and thanked him.

'Ach, nae bother.' He looked round. 'Ye're getting on a'richt, are ye?'

'Yes, thanks.' Past him, through the window of my front room, I could see the sprawl of Slains towards the north. I pulled my gaze away, deliberately avoiding it. It wasn't that I wanted to escape the book, exactly, but the things that had been happening these past few days had left me feeling overwhelmed, and desperately in need of a diversion. On impulse I said, 'Jimmy?'

'Aye?'

'I might be away for a few days.'

'Oh, aye? Far would ye be awa til?'

Where would I be away to? Good question. 'To Edinburgh,

maybe. There's some research for the book I need to do.'

'Ye'll be hame at the wikkend, then, will ye?'

I thought of the driving tour I had been promised on Saturday, and answered with certainty, 'Yes.'

'Because Graham, my ither loon, said he'd be up at the wikkend, and I thocht ye'd want tae meet him. He's a lecturer in history, like I telt ye, and I doot that he'll ken somethin aboot Slains that'll be o use tae ye.'

My first reaction was surprise that Graham hadn't mentioned that he'd met me, but I tried my best to hide that. He'd doubtless had his reasons.

Jimmy, unaware, said, 'I was thinking ye micht want tae come fer lunch on Sunday. Nothing fancy, mind ye. I can roast a bit o beef fin I'm in luck, but I'll nae promise mair than that.'

It was impossible to say no to his smile. I said, 'I'll be there.'

Truth was, I wouldn't have been likely, anyway, to say no to a chance to spend a bit more time with Graham. But I didn't tell his father that.

'Aweel,' said Jimmy, pleased, 'g'awa tae Edinburgh finever ye like, quine, and nivver fash. I'll keep the cottage snod, and yer lum rikkin.' Then he caught himself, as though he'd just remembered I was not a local, and started to rephrase that, but I stopped him.

'No, it's all right, I got all of that. I understand.'

'Oh aye? Fit did I tell ye, noo?'

'You told me not to worry, that you'd keep the cottage in good order and my chimney smoking.'

Jimmy grinned. 'Michty, ye've a rare grasp o the Doric fer a quine fa's nivver heard it afore.'

I'd never given it much thought, but I supposed that he was

right. And come to think of it, a few of my own characters – the servants up at Slains – spoke in the Doric in my mind, and though I modified their speech when I was writing so my readers wouldn't curse me, I still understood what they had said originally. Just as I understood everything Jimmy Keith said.

It was almost as if I *had* heard it before. Heard it spoken so often that I had remembered...

My gaze was pulled back to the window, and Slains.

Jimmy cheerfully said, 'Weel, that's me awa hame. Best o luck wi' yer research, my quine.'

And I thanked him.

But part of me wasn't so sure that I wanted good luck, at the moment. It was one thing, I thought, to ask questions, and look for the answers. It might be another to actually find them.

In the end, I decided the Duke of Hamilton would be the safest subject for my research. I *did* need to learn more about the man, since it appeared he was going to play a key role, whether onstage or off, in my novel. And I knew I'd have no trouble finding information on him down in Edinburgh.

I'd been there several times already, doing research for this book, but always I'd just flown across from France and stayed a few days in the flat that Jane still kept there for her use when she went down each month to work out of the office of her literary agency. Her agency was large and based in London, but she'd worked for them so long and so effectively that, when she'd married Alan, they had in effect created a new office for her private use, in Edinburgh. Since then, a few more agents had moved up to work in Scotland, so she didn't feel the pressure to come down from Peterhead as often as she had before, but she still came enough to need the flat.

It was a tidy little place, two rooms, conveniently central. If I'd wanted to, I could have walked the short way down to Holyroodhouse, which had stood in its imposing park for centuries behind its great iron gates. I could have walked around it, or even tried to get permission to tour the old apartments of the Duke of Hamilton himself, to get more detail for the scenes that happened there between Sophia and the duke at the beginning of my story.

But I didn't.

I would never have admitted that I stayed away in part because I didn't want to know what those rooms looked like, didn't want to take the chance that they, too, might be just the way I had imagined them.

Instead, I told myself I simply didn't have the time this week for sightseeing – I had too many documents to slog through.

So it was that Wednesday morning found me settled in the record office reading room, a comfortably familiar environment, happily sifting through the Duke of Hamilton's private correspondence.

The letters that he'd written and received gave me a clearer picture of the man – his double-edged role as the patriot and the betrayer, though I doubted he'd have ever judged himself like that. He'd simply served himself, I thought, before all others. His political and personal decisions, which so many of his own friends, in their letters, claimed they could not fathom, all could be reduced with mathematical precision to that one common denominator: what would best advance the duke's ambition.

Always short of money, he had married an heiress with

large estates in England, and he hadn't been likely to do anything to irritate the English into cutting off that prime source of his income. He gave speeches in the parliament against the Union, but when others wanted to oppose with force instead of words, he held them back with empty promises until their opportunity was lost, and so made certain that the Union went ahead. He had not been a stupid man, and in his letters he'd left no clear evidence that he'd been bribed by England to support the vote for Union, but I knew, just from his character, that he would not have risked his reputation if he hadn't stood to gain by it.

I knew exactly whom the countess had been speaking of to Hooke in that last scene I'd written, when she'd said, 'He is suspected of holding a correspondence with the court of London...'

Someone coughed.

I looked up from my work, and saw a youngish female clerk who looked a little nervous. 'You're...excuse me, but you're Carolyn McClelland, aren't you?'

'Yes, I am.' I smiled politely, understanding now. She was a fan.

'I've read your books,' she told me. 'Every one of them. They're marvellous.'

'Well, thank you. That's so nice to hear.'

'I love the history. Well, I would. That's why I work here. But you make it come to life, you really do.'

I thanked her once again, and meant it. When a person cared enough to stop and tell me that they liked my books, I valued that connection. Since I wrote in isolation, just myself and my computer, it was good to be reminded there were readers at the end of that long process who enjoyed the stories. And it was because of readers like this young clerk, after all, that my books had been successful.

So I put my pencil down, and asked her, 'What's your name?'

'Kirsty.'

'One of the characters in my new book is named Kirsty.'

She beamed. 'Is this for your new book, the research you're doing?' She glanced at my table. 'The Hamilton papers?'

'Yes, the 4th duke is one of my characters, too, so I'm getting my facts straight.' The people around us appeared to be packing up. I stole a glance at my watch. It *was* closing time. Where had the day gone, I wondered?

'I feel like I've only just started,' I told the girl Kirsty, and smiled. 'Guess I'll have to come back in the morning.'

Which made her look more pleased. 'Do you think...' she started, then broke off and tried again. 'If I brought one of my books in...'

I knew what she was asking me. 'Of course. Bring whatever you have, I'll be happy to sign them.'

'Oh, that would be wonderful.'

I had so clearly made her day that I left feeling happy, too, if humbled.

When I came back to the record office first thing the next morning, I felt humbled even more. It wasn't only that she'd brought my novels in for me to sign – all hardback copies, obviously read and re-read many times – but she'd gone to the trouble of arranging an assortment of materials she'd thought I might find useful in my research. 'They're mostly papers, family papers, that have some connection to your Duke of Hamilton. The letters aren't by anybody famous, and most people wouldn't know that they were here, but I remember someone else was looking up the duke last year and said that these were very helpful.'

I was touched, so I took extra care to sign all her books well, with my friendliest wishes and thanks for her help.

The papers she had found for me were of more interest, I discovered, than the letters the duke wrote himself. It was interesting, always, to learn about someone by how other people described him. By late morning, I had learnt so much I didn't think it possible that anything was left that could surprise me.

Till I turned to the next letter.

It was one of several written by an Edinburgh physician to his younger brother, and was dated 19th April 1707. After going on for half a page about a dying patient, he said, 'Coming home, I did meet Mr Hall, whom I am sure you will remember from our dinner with His Grace the Duke of Hamilton, and who is by the duke now greatly valued and esteemed. Mr Hall appeared quite pale, but when I questioned him he did assure me he was well, but only quite worn out from having travelled on His Grace's business. He has ridden these five days from Slains, the castle of the Earl of Erroll in the north, where he last month conveyed a young kinswoman of the earl who had come lately from the Western Shires. This lady, who is named not Hay but Paterson, had very much impressed the Duke of Hamilton as being of good character, and learning that her parents had both perished in the Darien adventure, which His Grace does hold to be our nation's greatest tragedy, His Grace did then endeavour to do all he could to aid the lady in her journey northward, and to that end did commission Mr Hall to be her guide.

'With such an act of kindness does His Grace reveal again

his true benevolence to those who do apply to him in need...'

The letter carried on to praise the Duke of Hamilton for fully one more page, but I just skimmed it to the finish, and went back.

I had to read that passage several times before I could believe that the words, the facts set down in front of me, were really there – that everything I'd written in my own book had been true in every detail, and not fiction.

But the line dividing fiction from the truth had blurred so badly now I didn't have a clue where it began, or where it ended. And I didn't know exactly how to deal with that.

My first thought was to share the news with Dr Weir, to tell him that I'd found what looked like proof Sophia Paterson *had* been to Slains. Not only that, but that she'd been there at the time and in the circumstances I had written down in my own story. But the doctor, when I called him, wasn't home. And likely wouldn't be, said Elsie, until sometime Sunday afternoon. He'd gone to see his brother, near Glasgow.

'Oh,' I said.

'If it's important, I could—'

'No, it's all right. I can wait till Sunday.' But it seemed a long way off. I could have used the doctor's counsel and encouragement when I came home to Cruden Bay late Friday night, too tired to take much notice of the apprehensive feeling that, as always, met me halfway up the path above the harbour.

The night was calm. There was a winter moon to see by, and as I drew closer to the cottage I could see that Jimmy had left lights on for me, spilling warmly out the front room windows. And inside, I found things looking just as I had left them. But the voices of my characters, beginning now to whisper in my mind, advised me differently. I heard the countess saying clearly: 'Much has changed since you were last at Slains.'

I didn't doubt that she was right.

And so I crossed to my computer, sitting patient on the long scrubbed table, waiting for me. And I switched it on.

V

All week there had been visitors.

They came on horseback, singly, from the shadowed lands that lay toward the north and the northwest. Sophia knew from their appearance and their bearing they were men of some importance, and although they were presented to her when they first arrived, as though they'd come for no more reason that to bid her welcome to the region, she knew well that this was simply a convenience, for each visitor was then conveyed to Colonel Hooke, in private, and remained with him some time.

The first to come had been announced as Lord John Drummond, which had stopped Sophia's heart an awful moment, till she'd calmed herself with the assurance that her Uncle John could not have left his grave and come to Slains in cruel pursuit of her. And then, the countess, too, had understood, and had been quick to say, 'Sophia, here is John, my nephew,' and the man who entered was a younger man, and pleasant in his manner. He was, Sophia learnt, the second son to that same Duke of Perth – the brother of the countess – who was spoken of so famously as living in such closeness with the exiled king, and young Lord Drummond did not hide the fact that he, too, was a Jacobite.

Sophia had suspected, these past days, beginning with the warning of the countess that she might hear things and see things that would play upon her conscience, that the coming of the colonel and of Mr Moray might, as its design, involve some plot among those nobles who would bring King James to Scotland and restore him to his throne.

Such things were never spoken of before her, but she'd noticed that, although the countess and the two men did not drink the king's health at the dinner table, they did pass their goblets casually above the water jug, and from her uncle's house Sophia knew this meant they drank the health of him 'over the water', meaning of the king in exile just across the English Channel.

She knew this, yet she held her tongue, because she did not wish to vex the countess by revealing what she understood of everything now happening at Slains. The countess was so occupied and busy with her guests and with the messengers who came and went at all hours from the castle that Sophia felt her own place was to keep herself well out of things and keep the countess happy by pretending to be ignorant.

She knew that Colonel Hooke did think her so, though she was not convinced of Mr Moray. His grey eyes were wont to watch her with a quiet concentration that did not appear to waver from its purpose, although what that purpose might have been, Sophia could not say. She only guessed that he saw much, and was not easily deceived. But in that instance, and if he was as intelligent a man as she believed, he also would have seen her feelings were in sympathy with theirs, and that they need have no worry that she would betray them.

Whatever Mr Moray's knowledge, he did nothing, for his part, to raise the question of her being trusted in their company.

And so the first days passed, and brought the visitors, with names belonging to the greater families of the north – the Laird of Boyne, and later, Lord Saltoun, the chief of one branch of the house of Fraser. And behind them all came the Lord High Constable himself, the Earl of Erroll.

Sophia thought him more impressive than his portrait; young, but careful with his actions and his words, and with his mother's independent mind. There was around the man a certain energy, as of a banked-up fire that might, at any moment, flare to life.

He made a vital contrast to poor Colonel Hooke, whose health, since his arrival at the castle, had continued to be troublesome.

The Earl of Erroll, noticing, remarked upon this, and the colonel answered him, 'I fear that I am still much out of order with my voyage. Indeed, I have been indisposed since we did leave Versailles.'

Which was the first time that the French king's court had been so openly referred to, and Colonel Hooke, as though just realising his carelessness, glanced quickly at Sophia, as did everybody else. Except the Earl of Erroll. He simply carried on to ask, 'And I do trust that you left both their majesties, the King of France, and our King James, in all good health and spirits?'

There was silence for an instant, then the countess warned him, 'Charles...'

'What, Mother?' Shrugging off his cloak, he turned his gaze toward Sophia, as the others had, his own expression showing no concern. 'She is a member of our family, is she not?'

The countess said, 'Of course, but—'

'Well, then I would warrant she has wit enough to know the way things are with us. She does not look a fool. Are you a fool?' he asked Sophia.

She did not know how to answer with so many eyes upon her, but she raised her chin a little and quite bravely shook her head.

'And have you formed your own opinion as to why these gentlemen have come to Slains?'

Although she faced the Earl of Erroll, it was not the earl's regard she felt just then, but that of Mr Moray, whose unyielding gaze would brook no falsehood, so she said, 'It is my understanding that they have come here from France to treat among the Jacobites, my Lord.'

The young earl smiled, as though her honesty had pleased him. 'There, you see?' he told the others. Then, returning to Sophia, asked, 'And would you then discover us to agents of Queen Anne?'

He was but baiting her, in jest. He knew the answer, but she told him very clearly, 'I would not.'

'I did not think so.' And the matter, from his tone, was settled. 'I do therefore feel at ease to speak my mind in this young lady's presence. As should all of you.'

If Colonel Hooke looked doubting, it was balanced, thought Sophia, by the faint smile of approval on the face of Mr Moray. Why it mattered to her so, that he approved, she did not seek to know, but turned her eyes and ears instead to Colonel Hooke, who had at last relented and was answering the earl as to the health of those whom he had last seen at the exiled Stewart court of Saint-Germain, in France.

'I am encouraged,' was the earl's reply, 'to hear that young King James is well. This country sorely needs him.'

Hooke nodded. 'So he is aware. He is now more convinced than ever that the time has come for Scotland to arise.'

'He was convinced of that, as I recall, two years ago, when we first started this adventure.' With a patient look, the earl went on, 'But it may be as well that he did hesitate, for he will find that there are many more who are now full prepared to stand for him, convinced that, at the worst, they will gain more with sword in hand than they are offered by this union with the English.'

'Is it true that the Presbyterians in the west might seek to join our cause?'

'I have heard whisperings to that effect. The Presbyterians were angered by the Union, and indeed, being among the best armed and the least divided forces in this country, they did intend to make their anger plain by marching upon Edinburgh, there to disperse the parliament.'

Mr Moray, who'd kept to the background until now, could not contain himself on hearing this. 'But surely, had they done so, that would then have stopped the Union taking place?'

'Aye, almost certainly. Especially,' the earl said, 'since no fewer than four nobles from the shires of Angus and of Perth proposed to do the same.'

'Christ's blood,' swore Mr Moray. 'Why then did they not?'

A quick glance passed between the young earl and his mother before he replied, 'They were dissuaded, by a man they did esteem.'

'What man?'

'His Grace the Duke of Hamilton.'

There was a swift response from Colonel Hooke. 'I'll not believe it.'

'Know it to be true,' the earl assured him. 'And know too that your friend the duke, who for these two months past has testified to such impatience that you should arrive, has changed his tone now that you are on Scottish ground. He says to all who care to listen that you come too late, and that the king no longer thinks about this nation, and we cannot hope for his return.'

'You lie.'

The earl's hand lightly touched his sword hilt in an answer to the insult, but the countess stepped between the two men.

Calmingly, she said, 'I told you, Colonel, much has changed since you were last at Slains.'

'So it appears.' He turned away, his face more drawn and troubled than could have been solely blamed upon his illness.

The earl said, 'I am mindful, Colonel, of your long acquaintance with the duke, but his discourse has given great offence to many, and his secret intrigues with Queen Anne's commissioner in Scotland do increase our noble friends' distrust. It was the Duke of Athol, whom you know to be an honest man, who did first discover that intrigue, with which he did reproach the Duke of Hamilton. He, at the first, denied it, but the Duke of Athol having proved it plainly, he was forced then to confess, though he entreated Athol to believe he sought no more than to mislead the English. This excuse, as you can well imagine, gave to no one satisfaction. The result is that most of his former friends have broken openly with him, and there are few of us who will still bear his visits.

'His credit with the people now comes mainly from your court of Saint-Germain. King James has made it plain that none in Scotland should declare themselves until the Duke of Hamilton declares himself, and that we all should follow his direction, as he has our king's good favour.'

'I believe,' said Hooke, 'those orders were repeated in a letter which was sent to you and others, to inform you of my voyage.'

'Aye, they were. And I stand ready to obey my king, as always. But I would have him know that what he wrote to us in confidence has already been passed, by a betrayer, to our enemies, for I have seen another letter, written by the secretary to Queen Anne's commissioner in Scotland, that does also speak about your voyage, and your purpose here. And names the man who travels with you.'

Hooke was speechless. 'But—'

'I do not seek to judge the conduct of the Duke of Hamilton, nor would I have you neglect him in your negotiations. I tell you only that the man is impenetrable, and that you would do well to make use of these things I have told you, and be upon your guard, and keep concealed from him all that you may transact with other lords.'

The interval between the time he said that and the time Hooke nodded and replied was little longer than the time it took to swallow, and Sophia could not see Hooke's face directly, yet she felt in that small moment he had weighed things in his mind, the way her Uncle John had craftily weighed any new development and turned it to his benefit. Hooke's voice, too, when he spoke, was like her uncle's in its tone, and for that fault it left Sophia unconvinced.

Hooke said, 'My Lord High Constable, your counsel is most useful. I do thank you for it, and will take the measures you suggest.'

Sophia had no proof that he was lying, nor was it her place to speak in such a gathering, but had she been a man, she might have warned the Earl of Erroll that His Grace the Duke of Hamilton was not the only person who should not be fully trusted.

'You look troubled,' said the countess.

When Sophia glanced up to reply, her embroidery needle slipped under the knot she was working and pricked at the edge of her fingernail, painfully. Clenching her jaw, she succeeded in holding her silence until the sensation had fled, then she said, 'I am not troubled, I assure you. It is only that this pattern is beyond me, and I cannot make my stitches come out evenly.'

The countess paused, and when she finally spoke her voice was fond. 'My son did right to trust you. You can tell no lie, my dear, without it showing plainly on your face.' Returning to her own needlework, she said decidedly, 'We ask too much of you, to keep our secrets. That is Colonel Hooke's opinion, and I do believe it true.'

Sophia took a cautious step into that opening. 'The colonel is a good friend of your family, so I understand.'

'A good friend of my brother James, the Duke of Perth. They have worked very much in step these past few years, toward a common end. It has been two years since my brother first sent Colonel Hooke across from France to visit us at Slains, and to begin to seek support among the nobles of this nation for our venture. Times were different, then. The Union was a subject only talked about, and none would have believed that it would happen, that the guardians of this country would sell Scotland's independence for the lining of their pockets. There was then no sense of urgency, as there is now among us. For when Queen Anne dies – and, from her health, that end will come upon her soon – the Stewart line upon the British throne will die, as well. The English mean to give a foreign prince of Hanover the crown, unless we bring King James back safe from France, to take his rightful place. We might have tolerated Mary's reign, and Anne's, for they were sisters of the true king, born of Stewart blood, but the throne is rightly James's, and not Anne's. It must be his when Anne is gone, for all of Scotland will oppose a Hanoverian succession.' She finished off a knot with force, and bit the thread to cut it. 'Colonel Hooke no doubt will have more luck this time in treating with our nobles, and persuading them to come to an arrangement with our friend the King of France, who waits to lend us his assistance should we move to rise in arms.'

Sophia did not question Colonel Hooke's intent. It was her intuition only that made her suspect his aims might not be as the others thought they were, and intuition, while it served her well, was not enough to justify the accusation of a man she did not know. Besides, 'He will be leaving soon, he says.'

'Aye. He starts tomorrow for Lord Stormont's house at Scone, to see the Duke of Athol. My son was asked to go, as well, but he thinks it unwise that he should undertake that journey, as he has but just come home after a session of more than six months. If he did return towards Edinburgh so soon, and to such an assembly of known Jacobites, it would give the government room for a suspicion that some plot was carrying on. It is enough of a risk that, with the parliament now finished, and the chief men of the nation dispersed over the different counties, Colonel Hooke must hazard himself in travelling through a great part of the kingdom to meet with our nobles. He has a design, I believe, to divide the country into two circuits – to visit one himself, and to desire Mr Moray to go through the other, but my son does view that plan with apprehension, also.'

'Why?' Sophia asked.

The countess was threading her needle with deep, blood-red silk. 'Mr Moray is a wanted man.' She said it as though none could deem it shameful; as though, greatly to the contrary, it were a thing of pride. 'The English for these three years past have put a price upon his head. They have offered, by proclamation, the sum of five hundred pounds sterling to any person who should seize him.'

Sophia's needle slipped again and speared her finger as she let her hands drop to her lap. 'Five hundred pounds!' She'd never heard of such a sum. A tenth of that would be a fortune to most men.

The names of those who'd wronged the Crown were often published, so she knew, with five pounds offered for their capture, and that commoner amount did often stir an honest person to betray a friend. What friends could Mr Moray hope to have, she wondered, with five hundred pounds upon his head?

'He is well known,' the countess said, 'south of the Tay, in his own country, but the colonel feels that Mr Moray could with safety make a progress through the northern provinces, and settle an agreement with the Highlanders.'

Sophia frowned. 'But why…?' She caught herself mid-sentence.

'Yes?' the countess asked.

'I do apologise. 'Tis none of my affair. But I was

wondering...there surely would be other men who might have come with Colonel Hooke. Why would King James send Mr Moray here to Scotland, and so set him in the path of danger?'

'Some men choose the path of danger on their own.'

Sophia knew this to be truth. She knew that her own father had been such a man. 'But if he should be captured...' she began, and then broke off again, because she did not want to think of what might happen to him if he should be recognised, and taken.

The countess, with no personal attachment, said, 'If he should be captured, then our plans may be discovered.' She had finished with the flower she was working, and she bit the blood-red thread through with precision. Her eyes upon Sophia's face held something of a tutor's satisfaction in a favoured pupil who showed ease in following a course of study.

'That,' she said, 'is why my son does feel uneasy.'

Sophia was uneasy in her own mind, still, when she awoke next morning. She'd been dreaming there were horses stamping restless on the ground outside the castle, with their warm breaths making mist each time they snorted, and men's voices calling out to one another with impatience. She woke to semi-darkness. From her window she could see a slash of palest pink across the water-grey horizon, and she knew that it would be another hour or more before the family and their guests began to stir and start the day's routine of morning draughts and breakfast. But her restlessness was strong, and within minutes she had up and dressed and left her chamber, seeking human company.

The kitchen was deserted. Mrs Grant had set a pot to boil,

but she herself was nowhere to be found, nor were the other servants of the kitchen. Nor was Kirsty. Thinking Kirsty might have gone to visit Rory in his stables, Sophia crossed the yard to look, but all she found was Hugo lying listless in his bed of wool and straw. There were no horses left for him to guard, except the one mare that had brought Sophia up to Slains from Edinburgh, and from whose back she'd tumbled when she'd ridden with the countess. That mare now dozed upon her feet, as though depressed to find the stalls to either side of her were empty. When Sophia touched the velvet nose, the mare's eyes scarcely flickered to acknowledge the caress.

'They've gone, then,' said Sophia. So it had not been a dream. Not altogether. In some half-awakened state, she truly had heard horses stamping, and the voices of the men, as Colonel Hooke and Mr Moray had struck out before the dawn on their respective missions – Hooke towards the south, and Mr Moray to the north.

She felt a sudden twist of loss, inside, although there was no cause for it. Unless it was because she'd had no chance to say goodbye. No chance to wish him well, and bid him keep his back well-guarded in that land of wild men, to whom five hundred pounds would seem the riches of a king.

She leant her head against the mare's soft muzzle, stroking still, and said, 'God keep him safe.'

The male voice seemed to speak out of the air behind her. 'Tell me, lass, what man does so deserve your prayers?'

She wheeled. It was no ghost. Within the stable doorway, Mr Moray leant one shoulder on the heavy post, arms folded and at rest across the leather of his buffcoat. Hugo hadn't stirred or barked, as he was wont to do when there were strangers in the stable, and the mare's soft head stayed steady in Sophia's startled hands.

'I thought that you had gone,' she blurted out, and then because as speeches went, she knew that sounded foolish, and because it might to certain ears reveal more than she cared to show, she gathered her composure and responded to his question with another of her own. 'Did Colonel Hooke take both the geldings, then?'

'He took the black. The young groom took the other, on an errand for the earl. And I, as you can see, am left behind.' He seemed to mock himself with that last statement, but Sophia had a sense that he was none too pleased about it. His features were more grim and unforgiving than she'd seen them, but they softened as he looked at her, and though he had not moved within the doorway, he still seemed a full step closer when he tipped his head and asked her, 'Is this some strange and curious custom of the Western Shires, to talk to God and horses when the sun is barely up?'

She turned her face away, and kept her focus on the mare. 'I could not sleep. I heard the horses.'

'Aye, there was a fair bit of confusion when they left. I do confess I might have raised my own voice, once or twice. 'Twas likely me that woke ye.' He was silent for a moment, then he said, 'That mare seems fond of ye.'

Sophia smiled. 'We have an understanding. She has thrown me once, though I admit the fault was mostly mine.'

'I am surprised. She does appear too gentle to so use a rider, and I cannot think ye capable of handling her too roughly.'

'No, I only fell because I could not hold her when she ran. She has a wildness that she keeps well hid behind this gentle face.'

'Aye, so it is with many women.' Moray did move, then. She heard the rustle of his boots upon the dampened straw, and when she dared to take a sideways glance his leather-covered chest was at her shoulder. He reached to stroke the mare's arched neck. 'It is as well for her I do not leave this morning, for however wild she thinks herself, she would not have a liking for the hard road through the highlands, and she'd like it even less to carry such a load as me.'

So that, Sophia thought, was why he had not gone. There was no mount for him. 'Then you must wait, and leave when Rory brings the other gelding back?'

'No, lass. I do not leave.' He dropped his hand and turned to lean with both his elbows on the cross-rail of the stall so that a fold of his black cloak swung round to rest upon Sophia's sleeve. 'The others felt it best that I remain at Slains.'

She was relieved to know that reason had at least prevailed. The earl must have persuaded Moray that to stay here would decrease the chance he might be captured, and although he did appear to be ill-pleased with the decision, from what she had observed of Moray these past days she knew his honour would compel him to abide with that which might best serve the purpose of the exiled king.

Not sure if she was meant to know he had a price upon his head, she only said, 'You'll doubtless find it safer.'

'Aye.' He seemed to find amusement in the word. 'Which minds me, ye've not told me yet whose safety ye were praying for.'

He was but teasing her, she thought. It mattered not at all to him who she'd been saying prayers for in the silence of the stable. But she could not school her voice to match his lightness, any more than she could keep her chin from lifting till her wide eyes met his quiet grey ones. And she saw he was not laughing. He was truly curious.

She could not tell a lie to him. But neither could she talk – her heart had risen to her throat, and beat so strongly there that speech was quite impossible.

Which was as well, for she could not have told him, 'It was you.' Not in this stable, with the warmth of his own cloak upon her arm, and his broad shoulders almost touching her, and his face but inches from her own. Time seemed suspended, and it felt to her that moment might have stretched until forever; but the mare, forgotten, nudged a softly questing nose between them, and Sophia found her wayward voice.

'The countess will be wanting me,' she said.

And taking one quick step back from the stall – so sharp a step that Hugo, drowsy in his bed of straw, came instantly alert – she turned and fled the stables, and the watchful mastiff, and the mare, and most of all, the man whose gaze she still could feel like warming fire upon her back.

Chapter Ten

I knew that he was watching me.

The rain was coming harder now. It beat upon the windshield with the force of fifty drummers, and the wipers could no longer clear it fast enough for us to have a good view of the road. Graham had tucked the car into a layby and idled the engine, and now he had turned in his seat and was watching my face while I looked out the window.

'I'm sorry,' he said. 'It's not much of a tour, in this weather. The countryside all looks the same when it rains.'

'That's all right. You can't control the weather.'

'We could try to wait it out.' But from his doubtful tone I knew that he felt fairly sure, as I did, that this rain had settled in to stay awhile, and he was not the sort of man to wait for long.

I had been looking forward to this morning more than I'd have wanted to admit. I'd been watching the clock till he'd come up half an hour ago and walked me down to where his beaten-up white Vauxhall waited parked beside the harbour wall, with Angus wagging happy in the back. But we had only gone a short way when the clouds that had been smothering the morning sun had opened. It was clear now that we'd have to end our driving tour before we'd even properly begun. I tried to hide my disappointment.

Graham must have seen it anyway, because he put the car in gear again and, turning up the wipers to their highest speed, eased back on to the narrow road. 'I tell you what. I've friends who have a farm not very far from here. We'll stop and visit them, all right? Put in a bit of time, till the rain eases.'

Angus, who'd stretched out along his blanket on the back seat, raised his head to note the changing of our course, and by the time we'd reached the farm's long lane was standing on the seat, tail wagging, obviously pleased by where he was.

The lane was rutted deep and muddy, ending in a neat square yard with sheds joined in a squat row to the front of us, and barns along our righthand side, and to the left a low-walled whitewashed farmhouse with a bright blue door.

'Sit tight,' said Graham, pulling up his jacket's hood, 'I'll see if they're about.'

He stood at the farmhouse door, with water sluicing down a drainpipe at his shoulder, and knocked. No one came, so with a shrug and quick smile of encouragement, he jogged across the hard-packed yard and through the open doorway of the nearest barn.

He hadn't been exaggerating when he'd said that Angus hated being left behind. The dog had merely sat and whimpered while his master had been knocking at the blue door, but when Graham disappeared into the barn, the spaniel stood and scrabbled at the window of the back seat and began to howl, a piteous, heart-rending noise designed to move the listener to action. I could only stand a minute of it – then I turned and rummaged for his leash. 'All right,' I said, 'all right, we'll go, too. Just hold on.'

I didn't have a hood. But I had boots, which I was thankful for, because my first few running steps were ankle-deep in rainwater. With Angus pulling hard against the leash, we moved with near-Olympic speed across the courtyard, and were through the door and in the barn before the rain had soaked me.

It was warmer inside, dusty from the hay and from the movement of the animals, and smelling sharply of straw and manure. After what I'd written last night, it seemed fitting, somehow, that I should now find myself confronted by a row of tidy horse stalls – three with horses, and one empty – and that one of the three equine faces turned to watch my entrance should look strangely like the mare that I'd created for Sophia, with the same great liquid eyes and coal-black mane and gentle features.

Graham wasn't anywhere in sight. He must, I thought, have gone the full way down the barn and round the corner, to the sheds, which I could see now were connected at the far end. Angus would have followed, but I held him back a moment, keen to have another minute with the horses.

I loved horses. Every young girl did, so I'd been told, and I had never totally outgrown the phase. My more discerning readers sometimes commented on how I always managed to work horses into all my plots, though I at least could claim that I could hardly write historicals without a horse or two. Truth was, they were my private weakness.

There was no great black gelding in any of the stalls, like the one I'd given to Nathaniel Hooke, and no bay gelding either. Only a tall chestnut hunter who eyed me, aloof, and a curious grey in the end stall, and standing between them, the mare – or the horse that I thought was a mare, since she looked like the one I'd imagined. She stretched out her nose as I offered my hand and with pure joy I petted the velvety hair by her nostrils and felt the warm push of her breath in my palm.

'That one's Tammie,' Graham said. He had, as I'd deduced, been in the sheds, and was returning now with his unhurried stride. 'You want to watch him, he's a ladies' man.'

I turned, surprised. 'He?'

'Aye.' Coming up, he took the dog's lead from me so I'd have both hands free for the horse.

I rubbed the side of Tammie's neck. 'He's much too pretty,' I declared, 'to be a boy.'

'Aye, but you'll wound his pride by saying so.' He glanced at me with interest. 'D'ye ride?'

'Not really.'

Grinning, he asked, 'What does that mean?'

'That means I can sit on horses if they let me do it. I can even hold on if they're only walking, but beyond a trot I'm useless. I fall off.'

'Well, that can be a problem,' he agreed.

'I take it no one's home?'

'No.' He glanced briefly at the open double doorway, where the rain was coming down now in an almost solid sheet, and then looked back at me and, seeing how absorbed I was in petting Tammie, said, 'But we can wait. We're in no hurry.' And he hitched a rough stool forward with one foot, and took a seat, while Angus settled on the straw-strewn floor beside him.

It was almost like my book, I thought. The stables, and the

mare – well, Tammie, looking like the mare – and me, and Graham, with his clear grey eyes that looked, by no coincidence, a lot like Mr Moray's. We even had the dog, curled up and sleeping in the straw. Life echoed art, I thought, and smiled a little.

'What about yourself?' I asked. 'Do you ride?'

'Aye, I won ribbons in my youth. I'm that surprised my dad's not had them out to show you.'

His voice, behind the dryness, held such fondness for his father that it made me wonder something. 'Maybe,' I ventured, 'he'll show me tomorrow. You know he's invited me over for lunch?'

'He did mention it.'

'You'll be there, too?'

'I will.'

'That's good. Because your dad's been trying very hard to help me with my research, and he seemed keen to have me meet you so we could talk history.' Pretending a deep interest in the horse's face, I asked him, without looking round, 'Why didn't you tell him we'd already met?'

I wished, through the long minute of the pause that followed, that I could have seen his face, and known what he was thinking. But when he spoke, his voice was hard to read. He only tossed the question back at me. 'Why didn't you?'

I knew why I'd kept silent, and it wasn't just because I hadn't wanted to conflict with his own story, or the lack of it. It was because...well, Graham, like the horses, was a private weakness, too. When he was near me I felt half-electric, half-confused, excited as a teenager caught up in a new crush, and I had wanted that to last a while, to hug it to myself and not let anyone intrude upon it. But I couldn't tell him that, so I said, 'I don't know. I didn't really think.' And then, like him, I threw the ball back. 'I assumed you'd had your reasons for not telling him.'

Whatever they had been, he didn't tell me. We were on a different subject. 'So,' he asked, 'how goes the book?'

Much safer ground, I thought. 'It's going really well. It kept me up till three o'clock this morning.'

'Do you always write at night?'

'Not always. When I get towards the last part of a book, I write all hours. But I do my best work late at night, I don't know why. Maybe because I'm half-conscious.' I'd said that last part as a joke, but he nodded, considering.

'It's possible,' he said. 'Maybe at night your subconscious takes over. A friend of mine paints, and he says the same thing, that it's easiest working at night, when his mind starts to drift and he's nearly asleep. Says he sees things more clearly, then. Mind you, I can't tell the difference myself from the pictures he paints in the daytime – they all look like great blobs of colour to me.'

After this past week and what I'd learnt about Sophia Paterson, I'd formed a few opinions on the subject of subconscious thought and how it ruled my writing, but I kept these to myself. 'With me it's habit, more than anything. When I first started writing – really writing, not just playing – I was still at university. The only time I had was late at night.'

'And what was it you studied? English?'

'No. I love to read, but all through school I hated it when books were pulled apart and analysed. Winnie-the-Pooh as a political allegory, that sort of thing. It never really worked for me. There's a line in *The Barretts of Wimpole Street* – you know, the play – where Elizabeth Barrett is trying to work out the meaning of one of Robert Browning's poems, and she shows it to him, and he reads it and he tells her that when he wrote that poem, only God and Robert Browning knew what it meant, and now only God knows. And that's how I feel about studying English. Who knows what the writer was thinking, and why should it matter? I'd rather just read for enjoyment. No, I studied politics.'

'Politics?'

'I had ideas of changing the world,' I admitted. 'And anyway, I thought it might come in handy, somewhere. Everything's political.'

He didn't argue that. He only asked me, 'Why not history?'

'Well, again, I'd rather read it for enjoyment. Teachers always knock the life out of the subject, somehow.' Then remembering what he did for a living, I tried softening that statement with, 'Not *all* teachers, naturally, but—'

'No, it's no use now, you've said it.' Leaning back, he studied me with obvious amusement. 'I'll try not to take offence.'

'I didn't mean—'

'You'll only dig yourself in deeper,' was his warning.

'Anyway, I never finished university.'

'Why not?'

'Because I finished my first novel first, and then it sold, and things just took off on their own after that. It bothers me sometimes that I didn't get my degree, but on the other hand I really can't complain,' I said. 'My writing has been good to me.'

'Well, you've got talent.'

'My reviews are mixed.' Then I paused, because I realised what he'd said, and how he'd said it. 'Why would you think I've got talent?'

I'd caught him. 'I might have read one of your books this past week.'

'Oh? Which one?'

He named the title. 'I enjoyed it. You impressed me with the way you did your battle scenes.'

'Well, thank you.'

'And you obviously did a thorough job with all your research. Though I did think it was hard luck that the hero had to die.'

'I know. I tried my best to make the ending happy, but that's how it really happened, and I don't like changing history.' Fortunately, many of my readers had approved and had, according to their letters to me, wallowed in the tragic end, enjoying a good cry.

'My mother would have loved your books,' he said.

My hand still idle on the horse's neck, I turned. 'Has she been gone for long?'

'She died when I was twenty-one.'

'I'm sorry.'

'Thank you. So am I. My dad's been lost these fifteen years. He blames himself, I think.'

'For what?'

'She had a problem with her heart. He thinks he should have forced her to slow down.' He smiled. 'He might as well have tried to slow a whirlwind. She was always into everything, my mum.'

That must be where he got it from, his restlessness. He flipped the conversation back to me. 'Are both your parents living?'

'Yes. I have two sisters, too.'

'They're all still back in Canada?'

'One sister's in the States, and one's in China, teaching English. My dad says it's our Scottish blood that makes us want to travel.'

'He may be right. Where's home for you, then?'

'I don't really have one. I just go to where my books are set, and live there while I'm writing.'

'Like a gypsy.'

'Sort of.'

'You must have some interesting adventures. Meet some interesting people.'

'I do, sometimes.' I could only hold his gaze a moment, then I turned away again to scratch round Tammie's forelock. Tammie nudged me, flirting, and I said to Graham, 'You were right, he is a ladies' man.'

'He is. He has a handsome face,' he said, 'and kens the way to use it.' He was looking at the open door again, and at the rain that was still pelting down upon the hard-packed yard. 'I think we're out of luck the day, for touring.'

He was right, I knew, but I said nothing.

Truth be told, I wouldn't have minded spending the rest of the day in this stable, with Graham and Angus for company. But he clearly wasn't one to sit still for that long, so when he stood, I gave the horse a final pat and turned my collar up, and made the dash, reluctantly, back through the rain to where we'd parked the Vauxhall.

I did a better job, this time, of hiding how I felt. And it seemed hardly any time at all before we were surrounded by the houses and the shops of Cruden Bay, and then we'd reached the bottom of the path up to my cottage and he parked and came around to let me out. Shrugging off his coat, he held it overhead so that it shielded both of us, and said, 'I'll walk you up.'

He left Angus in the car, though, and I knew that meant that Graham didn't plan on coming in. And that was fine, I thought, there was no reason for me to be disappointed. There'd be other times.

But still, I felt a little flat inside and had to force a smile to show him when we reached my front door and I turned to thank him.

Graham took the coat that he'd been holding overhead and put it on again. 'We'll try the tour another time,' he said.

'All right.'

'See you tomorrow, then. At lunch.'

'OK.'

He stood a moment longer, as though wanting to say something else, but in the end he only flipped his hood up, smiled, and started off again along the path while I turned round to fit my key into the cottage door.

My hands were cold and wet and couldn't work the lock, and then I dropped the key and heard it ping on stone, so that I had to crouch and search for it, and by the time I'd found it I was well and truly soaked.

I straightened, to find Graham standing once again beside me. Thinking he'd come back to help, I told him, 'It's all right, I found it.' And I raised the key to show him.

But when I began to try the lock again, his hand came up to catch my face, to stop me. I could feel the warmth of his strong fingers on my jawline, as his thumb traced very gently up my cheekbone.

'Look,' he said, 'I didn't tell my dad, because I didn't want to share you. Not just yet.'

I was convinced, at first, I hadn't heard him properly. And even if I had, I couldn't think of what to say. If I'd been writing this, I thought, I would have had no problem. It was easy writing dialogue for characters in books, but in real life, the words just never came to me the way I wanted them.

He took my pause for something else. 'I'm sure that sounds insane to you, but—'

'I don't want to share you either.' Which, considering the way that tumbled out, was not exactly the sophisticated answer I'd been aiming for, but seconds later I had ceased to care.

The kiss was brief, but left no room for me to misread his intentions. For that swirling moment, all I felt was him – his warmth, his touch, his strength, and when he raised his head I rocked a little on my feet, off balance.

He stood looking down at me as though he'd felt the power of that contact, too. And then his teeth flashed white against the darkness of his beard. The grey eyes crinkled. 'Put *that* in your book,' he dared me.

Then he turned and, shoving both hands deep into his pockets, walked off whistling down the wet path while I stood behind and watched him, standing speechless in the rain.

VI

'Ye've lost your mind,' said Kirsty. 'He's a handsome man. If I were of the proper birth, I'd smile for him myself.'

Sophia's own mouth curved. 'I doubt that would please Rory. And besides, you said you want a man who'll settle down, and give you bairns. I do not think that Mr Moray leads a settled life.'

'I'd take his bairns,' said Kirsty. 'Or the making of them, anyway.' She tossed her hair and smiled widely. 'But now I'll be shocking ye, to talk so like a wanton. And 'tis true, your Mr Moray is nae farmer.'

They were outside in the little kitchen garden, where Sophia had found Kirsty searching for mint leaves to season the dish Mrs Grant was preparing. The morning was fine, with a warm sun above and a gentle breeze blowing instead of the fierce wind that had for the past three days rattled the windows and rolled the sea into great waves that had looked, to Sophia, as high as a man. Wicked weather for May, she had thought it. She greatly preferred days like this one, that let her come out of the house and away from the whirling confusion of feelings that pressed her when she was confined to close company with Mr Moray.

Kirsty asked her, 'Did ye ken he was a colonel in his own right? A lieutenant-colonel, in the French king's service. Rory telt me.'

'No, I did not know that.' But she did know his first name, because the Earl of Erroll called him by it: John. She thought it suited him. A simple name, but strong: John Moray.

Now she added 'Colonel' to it, tried it in her mind, while Kirsty shot her one more disbelieving look and asked, 'Why did ye say ye would not ride with him?'

'I did not say I *would* not. I but told him I was occupied with other things this morning.'

Kirsty's eyes danced. 'Aye, 'tis fair important watching me pick mint.'

'I have my needlework.'

'And heaven kens the tides might stop their flow were ye to leave that for an hour.' She paused, and waited for the next excuse, and when none came she said, 'Now tell me why ye telt him that ye would not ride with him. The truth.'

Sophia thought of saying that she hadn't thought the countess would approve, but that was not the reason either, and she doubted Kirsty would be fooled. 'I do not know,' she said. 'He sometimes frightens me.'

That came as a surprise to Kirsty. 'Has he been unkind?'

'No, never. He has always been a gentleman towards me.'

'Why then do ye fear him?'

Sophia could not answer that, could not explain that it was not the man himself she feared but the effect he had upon her; that when he was in the room she felt like everything inside of her was moving faster somehow, and she trembled as with fever. She said only, once again, 'I do not know.'

'Ye'll never best your fears until ye face them,' Kirsty told her. 'So my mother always says.' She'd found her mint and taken what she needed. Now she stood. 'The next time Mr Moray asks,' she said, and smiled more broadly, 'ye might think to tell him yes.'

A week ago, Sophia would have followed her inside and spent a warm hour sitting chatting with the servants in the kitchen, but the protocol within the house had changed now that the Earl of Erroll had returned. Although the earl himself had never made a comment, it was plain that while he was in residence, the servants had resolved to run a tighter ship.

And so, when Kirsty left, Sophia stayed outside and wandered in the garden. Here at least there was fresh air and peace. The songbirds flitted round in busy motion, building nests within the shadowed crannies of the wall, and flowers danced among the grasses that blew softly by the pathways. The scents of sunwarmed earth and growing things were welcome to her senses, and she closed her eyes a moment, reaching back within her memory to the spring days of her childhood, and the fields that tumbled greenly down towards the River Dee...

A hand closed hard around her arm.

Her eyes flew open, startled, and she found the sharp face of the gardener close beside her own. She felt the sudden and instinctive crawl of fear that every animal must feel when in the presence of a predator. And then, because she would not show her fear to Billy Wick, she damped it down, but he had seen it and she knew it gave him pleasure.

'Have a care,' he said. His voice was not the scraping one that should have matched his face. It had a softer edge but to Sophia's ears its tone was yet unpleasant, like the whisper of a snake. 'Ye should keep both eyes open when ye're walking in my garden.'

She kept her own voice calm. 'I'll mind that, Mr Wick.'

'Aye, see ye do. I widna wish tae see ye come tae harm, a bonnie quinie like yerself.' His dark eyes stripped her with a slow glance as he held her by the arm.

She pulled away, but he did not release her and she knew that if she struggled it would only please him more. So, standing still, she told him, 'Let me go.'

'Ye look a bit unsteady on yer feet,' he said, and smiled. 'I'd nae want ye tae fall. Leastwyes, that's what I'll tell her ladyship, if ye should have a mind tae speak against me. I've been here at Slains a wee while longer than yerself, my quine. Her ladyship puts value on my word.' His other hand was reaching for her waist as he was speaking, and Sophia realised that, where they were standing, they were all but out of sight of anyone within the house. She felt the panic and revulsion rise like bile within her throat, and choke her words as she repeated, 'Let me go.'

'I dinna think I will, the now.' The hand had reached her waist and clasped it, and begun a progress upwards. 'I'd best be making certain ye've nae done yerself an injury.'

The footsteps on the pathway were a welcome interruption. In an instant Billy Wick had dropped his hands and moved away, so there was nothing untoward in the appearance of the scene that greeted Mr Moray when he came upon them. But he slowed his steps, and with a brief look at Sophia's face, stopped walking altogether, as his eyes swung, cold and watchful, to the gardener.

'Good morning, Mr Wick,' he said, but leaving no time for the other man to make reply, he added, 'I am sure this lady did not mean to keep ye from your work.'

The gardener scowled, but touched his cap respectfully and, picking up his tools from where he'd set them down beside the path, he slipped away as neatly as a viper in the grass.

Sophia's shoulders sagged a little with relief. Feeling Moray's eyes upon her once again, she waited for the questions, but they did not come. He only asked, 'Is everything all right?'

She could have told him what had happened, but she dared not, for beneath his calm she sensed that he was very capable of violence, in a just cause, and she dared not give him any reason to defend her honour, lest in doing so he called attention to himself. She would not have him be discovered.

So she told him, 'Yes,' and smoothed her gown with hands that barely trembled. 'Thank you. Everything is fine.'

He nodded. 'Then I'll not detain you, for I see you are, indeed, quite fully occupied this morning.'

He'd gone past her by the time she found her courage. 'Mr Moray?'

Once again he stopped, and turned. 'Aye?'

'I do find my situation changed.' She'd said it now. She could not lose her nerve. 'If you still wish to ride, I could come with you. If you like,' she finished, conscious of his steady gaze.

He stood a moment in consideration. Then he said, 'Aye, Mistress Paterson, I'd like that very much.'

She didn't bother changing from her gown into her borrowed habit. Dust and horsehair could not harm the fabric of her skirts more than the years themselves had done. This gown was the not the oldest one she owned, but she had worn it several seasons and had mended it with care because its colour, once deep violet, now a paler shade of lavender, did set off her bright hair to some advantage.

At the stables, Rory brought her out the mare, and ran his hands along the broad girth of the sidesaddle to see it was secure. But it was Moray's hand that helped Sophia to her mount.

She felt again that shooting charge along her arm that she had felt when they'd first touched, and as she drew her hand back he remarked, 'Ye should be wearing gloves.'

'I'll be all right. My hands are not so soft.'

'To mine, they are,' he said, and handed her the gauntlets from his own belt before swinging to the saddle of his gelding, where he sat with so much ease he seemed a part of the great animal. To Rory, he said, 'If her ladyship should ask, we'll not be riding far, and we'll be keeping close to shore. The lass is safe with me.'

'Aye, Colonel Moray.' Rory stepped well clear and watched them go, and though he made no comment, from the look of interest on his face Sophia guessed that Kirsty would soon hear of her adventure.

But while Kirsty would undoubtedly approve, Sophia did not know what thoughts the countess or her son might have upon the matter. True enough, the countess had been in the room when Moray had first asked her to go riding after breakfast, but Sophia had declined that offer with such haste the countess had not had the time or need to voice her own opinion. Nonetheless, Sophia reasoned, there could scarce be an objection. Mr Moray was an honourable man and of good family – a woman under his protection surely would not come to harm.

She told herself this last bit for a second time to fortify her confidence. They were beyond the castle now and heading to the south. He held the gelding to an easy walk although she sensed, had he been on his own, he would have settled on a pace more suited to his restlessness. It must, she thought, be difficult for someone such as him, a soldier, bred and trained for action, to be confined to Slains these past few days. She'd often seen him taking refuge in the library among the shelves of books, as though by reading he could give his mind at least a taste of liberty. But mostly he'd reminded her of some caged beast who could but pace the grounds and corridors without a worthy purpose.

Even now, he seemed to have no destination in his mind, as though it were enough for this brief time that he should breathe the sea air and be free.

He seemed in no great mood to break the silence, and indeed he did not speak till they had splashed across the burn and passed the huddle of small dwellings just beyond, and turned their mounts to where the soft beach grasses blew atop the dunes of sand. And then he asked, 'How do ye find those gloves?'

She found them warm, and overlarge, and rough upon her fingers, but the feeling had a certain sinful pleasure to it, as though his own hands were closed round hers, and she would not have wished them gone. 'They are a help to me,' she said. 'Though I confess I feel that I should have a falcon perched upon my wrist, to do them justice.'

She had never seen him smile like that – a quick and sudden gleam of teeth and genuine amusement. Its swift force left her all but breathless.

'Aye,' he said, 'they are not of the latest fashion. They were sent me as a Christmas present by my sister Anna, who greatly loves all tales of knights and chivalry, and no doubt chose those gloves with that in mind.'

She smiled. 'My sister's name was also Anna.'

'"Was"?'

'She died, last year.'

'I'm sorry. Did ye have no other family?'

'No.'

'Ye've but to ask, and ye may freely borrow some of mine.' His tone was dry. 'I have two sisters and three brothers.'

'It must vex you that you may not see them while you are in Scotland.'

'Aye. My elder brother William, who is Laird of Abercairney, has a wee lad not yet eighteen months of age, who would not ken me from a stranger. I had hoped that I might put that right this month, but it appears I will not have the chance.'

She tried to temper his regret with the reminder, 'But a lad so young, were he to meet you, still would not remember you.'

'I would remember him.' There was a tone within his voice that made her glance at him and wonder if he found it very hard to live in France, so far from those he loved. It was no strange thing for a Scottish man to live abroad, and younger sons of noble families, knowing well they never would inherit lands themselves, did often choose to serve in armies on the continent, and build lives far from Scotland's shores. The Irish Colonel Hooke, so she'd been told, had done just that and had a wife and children waiting now for him in France. She did not know for certain that John Moray did not have the same.

'Have you any sons, yourself?' she asked, attempting to speak lightly so that it would seem his answer did not matter.

He looked sideways at her. 'No, I have no sons. Nor daughters either. Or at least no lass has yet presented me with such a claim. And I'd think my mother would prefer it were I married first, afore I brought new bairns into the family.'

'Oh,' Sophia said, because she could not think of any other thing to say.

She felt him watching her, and though he had not altered his expression she could sense he was amused by her confusion, so she turned their talk along a different course.

She asked, 'And do you live at Court?'

'At Saint-Germain? Faith, no,' he said. ''Tis not a place for such as me. I find my lodgings where the King of France sees fit to send my regiment, and am content with that, although I do admit that when, from time to time, I am called back to Saint-Germain, I find King Jamie's court a grand diversion.'

She had heard much of the young King James – the 'Bonny Blackbird', so they called him, for his dark and handsome looks – and of his younger sister, the Princess Louise Marie, and of the grandeur and gay parties of their exiled court in

France, but she had never had occasion to meet someone who had been there, and she longed to know the details. 'Is it true the king and princess dance all night and hunt all morning?'

'And make promenades all afternoon?' His eyes were gently mocking. 'Aye, I've heard it rumoured, too, and it is true they both are young and on occasion have a mind to take such pleasure as they can, and who can blame them, after all that they have lived through. But the duller truth be told, the princess is a lass of charming sensibility, who does comport herself in all ways modestly, and young King Jamie spends his hours attending to his business matters, foreign and domestic, with the diligence that does befit a king. Although,' he added, so as not to disappoint her, 'I recall that Twelfth Night last, there was a ball held at Versailles at which King Jamie and the princess danced past midnight, and at four o'clock were dancing still, the princess all in yellow velvet set with jewels, and diamonds in her bonny hair, and some two thousand candles burning round the hall to give the dancers light. And when the ball was over and the king and princess came out in the torchlight of the Cour de Marbre, the Swiss Guard of the French king did salute them to their carriage, and they drove back home to Saint-Germain surrounded by a company of riders, richly dressed, and with the white plume of the Stewarts in their hats.'

Sophia sighed and briefly closed her eyes, imagining the picture. It was so removed from all that she had known, and so romantic. How incredible it all would be, she thought, to have the king at home again. The first King James had fled to exile in the year Sophia had been born, and in her lifetime there had been no King of Scots upon the ancient throne in Edinburgh. But she had listened, raptured, to her elders, as they reminisced about the days when Scotland's destiny had been its own to manage. 'Will he truly come?' she asked.

'Aye, lass. He'll come, and set his foot on Scottish soil,' said Moray. 'And 'tis my resolve to see the effort does not cost his life.'

She would have asked him more about the court at Saint-Germain, but Moray's gaze had swung away and out to sea, and suddenly he pulled upon the gelding's reins and brought him to a standstill.

Stopping too, Sophia asked, 'What is it?'

But whatever it was that John Moray had seen, I decided, would just have to wait until later. With reluctance I depressed the keys to save my work, and switched off my computer.

I was nearly late for lunch.

Chapter Eleven

Angus set up an alarm at my first knock, and went on barking steadily till someone came to answer. Jimmy held the door wide with a smile of welcome. 'Aye-aye, quine. Come in, and dinna fash yersel aboot the dog, it's only Angus. He'll nae bite. Here, gie us yer coat and umbrella, I'll hang them tae dry.'

It was good to step in from the grey mist and rain to the warmth of the bright narrow hall with its yellowing wallpaper. Today the smells of cooking were not lingering, but fresh and strong. He'd kept his promise, so it seemed, to do a roast of beef, and the richly brown aroma of it met me where I stood, reminding me that I'd been so absorbed in writing that I had forgotten to eat breakfast, and was starving.

Angus, seeing it was me, had stopped his barking and came forward now, tail wagging, to nose round my legs in search of some attention. I bent down to scratch his ears and said, 'Hi, Angus.' Then I caught myself, and ran the conversation back a few lines in my mind to reassure myself that Jimmy had made mention of the dog's name. And he had, but I would have to be more careful, I thought, if I was supposed to be pretending that this was the first time I was meeting Graham.

'Will ye have a bittie sherry?' Jimmy offered. 'My wife aye liked a wee bittie sherry afore Sunday lunch.'

'Yes, please.'

Following him through into the sitting room, I felt a clutching of anticipation at my ribcage, so I had to draw my breath in deeper, to prepare myself. It might not be the first time I was setting eyes on Graham, but it would be the first time that I'd seen him since he'd kissed me, and I found that I was nervous.

If I hadn't been so occupied with writing last night, I'd have likely analysed that kiss to death. I'd know today if he had meant it, or if he was having second thoughts about the change of course we had just made in our relationship.

He had his father's manners. As I came into the sitting room, he stood, and when his eyes met mine they laid my doubts to rest. We might have been the only people in the room.

Except we weren't.

I hadn't seen the other person standing to my left until a hand reached out to claim my shoulder, and I felt the brush of Stuart's breath against my cheek as he bent down to greet me with a smiling kiss that faintly smelt of beer. 'You see? I told you I'd not be away too long.' With the hand still on my shoulder, he said, 'Graham, this is Carrie. Carrie, meet my brother, Graham.'

Thrown off balance by this new turn of events, I went through the motions of the introduction by pure reflex, till the firm electric warmth of Graham's handshake steadied me. Politely but deliberately, I took a step forward that brought me out of Stuart's hold, and chose the armchair closest to the one where Graham sat. I then aimed my smile beyond both brothers to their father, who had crossed to offer me the glass he'd filled with care from what appeared to be a newly purchased bottle of dry sherry on the sideboard.

'Thanks,' I said, to Jimmy. 'Lunch smells wonderful.'

'Ye'll nae be filled wi' sic praise efter ye've aeten it.'

'That's why he's got us drinking first,' said Stuart, holding up his own half-finished glass of ale as evidence. Oblivious to my manoeuvre with the chairs, he took the one that faced me, stretching out his legs and shifting Angus to the side. The dog moved grumpily.

'So,' Stuart asked me, cheerfully, 'how did you get along this week, without me?'

'Oh, I managed.'

Jimmy said, 'She's been tae Edinburgh.'

I felt the brush of Graham's gaze beside me, before Stuart said, 'To Edinburgh?' His eyebrows lifted, curious. 'What for?'

'Just research.'

'Aye,' said Jimmy, 'awa all the wik she wis, and she didna get hame till late on Friday. Had me fair worriet. I nivver like tae see a quinie travel on her ain at nicht. Fit wye didna ye wait and come up in the morning?' he asked me.

'I was ready to come home,' was all the explanation I could give without revealing that I'd only wanted to get back in time to keep my date with Graham for our driving tour on Saturday.

If he suspected it himself, he kept it hidden. 'Did you find what you were after?' Graham asked, and as my head came round he added calmly, 'With your research?'

'I found quite a bit, yes.' And, because it gave me something useful I could focus on, I told him a little of what I had learnt from the Hamilton papers.

Stuart, settling back, asked, 'And who was the Duke of Hamilton?'

'James Douglas,' Graham said, 'Fourth Duke of Hamilton.'

'Oh, *him*. Of course.' He rolled his eyes, and Graham grinned and told his brother, 'Don't be such an arse.'

'We don't all sleep with history books.'

'The Duke of Hamilton,' said Graham slowly, as though speaking to a child, 'was one of Scotland's most important men, around the turning of the eighteenth century. He spoke out as a patriot, and had a place in line to Scotland's throne. In fact, some Protestants, himself included, thought he'd be a better candidate for king than any of the exiled Stewarts.'

'Aye, well, anyone would have been better than the Stewarts,' Stuart said, but as he raised his glass the curving of his mouth showed he was goading Graham purposely.

Ignoring him, Graham asked me, 'Does he play a great role in your book?'

'The duke? He's around in the background a lot. The story, so far, has kept pretty much to Slains, but there's a scene at the beginning where he briefly meets my heroine in Edinburgh. And my characters, of course, all have opinions on the duke's connection to the Union.'

'So do some historians.'

Stuart drained his glass and said, 'You're losing me, again. What Union?'

Graham paused, then in a dry voice told me, 'You'll excuse my brother. His appreciation of our country's past begins and ends with *Braveheart*.'

Stuart tried his best to look offended, but he couldn't. In his easy-going way, he said, 'Well, go on, then. Enlighten me.'

Graham's eyes were indulgent. 'Robert the Bruce was in *Braveheart*, so you'll ken who he was?'

'Aye. The King of Scotland.'

'And his daughter married the High Steward, so from that you've got the "Stewart" line, which went through two more Roberts and a heap of Jameses before coming down to Mary, Queen of Scots. You've heard of her?'

'Nice girl, bad marriages,' said Stuart, sitting back to play along.

'And Mary's son, another James, became the heir to Queen Elizabeth of England, who died without a child. So now you've got a Stewart being King of Scotland *and* of England, though he acts more English, now, than Scots, and rarely even sets a foot up here. Nor does his son, King Charles the First, who gets a bit too cocky with his powers, so along come Cromwell and his men to say they've had enough of kings, and they depose King Charles the First and cut his head off.'

'With you so far.'

'Then the English, after years of Civil War and having Cromwell and his parliament in charge awhile, decide that they'd be better off with kings, after all, so they invite the old king's son, Charles Stewart – Charles the Second – to come back and take the throne. And when he dies in 1685, his brother James becomes the king, which would be no real problem, only James is Catholic. *Very* Catholic. And not only do the English fear he's trying to edge out their hard-won Protestant religion, they also fear he'll enter an alliance with the Catholic King of France, who's their worst enemy.'

He paused to take a drink from his own glass which, like his father's, held neat whisky. Then he went on with the story.

'The aristocracy in England starts to think of getting rid of James and putting someone on the throne who'll be a Protestant, as they are, and against the French. And they have the perfect candidate in front of them, for James's eldest daughter, Mary, has a Protestant husband who's been waging war against the French for years, and who has had his eye upon the English throne since long before that – William, Prince of Orange. It doesn't matter that he's Dutch because he's Mary's husband, so if she's made queen, he'll only need an act of Parliament to rule as king beside her.

'But just as the aristocrats are making all their plans, King James's second wife gives birth to a son. Now the English have a problem, because male heirs trump females. So they put around a rumour that the newborn prince is not a prince at all, but just a common child that James had smuggled into his queen's chamber in a warming pan, to give himself an heir. It's not the most convincing story, but to those who want a reason to rise up against James, it's enough.

'What follows isn't quite a war – it's more a game of chess, with knights and nobles changing sides – and within six months James, his queen, and their wee heir have fled to France. It's not the first time James has done this, mind – when he was just a lad and his own father, Charles I, was in the middle of a Civil War, James was taken by his mother into France for safety. And although his father was beheaded and the Stewarts had to live awhile in exile, in the end the English asked them to come back and take the throne. So James remembers this, and trusts the same will happen now if he just keeps his head down, waits things out. And so he takes his queen and prince to live at Saint-Germain, where he spent his own exile as a lad, and by the spring of 1689 his daughter

Mary and her husband William have the English throne, and Scotland, having held a vote, declares for William, too.

'So now,' he said, 'our country's split in factions – those who, mostly Presbyterian, can stomach having Mary for a queen because she's Scottish and a Protestant besides, and those who think she's got no right to rule, not with her father living and a brother who's ahead of her in line. This second group, the ones who want to put King James back on the throne, are called the Jacobites,' he said, 'from "Jacobus", the Latin name for "James".'

Stuart raised his hand. 'Am I allowed another drink?'

'Aye.' Graham smiled, and took another swig of whisky while his brother briefly left the room, returning with a full glass and a question for their father.

'Should the oven still be on?'

'Ach, na.' And rising, Jimmy left the room with urgency.

As Stuart took his seat again, he said to me, 'He's never met a roast he hasn't burnt past recognition.'

Graham shared the joke and shrugged. 'We eat them, all the same.'

'I'm only warning her,' said Stuart. 'Anyhow, where were we? I was asking, I believe, about the Union, and so far you haven't mentioned it.' To me, as an aside, 'These academics always ramble on.'

'So, with King William on the throne,' said Graham, patiently recapping, 'we've got Scotland in a muddle, and enjoying one long chain of rotten luck. Towards the last years of the century, the harvests are so poor that people starve to death in droves, while English laws and tariffs choke out Scottish trade and navigation. And when a Scottish company scrapes up enough investment for a colony at Darien, in

Panama, to take a bit of trade away from England's East India Company, the English slam it hard by cutting off supplies and aid that might have helped the colonists survive. When Darien fails, the investors lose everything. Scotland is not only broke, but in debt, and we have nothing left to sell,' he said, 'except our independence.

'William's a widower now, but still fighting with France. He doesn't want to die and leave the French king any cards to play with, and so long as Scotland is a separate country, there will always be the threat that King James Stewart or his son, young James, might, with the backing of the French, return and cause the English trouble. It makes sense, in William's mind, that since the thrones of England and of Scotland had been joined some hundred years before, that now the parliaments should join as well, and make one single country of Great Britain.'

'Ah,' said Stuart, beginning to comprehend.

'And when William dies, he passes on this policy of Union to Queen Anne, his wife's sister and the second daughter of the old King James. Anne's a little nicer than her sister. She at least admits in private that young James is her half-brother, and it's widely hoped that, since she has no living children of her own, she'll name him as her heir. But her advisors have their own agenda, and they quickly see to it she chooses as her heir another relative, from the German House of Hanover.

'The Scottish parliament replies it won't accept the Hanoverian succession unless Scotland has the freedom to opt out of foreign policies that go against our interests, like the war Queen Anne's still waging with the Spanish and the French.'

'And I'm guessing,' Stuart ventured, 'that the English didn't go for that.'

'They hit us,' Graham said, 'with the Alien Act, which said in effect that unless we Scots came to the table to talk about a Union, every Scot who lived in England would be treated as an alien, and all estates in England owned by Scots would be repatriated, and our exports banned.'

'We had no choice, then,' Stuart said.

His brother looked at him. 'There is always a choice. But Scotland's nobles, as ever, were rich on both sides of the border, and few of them wanted to risk their own fortunes, so in the end, they sat down at the table. And our friend the Duke of Hamilton proposed that the selection of commissioners to talk about the Union should be left up to Queen Anne herself. He put it to a snap vote in the parliament when the opposition weren't all in their seats, and so it passed by a few votes, and that meant virtually all the commissioners were pro-Union. That,' Graham said, 'was just one of the small, sneaky things that he did.'

'So the Union went through.'

Graham grinned. 'Did ye not go to school?'

'Well, we have our own parliament, now.'

'Aye, but that's only recent. Christ, Stuie, you're not *that* young, surely, that you can't remember the whole campaign around the country for home rule? The Scottish National Party? Everybody marching in the streets?' When Stuart looked back at him blankly, Graham shook his head. 'You are a lost cause, aren't you?'

Shrugging, Stuart took it in good part, and told his brother, 'I was likely overseas, when all of that was going on.'

'More likely sitting in the pub.'

'It's possible,' said Stuart. 'Does it really matter?'

'Not unless your children ask you where you were the day our parliament re-opened after nearly three full centuries without one.'

I was privately inclined to think it wouldn't be a problem. Stuart Keith was not the kind of man who married and had children. With him, life was all great fun and play, and staying with one woman while she aged, or sitting up with crying babies, simply wasn't in his cards.

It had been interesting to sit here in my chair and watch the two of them while Graham gave his history lesson – both men with their different personalities, yet brothers through and through. Beneath the banter ran a deeper vein of genuine affection and respect, and it was clear they truly liked each other.

Jimmy, when he came back in to tell us lunch was ready, made the triangle complete, and from the way the three men interacted, I could tell that this had always been a happy home.

Could tell, too, that it hadn't seen a woman's touch in quite some time. This was a man's house now, from the mismatched and practical earthenware dishes to the no-nonsense table we ate on.

From the sideboard, a silver-framed photograph smiled at us all. Jimmy noticed me looking. 'My wife,' he said. 'Isobel.'

I would have known that without being told. I was already closely acquainted with eyes that, like hers, were the grey of the North Sea in winter. I said, 'She was lovely.'

'Aye. It's a shame she's nae here, the noo. She'd've hid a puckle questions tae speir at ye, about yer books. Allus wantit tae write one hersel.'

Graham said, 'She likely could have helped you with your research, come to that. My mother's family go a long way back, here.'

'Fairly that,' said Jimmy, nodding. 'She'd've telt ye stories, quine. And she'd've geen ye a better meal.'

'There's nothing wrong with this one,' I assured him. The roast beef, as Stuart had warned, was a little bit blackened and dry, but with gravy it went down just fine, and the carrots and roasted potatoes, though overdone too, were surprisingly good.

'Don't encourage him,' Stuart advised. He had taken the chair at my side, and from time to time his arm brushed mine. I knew the show of closeness was no accident, but short of picking up my chair and moving it away there wasn't much that I could do. I only hoped that Graham, facing me across the table, understood.

I couldn't tell what he was thinking.

This was not the way I'd hoped this afternoon would go. I'd thought it would be only Jimmy, me, and Graham; that we'd have a chance to talk, and maybe afterwards he'd walk me home, and…well, who knew what might have happened, then.

But Stuart had his own ideas. While he'd been content enough to sit through Graham's history lesson earlier, he now appeared determined not to share the limelight. Every time the conversation turned away from him he deftly drew it back again, and Graham, calmly silent, let him do it.

By the time the meal had ended I was frustrated with both of them – with Stuart's all but marking out his territory round me, like a dog, to warn his older brother not to trespass, and with Graham's sitting back and letting Stuart get away with it.

For Jimmy's sake, I stayed until we'd finished with our coffee, and he'd started clearing plates away to do the washing up. I offered to help, but he shook his head firmly. 'Na, na, nivver fash, quine. Keep yer strength fer yer writing.'

Which gave me an opening, when I had thanked him for lunch, to announce that I ought to be going. 'I left my book this morning in the middle of a chapter, and I ought to get it done.'

'A'richt. Jist let me put these in the kitchen.' Jimmy, with the plates piled in his hands, looked down at Stuart. 'Stuie, quit yer scuddlin, loon, and go and fetch her coat.'

Stuart went, and Jimmy followed after him, which left me on my own, with Graham.

I felt him watching me. My own gaze stayed quite firmly on the tablecloth in front of me, as I sat sifting words, and then discarding them again while I tried hard to think of what to say.

But he spoke first. He said, 'The best laid schemes o' mice an' men…'

He'd meant for me to smile, I knew. I didn't.

Graham said, 'You realise Stuart thinks of you as being his?'

'I know.' I raised my head at that, and met his eyes. 'I'm not.'

'I know.' His voice was quiet, willing me to understand. 'But he's my brother.'

And just what, I thought, was *that* supposed to mean? That since his brother had such clear designs on me, he didn't think it right to interfere? That, never mind *my* preference, or the fact that something seemed to be developing between us, Graham thought it best to just forget it, give it up, because his brother might object?

'Here you are,' said Stuart, breezing through the doorway of the sitting room, my coat in hand. The one good thing about self-centred men, I thought, was that they were oblivious to everything around them. Any other person walking into that room at that moment would have surely been aware of something hanging in the air between myself and Graham.

But Stuart only held my coat for me, while Jimmy, coming back, said, 'Div ye want one o the loons tae walk ye hame?'

'No, that's all right.' I thanked him once again for lunch and shrugged my coat on and, still with my back to Stuart, somehow summoned up the thin edge of a smile to show to Graham. 'I'll be fine,' I told them, 'on my own.'

So, not a problem, I assured myself. I'd come to Cruden Bay to work, to write my book. I didn't have the time to get involved with someone, anyway.

My bathwater was cooling, but I settled deeper into it until the water lapped my chin. My characters were talking, as they always did when I was in the bath, but I tried shutting out their voices – in particular the calm voice of John Moray, whose grey, watchful eyes seemed everywhere around me.

I regretted having made him look like Graham. I could hardly change it now, he'd taken shape and would resist it, but I really didn't need an everyday reminder of a man who'd thrown me over.

Moray's voice said something, low. I sighed, and rolled to reach the pen and paper that I kept beside the tub. 'All right,' I said. 'Hang on.'

I wrote his words down, and Sophia's voice spoke up with a response, and in a minute I had pulled the plug and stepped out of the bathtub and was buttoning my clothes so I could head for the computer, smiling faintly at the thought of how the worst things in my life sometimes inspired the best plot twists.

When I'd stood and talked to Graham in the stables, only yesterday, surrounded by the horses and the dog curled in the hay, so like the scene that I'd just written in my book, I had been thinking how life echoed art.

And now the time had come, I thought, for art to echo life.

VII

Moray's gaze had swung away and out to sea, and suddenly he pulled upon the gelding's reins and brought him to a standstill.

Stopping too, Sophia asked, 'What is it?'

Even as she spoke the words, she saw it, too – a ship, just coming into view around the jagged headland to the south. She could not see its colours yet, but something in the way it seemed to prowl the coastline made her apprehensive.

Moray, with no change of his expression, turned his horse. ''Tis time we started back.'

She made no argument, but turning with him, followed at that same slow, measured walk that gained them little ground before the silent, purposeful advance of those full sails. Sophia knew he only held them to that pace for her own comfort, and that chivalry would keep him from increasing it, so of her own accord she urged the mare into a rolling canter that would speed their progress.

Moray, left behind a moment, unprepared, was quickly at her side again, and when they reached the stableyard of Slains he stretched a hand to take the bridle of the mare and hold her steady as she halted.

He was not exactly smiling, but his eyes held deep amusement. 'I believe 'tis proper form, when running races, to inform the other party when to start.' Swinging himself from the saddle, he came and put his two hands round her waist to help her down.

Sophia said, 'I did not mean to race. I only—'

'Aye,' he said. 'I ken what ye intended.' She was standing on the ground now, but he did not take his hands away. He held her very differently than Billy Wick had done – his hands were gentle, and she knew that she had but to move to step clear of their circle...but she felt no will to move. The horse, still standing warm against her back, became a living wall that blocked her view of everything except John Moray's shoulders, and his face as he looked down at her. 'If ever ye do find my pace too slow,' he told her, quietly, 'ye only have to tell me.'

She knew he was not speaking of their ride. She felt the flush begin to rise along her throat, her neck, her cheeks, while in her chest her heartbeat leapt against her stays with...what? Not fear, but something strangely kin to that emotion, as she thought of what might happen if she were to give him any answer.

'Colonel Moray!' Running feet approached and Rory broke upon them, taking little notice this time of their close position. Other things of more importance occupied him now. He said, 'Her ladyship does ask for you, without delay.'

Sophia felt the hands fall from her waist as Moray gave a formal nod and took his leave of her. 'Ye will excuse me?'

'Certainly.' She was relieved to find she had a voice and that it sounded almost normal, and was more relieved yet to discover, when she took a step, that her still-trembling legs could move at all, and hold her upright.

She was still wearing Moray's gloves. She drew them off reluctantly, but by the time she'd turned to give them back he had already gone halfway across the yard, the black cape fastened to his shoulders swinging evenly in rhythm with his soldier's stride. Sophia tore her gaze from him and, folding the worn leather of both gauntlets in her hand, she turned back, meaning to ask Rory if he knew what ship was now approaching Slains. But he had left her, too, and now had nearly reached the stable door, with both the horses safe in hand.

Standing in the yard there by herself she felt a moment's panic, and it spurred her on to lift her skirts and run, as reckless as a child, toward the great door through which Moray had just passed.

Inside, the sudden dimness left her blind, and she collided with the figure of a man. It was not Moray.

'Cousin,' said the Earl of Erroll, in his pleasant voice. 'Where would you seek to go in such a hurry?'

'Do forgive me,' said Sophia, with the hand that held the gloves behind her back. 'There is a ship...'

'The *Royal William*, aye. I am just come to find you, as it happens, since my mother does inform me that the captain of this ship does take an interest in your welfare, and will surely wish to see you in attendance with the family when he comes ashore.' His smile was kind, and teasing as a brother's. 'Do you wish to change your gown?'

She smoothed the fabric with her free hand, conscious of the dust from riding, but her fingers, when they reached her waist, recalled the warmth of Moray's hand upon that place, and suddenly she did not wish to change her gown just yet, as though by doing so she stood to lose the memory of his touch. 'I thank you, no,' she said, and clenched her hidden hand more firmly round the leather gloves she held.

'Then come.' The earl held out his arm. 'We will await your Captain Gordon in the drawing room.'

The countess joined them there some minutes later. 'Mr Moray,' she announced, 'agrees to keep to his own chamber till we know that Captain Gordon comes alone.'

''Tis wise,' her son agreed. 'Though I am not so sure that even Captain Gordon should be introduced. Are you?'

'He is a friend.'

'Five hundred pounds is yet five hundred pounds,' the earl reminded her. 'And lesser men have turned for lesser fortunes.'

'Thomas Gordon is no traitor.'

'Then, as always, I must bow to your good judgement.' With his hands laced at his back, he crossed to stand beside the window, looking out toward the ship now anchored off the shore. 'I see the *Royal William* does no longer fly the white cross of Saint Andrew on the blue field as its flag.'

His mother came to look. 'What flag is that?'

'The flag of the new Union, with the crosses of St Andrew and St George combined,' her son replied, his voice hard-edged with bitterness. 'Which means that our Scots navy is no more.'

'Ah, well.' His mother sighed. ''Twas only the three ships.'

'Aye, but those three ships were our own,' he said, 'and now they, too, are lost to us. I wonder if our friend the Duke of Hamilton appreciates the price that has been paid that he may keep his lands in Lancashire.'

Sophia, while they talked, had been deciding what she ought to do with Moray's gloves, still clutched within her hand. She did not think the countess or the earl would take exception to the fact that she'd been riding with the man, but they might question why she was now in possession of his personal accessories. Not seeing any place where she could easily conceal the gloves, she sat, and tucked them safely underneath her on the chair.

She was still sitting there when Captain Gordon was announced.

He strode into the room with all the swagger she remembered, handsome in his long blue coat with the gold braid and polished buttons gleaming bright against the fabric. Greeting first the countess, then the earl, he came across to take Sophia's hand and raise it to his lips as he bowed low before her, smiling with great charm. 'And Mistress Paterson, I trust you have recovered from your late attempt at horse-racing?'

'I have, sir, thank you.'

'I am glad to hear it.'

As he straightened and released her hand, the earl asked bluntly, 'Do you come alone?'

'Aye. Captain Hamilton is yet some hours behind me.'

'Then,' the countess said, 'you will have time to dine with us, I hope.'

'I should be honoured.' Looking at her levelly, he said, 'I was informed that you might have another visitor.'

'We do.'

'I came as soon as I was able.' Before saying more, he glanced towards Sophia, and the earl, observing this, remarked, 'You may feel free to speak when Mistress Paterson is with us, as you'd speak were we alone. She has our confidence, and trust.' And with these words the earl moved forward so he stood beside Sophia's chair, with one hand resting on it as a mark of his endorsement. 'Colonel Hooke arrived some days ago, and is now gone to make a progress through the country, treating with our well-affected nobles. But he has left with us another, who, should you desire it, will be able to acquaint you with the mind of our young king.'

Captain Gordon frowned. 'Who is this person?'

From the doorway, Moray's voice said calmly, 'I believe he speaks of me.' Then, to the countess, 'Ye'll forgive me, but I did see clearly from my chamber window that the captain came ashore alone.'

The captain's eyes were slightly narrowed as with recognition. He said, 'Your servant, Mr...?'

'Moray.'

Certain now above the handshake, Captain Gordon said, 'I do believe we met three years ago, before your father's death.'

'I do recall our meeting.' Moray's voice, though even, held no warmth, and sounded to Sophia's ears a little like a challenge.

Captain Gordon, having thought a moment, said, 'At the time, as I remember, you were in the service of the King of France.'

'Aye. I serve him still.'

'And was it he who ordered you to Scotland, with a price upon your head?'

''Tis not a soldier's place to ask who gives the order,' Moray said. 'My duty but demands that I do follow it. I could no more have refused to come than ye could have refused to hoist the Union flag upon your mast.'

The countess, stepping in, said, 'Thomas, Mr Moray does well understand the many dangers of his being here. 'Tis why he did decide it best that he remain with us at Slains.'

Her voice, as always, calmed the waters. Captain Gordon said to Moray, 'I did not mean to suggest that you were reckless.'

'Did ye not?'

'No.' With a charming smile, the captain added, 'And you are quite right – were it my choice, I would not sail beneath the Union flag. In confidence, I may not sail beneath it long.'

The earl asked, 'Why is that?'

'I may soon be obliged to quit the service.' Captain Gordon's shoulders lifted lightly in a shrug that held regret. 'In consequence of the Union, I soon shall be required, as will all officers, to take an oath of abjuration which demands that I renounce King James, and say that he has no right to the throne.'

The countess said, 'Oh, Thomas.'

'I have worn this uniform with pride for many years, but I do not intend to now betray my conscience,' Captain Gordon said. 'I will not take the oath.'

'What will you do?' the countess asked him.

Captain Gordon glanced again at Moray, and for a moment Sophia was afraid he might be thinking, as the earl had feared, of those five hundred pounds, and of the life of comfort they might buy him. But the captain's thoughts were something different. He said, 'If I did believe the French king would accept my service, I would gladly sail my frigate straight to France at the first notice of his pleasure.'

Stepping round Sophia's chair, the earl reminded him, 'It

may well be that you shall find yourself in service to the King of Scotland, if God favours us.'

'Then let us hope for that.' The captain turned his thoughts to other things. 'What has become of the French ship that did deliver Colonel Hooke and Mr Moray to you?'

The earl replied, 'We did desire the captain of that ship to sail to Norway, and return to us in three weeks' time. It is our hope you will be able to avoid him.'

A faint frown settled on the captain's handsome face. 'I can but promise you I will appear no more upon this coast for fifteen days, and I do beg you to contrive that your French captain should not stay long in these seas, for if we meet too frequently I do not doubt but that young Captain Hamilton, who sails behind me in the *Royal Mary* and shares not my loyalties, will grow suspicious. As indeed,' he added, 'will my crew. I have on board my ship an officer, three sergeants, and three corporals and two drums, along with forty-one good sentinels, who must remain with me for the duration of my cruise. To keep so many men in ignorance,' he said, 'will not be easy.' After thinking for a moment, he went on, 'The last time Colonel Hooke did come to Slains, I gave to his ship's captain certain signals to display, that I should know him if we met upon the seas. Do you remember them?'

The earl looked less than certain, but the countess nodded. 'Yes, we have them still preserved.'

'Then, if you will communicate those signals to the captain of your French ship when he does return, I will try to avoid him, should we meet.' That said, he turned and let his smile fall warmly on Sophia. 'But our talk, as always, grows too dreary to amuse such gentle company. And I would rather hear of Mistress Paterson's adventures here at Slains.'

She saw the countess smiling, too, appearing pleased by the attention that Sophia was receiving from the captain.

'Sir,' Sophia said, 'I have had no adventures.'

'Then,' he told her, 'we must see that you do have some.'

Moray stood and watched without expression, but Sophia felt the weight of his grey eyes upon her, and she felt relief when a young maid appeared within the doorway to announce that dinner was now ready to be served.

But her relief did not last long. The captain offered her his arm. 'May I escort you?'

She could not have told him no without offending nearly everybody present, so she nodded, rising, but she had forgotten Moray's gloves, beneath her. When she stood, one fell, and Captain Gordon bent to pick it up. 'And what is this?'

Sophia could not think of what to answer. Trapped, she kept her eyes intently on the floorboards while she tried hard to compose a fitting explanation, but before she found the words, she saw two boots step casually in front of her as Moray crossed to take the other glove from the chair on which Sophia had been sitting.

'I did wonder what became of these,' said Moray.

'They are yours?' asked Captain Gordon.

'Aye. Ye surely did not think that they belonged to Mistress Paterson, with hands so small as hers?' His tone dismissed the notion of her having been connected to the gauntlets, but it did not keep the captain from regarding him with keener interest, as a swordsman might assess the strength of a new challenger.

The captain smiled thinly. 'No.' And raising up Sophia's fingers in his own, he said, 'Such hands as these would want a softer covering.' He handed back the second glove to Moray. 'You must take better care, in future, where you leave these, else you'll lose them.'

Moray said, 'No fear of that.' He took the glove from Gordon's hand, and folding it together with the other, tucked them both into his belt. 'I do not lightly lose the things that are my own.'

And having said that, he stepped back to let Sophia pass on Captain Gordon's arm and with the faintest smile fell in behind them.

Chapter Twelve

There, I thought, with satisfaction, printing off the pages I'd just written. Now Sophia's love life was as messed up as my own. Just as I'd had to deal with Stuart's coming back, she'd have to deal with Captain Gordon, though admittedly John Moray had reacted to the challenge rather differently than Graham had. The benefit, I thought, of writing fiction was that I could twist my characters to do the things real people never did in life.

The printer finished humming and I shut down my computer, arching back against the chair to stretch my shoulders, arms upraised.

I didn't know what time it was. It had been light outside my windows for a while now, but the sky was flatly grey and there was no way I could judge how high the sun had climbed behind the clouds.

I only knew that it was morning, and I hadn't been to bed, and all I wanted was a piece of toast, a glass of juice, and several hours of sleep. So when the shadow of a person passed my window, my first impulse was to let the knocking go unanswered and pretend I wasn't home. But curiosity won out.

'I've brought you lunch,' said Stuart, standing on my doorstep with a winning smile and something wrapped in newspaper that smelt so good my stomach flipped. It wasn't exactly a peace offering, since Stuart, I felt certain, didn't realise he'd done anything to warrant one – but in return for fresh-made fish and chips, I might forgive him for the trouble he had caused me.

'Come on in.' I pushed the door wide. 'Your timing's amazingly good, by the way. But it's breakfast, for me.'

Stuart arched a dark eyebrow. 'It's nearly twelve-thirty.'

'That late?'

'D'ye never go to bed?'

I took the fish and chips from him and crossed to the kitchen while he shrugged off his coat by the door. As I parcelled the food out on plates, I explained, 'I got into the flow last night. I didn't want to stop.'

His eyes danced as though I'd just made a dirty joke. 'That happens to me sometimes. Not with writing,' he admitted, with a Casanova smile, 'but it does happen.'

Indulging him, I let the double meaning slide and handed him his plate. 'You'll either have to eat it standing up, or sitting by the fireplace,' I apologised. 'There's no room on the table.'

'So I see.' He chose an armchair, settling back and nodding pointedly towards the mess of papers that was covering my writing table. 'How far along are you, then?'

'Maybe a third of the way, I don't know. I never know how long a book will be until I've finished it.'

'Don't you don't work to a plan?'

'No. I've tried, but I'm no good at it.' My characters refused to be contained by any outline. They were happiest when charting their own course across the page.

Stuart grinned. 'I'm not much good at planning either. Graham's the organised one of the family.' He glanced at me. 'What did you think of him?'

'Graham?' I opened the door of the Aga and prodded the coals with a bit too much force before saying, 'I thought he was nice.'

'Aye, he is that.' My bland choice of words had apparently satisfied Stuart. 'The only time I ever saw him lose his manners, to be honest, was when he played rugby. And even then I don't doubt he apologised to everyone he stomped on.'

I'd been right, then, thinking Graham was an athlete. 'He played rugby?'

'Oh, aye, he almost went professional.'

Clanging the Aga door shut, I crossed to join Stuart, my plate in my hand. 'Really?'

'Aye, he was recruited, had the papers nearly signed, but then Mum died, and Dad...well, Dad, he didn't do so well. And rugby would have meant that Graham had to live away, so he just turned the offer down,' he said, 'and stayed at university until they took him on there as a lecturer. I'd not say that it would have been his choice, but then, you'd never hear him moan. He's too responsible. He sees his job as taking care of Dad, that's all. He comes up every weekend to look in on him.' A sideways glance, and smile. 'He's given up on taking care of me.'

I could have told him no, he hadn't, but I kept my concentration on my plate. 'He's never been married, I take it?'

'Who, Graham? He's never come close.' His initial amusement changed, slowly, to something approaching suspicion. 'Why do you ask?'

'I just wondered.' To soothe his pricked ego, I asked, 'What about yourself? Ever been married?'

Back on his own favourite subject, he shook his head. 'No, not yet.' And unable to pass up the chance for a play, he said, catching my gaze with his own, 'I've been waiting to find the right woman.'

I didn't swing at that pitch either. 'How was London?'

'Murder. It's a busy time for us. I'll be off again tomorrow night, to Amsterdam, and then from there to Italy.'

In scheduling at least he seemed to match my novel's Captain Gordon, turning up just long enough to have an impact on the plot before he dashed away.

He started telling me about what he'd been up to in London, but I was only half-listening, trying to hold back a yawn that brought blood drumming loudly inside my ears. Stuart, not noticing, carried on talking, and although I tried from politeness to follow along, I was fading, and fast, as my long night of no sleep caught up with me. Resting my head on the chair back, I nodded at something that Stuart was saying.

And that was the last thing I really remembered.

The next thing I knew I was waking up, still in my chair, and the armchair that faced me was empty. The daylight had faded to dusk. As I moved, I discovered that Stuart was more of a gentleman than he would likely have cared to admit – he had taken a spare blanket out of the cupboard and covered me with it, to make me more comfortable. And when I made my way into the kitchen and opened the fridge, I discovered my half eaten fish and chips still on the plate, sealed with cling film, and waiting for me to reheat them for supper.

However irritated I had been with Stuart yesterday, there simply was no way that I could go on being mad at him when he did things like this. Nor could I muster more than faint exasperation when, a little later, Dr Weir phoned up and started off with, 'I ran into Stuie Keith coming out of the Killie, and he said he'd left you fast asleep, and so I thought I'd best call first.'

Trust Stuart, I thought, to put his own twist on what had happened. But I was glad to finally hear the doctor's voice.

'I've been away a few days,' he said, 'visiting my brother, but I've done a bit of reading on the subject of genetic memory and I've found a few things that might interest you. I could come round right now, if that's all right?'

It was more than all right. I'd been waiting to talk to him, wanting to hear his opinion on what I'd discovered in Edinburgh. There wasn't anybody else I *could* talk to about it, really – no one else who'd listen in the patient, non-judgemental manner of a trained physician and be able to discuss things from the medical perspective.

I had the tea brewed by the time he arrived with a folder of what looked like photocopied pages from assorted books. And before he could tell me what *he'd* found, I told him my news about Mr Hall's letter describing how he'd brought Sophia to Slains.

Dr Weir was delighted. 'That's wonderful. Wonderful, lass. I'd have never believed you could find such a thing. And it actually said that she came from the west, and that both of her parents had died in connection with Darien?'

'Yes.'

'How incredible.' Shaking his head, he said, 'Well, there

you are. There's your proof that you're not going mad.' He smiled. 'You simply have the memory of your ancestor.'

I knew, deep down, that he was right. I even shared his obvious excitement at my find, but it was tempered by a sense of hesitation. I wasn't sure I wanted such a gift, or knew the way to deal with all its implications. And my mind was still resisting the idea. 'How could something like that happen?'

'Well, it has to be genetic. Do you know much about DNA?'

'Just what I see on crime shows.'

'Ah.' He settled in, balancing his folder for the moment on the broad arm of his chair. 'Let's start with the gene, which is the basic unit of inheritance. A gene is nothing but a length of DNA, and we've thousands of genes in our bodies. Half of our genes we inherit,' he said, 'from our mother, and half from our father. The mix is unique. It determines a whole range of characteristics: your eye colour, hair colour, whether you're left- or right-handed.' He paused. 'Countless things, even your chance of developing certain diseases, are passed down to you in your genes from your parents, who got their own genes from *their* parents and so on. Your nose may be the same shape as your great-great-great-great grandmother's. And if a nose can be inherited,' he said, 'who knows what else might be?'

'But surely noses aren't the same as memories.'

He shrugged. 'It's been discovered, so I've learnt, that there's a gene that plays a part in making people thrill-seekers, or not. My eldest daughter, now, she always loved a bit of danger, from the time that she was born. Always climbing, she was – we had to harness her to keep her in the pram. She climbed out of her cot, up the bookcases, everywhere. Now that she's grown, she climbs mountains, and jumps out of airplanes. Where did she get that from? I don't know. Not her environment,' he told me, with a certain smile. 'My wife and I are hardly what you'd call the mountaineering type.'

I shared the smile, imagining the gnome-like doctor or his wife suspended from a cliff by ropes.

'My point,' he said, 'is that some aspects of our nature, of our temperament, are clearly carried in our genes. And memory, surely, is no more intangible than temperament.'

'I guess you're right.'

He reached to open up his folder and began to sort the photocopied pages. 'I did find some very interesting articles on the subject. For instance, here's a piece by an American professor who believes that the abilities of some savants – autistic savants, who are mentally and socially shut off from all the rest of us, and yet have these strange, unexplainable gifts in one area, music, or maths, for example – this professor thinks their abilities may be the product of some form of genetic memory. He actually uses the term.

'And here's another piece that caught my fancy. I tried to keep strictly to science, but even though this is a bit more new-age, it did raise what I thought were some valid possibilities. It suggests that the entire past-life phenomenon, where people are "regressed" under hypnosis and recall what they believe are former lives in other bodies, may in fact be nothing more than their remembering the lives of their own ancestors.' He handed me the folder, sitting back again to watch me while I sifted through the articles myself. Then he said, 'Maybe I should start my own wee study, hmm?'

'With me as your subject, you mean?' I was briefly amused by the thought. 'I'm not sure how much use I'd be to science.'

'Why is that?'

'Well, there'd be no way to prove just how much of the story was coming from memory, and how much was my own creation,' I said, thinking now of how I had deliberately brought Captain Gordon back into the plot to stir the waters. *That* had come from my frustration with Stuart and Graham, and not from Sophia. 'The family history details, fair enough, those can be checked, but when it comes to things like dialogue...'

'I should imagine it would be a mixture of your memory, and your writer's art. And what of that? We tinker with our memories all the time. We add embellishments – that fish we caught gets larger, or the faults we had get fewer. But the basic event...well, that is what it is. We can't turn sad memories to happy ones, no matter how we try. So I'd wager what you'll write about Sophia, at its essence, will be truth.'

I thought about that later, when he'd gone and I was sitting at my writing table, staring at the screen of my computer while the cursor blinked expectantly.

I wasn't in the trance, tonight. My conscious mind was uppermost, and I could feel it pushing at my characters while they dug in their heels. They wouldn't walk the path I tried to put them on. I'd meant to write the dinner scene, with Captain Gordon sitting at the table with John Moray and Sophia, so the two men could continue their competitive exchange.

But neither man was keen to speak, and in the end I had to go and fetch *The Old Scots Navy* book that Dr Weir had loaned me, thinking I might come across some interesting naval going-on that Captain Gordon could be telling everyone about, to get the conversation going.

I hadn't had the nerve to read the book since that first night

when I had opened it and learnt that all the details I had
written about Captain Gordon had in fact been real, and not
of my creation. That knowledge had been too much for my
troubled mind to process at the time, and after that I'd left the
book untouched beside my bed.

But desperation drove me now to scan the index, searching
for a Captain Gordon reference that might give me what I
needed. And I found a document appended to the text, that
seemed to be of the right date. It started:

*'During Hooke's absence in Edinburgh Captain Gordon,
commander of the two Scotch frigates on guard upon the coast
(the one of 40, the other of 28 cannon) had come ashore to the
Earl of Erroll...'*

I could feel the now familiar creeping chill between my
shoulder blades.

It was all there, as plain as day.

The captain promising the earl that he'd stay off the coast
for fifteen days, and the exchange of signals to be used in case
he met the French ship, and the fact that Captain Hamilton
was bound to grow suspicious if the French ship stayed too
long in Scottish waters. Even Captain Gordon's statement that
he might soon have to leave the naval service, since he would
not take the oath against King James.

I read it with the same sense of surrealism I'd felt when I'd
been sitting in that reading room in Edinburgh with Mr Hall's
old letter. Because I knew for certain I had never read *this*
document before. I hadn't gotten this far in the book on my
first reading. I had gotten spooked and closed it, as I closed it
now. I pushed it far away from me across the table.

'Damn.'

I'd honestly believed that scene had been my own invention, that I'd made the captain come back just to complicate the plot. I'd been so proud of how I'd worked the whole thing in. And now I found I hadn't done such an amazing thing.

It looked as though I'd have to face the fact that Dr Weir had hit the nail more squarely on the head than I'd have liked. It might be that I was not to have a hand at all in the creation of this story.

Maybe all that I *could* do was write the truth.

Deleting the few stilted lines I'd written so the cursor sat once more at the beginning of the chapter, I closed my eyes and felt the silence of the room press round me like a thing alive.

'All right,' I said. 'What scene *should* I be writing?'

VIII

The countess looked round, smiling, as Sophia passed the doorway of her private rooms. 'My dear, would you have seen Monsieur de Ligondez?'

She meant the captain of the French ship, the *Audacious*, which that morning had, unheralded, returned from Norway, sliding down the coast so very stealthily that none at Slains had noticed it until the boat that bore the captain had been rowed halfway to shore. The earl, who had not risen from his bed yet, had been forced to beg Monsieur de Ligondez's indulgence for the short while it would take to dress and drink his morning draught and make himself prepared.

The countess, also, had just finished dressing.

But Sophia had herself been up some time, and knew exactly where the French ship's captain was. 'I do believe,' she said, 'that he is walking now with Mr Moray, in the garden.'

'Then would you be good enough to go and seek him there, and tell him that my son and I are ready now to welcome him.'

Sophia hesitated. She had not been in the garden these three days since Billy Wick had put his hands on her, and she had no desire to go there now in case he tried it once again. But she could not refuse the countess. With a brave lift of her chin, she answered, 'Yes, of course,' and did as she'd been asked.

It was another fair spring morning. Songbirds greeted her with twittering more cheerful than the crying of the gulls that wheeled, high specks of white, above the cliffs beyond the garden wall. Her shoulder brushed a vine that loosed a fragrance sweetly unfamiliar from its soft, unfolding leaves, and when she walked her gown brushed lightly over bluebells growing close against the ground.

She did not give herself to daydreams this time, though, but kept her eyes fixed open, and her ears alert. Not far off, she could hear the quiet voices of Monsieur de Ligondez and Moray, though she could not understand their words, and so presumed they must be speaking in the language of the French. She turned her steps towards the sound, and felt so near her goal that she had almost let her guard down when the heavy steps fell in behind her on the path.

She would not show him fear again, she thought. Not looking round, she kept her shoulders square and walked more briskly, heading for the voices with such single-minded focus that she burst upon the speakers like a pheasant flushed by dogs out of the underbrush.

The French ship's captain stopped mid-sentence, startled. Moray turned to look first at Sophia, then beyond her to the gardener, who had changed his course unhurriedly away from them, towards the malthouse.

Quickly, to distract his narrowed gaze, Sophia said, 'The countess sent me here to find you.'

Moray's grey eyes settled once more on Sophia's face. 'Did she, now?'

'She would inform Monsieur de Ligondez that she is ready, with the Earl of Erroll, to receive him.'

Moray translated her message for the Frenchman, who bowed low and left them.

Moray made no move to follow. Squinting upwards at the sky, he said, 'The day is wondrous fair.'

She could do nothing but agree with him. 'It is.'

'Have ye yet breakfasted?'

'I have, sir, yes.'

'Then come,' he said, 'and walk with me.'

It was no invitation, she decided, but a challenge. He did not make a formal offer of his arm, but shifted, with his hand firm on his sword hilt, so his elbow lifted slightly from his body.

She considered. She had well observed that there were roads in life one started down by choice, that led to ends quite different from what might have been if one had chanced to take another turning. This, she thought, was such a crossroads. If she were to tell him no, and stay behind, the comfort of her world would yet continue, and she'd surely be the safer for it. If she told him yes, she had a fair idea where that road would lead, and yet she felt the stirring of her father's reckless blood within her and she yearned, as he had done, to set her course through waters yet uncharted.

Reaching out, she set her hand upon the crook of Moray's elbow, and the look he angled down at her was briefly warm.

She asked, 'Where would you walk?'

'Away from here.'

Indeed, the ordered garden seemed too small for him. Within it, he was as the bear she'd once seen caged for baiting, pacing ceaselessly around its strong-barred prison. But the garden walls proved easier to breach than iron bars, and in a moment they had passed beyond its boundaries to the wider sweep of greening cliff that dipped towards the village and the pink sand beach beyond.

It was yet early, and Sophia saw no faces in the windows of the village peering out to mark their passage. Likely everyone was still abed, she thought, and just as well, at that. Her cautious glances did not go unnoticed.

Smiling, Moray asked her, 'D'ye fear that being seen with me will harm your reputation?'

'No.' She looked at him, surprised. 'It is not that. It—' But she could not bring herself to tell him of her true fear, that behind one of these curtained windows, someone even now was taking note of him and planning to expose him. She had heard the tales of other captured Jacobites, and how they had been cruelly tortured by the agents of the Crown who had put one man to the boot and shattered both his ankles when he would not talk. And she could not imagine Moray talking, either.

Looking down, she said, 'I do not fear your company.'

'I'm glad to hear it, lass.' He brought his arm against his side and kept her hand close to him as he steered their steps between the sleeping cottages and down again onto the beach.

The sea was wide. Sophia could no longer see the bare masts of the French ship brought to shelter on the far side of the castle rocks. She only saw the bright sky and the water, with its endless waves that rolled to shore in white-curled ranks that fell in foam against the sand and then retreated to the broad horizon.

As she watched, she felt again the pulsing of her father's blood within her veins, and asked impulsively, 'What is it like to sail upon a ship?'

He shrugged. 'That does depend on whether ye do have the constitution for it. Colonel Hooke would no doubt say it is a wretched way to travel, and I would not call him wrong. To be so close confined with many men and little air does not improve my temper. But to be on deck,' he said, 'is something altogether different. When the ship is running fast, sails filled with wind...' He searched for words. 'It feels, then, like to flying.'

She did not suppose that she would ever know that feeling, and she told him so.

He said, 'Ye cannot ever say which way this world will take ye. Had ye told me when I was a lad that I would leave the fields of home to fight the battles of a foreign king, I would have called ye mad.' He slanted a kind look at her. 'Mayhap ye'll walk a ship's deck, after all.' And then he looked ahead, and added in an offhand tone, 'I've no doubt Captain Gordon could arrange it, if you asked.'

Sophia shot a quick look upwards, searching for some clue in his expression as to why he felt so cold towards the captain. There was more between the men, she knew, than could be laid to her account. She said, 'You do not like him.'

'On the contrary, I do admire him greatly.'

'But you do not like him.'

He took several strides in silence. Then he said, 'Three years ago I came here by the order of King Jamie, in the company of Simon Fraser. D'ye ken the name?'

She knew it well, as did the whole of Scotland. Even in a nation such as theirs, where the rough violence of the past ran like a stream submerged beneath the everyday affairs of men, a rogue like Simon Fraser set his deeds apart by their depravity. To gain himself the title of Lord Lovat, he had sought to kidnap and marry his own cousin, the heiress to the last lord, but his plot had gone awry and he had taken, in her stead, her widowed mother. All undaunted, he'd decided that the mother was as useful as the daughter to his purposes, and calling on his pipers to play forcefully to drown the lady's screams, he had subjected her to brutal rape before a band of witnesses, and claimed the weeping woman for his wife.

Fraser had not kept his title long and had been outlawed for his deeds. He had fled to exile before finally being pardoned, but the black stain of such villainy would not soon be erased.

Sophia's pale, set face showed plainly that she knew whom Moray spoke of.

'Aye,' he said, ''twas all the time like walking with the devil, but the devil kens the way to charm when it does suit his purpose, and to most at Saint-Germain that year it seemed that Simon Fraser was the key to raising Scotland for the king. He had a plan, he claimed, and he convinced the king's own mother of its virtues, so she sent him here to test the ground. They chose me to come with him, I was later told, because it was believed that by my honour and my family's reputation I'd more easily commend myself to those we wished to meet with than would such a man as Fraser. They were right.' The reminiscence set a shadow on his face. 'We were received by many honourable men. And Simon Fraser did betray them all. And me.' His smile was thin. 'He was, throughout our visit, telling all he knew to agents of Queen Anne.'

That, thought Sophia, must have been how Moray had been branded as a traitor to the queen, and earned the price upon his head.

'I was full ignorant of this. 'Twas Captain Gordon who enlightened me,' he said. 'At table with my father, he did call me fool, and worse, that I would let myself be so used by a man who, by his treachery, would surely bring to pain and ruin men of better character. And so it came to pass. I saw good men of my acquaintance taken prisoner, and battered in the pillory, and sentenced to be hanged. And though I managed to escape, my father took my shame upon himself and bore it with him to his grave.'

Sophia felt a pang for him. 'I'm sorry.'

'No,' he said, 'It was no lie, what Gordon said – I was a fool. But life does carry lessons with it. Never since that time have I been easily deceived.'

She chose her next words carefully, because she did not know if Moray shared her own distrust of Colonel Hooke. ''Tis well, then, Colonel Hooke is not like Simon Fraser.'

'He is not.' Another slanting look, that seemed to somehow be assessing her. 'But Colonel Hooke's design is to restore a king to Scotland, and I'll wager he himself cares little whether 'tis King Jamie or His Grace the Duke of Hamilton who takes the throne when all the cards are played. Hooke has gone now, I believe, to judge where lie the loyalties of your good people of the Western Shires, for it is on the Presbyterians our planned rebellion hangs. They are well-organised, and having not before this time aroused the temper of the Crown they have been left well-armed. If they declare for Jamie Stewart, all is well. But if they do declare for Hamilton, then I ken well where Hooke will stand.'

The prospect left her troubled. 'But that will mean civil war.'

'Aye, lass. And that,' he said, with cynicism, 'may be what the French king did design from the beginning.'

Sophia frowned. They'd come along the beach now to the windblown drifts of sand that marked the edges of the dunes. She did not notice for a moment that they were no longer walking. It was only when her hand was given back to her, and Moray started taking off his boots, that she came fully to awareness.

With a glance at her wide eyes, he said, 'I'm not about to ravish ye. I did but think to try the water. Will ye join me?'

She did not understand at first, and stammered in alarm, 'You mean to bathe?'

Which brought one of those rare, quick smiles to light his face with pure amusement. 'Christ, lass, if the sight of me without my boots is giving ye the vapours, I'd not want to risk removing something else.' Then, as she flushed a deeper red, he added, 'I mean to wet my feet among the waves, and nothing more.' He held his hand out. 'Come, 'tis safe enough. Ye said ye did not fear me.'

He was testing her, she knew. It was another of those challenges with which he seemed determined to present her, as if seeking to discover just how far she could be pushed beyond propriety.

She raised her chin. 'I'll have to take my slippers off.'

'I'd think it most advisable.'

He turned his head and watched the hills while she rolled off her stockings, too, and tucked them in her slippers, which she left upon the sand beside his boots. There could be no disgrace in going barefoot, she decided. She had known of several ladies of good quality who went unshod within their homes and in full view of company, though that, she did admit, was for economy, and not because they wished to show a man he could not best them.

In the end, though she had come to it reluctantly, it proved to be the greatest pleasure that she could remember since her childhood. The water was so cold it struck the breath out of her body when she stepped in it, but after some few minutes it felt warmer to her skin, and she enjoyed the wetly sinking feel of sand beneath her feet and was refreshed. Her gown and skirts were an impediment. She lifted them with both hands so the hemline cleared the waves, and like a child, cared little that it gave a wanton view of her bare ankles. Moray seemed to take no notice. He was walking slowly through the water, looking down.

'What are you searching for?' she asked.

'When I was but a lad, my mother told me I should keep my eyes well open for a wee stone with a hole in it, to wear around my neck, as it would keep me safe from harm. 'Tis but a tale, and one she likely did invent to keep her wild lad occupied, and out from underfoot,' he said. 'But having once begun the search for such a stone, I do confess I cannot end the habit.'

She looked at him, barefooted in the sea and with his head downturned in concentration, and it was not difficult to glimpse the small, determined lad he must have been once – perhaps walking on a beach like this one, with the sun warm on his shoulders and his breeks rolled to his knees, and with no worry in his mind save that he had to find a pebble with a hole in it.

He cast a brief look back at her. 'Do I amuse ye?'

'No,' she said, and dropped her own gaze. 'No, I only—' Then she stopped, as something in the water drew her eye. She quickly bent to scoop it up before the sand should shift again to cover it. She'd let go one side of her gown to have a hand free, and she let drop both sides now, and raised the other hand to turn her find against her palm.

It gleamed like black obsidian, an oblong pebble half the size of her own thumb, held by its weight within her hand while grains of wet sand trickled through her fingers to all sides.

Moray turned. 'What is it?'

And Sophia, with a smile of triumph, stretched her palm towards him. 'Look.'

He looked, and with a cheerful oath splashed back to have a better look. He did not take the stone from her, but cupped his larger hand beneath her wet one and with gentle fingers turned the stone, as she had done, to see the hole carved through it by some trick of nature, just above its centre.

She said, 'Now you have your stone.'

'No, lass. It does belong to you.' He closed her fingers round it with his own, and smiled. 'Ye'd best be taking care of it. If what my mother said was true, 'twill serve ye as a talisman against all evil.'

His hands were warm, and spread their heat along her arm so that she scarcely felt the wet cold of the waves that dragged against her heavy gown. But still she shivered, and he noticed.

'Christ, you're wetted through. Come out and let the

sunshine dry you, else her ladyship will have my head for giving ye the fever.'

In the shelter of the dunes, she sat and spread her gown upon the sand while Moray pulled his boots back on and came to sit beside her. 'There,' he said, and tossed her slippers and her stockings in her lap. 'Ye'd best put those on, too. The wind is chill.' Again, he turned his eyes away to let her keep her modesty, but commented, 'If ye do mend those slippers any more, they'll be but seams of thread.'

She only said, 'They were my sister's.' But she fancied, from his silence, that he understood why she had sought to keep them whole.

More soberly, he asked, 'How did she die?'

Sophia did not answer him for so long that she knew he must be wondering if she had heard him, but the truth was that she did not know the way to tell the story. In the end, she tried beginning with, 'Anna was thirteen, two years my elder, when my mother went aboard the ship to Darien. We were then living with our aunt, my mother's sister, and a woman of good heart. And with our uncle, who was—' Breaking off, she looked away, across the endless water. 'He was nothing like my aunt. He was a Drummond, and it is by grace of his connection to the countess that I now do find myself at Slains, but that is all the kindness he did ever show me, and he did not show me that till he himself was dead.' She turned her sleeve above the elbow, so that he could see the slash of puckered skin. 'He showed me this, instead.'

She saw the flash of something dark in Moray's eyes. 'He burnt you?'

'I was slow,' she said, 'in bringing him his ale. This was my punishment.'

'Was there no one to aid you?'

'He did use my aunt the same. He had been careful not to do so when my mother had been with us, for my father had left money for our keeping and he did not wish to lose so great an income. But when news came that my parents both were lost...' She raised one shoulder in a shrug, to hide the pain that had not eased. 'His rages did increase with my aunt's illness and her passing, but my sister bore the worst of it to shield me. She was beautiful, my sister. And she might have made a loving wife to any man, had not—' She bit her lip, and called upon her courage to go on, 'Had not my uncle used her in that way, as well.'

She did not look at Moray, and he did not speak, but in the silent air between them she could sense his question.

'He did never touch me as he touched her. She had made him promise not to, in exchange for her compliance, and for all he was a villain he did keep his word.' The next part was more difficult. 'But Anna was with child when she died. My uncle's child. He would not have the neighbours know it, and so he did call upon the knowledge of a woman who did claim that she could stop the bairn from growing.' There was sunlight on the crest of the horizon, but Sophia's eyes, while fixed upon it, only saw the darkness of that awful night – the dirty, grinning woman with her evil-smelling potions. Anna's terror as their uncle held her down. Her screams. The stench of death. Sophia finished quietly, 'If I did still believe in God, I would have said He took my sister to Himself from pity.'

Moray, looking at her steadily, said nothing, and she took the little pebble in her hand and clutched it tightly, till she felt its hard impression. ''Tis an ugly tale,' she said, 'and likely I should not have told you.'

'Ye surely did not stay,' he asked her, 'in that house?'

'I had no choice. But Uncle John fell ill himself soon after, and so lost his power to harm me.'

Moray did not touch her, but she felt as though he had. 'Ye have my word,' he said with quiet force, 'that no man ever will again do harm to ye, while I do live.' His eyes were hard, and dark with what she took for anger, but it was not meant for her. 'And ye can tell that to the gardener up at Slains, for if he—'

'Please,' she interrupted him, alarmed. 'Please, you must promise you'll not fight with Billy Wick.'

His eyes grew harder still. 'Ye would protect him?'

'No, but neither would I have you make an enemy of such a man on my account, for he would seek his vengeance, then, and you have much to lose.'

The pebble in her hand was hurting now. She loosed her grip, and braved a glance at Moray. He was watching her, his grey eyes still a shade too dark, but not, she thought, with anger. When he spoke, his voice was gentle. 'Are ye worried for my safety?'

She had no voice to answer him. She nodded, once, but faintly.

'Lass.' And then she saw the memory strike him, and he asked her slowly, as though he yet disbelieved it, 'Was it me that ye were praying for, that morning in the stables?'

She tried to look away, but he reached out to hold her face within his hand and turn it back again. He asked her, low, as though it mattered, 'Was it me?'

He was too close, she thought. His eyes were too intense upon her own, and held her trapped so that she could not look away, or move, or breathe in proper rhythm. And she could think of no defence to offer but, 'I do not pray,' she told him, though her voice was none too steady and without conviction. 'I do not believe in God.'

He smiled, in that quick and blinding flash that left her speechless. 'Aye,' he said, 'so ye did tell me.' And he took her face in both his hands and brought it to his own, and kissed her.

It was no hardened soldier's kiss. His mouth came down on hers with care, with something close to reverence, mindful of the fact that she had never been so touched before, and it was like a wave had rolled upon her in the sea and sent her tumbling underwater. For that swirling moment, all she felt was him – his warmth, his touch, his strength, and when he raised his head she rocked towards him, helplessly off balance.

He looked down at her as though he'd felt the power of that contact, too.

Sophia felt a sudden need to speak, although she knew not what to tell him. 'Mr Moray—'

But his dark eyes stopped her. 'I've a name, lass,' he replied, 'and I would hear ye say it.'

'John—'

But even as she spoke the word, she knew that it was ill-advised, for once again he stopped her with a kiss that shook her senses still more deeply than the first, and she found herself with no more will to speak for quite some time.

Chapter Thirteen

My father, on the phone, had no idea. 'I don't know,' he said. 'I thought he read it, somewhere. Wasn't there a piece in one of Greg Clark's books about a little stone that had a hole in it?'

'The Talisman,' I named the story by one of my favourite Canadian writers. 'Yes, but Grandpa didn't get it from there. Don't you remember, he always used to say he liked that story because his own father had told him the same thing – that if you found a little stone that had a hole in it, it would protect you, keep you safe from harm.'

'Well, there you go. My father never talked to me the way he talked to you girls, but if he said that *his* father told him, that's your answer, isn't it?'

'But how far back,' I asked him, 'does the thing about the stone go, in our family? Who first started it?'

'I couldn't tell you, honey. Does it matter?'

Looking down, I smoothed my thumb across the little worn pebble in my hand. I'd found it just last year in Spain, though I'd been looking for one ever since my grandfather had told me of it when I was a child. He'd never found one of his own. I'd often seen him strolling, head bent, at the water's edge, and I had known what he was searching for. He'd told me if I found one, I should wear it round my neck. I hadn't done that, yet. I'd been afraid the cord I'd threaded through the hole would break, and so I'd kept the stone safe in the little case I used to carry jewellery when I travelled, and had trusted it to do its job from there.

I closed my hand around it, briefly. Put it back among the necklaces. 'Not really, no,' I told my father. 'I just wondered, that's all.' Wondered if that superstition had come down to me from a bright-haired young woman who'd heard it told once while she'd walked on the beach with a soldier, a long time ago...

'Hey,' my father said, and changed the subject, keen to share the satisfaction of discovery. 'I've got another generation back on our Kirkcudbright bunch. Remember Ross McClelland?'

'Yes, of course.' We shared an ancestor in common, and my father, having first run into Ross back in the sixties on an early trip to Scotland, had been writing to him ever since. I'd never met the man myself, but I recalled the Christmas cards. 'How is he?'

'Fine. It sounds like his wife's not too well, but you know Ross, he doesn't complain. Anyhow, I called him up last week to tell him I'm back working on that branch of the family tree again, and I told him what we'd managed to find out about the Patersons – not that they're really connected to him, but he still found it all interesting. And when I said I'd ordered Sophia Paterson's baptism record through the LDS library here, and was just waiting for it to come in, he said he had some time free and, since he was right there anyway, he might just poke around himself and see what he could find.'

I shifted the phone on my shoulder, smiling at the faint tone of envy that had crept into my father's voice. I knew how much he would have loved to be poking around, too, in churchyards and reading rooms. Toss in a sandwich for lunch, and the odd cup of coffee, and he'd be in heaven. 'That was nice of him,' was all I said.

'You're telling me. I just got off the phone with him. Sophia Paterson,' he told me, reading off the details, 'Baptised thirteenth June, 1689, daughter of James Paterson and Mary Moore, and it lists both the grandfathers, too – Andrew Paterson and William Moore. I've never seen that in a register before.' He was beaming, I could tell. 'Ross hasn't found James and Mary's marriage yet, but he's still looking, and at least with all those names it will be easier to verify.'

'That's great,' I said, and meant it. 'Really great.' But I was thinking, too. 'I wonder...'

'Yes?'

'Could you ask him to keep one eye open for the death,' I asked, 'of Anna Paterson?'

'Of who?'

'Sophia's sister. She was mentioned in their father's will, remember?'

'Oh, right. Anna. But we don't know when she died.'

I bit my lip. 'Try the summer of 1706.'

There was a long pause. 'Carrie.'

'Yes?'

'Why won't you tell me where you're getting all this from?'

'I've told you, Daddy,' I said, wishing I could lie more convincingly, 'it's just a hunch.'

'Yes, well, so far all your hunches have hit the bull's-eye. You're not turning psychic on me, are you?'

I tried for a tone that implied the idea was nonsense. 'Daddy.'

'All right.' He gave up. 'I'll see if Ross will take a look. You don't know where, exactly, she'd be buried?'

That last bit was faintly sarcastic, but I answered anyway. 'No. I don't think in the town itself, though. Maybe just outside Kirkcudbright. Somewhere in the country.'

'Right. And Carrie? If you nail this one, we'll have to have a little talk,' he said, 'about your hunches.'

The week flew by more quickly than I'd thought it would. The story was in full run, now – I wrote until the need for sleep took hold of me, and slept till noon, then woke and got back at it, rarely bothering with proper meals, preferring bowls of cereal instead, and pasta eaten with a spoon straight from the tin, things I could eat while I was working and that didn't leave a lot to clean up, afterwards. The coffee cups and spoons began to gather in the sink, and by week's end I didn't bother looking for a clean shirt but just took the one I'd worn the day before, the one that I'd left slung across the bedroom chair, and shrugged it on again.

I didn't care. I wasn't in the real world, any longer. I was lost within my book.

Like someone living in a waking dream, I walked among my characters at Slains, and gained increasing admiration for the countess and her fearless son as they involved themselves more deeply than before in secret preparations for the coming of King James. That angle of the plot, as always, held me fascinated. But this week, my storyline kept turning more and more upon the growing love between John Moray and Sophia.

How much of that was memory, and how much was my imagining the romance that I might have had myself, I didn't know, but their relationship developed with an ease that drove my writing as a fair wind blows a ship upon its course.

They were not lovers, yet. At least, they hadn't shared a bed. And in the castle, in the presence of the others, they did nothing that would give away their feelings. But outside, beyond the walls of Slains, they walked, and talked, and stole what moments they could make their own.

I didn't like repeating scenes, and so I hadn't put them on the beach again, although I sensed they'd been there. I could see them in my mind's eye with such certainty, and always in the same spot, that when I woke up one morning, restless, earlier than usual at nine o'clock instead of noon, I took my jacket from its peg and went to see if I could find the place.

I hadn't been outside in days. My eyes were unaccustomed to the light, and I felt cold despite my heavy sweater. But my mind, fixed firmly on the past, ignored these things. There were still dunes that ran above the beach, but not in the same places they had been three hundred years ago. The sands had blown, and shifted, and the tides had come to claim them, and left little I could use to judge position by. But inland, there were hills I found familiar.

I was studying the nearest of them when a blur of brown and white streaked past me, snatched a rolling bit of yellow from the sand, and sharply wheeled to change its running course and come and pounce on me, with muddy feet and wagging tail.

I had stiffened at the sight of him. He'd caught me unprepared. I'd known that Graham would be back to visit

Jimmy, but I'd hoped I could avoid him. And the way that we had left things, I'd been sure that he would be avoiding me.

The spaniel nudged my knee with an insistent nose.

'Hi, Angus.' Reaching down, I gave his ears a scratch and took the tennis ball he offered me and threw it out again for him as far as I could throw. As he dashed happily away in close pursuit, the voice that I'd been bracing for spoke, coming up behind me.

'Good, you're up. We were just coming to collect you.'

His tone, I thought, was so damned normal, as though he'd forgotten what he'd told me at his father's. I turned my head and looked at him as though he were insane.

He'd been starting to say something else, but when he saw my face he stopped, as someone does who's put a foot down on uncertain ground. 'Are you all right?'

The dog was back. I turned again to take the ball and throw it out along the beach for Angus, grateful to have some excuse to look away from Graham's steady gaze. I shook my head and bit my tongue to keep from saying something I'd regret. And then I calmed my temper and said, 'Look, just let it go, OK? If you don't want to see me anymore, that's fine. I understand.'

There was a pause, and then he came around to stand so that he filled my field of vision.

'Who said,' he asked, evenly, 'I didn't want to see you?'

'You did.'

'I did?' Forehead creased, he shifted slightly as though needing space to concentrate, as though he'd just been handed something written down in code. 'And when did I say that?'

I was beginning to feel less than certain of the facts myself. 'At your father's, after lunch, remember?'

'Not exactly, no.'

'You said that Stuart was your brother.'

'Aye?' The word came slowly, prompting me to carry on. 'Well...'

'Stuart was behaving like himself on Sunday, meaning he was something of an arse. But he was doing it,' said Graham, 'to impress you, and I didn't have the heart to knock him down for it. That's what I thought I'd told you.' With a step he closed the space between us, and he lifted one gloved hand to tip my face up so I wouldn't look away. 'What did ye think I meant?'

It wasn't that I didn't want to tell him, but his nearness had the power of a magnet on my brainwaves, and I couldn't even phrase a decent sentence.

Graham took a guess. 'You thought that I was giving you the push, because of Stuie?' There was disbelief in that, until I answered with a tiny nod.

He grinned, then. 'Christ,' he said, 'I'm not so noble.'

And he brought his mouth to mine, and kissed me hard to prove the point.

It was a while before he let me go.

The dog, by then, had given up on both of us, and trotted off some distance to explore along the ridge of dunes that edged the beach. Graham turned and, slinging one arm warm around my shoulder, set us strolling in the same direction.

'So,' he asked, 'we're good?'

'You need to ask?'

'I'm thinking, now, I'd best not be assuming anything.'

'We're good,' I said. 'But Stuart won't—'

'Just let me handle Stuie.'

I decided I should mention, 'He's been giving everybody the impression that he tucks me in at night.'

'Aye, so I've heard.'

I glanced up quickly, but I wasn't quick enough to catch the smile. He said, 'I ken my brother, Carrie. He'll not be a problem. Give it time.' He drew me closer to his side, and changed the subject. 'So, if you weren't out here waiting for me, what brought you down to the beach?'

'I was getting a feel for the setting,' I said. 'For a scene I've been writing.'

I looked at the dunes, and the rough waving grass, and the clifftops beyond, and I had the strange feeling that something was missing, some part of the landscape I'd seen in my mind when I'd written the scenes between John and Sophia.

I narrowed my eyes to the wind, as I tried to remember. 'There used to be a rock, up there, didn't there? A big grey rock?'

Turning his head, he looked down at me, curious. 'How did ye know that?'

I didn't want to tell him I'd inherited the memory of its being there. 'Dr Weir loaned me some of his old photos...'

'Aye, they'd have had to be old,' he said, drily. 'That stone's not been there since the 1700s.'

'It must have been a drawing, then. I just remember seeing some view of this shoreline with a big rock, just up there.'

'Aye, the grey stone of Ardendraught. It used to lie in that field, up at Aulton farm,' he said, pointing out a spot above the far curve of the beach. 'A great granite boulder, so large that the sailors at sea steered their course by it.'

'Where did it go?' I asked, gazing upwards at the empty hillside.

Graham smiled at me, and whistled for the dog. 'Come on, I'll show you.'

* * *

The ancient church sat in its own little hollow of trees, with bare farmland rising all round and no neighbours except for a plain-looking house and a grander home built of red granite that stood on the opposite side of the narrow curved road, which was edged by the high granite wall of the kirkyard so closely that Graham had to park the car a short way down, beside a little bridge.

He wound the windows down a bit for Angus, who looked weary from his run along the beach and seemed content to lie back, uncomplaining, while we left him there to walk back up the winding road.

It was a peaceful place. There was no sound of traffic, only birds, as Graham swung the painted green gate open and stood back so I could go ahead of him into the quiet kirkyard.

The church was graceful, built with rounded towers at each side, with pointed tops that made it look a lot like the old pictures I had seen of the Victorian façade of Slains. Around the church and out behind, the standing headstones stretched in ordered ranks though some were old and weathered, spotted white with lichen, and some leant, and some had fallen altogether with their age and had been taken up and propped against the inside of the kirkyard wall.

The setting was familiar, and yet somehow wrong.

Behind my shoulder, Graham said, 'This entire church was built out of that one great stone of Ardendraught, which gives you some idea of the size of it.'

It also explained why I hadn't recognised it, I thought. The stone had still been on the hill overlooking the shore, when Sophia and Moray had walked there. It hadn't been broken away yet by stonemasons' hammers.

'What year was the church built?' I asked.

'In 1776. There was a church here before that, but no one knows exactly where.'

I could have told him where. I could have traced the outline of its walls beneath the present ones. Instead, I stood in silent thought while Graham showed me some of the more interesting features of the parish church.

I didn't catch it all – I drifted in and out of daydreams, but a few things stuck. Like when he pointed out a marble slab that had been sent across the sea to mark the grave site of a Danish prince, killed in the battle that had given Cruden Bay its name in the eleventh century.

'It means "the slaughter of the Danes", does Cruden,' Graham told me. 'Cruden Water runs close by the battlefield.'

I looked where he was looking, at the quiet stream that ran beneath the bridge where we had parked the car – a little unassuming one-arched bridge that struck a stronger chord within my memory when I viewed it from this angle.

Curious, I asked, 'Is that an old bridge?'

'Aye. The Bishop's Bridge. It would have been here at the time your book is set. You want to take a closer look?'

I did, and so we left the quiet of the kirkyard and walked the winding road that made a narrow S-curve at the bridge itself. It wasn't more than ten feet wide, with worn and crusted sides of stone that rose to Graham's elbow height. The Cruden Water underneath was muddy brown and gently running, swirling into eddies that moved lazily along the reedy shore beneath the overhanging bare-branched trees.

Graham stopped halfway across, leaning over the edge like a schoolboy to watch the water slipping into shadow underneath us. 'It's called the Bishop's bridge for Bishop Drummond, since he was the one who had it built, although it wasn't finished until 1697, two years after he was dead. He retired up to Slains,' he offered.

But that would have been before the time I needed. Bishop Drummond would have died more than ten years before Sophia had arrived. Besides, there wasn't anything about his name that rang a bell for me. Another name was rising in my mind, and with it came a hazy image of a kind-faced man with weary eyes.

I asked, 'Was there a Bishop Dunbar?' When I spoke the name I knew that it was right, somehow. I knew it before Graham answered, 'William Dunbar, aye. He was the minister of Cruden at the time of the '08.' The look he angled down at me appeared to be acknowledging the thoroughness of my research. 'By all accounts, he was well-liked. It caused a bit of a stir when the Church forced him out of the parish.'

'Why did they do that?'

'He was Episcopalian, as was Drummond before him, and as were your Errolls at Slains. If you lean over here, in fact, you can still see what's left of the Earl of Erroll's coat of arms, carved in the side of the bridge. See that square?'

I leant over as far as I dared, and Graham kept a safe hold on my shoulder, and I saw the square he meant, although the carving was so worn inside I couldn't see the detail. I was about to say so when the movement of the water underneath me stirred a sudden memory of a different stream, a different bridge, and something that had happened...

Damn the Bishop, Moray's voice said calmly, and I tried to catch the rest of it, but Graham pulled me back. When I was standing upright once again he asked me, 'D'ye deal with that, then, in your book? The religious divisions?'

It took me a moment to bring my thoughts back, but my

voice sounded normal when I said, 'They're there, yes. They have to be.'

'Most of my students, when they're coming new to my lectures, don't realise how much of an issue it was,' Graham said. 'How much fighting went on because somebody read from the wrong prayerbook. If you and I had lived back then, and you'd been Presbyterian and I Episcopalian, we'd not have stood together on this bridge.'

I wasn't sure of that myself. The fear of hellfire and damnation notwithstanding, I'd have lain odds that the eighteenth-century version of myself would have had the same weakness for Graham's grey eyes.

The hard stone of the bridge had passed its chill into my fingers, so I hugged them to my chest. 'I am, actually.'

'What?'

'Presbyterian.'

He smiled at that. 'We call it Church of Scotland here. And so am I.'

'So we're all right to stand on the same bridge, then.'

'Aye.' His glance was warming. 'I suppose we are.' He looked me over. 'Are you cold?'

'Not really. Just my hands.'

'You should have said so. Here, take these.' And tugging off his gloves, he passed them over.

I looked at them, remembering how Moray, in my book, had made a gesture much the same when he'd gone riding with Sophia that first time. And putting on the gloves, I found, as she had found, that they were warm, and overlarge, and rough upon my fingers, and the feeling had a certain sinful pleasure to it, as though Graham's hands had closed around my own.

'Better?' he asked.

Wordlessly I nodded, struck again by all the little intersecting points between the world that I'd created and the world that really was.

He said, 'You look half frozen. Want to get a cup of coffee?'

My thoughts were with Sophia still, and Moray, and the moment when he'd asked her to go riding, and she'd known that she was standing at a crossroads of a kind, and that her answer made a difference to the way that she would go. I could have simply told him yes, and we'd have found a place somewhere to stop and buy a cup of coffee on our way back down to Cruden Bay. But like Sophia, I decided that the time had come to choose the unknown path.

And so I told him, 'I have coffee at the cottage. I could make you some.'

He stood there for a moment looking down at me, considering.

'All right,' he said, and straightened from the bridge, and held his hand to me, and smiled when I took it. And we left behind the little church that had once been the great grey stone of Ardendraught above the windblown shore, and in whose shadow other lovers, not so different from ourselves, had moved in step three centuries before.

IX

He was waiting for her on the beach.

He'd stretched himself full length upon the sand, boots crossed, arms folded underneath his head, and when she came around the grassy dune she nearly fell upon him.

'Faith!' she said, and laughed, and let him pull her down to rest beside him.

In a lazy voice he said, 'You're late.'

'The countess wanted my opinion on a newly published tract that she has lately finished reading, on the Union.'

Moray's mouth curved. 'She's a rare sort of woman, her ladyship.'

Sophia agreed. She had never known a woman as intelligent, or capable, or fearless, as the Countess of Erroll. 'I do not like deceiving her.'

He rolled his head upon his arms to look at her. 'We've little choice.'

'I know.' She looked down, sifting the warm sand between her fingers.

'She thinks only of your happiness,' he said, 'and to her mind an outlawed soldier who must soon return to France, and to the battlefield, would hardly be as suitable a match as...well, the commodore, let's say, of our Scots navy.'

'British navy, now,' she absently reminded him, not liking to imagine him at war. 'And though she favours Captain Gordon, I do not.'

His smile flashed as he settled back again, eyes closed. 'And glad I am to hear it. It would pain me to discover that I'd wasted so much effort on a lass for naught.'

Playfully, she struck him on his chest. 'And am I so much effort, then?'

'In ways ye can't imagine.' He was teasing still, but when his eyes came open to her own she saw the warmth in them, and knew what he intended even as his hand reached up to weave itself into her hair and draw her down. His kiss yet had the power to stop her breath, though she'd grown used to it by now and had the knowledge to return it.

When it ended, Moray slid his arm around her back to keep her close against him, and she rested with her cheek against the fine weave of his shirtfront, with his heartbeat sounding strongly at her ear. Above, a gull was hanging on the wind, its outspread wings appearing not to move at all. Its solitary shadow chased across the sand beside them.

Theirs was stolen time, Sophia knew. It could not last. She had not wished to think of it, herself, but since he'd raised the issue, she asked, 'Will you leave soon, do you think?'

His shoulder moved a little in a shrug. 'By his last letter, Hooke will be already on the road to Slains, and Captain Ligondez of our French frigate was instructed to keep off the coast three weeks and then return, which means he, too, can be expected any day.'

'And then you will be gone.'

He did not answer her. He held her closer, and Sophia, saying nothing, closed her eyes and tried to hold the moment. She was used to losing those she loved, she told herself. She knew that when he'd gone the sun would rise and set as it had done before, and she would wake and live and sleep in rhythm with its passing. But this loss, coming forewarned as it did, evoked a different kind of sadness, and she knew that it would leave a mark upon her very different from the rest.

He shifted underneath her. 'What is that?'

'What?'

'That.' His hand moved to her throat, and lower, till it felt the small, hard object pressing at the fabric of her gown. His fingers found the cord strung round her neck, and slipped beneath it to draw forth the makeshift necklace. She had lifted up her head to watch him, and she saw the change of his expression as he studied the small pebble, gleaming black, warmed by its closeness to her skin. She'd found a leather lace to string it with, and wore it tucked well underneath her bodice, where no one would chance to see it.

He seemed about to say something, then thought the better of it, and asked lightly, 'Does it work, I wonder?'

'It well might,' Sophia told him, holding up her hand as evidence. 'This afternoon has been the first time I can yet recall that I've not pricked myself to pieces at my needlework.'

He caught her fingers lightly, turned them as if to examine them, then flattened his own hand to hers, as if to test the difference in their sizes. She could feel the pressing coolness of the ring he always wore on the last finger of his right hand – a heavy square of silver with a red stone at its centre, on a plain, broad silver band. It had been, he had told her once, his father's ring, a small piece of his family he could carry with him in a foreign land.

She wished she had some way to know what he was thinking, with his grey eyes fixed so seriously on their hands together, but he made no comment, and at length he simply twined his fingers through her own and brought her hand to rest above his heart.

The light was changing all around them to the light of early evening, and she knew they did not have much time before they'd be expected back for supper. She asked, 'Shall we walk again to Ardendraught?'

'No. Not today.' He did not loose his hold on her, but closed his eyes again in such a way that she knew, from these past days of observing him, that he was deep in thought.

She waited, and at last he said, 'When I am gone, what will ye do?'

She tried to keep her answer light. 'I'll throw myself at Rory.'

Moray's chest moved with his laughter, but he turned her face to his. His eyes were open now. 'I would be serious. The countess will want to be seeing ye married, for your sake. Will you take a husband?'

'John…'

'Will you?'

Pushing at him suddenly, she made him let her up and sat so that her back was to him and he could not see her face. 'How can you ask me that?'

'I think I have a right.' His voice was quiet, and it gave her hope that he, too, might be looking on the prospect of his leaving with regret.

Head down, she answered, 'No. When you have gone, I will not marry someone else.'

'Why not?' His question gave no quarter, and Sophia knew he would not let the subject rest until he'd had a truthful answer.

Sifting sand again, she watched it spilling freely from her palm, unwilling to be held. 'Because,' she said, 'my sister made me promise her I'd never give my hand unless I also gave my heart. And you have that.' She spread her fingers, setting loose the final fall of sand, and Moray, raising himself up on to one elbow, caught her hand in his again.

'Ye give me more than I deserve,' he said.

'You have a poor opinion of yourself.'

'No, lass. An honest one.' With eyes still darkly serious, he contemplated their linked hands a second time, and then in one swift rolling motion stood, and helped her up to stand beside him. 'Come.'

She saw their shadows stretching long across the sand,

towards the sea, and knew the sun was moving ever lower in the west, above the line of distant hills. It touched the sky and clouds with gold, and caught her vision in a burst of shifting rays when Moray turned her to its light, and set her hand upon his arm, and led her back along the beach.

He did not take her by the main path that went up and through the crow's wood, but along the shore itself and up the hill that stood between themselves and Slains. From here she saw the castle stretched before them in the distance, and the gardens running down to meet the dovecote that clung bravely to the gully's edge, among the gorse and grasses. Then the path was leading down again. It brought them to the bottom of the gully with its quiet grove of chestnut, ash and sycamore trees blotting out all sound except their footsteps and the cooing of the wood doves and the gurgle of the burn whose water ran to meet the sea.

As they approached the footbridge set across the water, Moray asked her, without warning, 'Do ye love me?'

She stopped walking. 'John.'

'"Tis but a simple thing to answer. Do ye love me?'

He was mad, she thought, completely mad, to ask her such a question in the open, here, but looking in his eyes she lost the will to tell him so. 'You know I do.'

'Then, since I have your heart already, let me have your hand.'

She stared, and told herself that she could not have heard him properly. He surely only meant to hold her hand, she thought, and not—

'Sophia.' With a careful touch he smoothed a strand of hair behind her ear, as though he wished to better see her face. 'I'm asking if ye'll marry me.'

A woman who was sane, she knew, would have the wit to tell him that they could not hope to marry, that the countess and the earl would not permit it, that it was a lovely dream, and nothing more...but standing now as she was standing, with her face reflected in the grey eyes fixed with steady purpose on her own, she could not bring herself to think the thing impossible. She swallowed back the sudden swell of feeling that was rising in her chest, and gave her answer with a wordless nod.

The smile that touched his eyes was one she never would forget. 'Then come with me.'

'What, *now*?' That was enough to free her from the spell. 'Oh, John, you know that we cannot. The Bishop never will agree to—'

'Damn the Bishop,' was his mild reply. 'He has no say in our affairs.'

'And who will marry us, if not the Bishop?'

'My brother Robert makes his living in the law, and he would tell you that a marriage made by handfast is as binding as a marriage made in Kirk.'

She knew of handfasting. She'd even seen it done when she was but a girl, and she recalled her mother's explanation that the sacrament of marriage was the only one that did not need a priest, because the man and woman were themselves the ministers, and bound themselves together by their words. Handfast was frowned upon these days, but practised still – an old tradition of a bygone age when priests were not so plentiful, especially in lonelier locations, and the joining of a man's hand to a woman's was a simpler thing.

'Sophia.' Holding out his hand to her, he said, 'Will ye come with me?'

'Where?'

''Tis best done over water.'

In the middle of the bridge he stopped, and drew her round to face him, while beneath their feet the water, turned half-golden by the sun, slipped through the shadow of the arch of wood and flowed on without care towards the sea.

They were alone. He took her two hands in his larger ones.

'I take ye to my wedded wife,' he said, his voice so quiet that the water sang above it. 'Now, lass, tell me that ye'll have me for your husband.'

'Is that all?'

'That's all.'

She raised her gaze to his. 'I take you to my wedded husband.' Then, because that seemed unfinished somehow, she invoked the name of God the Father, and the Son, and of the Holy Spirit.

'I thought,' said Moray, 'ye did not believe.'

'Then it can do no harm to ask His blessing.'

'No.' His fingers tightened briefly on her own, as if he understood her need to hold, by any means, this little piece of happiness. 'No, it can do no harm.'

Sophia looked at him. 'Are we then married?'

'Aye,' he said. 'We are.' She heard the pride, and a faint challenge, in his words. 'And ye can tell that to the countess when she comes to try to marry ye to someone else.' His kiss was warm, and deep, and too soon ended. 'That's for now. The rest will have to keep, else we'll be late to Erroll's table.'

So then, thought Sophia, it was done. A touch of hands, words over water, and a kiss, and everything was changed. It was a little thing, and yet she felt the change within herself so very keenly she was sure the Earl of Erroll or the countess would be quick to see it also, and remark upon it. But the evening passed without an incident.

At supper, Moray and Sophia sat in their accustomed chairs, across from one another, and behaved for all the world as if things were the same as they had been that morning, though Sophia feared that, in her effort not to stare and so betray her feelings, she had erred too far the other way, and hardly looked at him at all.

The only person who had taken note was Kirsty. After supper, in the corridor, she caught Sophia passing. 'Have ye quarrelled?'

'What?' Sophia asked.

'Yourself and Mr Moray. Ye were quiet all the meal. Has he upset ye, in some way?'

'Oh. No,' she said. 'He has done nothing to upset me.'

Kirsty, unconvinced, looked closely at Sophia's flushing face. 'What is it, then? And I'll not have ye say 'tis naethin,' was her warning, as Sophia made to speak.

She wanted desperately to tell, to share some measure of her happiness with Kirsty, but her fear of putting Moray into danger bound her tongue. She summoned up a weary smile and said, ''Tis only that my head aches.'

'And nae wonder, with the walks that ye've been taking in all weathers. Ye'll be bringing on a fever,' Kirsty chided her. 'No matter what the bards may say, there's no romance in dying for a man.'

It was pure instinct made Sophia lift her head. 'What do you know about my walks with Mr Moray?'

'Ye can put the blame on Rory. He's aye seeing things, he is, though he'll not speak of them to any soul but me, and that but rarely.'

Glancing up and down the corridor for reassurance that they were alone, Sophia asked, 'And what does Rory tell you?'

'That yourself and Mr Moray were this evening on the bridge down by the burn, and holding hands, and talking serious. 'Tis why I thought ye must have quarrelled after, for ye did not seem, tonight, as if—' She broke off, as though something had just suddenly occurred to her, and as her eyes were widening, Sophia pleaded,

'Kirsty, you must promise me you'll never say what you've just said, to anyone. Not anyone.'

'Ye've married him!' The words came in a whisper, half accusing, half delighted. 'Ye've married him by handfast, have ye not?'

'Oh, Kirsty, please.'

'I'll never tell. Ye needn't fear I'll tell, nor Rory, either. But Sophia,' she said, in a whisper still, 'what will ye do?'

Sophia did not know what she would do. She had not planned this. It had happened of its own accord, and she'd had little time to think about the future.

Kirsty looked at her with sympathy, and envy, and then, breaking forth a smile, reached out to grab her hand. 'Come now, I've something I would give ye for a wedding present.'

'Kirsty...'

'Come, his lordship and her ladyship do have your Mr Moray deep in conference in the drawing room. Ye'll nae be missed. And anyway, ye have an aching head,' she nudged Sophia's memory, 'do ye not?'

The servants' rooms were at the far end of the castle. Kirsty's window overlooked the stables, where she nightly would see Rory tending to the stalls and horses. Underneath the window stood a simple box, and from this Kirsty drew a length of fine white fabric. When she held it up, Sophia saw it was a nightgown, delicately broidered with pale vines and flowers intertwined, and edged at neck and sleeves with bits of lace.

''Tis my own work,' said Kirsty proudly. 'I've not yet finished all the flowers, but I'd thought I'd have more time afore the countess planned a marriage for ye. I didna ken that ye would be arranging one yerself.'

The holland fabric ran like silk between Sophia's fingers. 'Kirsty, it is beautiful,' she said, so touched that she could feel the spring of tears behind her eyes. 'Wherever did you find the time, with all your duties?'

'Well, now,' Kirsty turned the praise aside, self-consciously, 'it helps me to relax at night. I made one for my sister when she married, and ye've been a second sister to me since ye did arrive, and so I thought it only right that ye should have one, too. I ken ye canna wear it here at Slains, but when ye've gone to France...' She paused then, as Sophia turned her gaze towards the floor. 'He will take ye to France when he goes, will he not?'

Sophia thought of what he'd told her on the bridge when she had asked if they were truly married: *Ye can tell that to the countess, when she comes to try to marry ye to someone else.* Still looking down, she said to Kirsty, 'No. He does not mean to take me with him.'

'But why not?'

She did not know. She only knew that Moray came to no decision lightly, without cause. She raised her head, and showed a smile she did not feel. 'It is enough that he did take me for his wife.'

Fine words, she thought, and bravely spoken, but they did

not cheer her then, nor yet an hour later, when she summoned them a second time within her mind as she stood lonely in her chamber.

The wind had changed from off the sea, and cooled the air so sharply that, although it was now early June, the fires had been lit. She shivered out of gown and shift beside the warmth of her small hearth, and let the lovely nightgown slide like satin down her arms, her shoulders, till its hemline softly brushed her feet. Before the looking-glass, she stood and stared at her reflection, seeing not herself but an uncertain bride, with brightly curling hair and shining eyes and cheeks that seemed so highly coloured that she raised her hands to cover them.

A voice spoke from the darkness. 'Christ,' said Moray, 'you are beautiful.'

Sophia dropped her hands, and wheeled about. She could not see him clearly, just his shape, deep in the shadows of the corner of the chamber. He was standing with his back against the wall, beyond the flicker of the firelight.

His quiet voice would not have carried through the walls, she knew, and she took care to keep her own voice just as low. 'How long have you been here?'

'Ye needn't look so nervous. 'Tis no crime,' he said, 'for me to watch my wife prepare for bed.'

Her face grew warmer still within the pause that followed, and she felt his eyes upon her.

'Where,' he asked her, slow and with appreciation, 'did ye get that garment?'

Smoothing both her hands along the soft folds of the nightgown, she replied, 'It was a wedding gift, from Kirsty.'

'So ye've told her, then.' His voice held mild surprise.

'She knew already. Rory saw us on the footbridge.'

'Well, I don't doubt they'll keep the secret. And 'twill be some comfort to ye, having Kirsty to confide in.' *When I'm gone.* He did not speak the words, and yet they hung as clearly in the air between them as if they'd been said aloud.

Sophia wrapped her arms around herself as though she'd felt a sudden chill. 'Will you not come into the light? I cannot see you. 'Tis like talking to a ghost.'

She heard the slight, half-laughing breath that told her he was smiling, but he did not leave his place against the wall. 'Two years ago,' he said, 'when Colonel Hooke first came to treat in Scotland, he did set a secret meeting with the Duke of Hamilton at Holyroodhouse. A daring thing, and dangerous for both of them if they had been discovered. Hooke did tell me that the chamber where they met was kept in darkness, by the order of the duke, so that if he were later asked if he had seen Hooke, he could answer with full honesty that he had not.'

'And do you then intend that we should do the same?' she asked him lightly. 'So that if the countess asks me, I can tell her with my conscience clear that I did never see you in this room?'

'It is a thought, at that.' His tone was quietly amused. 'Ye've no great gift for lying, lass.'

'I'll have no need to lie. And you already gave me leave to tell the countess we were man and wife.'

'Aye, so I did, but only if she aims you at the altar with another man. Till then, 'tis best we keep it private. Just for us.' She heard his shoulders shift against the stone, and then he stepped into the light, and smiled. 'This night is ours alone.'

And she *did* close her eyes, although she had not meant to, and stood trembling while he came to her, his hardened hands not hard at all as they brushed warm upon her hair, her upturned face, her shoulders. There they stopped, and slipped beneath the lace-edged neckline of the nightgown. Moray's head bent so the angle of his jawline pressed her cheek, his mouth against her ear. She felt his warm breath stir her hair. He asked, 'Why are ye shaking? Are ye frightened?'

Not quite trusting to her voice, she shook her head.

He said, 'I would not have ye fear me.'

'I do not.' She found the words, but in a voice that trembled, too. 'I do not fear you, John. I love you.'

His mouth travelled in a smile across her cheek, and once again the hands upon her shoulders moved beneath the nightgown, and the silken fabric whispered to the floor. And as he lifted her, his mouth came down on hers with so much strength of feeling that the world behind her tight-shut eyes began to spin, and seemed no longer dark, but filled with bursting lights of wonderment.

Against her lips he breathed, 'I love ye more.'

The time for words was over.

She woke, to hear the roaring of the sea beneath her windows and the raging of the wind against the walls that made the air within the room bite cold against her skin. The fire was failing on the hearth, small licks of dying flame that cast half-hearted shadows on the floorboards and gave little light to see by.

She shivered at the thunder of the passing storm, and stirred to rise and tend the fire, but Moray stopped her.

'Let it be,' he mumbled, low, against her neck. 'We will have warmth enough.' And then his arm came round her, solid, safe, and drew her firmly back against the shelter of his chest, and she felt peace, and turned her face against the pillow, and she slept.

Chapter Fourteen

With my hand I smoothed the scrap of paper on which I had scribbled those few lines, when I had woken from the dream I'd had that final night in France. It seemed an age ago, in some ways, that I'd dreamt it, and in other ways it seemed like only yesterday.

I'd wondered where that fragment would fit in, and now I knew.

Knew, too, why that one night had left so strong a memory it had travelled down the centuries to haunt my dreams, as well.

'Good morning.' Graham's voice was rough with sleep. He had his jeans on, and a shirt, but it was hanging open, and his chest and feet were bare. 'Have you seen Angus?'

'He got up with me. And he's been out,' I said. 'He's fine.' The spaniel, curled beneath my work table, rolled both his eyes up without stirring from his comfortable position and, convinced that no one needed him, went back to his contented daydreams.

Graham said, 'You should have woken me, as well.'

'I figured you could use the rest.'

'Did you, now?' His grey eyes met mine, laughing, making me blush. 'After all my exertions last night, d'ye mean?'

'Well...'

'I'm not such an old man as all that,' he said, and came over to prove it. He leant with both hands on the arms of my chair and bent down for the kiss, and it still stole my breath. And he knew it. He drew back and smiled, looking boyishly rumpled and happy. 'Good morning,' he said again.

Somehow I managed to answer. 'Good morning.'

'Want coffee?'

'Yes, please.'

Graham straightened, and crossed to the kitchen. The cups I'd set out for us yesterday still sat untouched on the counter, beside the full kettle. We'd never gotten round to it. Five minutes through the door I had been standing where he stood right now, with my back to the sitting room, nervously chattering on like an idiot, and the next thing I'd known he had been there behind me, his arms coming round me to turn me towards him, and then he had kissed me, and I had been lost.

It had been, in a word, unforgettable. And it would not have surprised me at all if the memory of what I had just shared with Graham survived me as strongly as Sophia's memories of her night with Moray.

I was watching his back and the way that he moved, when he asked, 'Did you get a lot written?'

'I did, yes. I finished the scene.'

'Am I in it?'

He'd meant that, I knew, as a joke, but I answered him honestly. 'Sort of.'

Graham half-turned to look at me, raising an eyebrow. 'Oh, aye? Who am I, then?'

'Well, it isn't you, exactly, but he looks a lot like you.'

'Who does?'

'John Moray.'

'Moray.' He seemed to be searching his archive of knowledge.

'He's a soldier in the Regiment of Lee, in France. They sent him over here with Hooke, to get the nobles ready for the king's return.'

'A soldier.' Graham grinned, and turned back to his coffee making. 'I can live with that.'

'He was an officer, actually. A Lieutenant-Colonel.'

'Even better.'

'His big brother was the Laird of Abercairney.'

'Ah, *those* Morays,' Graham said, and gave a nod. 'From Strathearn. I don't ken too much about the family, other than that one of the later Lairds, James Moray, was famously kept from the field at Culloden – his manservant scalded his feet so he couldn't go fight along Bonnie Prince Charlie – but he'd have been only a lad, at the time of the '08.'

I wondered in silence if that later Laird might have been 'the wee lad not yet eighteen months of age' whom Moray had been speaking of that day he'd first gone riding with Sophia, and who, he had complained, would not have known him from a stranger.

'I'll have to read up on the family,' said Graham, 'and see what sort of character you'd be giving me. John Moray, you said?'

'That's right.'

'And what's the part that he plays in your book?'

'Well…he's kind of the hero.'

The kettle was boiling, but Graham ignored it. He looked round again, eyes warm. 'Is he, now?'

I nodded.

'I thought you were writing everything around Nathaniel Hooke.'

'Hooke wasn't here much. He was off around the country, meeting nobles. Moray stayed at Slains all through the month of May, and into June.'

'I see.' The kettle clicked off, sullenly, as though it somehow knew we wouldn't want it this time either. Graham turned to fully face me, leaning back against the counter, arms folded comfortably over the unbuttoned shirt. 'And just what did he get up to, your John Moray, in the time that he was here?'

'Oh, this and that.' I didn't blush this time, but from his knowing eyes I knew I might as well have done.

'Is there a woman in all this?'

'There might be.'

'Well, then.' His intent was clear before he'd straightened from the counter, but that didn't stop me laughing when he lifted me, as easily as if I had weighed nothing, and cradled me warm to his half-bare chest.

'Graham!'

His arms tightened. 'No, you've said already that you like your writing to be accurate.' He headed for the bedroom. 'And my Dad did say,' he added, with a wicked smile, 'that I should help ye any way I could, with your research.'

The phone was ringing.

Barely conscious, I rolled over on the bed, my body weighted by the tangled sheets and blankets. I could see the indentation on the pillow where Graham's head had rested close beside mine while we'd slept. But he was gone.

I had a recollection, vaguely, of his leaving. Of his kissing me, and tucking in the blankets, but I couldn't for the life of me remember what he'd said. And I had no idea, now, what time it was, what day it was. The room was nearly dark.

The phone kept ringing, from the front room, and I rose and went to answer it.

'Oh, good. You're there,' my father said. 'I tried to call you earlier, but you weren't home. Where were you?'

I could hardly tell him where I'd really been, or why I had ignored the phone the first time it had rung, just after lunch. And I was glad he wasn't in the room to see my face when I said, 'Oh, just out.'

'More research?'

It was a good thing he couldn't see my face then, either. 'Something like that.'

'Well, dear, it's time for us to talk. I've had a call from Ross McClelland.'

Bracing myself for the coming questions, I said, 'Yes?'

'He found a burial for Anna Mary Paterson, in August, 1706. Not far outside Kirkcudbright. In the country.'

'Oh.'

'So now, I think it's time you told me where you're getting all of this.'

'I can't.'

That threw him off. 'Why not?'

'Because you'll think I'm crazy.'

'Sweetheart.' I could hear the dryness of his tone across the line. 'Do you remember when you first got published, and I asked you where you got your stories from, and you said you just heard the voices talking in your head and wrote down what they were saying?'

I remembered.

'Well,' he told me, 'if I didn't pack you off to the asylum *then*, what makes you think I'll—'

'This is different.'

'Try me.'

'Daddy, you're an engineer.'

'And what does that mean? I can't have an open mind?'

'It means you don't believe in things that can't be proven.'

'Try me,' he repeated patiently.

I took a breath and told him. For good measure, I threw in the bits of information Dr Weir had scrounged for me, in hopes they'd make things sound more scientific, but the essence of it was, 'And so I seem to have inherited her memories, and my being here at Slains has somehow called them to the surface from wherever they've been stored.'

A pause. Then he said, 'Interesting.'

'See? You think I'm crazy.'

'Did I say that?'

'You don't have to. I remember your reaction when Aunt Ellen said she'd seen a ghost.'

'Well, a ghost is one thing. This is DNA,' he said. 'And anything is possible, with DNA. You know they use it now, in genealogy, to trace specific lineages? If Ross McClelland and I had our blood tested, we'd show the same markers on our DNA, because we're both descended from the same man.'

'David John McClelland's father,' I said, frowning.

'That's right. Hugh. He had two sons, David John and William, but he died when they were young, and both the boys wound up in Northern Ireland somehow. Sent to be raised up by their relatives, I guess. The Scottish Presbyterians had settled into Ulster by that time, but they still liked to send their sons across to Scotland to find wives, and likely that's why our McClellands came back over to Kirkcudbright. William found his wife, and never did go back to Ireland. And David found Sophia.'

If I didn't answer right away, it was because I didn't want to be reminded that Sophia hadn't ended up with Moray. I had gotten so caught up in their romance, I didn't like to think of any ending for them but a happy one.

'It's too bad,' said my father, not quite serious, 'you didn't get *David's* memory. I'd love to find out anything about his early years in Ireland, before he got married. The family Bible doesn't start till then.'

I said, reacting to his tone of voice, and not his words, 'I knew it.'

'What?'

'You don't believe me, do you?'

'Honey, whether I believe or not, it doesn't matter. I can't offer any explanation of my own, how you came up with all those names and dates from nowhere, so I guess that your genetic memory theory makes about as much sense as anything.'

'Well, thanks.'

'I mean, I'd hoped it was a book you'd found, or something.'

'Sorry to disappoint.'

'You haven't disappointed me,' he said. 'You've got me back two generations on the Patersons. And like I said, I'll keep an open mind.'

I knew my father well enough to know he'd keep that

promise, and that if I passed on any other details I 'remembered' from Sophia's life, he'd search for documenting evidence, the same as he'd have done if I *were* finding information in a book.

But I didn't choose to tell him, yet, that it might just be possible Sophia's marriage to our own McClelland hadn't been her first; that three years earlier, she might have bound herself by handfast to a young Lieutenant-Colonel in the French king's service.

That was knowledge that I wanted to hold closely to myself a while longer.

There was nothing that my father could have found to prove it, anyway, and even if there had been, something deep within me wanted me to keep Sophia's secret, as she'd kept it for herself, those many years ago.

And I obeyed the instinct, though I knew it was irrational. I had already written down the scene, and when the book was published there'd be other people reading it, and nothing would be secret. But for this small time between, I felt responsible to Moray and Sophia to protect their hour of happiness, to help them hold it just a little longer...though I knew that like the beach sand that had slipped between Sophia's fingers, it could not be held.

X

It was, Sophia thought, like waiting for the headsman's axe to fall.

It had been but a day since Colonel Hooke had made a safe return to Slains, looking ill and weary from his days of horseback travelling among the Scottish nobles. And this morning, shortly after dawn, Monsieur de Ligondez's French frigate, the *Heroine*, had reappeared in full sail off the coast, having kept strictly to his earlier instructions to remain three weeks at sea.

Sophia's heart felt like a stone within her chest. She could not look at Moray, who sat now in his accustomed place across the dinner table, for she would not have him see the wretched nature of her misery. It was as well, she thought, that all the others were so focused on their conversation that they took no notice of the fact she had no appetite for any of the fine food Mrs Grant had set in front of them – oysters and mutton and wildfowl in gravy, a swirl of rich smells that would normally stir her, but which, on this day, failed to tantalise. Pushing the meat round the plate with her fork, she listened while the Earl of Erroll questioned Hooke about his meetings with the other chieftains.

'Nearly all,' said Hooke, 'have signed their names to a memorial whereby they pledge King James their swords and loyalty, and lay out their requests for arms and aid, to guard his person when he lands. If you will sign it for yourself, and for those others who did give you leave to sign for them, then I will gladly carry it with me to Saint-Germain, and give it by my own hand to the king.'

The earl was sitting back, his keen eyes deep with thought. 'Who has not signed?'

'I beg your pardon?'

'You said, "nearly all" had signed. Who did not choose to put their name to this memorial?'

'Ah.' Hooke searched his memory. 'None but two. The Duke of Gordon and the Earl of Breadalbane, though both did pledge me their support. The Duke of Gordon said he could not in good conscience sign a document that calls upon King James to come to Scotland and so put himself in danger.'

The young earl glanced along the table to where Moray sat, and in a calm, impassive voice, reminded Hooke, 'I know of many in this country who do risk as much, for lesser gain.'

Hooke nodded. 'And I'm well aware of that. I tell you only what the Duke of Gordon said to me. 'Twas my opinion that both he and Breadalbane would not sign more from caution than from any great concern about the king.'

The earl shrugged. 'Aye, well, Breadalbane has kept his head and health for eighty years, and in that time I do not doubt he's grown too canny to affix his name to anything except his correspondence.'

'You may be right.' Hooke cocked a look towards the earl. 'Do you then share his cautious nature?'

'If I did,' the earl said, 'you would not be here, nor would there be a French ship anchored now below my castle. Do you honestly suppose that, in these times, no one has whispered to Queen Anne of our involvement? It is sure she knows, or does suspect, and only my position keeps our lands from being forfeit. Yet for these past years my mother and my father, heaven rest his soul, and now myself, have ventured all to aid our king however we are able.'

'And I do know the king is duly grateful.' Hooke said hastily, as though he realised he had pressed the younger man too firmly.

It was true, Sophia thought. If it had not been for the countess and her son, King James would have found it more difficult sending his agents across into Scotland to raise the rebellion. At Slains they were sheltered and aided. The countess had even brought in, for Hooke's comfort, an old Catholic priest, who could yet say the mass. For so long now, Sophia had worried for Moray, and what would become of him if he were taken. She hadn't considered, till now, just how greatly the earl and his mother might suffer if they were to be convicted of high treason.

They would be called to pay, she thought, with more than just their lands. A noble birth had never been a guard against a sharp drop from the gallows – it but made the fall the greater.

From the head of the table, the earl said to Hooke, 'I will read your memorial, and if I do approve its terms, I'll sign, both for myself and for the others who do trust me.' With that settled, he returned to eating, spearing up a chunk of roasted mutton with his knife-point. Casually, he added, 'I confess I am surprised you did convince the Duke of Hamilton to sign.'

Hooke paused. It was the faintest wobble of his confidence, but still Sophia saw it. Then his features found their place again. He said, 'When I did speak of those two lords who did not sign, I meant those lords among the ones I had the chance to meet, and speak with. I regret the Duke of Hamilton did not feel well enough to meet with me.'

'And so he has not signed?' the earl asked.

'No.'

'I see. Well, *that*,' the earl said, smiling, 'is no more than I expected.' He stabbed another piece of mutton. 'Did my mother tell you we have had a letter from the duke's friend, Mr Hall?'

Hooke raised an eyebrow to the countess. 'Have you, now?'

She said, 'You must forgive me, it did come to us by night, while you were sleeping, and with the arrival this morning of

Monsieur de Ligondez, it had escaped my mind. Yes, Mr Hall did write to beg a favour of me, that I tell you he is coming north, by order of the duke, to renew the negotiation with you, and that he hopes you will not leave before he does arrive, and that you will not conclude anything with the rest of us, for he is sure you will be satisfied with the proposals he will bring.'

'Indeed.' Hooke's eyes betrayed his interest. Thinking for a moment, he addressed Monsieur de Ligondez. 'Well, then, I wonder if you could see fit to cruise off the coast for a few days longer?'

It must, Sophia thought, be rather wearying for the French ship's captain, forever coming back to Slains and being sent away again, and she would not have blamed him had he told Hooke to be damned, although she privately would not have minded if the ship had kept to sea another month. Whatever thoughts de Ligondez himself might have, he kept them closely shuttered, and with one curt nod, said, 'Very well.' He spoke, in English, carefully and slowly, as though forced to think of every word, although Sophia guessed his understanding of the language was quite fluent. He'd been following along with ease, while they had talked – he'd laughed at the earl's jokes, and his black eyes had shown an admiration of the clever comments of the countess.

And he'd seemed to have a great respect for Moray, who asked Hooke, 'Ye cannot think the duke will give ye satisfaction now, when he has kept ye hanging in the hedge so long?'

Hooke said, in his defence, 'I met the Duke of Hamilton when we were both much younger men, and sharing prison quarters in the Tower. I do know his faults, believe me, but I owe him still some measure of that friendship. If he but asks me to remain a few more days that I may hear his own proposals, I can surely do that much.'

The earl replied, 'Perhaps the duke does fear that your design may find success without him, Colonel Hooke, for I do think that nothing but that fear could make him take such a step as to send Mr Hall to you.'

Moray had read the move differently, and said so now. 'And has it not occurred to ye, the duke might mean no more than to delay us?'

'To what end?' asked Hooke.

'His lordship has already said, there is no safety here. And many of those men whose names are signed to your memorial would pay a bitter price if that same document were set before Queen Anne.' His level gaze met Hooke's. 'My brother William signed for you, as Laird of Abercairney, did he not?'

'He did.'

'Then ye'll forgive me, Colonel, if I do not hold your friendship with the duke as being worth my brother's life. Or mine.'

There was a pause, while Hooke at least appeared to be considering the argument. 'I take your point,' he said, at last, 'but I must keep my conscience. We will wait for Mr Hall a few days more.'

And so, Sophia thought, she was reprieved, but her relief was tempered by the knowledge that it was but temporary, time enough to thread a few more days like beads of glass along the fragile string of memories that would be her only joy to hold, when he had gone. For in the end, she knew, the axe *would* fall, and there would be no rider bearing one last pardon to relieve her of the pain of it.

He would not take her with him.

She had asked him, in a foolish moment while they'd lain in bed last night, aware that Hooke's returning meant their time was growing short. She had been watching him, and trying with a fierceness to commit to memory how he looked, his head upon her pillow, with his short-cropped hair that would have curled itself if he had let it grow, not kept it shorn with soldier's practicality beneath the wig. She knew the feel of that dark hair against her fingers now, and knew the hard line of his cheek, and how his lashes lay upon that cheek in stillness, like a boy's, when he had spent himself in loving her and stretched himself along her side, and breathed in gentle rhythm, as though sleeping.

But he did not sleep. Eyes closed, he asked, his voice a murmur on the pillow, 'What are ye looking at?'

'You.'

'I'd have thought ye'd have seen more of me than was good for a lass, these past days.' His eyes drifted half-open, lazily, holding a smile. 'D'ye fear ye'll forget what I look like?'

She could not answer him so lightly. Rolling to her back, she focused on a faint crack that had spread across the ceiling as a rip might run through fabric. 'John?'

'Aye?'

'Why have you never asked me to go with you?'

'Lass.'

'I am not rooted here at Slains, I've only just arrived, and none would miss me overmuch if I should leave.'

'I cannot take ye.'

She could feel a crack begin to spread across her heart as well, just like the one that marred the ceiling. Moray reached a hand to touch her hair and turn her face towards him. 'Look at me,' he said, and when she did, he told her quietly, 'I would not take you into France, or Flanders, to a field of war. 'Tis no life for the lass I love.' His touch was warm against her skin. 'Before this year is out, the king will be on Scottish soil again, and I will be here with him, and he'll have his crown, and there will be a chance for you and me, then, to begin a life together. Not in France,' he said, 'but here, at home, in Scotland. Will ye wait for that?'

What else could she have done, she thought, but nod, and let him kiss her? For when she was in his arms it seemed the world was far away from them, and nothing could intrude upon the dream.

She would have given much to have that feeling now.

The talk around the dinner table had reverted to the war upon the continent, and how things stood for France, and of the word, just lately come across the water, that there had been a decisive victory for the French and Spanish forces at Almanza.

''Twas the Duke of Berwick's doing,' Hooke remarked with admiration.

Everyone admired the Duke of Berwick. He was half-brother to the young King James, born to their father by his mistress, Arabella Churchill, and although he was denied, by virtue of his bastard birth, a claim upon the throne, he had, by virtue of his courage and intelligence, become his younger brother's best defender, and in doing so had earned himself the love and great respect of all the Scots.

The Earl of Erroll gave a nod. 'You do know that our nobles wish the Duke of Berwick to be put in full command of bringing King James back to us?'

'It is already known at Saint-Germain,' said Hooke, 'and

several of the chieftains here did mention it again to me, when we did meet.'

The countess said, 'He is the only choice, the king must see that.'

'And I have no doubt the king will choose him, if it is his choice to make,' said Hooke.

Sophia knew that when the countess smiled like that, it was designed to hide the workings of her intellect from those she meant to question. 'And who else would make the choice for him?'

Hooke shrugged. 'The King of France will have some say in it, if he is to provide the arms, and ships, and all the funds for our success.'

'I see.' The countess, smiling still, asked, 'And in your opinion, Colonel, does the King of France desire success?'

Not for the first time, Sophia saw Moray's grey eyes fix in silence on the countess, with respect. Then, still in silence, his gaze travelled back for the Irishman's answer.

Hooke appeared surprised. 'Of course he does, your Ladyship. Why would he not?'

'Because his purpose will be served as well if England only hears that we do plan the king's return, for then the English surely will call some of their troops home to guard against it, and the King of France will find it somewhat easier to fight their weakened forces on the continent. He does not need to fight our war. He has but to suggest it.' She ended her remark by neatly forking up a piece of fowl, as though she had been speaking of some trifle, like the weather, and not making an analysis of France's foreign policy.

The earl, his voice amused, said, 'Mother.'

'Well, 'tis time that someone at this table did speak plainly,' was her calm defence. 'You do forget my brother is the young king's chancellor, and I am well aware that there are those among the French king's court who, for their varied purposes, would see this venture fail. We cannot think it was an accident that Mr Moray was sent over to us this time, when his capture would have ruined all. We can but thank God Mr Moray has the sense to know when he is being played.' Her eyes, here, fixed on Hooke's face with a patience that was motherly. 'Not all men are so worldly wise.'

The earl leant forward once again as if to speak, but she held up her hand.

'A moment, Charles. Before you put your name to this memorial, and risk your head and mine still further, I would ask the colonel if he is content, in his own mind, that the French king will keep its terms, and bring our young king safely to our shores?'

Even Monsieur de Ligondez looked round at Hooke, to wait for his reply. Hooke thought a moment, and appeared to choose his words with care. 'I cannot give you promises, your Ladyship. I can but tell you what I have observed, and what I feel in my own heart. The King of France has raised young James with his own children, and he loves him like a son. I would not think that, for the sake of politics, he'd risk our young king's life.'

The countess asked, 'But would he risk our own?'

'I do not know.' An honest answer, thought Sophia. She could see it in his eyes, which were no longer set to charm, but held the doubts of all the others round the table. 'I only know that if we do not seize this moment, if we do not try, then it will pass, and may not come again. I do not think your Robert Bruce was certain he would win, when he did set his foot upon the field at Bannockburn, but he did set his foot upon it, all the same. And so must we.'

By which he meant, Sophia knew, the safer path did rarely lead to victory.

She'd thought on that herself the day she first had taken Moray's invitation to go riding. She had known that she was choosing an untravelled path that did not promise safety, but she'd set her course along it and her life had been forever changed. There was no turning back.

She felt a warmth upon her face and knew that he was watching her, and bravely lifting up her chin, she met his steady eyes and drew her courage from the light in them that burnt for her alone.

No *turning back*, she thought again, although, like all the others at the table who would choose the yet untrodden way and follow young King James, she could not see along the winding path to know the way that it would end.

Mr Hall came two days later.

He stayed closeted some time with Colonel Hooke and then departed, pausing only long enough to pay his respects to the countess, who was sitting reading with Sophia in the sunlight of the drawing room.

'You will stay and dine with us, surely?' she asked him.

'Forgive me, but no. I must start back as soon as I am able.'

With an eyebrow arched, the countess said, 'Then do at least allow my cook to make a box for you. It will take no more than a few minutes, and the duke will surely not begrudge you that.' She called to Kirsty, and with her instruction given, asked the priest to sit. 'I have been reading to Miss Paterson some pages of Mr Defoe's excellent reportage of the hurricane in England, of a few years back. She did lead a sheltered life before she came to us and had not heard the fullness of the tales.'

He nodded. 'Yes, it was God's punishment upon a sinful people who have put away their rightful king and will not see the error of their ways.'

The countess looked at him, and glancing up, Sophia saw the humour in her eyes. 'Good Mr Hall, you cannot think that God would send so fierce a wind against a country for its sins? Faith, all the world would be so plagued with winds no house would stand, for we are none of us unstained. 'Twas not the English who sold Scotland's independence, in our Parliament.' She smiled, to soften her reminder of the way the duke had voted. 'Still, if God does send us wind, we can but hope he'll put it at the back of young King Jamie's sails, to bring him to us faster.' Turning the book in her hand, she regarded it. 'Mr Defoe is a very good writer. Have you had occasion to meet him, in Edinburgh?'

'Daniel Defoe? Yes, I have met him a few times,' said Mr Hall. 'But I confess I do not like the man. He is canny, and watchful. Too watchful, I thought.'

She took his meaning, and, with interest, asked, 'You do believe he is a spy?'

'I've heard he owes much, for his debts, to Queen Anne's government, and is not to be trusted. And the duke does share my views.'

'No doubt he does.' The countess closed the book and set it to one side. 'Perhaps the duke will see his way to warn me if he knows of any others who are spying for the queen,' she said, 'so that I may be careful not to have them here at Slains.'

Sophia held her breath a moment, because she felt sure that

from the smooth challenge of the countess's tone, Mr Hall could not have failed to guess the countess's opinion of his master and of where the duke's own loyalties did lie. But Mr Hall appeared to miss the thrust entirely. 'I shall ask him to,' he promised.

Whereupon the countess smiled, as though she could not find the heart to spar with such a gentle man. 'That would be kind of you.'

The conversation ended there, for Kirsty reappeared with a packed box of Mrs Hall's good food – cold meat, and cakes, and ale to keep him nourished on his journey.

They went out into the yard to see him off, as did the earl and Colonel Hooke – and even Moray, who stayed back a pace. The mastiff, Hugo, having come to view him with affection, circled round and barked as though to call him to a game, but Moray only gave the dog an absent pat. After watching Mr Hall ride out of sight, he turned on his heel and, with a few words, took his leave with a shuttered sideways glance toward Sophia that she knew was his unspoken signal she was meant to follow.

Hugo helped. He was still circling, and the countess, taking pity on him, said, 'Poor Hugo. Every time young Rory goes away, he is fair desolate.'

It wasn't only Hugo, thought Sophia. Kirsty, too, had been at odds these past two days, with Rory sent to carry messages to all the lords on whose behalf the Earl of Erroll had just signed his name to Hooke's memorial, so they would know the business was concluded. But Kirsty, at least, had her work to attend and Sophia to talk to. The mastiff was lost.

'Shall I take him for a walk?' Sophia offered, on a sudden

inspiration. 'He would like that, and we'd not go far.'

The countess gave consent, and having fetched Hugo's lead from the stables, Sophia set forth with the great dog beside her, taking care to appear to be taking a different direction than Moray had. 'Now, then,' she said, to the mastiff, 'behave yourself, or you'll be bringing me trouble.'

But Hugo, so happy to be in human company, seemed perfectly content to go wherever she would lead him, and when they came out at last upon the beach, amid the dunes, and he discovered Moray sitting waiting for them, Hugo's joy exploded in a burst of body-wagging gladness. Grovelling in the sand, he stretched his full length with a grunt of satisfaction, rolling to be petted.

'Away with ye, great foolish beast,' said Moray, but he gave the massive barrel of a chest a scratch. 'I'm not so fooled. Ye'd tear me limb from limb if someone told you to, and never shed a tear.'

Sophia took a seat beside them. 'Hugo would not do you harm,' she said. 'He likes you.'

'It's got naught to do with liking. He's a soldier like myself. He follows orders.' He looked seaward, and Sophia did not ask what his own orders were. She knew, with Mr Hall gone, there was no cause now for Colonel Hooke to linger here at Slains, and when the French ship came again it would take Hooke and Moray with it.

But he had not brought her here to tell her what she knew already, and she'd learnt his moods enough to tell that something else lay heavy on his mind. 'What is it, John? Do the proposals Mr Hall brought with him worry you?'

He seemed to find some cynical amusement in the thought. 'The Duke of Hamilton's proposals were a waste of ink and paper, and he knew it when he wrote them. *That*,' he told her, 'is what has me worried.'

'Do you still believe that he did mean but to delay you?'

'Aye, perhaps. But it is more than that. I've no doubt the duke has been gained over by the court of London, and that he seeks to play us all as neatly as a deck of cards – but what his own hand is, and what the rules, I cannot yet discover.' The frustration of that limitation showed upon his face. 'He knows too much already, but he knows that he does not know all, and that, I fear, may drive him to new treachery. Ye must be careful, lass. If he does come here, guard your words, and guard your feelings. He must never learn,' he said, 'that you are mine.'

The deep, protective force with which he said that warmed her spirit, even as his words ran cold across her skin, more chilling than the swift breeze from the sea. She had not thought of danger to herself, but only him. But he was right. If it were known that she was Moray's woman, she would be a playing piece of value to the men who wished to capture him.

He held her gaze. 'I would not have ye suffer for my sins.'

'I promise I'll be careful.'

Seeming satisfied, he gave the mastiff lying at his side another thump, and in a lighter tone remarked, 'I had a mind to tell ye not to walk so far from Slains, while I'm away, without this beastie with ye, but I'm thinking now he'd be of little use.'

She couldn't help but smile. 'You said before you had no doubt he'd kill you, if he were so ordered.'

'Aye, but look at that.' He rocked the lazing dog from side to side, in evidence. 'He's barely conscious.'

"'Tis because he trusts you,' said Sophia, 'and he knows that I am safe. If I were truly threatened, he would be the first to rise to my protection.'

'Not the first,' said Moray. Then he looked away again, towards the distant line of the horizon, and Sophia, falling silent, looked there, too, and found some peace by watching swiftly scudding clouds, small wisps of white, dance in their free and careless way above the water, running races with each other as they caught, and held, and changed their shapes at will.

And then one cloud, which seemed more steady than the others, drew her eye, and as it moved, she saw it was no cloud.

'John...'

'Aye,' he said. 'I see it.'

Hugo caught the change in Moray's tone, and rolled in one long motion to his feet, nose raised to test the wind – the same wind that was bearing those white, billowed sails toward them.

'Come,' said Moray, standing, holding out his hand. 'We'd best get back.'

His voice was clipped, as though he wished to waste no time, and dreading as she did the time that he must leave, she could not help but find his cold reaction to their sighting of the ship a disappointment.

'I had hoped that you might not be so pleased,' she told him, stung, 'to see Monsieur de Ligondez return. Are you so eager, then, to be away?'

His gaze had narrowed on the distant ship, and now it swung to hers with patient tenderness. 'Ye know that I am not. But that,' he said, and nodded seaward to the swift-approaching sails, 'is not Monsieur de Ligondez.'

The ship was yet too far away for her to see its ensign, but she trusted Moray's eyes enough to scramble to her feet and take the hand that he was offering, and feeling as a fox might when it runs before the hounds, she followed him, with Hugo, back along the path that climbed the hill above the shore.

'I wonder why your Captain Gordon does not come ashore to us,' the Earl of Erroll asked his mother, who, like him, was standing at the window of the drawing room, her hands behind her back, brow furrowed slightly as she gazed in consternation at the ship that lay now anchored off the coast.

'I do not know,' the countess said. Her voice was quiet. 'How long has it been, now, since he did appear?'

'An hour, I think.'

'It is most strange.'

Sophia did not like the tension that had fallen on the room. It was not helped by Moray's choice to stand so close behind her chair that she could all but feel the restless energy within him, held contained by force of will.

Colonel Hooke had given up on standing and was sitting now beside Sophia in a rush-backed chair, his face still bearing witness to the illness that had plagued him through this journey, and which would, no doubt, be worsened by his passage on the sea. His mood had altered since his talk with Mr Hall. He seemed less patient, and had gained the air of one who had been sorely disappointed.

This new turning of the tide, with Captain Gordon's ship, bearing all its great guns and its forty-odd soldiers, appearing from nowhere to stand between Slains and the open North Sea, all but drove Hooke's raw temper to breaking point.

'For God's sake,' he said, 'can we not send a boat out ourselves to ask what he intends?'

The countess turned, and in the face of Hooke's impatience seemed herself more calm. 'We could, but I have never yet had cause to doubt the captain's loyalties. If he does keep himself aloof, I'm sure he has good reason, and if we were to blunder in, we may yet do ourselves the greater harm.'

Her son agreed. 'We would be wisest,' said the earl, 'to wait.'

'Wait!' echoed Hooke, in some disgust. 'For what? For soldiers to approach by land, and trap us here like pigeons in a dovecote, with no window left to fly through?'

Moray's voice, behind Sophia, held a quiet edge. 'If we are trapped, 'tis no fault of our hosts,' he said, as though he would remind Hooke of his manners. 'They had no part in keeping us at Slains these few days past our time. That was, as I recall, your choice, and ye'd do well to pick that up and carry it yourself, not seek to lay the burden and the blame on those who've shown us naught but kindness.'

It was, Sophia thought, one of the longest speeches he had made before the others, and they seemed surprised by it. But it had hit the mark, and, chastened, Hooke said, 'You are right.' The fire fading from his eyes, Hooke told the earl, 'I do apologise.'

Accepting, the earl sent a glance of gratitude to Moray before turning once again to the long window, and its view upon the sea. He watched a moment, then Sophia saw him frown. 'What is he doing now?'

His mother, watching too, said, 'He is leaving.'

Hooke sat upright. 'What?' He rose and went to look himself. 'He is, by God. He's getting under sail.'

They all looked then, and saw the white sails rise and fill with wind, and watched the great ship roll away from shore, while on her tilting deck the moving figures of the men worked hard to set her course. Sophia could not see the blue of Captain Gordon's coat among them.

It was Moray who first saw the second ship, just rounding into view around the southern headland. It was another frigate, and the countess said, 'I'll wager that is Captain Hamilton, the colleague of whom Captain Gordon told us when he was last here.'

Sophia remembered how Gordon had said that his younger associate, sailing so often behind him, would soon grow suspicious if French ships were spotted too often off Slains, and might prove himself to be a problem.

'Captain Hamilton,' the countess said, 'is no friend of the Jacobites.' She had relaxed. 'This does explain why Captain Gordon did not come ashore.'

The second frigate passed the castle by. It flew the ensign of the new united British navy, bright against the sky, and followed swiftly on in Gordon's wake – a smaller ship, but seeming to Sophia more the predator, and she was glad when it had gone.

The Earl of Erroll was the first to turn away. 'At least,' he said, 'we know, now, where the frigates are, and likely we will have some days before they do return. Monsieur de Ligondez should find his way the clearer, now.'

Which doubtless pleased the others. But Sophia, standing there before the window, found no comfort in the knowledge, and the brightness of the sun upon the water hurt her eyes.

* * *

She was shaken awake by a hand on her shoulder.

'Sophia!' The countess's voice, close beside her. 'Sophia!'

Her eyes fluttered open, confused for a moment, then coming alert quickly glanced to the side in remembrance, but Moray was gone, and the pillow showed barely an imprint of where he had lain. With an effort, she pushed herself up till she sat in the tangle of blankets.

The sun was not long up, and slanted low across the window-sill, its light still pale and tinged with all the splendour of the dawn. 'What is it?'

'The French ship is come.'

She noticed now the countess, for the early hour, was fully dressed and wide awake. Sophia, in her shift, stood from the bed and slowly crossed to her long window. She saw the high masts of the *Heroine* some distance still off shore, but bearing steadily towards them.

'Get you dressed,' the countess said, 'and come downstairs. We will have one last meal together, and wish Colonel Hooke and Mr Moray well before they must depart.'

Sophia nodded, and she heard the door close as the countess left the chamber, but she seemed to be stuck fast upon the spot, her gaze fixed fiercely to the French ship's sails, as though she somehow could hold back its progress, if she tried.

She was so focused on it that she nearly failed to see the sweep of movement at the far edge of her vision, as another ship came darkly round the shoreline, like the shadow of a shark. It was the second British ship that they had seen the day before, not Gordon's ship but Captain Hamilton's.

Monsieur de Ligondez had seen it, too, and must have known he'd get no friendly welcome from this interceptor bearing down upon him. French ships on the coast of Scotland were but seen as privateers, rich prizes for a man like Captain Hamilton to capture. Sophia, with her breath held, watched the great prow of the *Heroine* begin to turn about, sails changing shape and swinging desperately to catch the wind. *Go on*, she urged, *go on!*

But Captain Hamilton was closing. In a few more moments he would surely be in range to use his guns.

Sophia's knuckles whitened as her fingers gripped the window-ledge, as though she could herself control the French ship's helm, and turn it with more speed.

There seemed to be a rush of new activity aboard the *Heroine*. The flags at both the topmast and the mizzen fluttered downward to the deck, and different colours were hauled up the ropes to take their place against the sails. Sophia recognised the Holland ensign, and the old Scots blue and white. The signal, she thought suddenly – the signal that had been arranged between Monsieur de Ligondez and Gordon so the ships would know each other when they met.

Except the ship that now had the French frigate in its sights was not in the command of Captain Gordon.

Captain Hamilton took no apparent notice of the changing of the ensigns, but continued on his course to close the distance between his ship and the *Heroine*.

And then, across the water, came the rolling boom and echo of the firing of a gun.

Sophia jumped, she could not help it. She could feel the very impact of that shot within her chest, and feeling helpless, turned her eye towards the *Heroine*, to see the damage done.

To her relief, she saw the French ship sailed as swiftly as before and seemed unharmed. And then a third and even larger ship slid smoothly from behind the northern headland and came fully into view, its great sails billowed with the morning wind. Again a great gun sounded, and Sophia this time saw it was the third ship that was firing – not upon Monsieur de Ligondez but out to sea, apparently with no intent of hitting anything.

The ship was Captain Gordon's, but she did not understand his purpose until Captain Hamilton began to turn, reluctantly, and change his course.

And then she knew. The gun, she thought, had been a call for Hamilton to give up his pursuit. How Captain Gordon would explain that to his colleague, she could not imagine, but she did not doubt that he would find some passable excuse.

His ship was running close along the shore of Slains now, close enough for her to see him standing to the starboard of the mainmast. And then he turned, as though to give an order to his crew, and in a crashing spray of white the great ship passed, and headed south behind the ship of Captain Hamilton, while out to sea the white sails of the *Heroine* danced lightly on the fast-receding waves.

'They'll hear us, John.'

'They won't.' He pressed her close against the garden wall, his shoulders shielding her from view, while at his back and overhead the thickly laden branches of a lilac tree hung round them, filling all the shadowed corner with a sweet and clinging scent.

All around, the final dying light of day was giving way to darkness, and Sophia found she could not take her eyes from Moray's face, as someone going blind might look her last upon the things best loved, before night fell. And night, she knew, was falling. In the shelter of the cliffs below the castle walls, the *Heroine* was back, and riding silent on the waves. When it grew dark enough, the boat would come to carry Hooke and Moray from the shore.

She did not wish him to remember her in tears. She forced a smile. 'And what if Colonel Hooke is looking for you now?'

'Then let him look. I have my own affairs to tend before we leave tonight.' He touched her hair with gentle fingers. 'Did ye think that I'd be parted from my lass without a farewell kiss?'

She shook her head, and let him raise her face to his, and kissed him back with all the fierceness spilling from her soul, the wordless longing that would not be held, but rushed upon her like the flooding tide. There was a quiver in her lips, she knew, but when he raised his head she'd overcome it and was trying to look brave.

She might have saved herself the effort. Moray studied her in silence for a moment with his solemn gaze, then gathered her against his chest, one arm around her shoulders and the other hand entangled in her hair, as if he sought to make her part of him. His head came down so that his breath brushed warm against her cheek. 'I will come back to ye.'

She could not speak, but nodded, and his voice grew more determined still.

'Believe that. Let the devil bar my way, I will come back to ye,' he said. 'And when King Jamie's won his crown, I'll no more be a wanted man, and I'll be done with fighting. We'll have a home,' he promised her, 'and bairns, and ye can wear a proper ring upon your finger so the world will see you're mine.' Drawing back, he brushed a bright curl from her cheekbone with a touch of sure possession. 'Ye were mine,' he told her, 'from the moment I first saw ye.'

It was true, but she did not yet trust her voice to tell him so. She could but let him read it in her eyes.

His hand withdrew a moment, then returned, to press a small, round object, smoothly warm, into the yielding softness of her palm. 'Ye'd best take this, so ye'll not doubt it for yourself.'

She did not need to look to know what he was giving her, and yet she raised it anyway and held it to the fading light – a heavy square of silver, with a red stone at its centre, on a plain, broad silver band. 'I cannot take your father's ring.'

'Ye can.' He closed her fingers round it with his own, insistent. 'I'll have it back when I return, and bring a gold one in its place. Till then, I'd have ye keep it with ye. Any man who knew my father knows that ring, as well. While I'm away, if ye need help of any kind, ye've but to show that to my family, and they'll see you're taken care of.' When he saw that she still hesitated, he went on more lightly, 'Ye can keep it safe for me, if nothing else. I've lost more things than I can name, on battlefields.'

She clenched her fingers round the ring, not wanting the reminder of the dangers he would face. 'How soon must you rejoin your regiment?'

'As soon as I am ordered to.' He met her eyes and saw her fear and said, 'Don't worry, lass. I've kept myself alive this long, and that was well before I had your bonnie face to give me better cause. I'll keep my head well down.'

He wouldn't, though, she knew. It was not in his nature. When he fought, he'd fight with all he had, and without caution, for that was how he'd been made. *Some men*, the countess had once told her, *choose the path of danger, on their own.*

Sophia knew that he was only seeking now to lift a little of the heaviness that weighed upon her heart, so she pretended to believe him, for she would not have him bear her worries, too, beside his own concerns, however broad his shoulders. 'Will you write to me?' she asked.

'I wouldn't think it wise. Besides,' he said, to cheer her, 'likely I'd be back myself before the letter found ye here. 'Tis why I thought to leave ye this.' He took a folded paper from his coat and passed it over. 'I've been told by my sisters a lass likes to have things in writing, to mind her of how a man feels.'

She was struck silent for a second time, the letter feeling precious beyond measure in her hand.

He said, 'Ye burn that, if the castle's searched. I'd not have Queen Anne's men believing I'm so soft.' But underneath his stern expression she could sense his smile, and she was well aware her shining eyes had pleased him.

She did not try to read the note. The light was too far faded, and she knew she'd have more need of it when he had gone, and so she kept it folded in her hand, together with the ring that still felt warm from being on his finger. Looking up, she said, 'But I have nothing I can give you in return.'

'Then give me this.' His eyes held all the darkness of the falling night as, lowering his head once more, he found her mouth with his, there in the closely scented shelter of the lilac tree against the garden wall. His movement freed a fragrant scattering of petals that fell lightly on Sophia's face, her hair, her hands. She hardly noticed.

Moray, when he finally raised his head, looked down at her

and half-smiled in the darkness. 'Now ye look a proper bride.'

She did not understand at first, but coming slowly to awareness of the feathering of lilac petals, moved to shake them off.

He stopped her. 'No,' he said. ''Tis how I would remember ye.'

They stood there, in the little silent corner of the garden, and Sophia felt the world receding from them as a wave withdraws along the shore, till nothing else remained but her and Moray, with their gazes bound together and his strong hands warm upon her and the words unspoken hanging still between them, for there was no need to speak.

The night had come.

She heard the sound of someone opening a door, and footsteps starting out on gravel, and the hard, unwelcome sound of Colonel Hooke's voice, calling Moray.

Moray made no move to answer, and she tried again to find a smile to show him, and with borrowed courage, told him, 'You must go.'

'Aye.' He was not fooled, she thought, by her attempt at being brave, yet he seemed touched by it. ''Tis only for a while.'

Sophia held her smile steady when it would have wavered. 'Yes, I know. I will be fine. I've grown well used to being on my own.'

'Ye'll not be that.' He spoke so low his words seemed carried by the breeze that brushed her upturned face. 'Ye told me once,' he said, 'I had your heart.'

'You do.'

'And ye have mine.' He folded one hand over hers and held it close against his chest so she could feel its beating strength.

'It does not travel with me, lass, across the water. Where you are, it will remain. Ye'll not be on your own.' His fingers held the tighter to her smaller ones. 'And I'll no more be whole again,' he said, 'till I return.'

'Then come back quickly.' She had not meant for her whispered voice to break upon those words, nor for the sudden tears to spring behind her eyes.

Hooke called again, some distance still behind them, and she tried to step aside to let him go, but Moray had not finished yet with his farewell. His kiss, this time, was rougher, raw with feeling. She could feel the force of his regret, and of his love for her, and when it ended she clung close a moment longer, loathe to leave the circle of his arms.

She'd told herself she would not ask again, she would not burden him, and yet the words came anyway. 'I would that I could go with you.'

He did not answer, only tightened his embrace.

Sophia's vision blurred, and though she knew he would not change his mind, she felt compelled to say, 'You told me once I might yet walk a ship's deck.'

'Aye,' he murmured, warm against her brow, 'and so ye will. But this,' he said, 'is not the ship.' His kiss, so gentle on her hair, was meant for comfort, but it broke her heart.

Hooke's steps were coming closer on the gravel.

There was no more time. Sophia, moved by impulse, freed her hands and reached to draw from round her neck the cord that held the small black pebble with the hole in it she'd found upon the beach.

She did not know if there was truly magic in that stone, as Moray's mother had once told him, to protect the one who wore it from all harm, but if there was, she knew that Moray had more need of it than she did. Without words, she pressed it hard into his open hand, then quickly pushed away from him before her tears betrayed her, and ran soundlessly between the shadows to the kitchen door.

Behind her, she heard Hooke call Moray's name again, more loudly, and an instant later Moray's steps fell heavily along the garden path, and in a voice that sounded rougher than his own, he said, 'I'm here. Is everything then ready?'

What came after that, Sophia did not hear, for she was through the door and running still, past Mrs Grant and Kirsty, and she did not stop till she had reached the solace of her chamber.

From her window, she could see the trail of moonlight on the sea, and rising dark across its silver path the tall masts of the *Heroine*, her sails now being raised to take the wind.

She felt the small, warm hardness of his ring, clenched in her fist so tightly that it bit into her hand and brought her pain, but she was grateful for the hurt. It was a thing that she could blame for all the tears that swam against her vision.

There was nothing to be gained, she knew, by weeping. She had wept the day her father, with one last embrace, had sailed for unknown shores, and she had wept still more the day her mother had gone after him, and weeping had not given them safe passage, nor yet brought them home again. She'd wept that black night that her sister, with the unborn bairn inside her, had been carried off in screams and suffering, and weeping had not left her any less alone.

So she would not weep now.

She knew that Moray had to leave, she understood his reasons. And she had his ring to hold, his unread letter to remind her of his love, and more than these, his promise that he would come back to her.

That should have been enough, she thought. But still the hotness swelled behind her eyes. And when all the frigate's sails were filled with wind, and set for France, and the dark ship was loosed upon the rolling sea, Sophia blinked again, and one, small traitor of a tear squeezed through the barrier of lashes and tracked slowly down her cheek.

And then another found the path that it had taken. And another.

And she had been right. It did not help. Although she stood a long time at her window, watching steadily until at last the winging sails were swallowed by the stars; and though her tears, the whole time, slid in silence down her face to drop like bitter rain among the lilac petals scattered still upon her gown, it made no difference, in the end.

For he was gone from her, and she was left alone.

Chapter Fifteen

I'd never done much gardening. My mother had, when I was young – but being young, I hadn't paid attention. I'd assumed that, in the winter, there was nothing to be done, but Dr Weir was bent and busy in his shrubberies when I walked over in the afternoon.

'We've not seen you about these past few days,' he said. 'Have you been away?'

'Well, in a sense. I've been at Slains,' I said, 'three hundred years ago. That's why I'm here, because a couple of my characters, so far, have mentioned spies.'

'Oh, aye?'

'Daniel Defoe, in particular.'

'Ah.' He straightened. 'Well, I might be able to assist you there. Just bear with me a minute while I check the stakes and straps on Elsie's lilac, after last night's wind.'

I followed him with interest to the bare-branched shrub, much taller than the others, at the far end of the border, by one window of the bungalow. 'That's a lilac?'

'Aye. I haven't had much luck with it. It's meant to be a tree, but it's a stubborn-minded thing, and it won't grow.'

The bark felt smooth against my fingers, when I touched it. Leafless, it stood half the height of that which I'd remembered in the garden up at Slains, against the wall where Moray and Sophia had said their farewells. But even so, it touched a chord of sadness in my mind. 'I've never liked the smell of lilacs,' I confessed. 'I always wondered why, and now I think I've found the answer.'

'Oh?' The doctor turned. His eyes, behind the spectacles, showed interest. 'What is that?'

And so I told him of the scene I had just written.

'Ah,' he said, 'that's very telling. Scent is a powerful trigger for memory.'

'I know.' One whiff of pipe tobacco could transport me straight back to my childhood and my grandfather's small study, where we'd sat and eaten cookies and discussed what I had thought were grown-up things. It had been there that he'd first told me of the small stone with a hole in it, and how it would protect me if I ever chanced to find one.

Dr Weir asked, 'What becomes of him, the soldier in your book?'

'I don't know, yet. He must not have come back, though, because three years after he left Slains, the real Sophia was back in Kirkcudbright,' I said, 'marrying my ancestor.'

He shrugged. 'Well, they were dangerous times. He most likely got killed on the Continent.'

'You don't think he could have died in the '08, do you? In the invasion attempt, somehow?'

'I don't think that anyone died in the '08.' He gave a faint frown as he tried to remember. 'I'd have to read over my books, to be sure, but I don't mind that anyone died.'

'Oh.' It would have been a nice romantic feature for my plot, I knew, but never mind.

The doctor straightened from his work, his round face keen. 'Now, come inside and have a cup of tea, and tell me what you'd like to know about Daniel Defoe.'

Elsie Weir had a decided opinion of the man who had written such classics as *Robinson Crusoe* and *Moll Flanders*. 'Nasty little weasel of a man,' she called him.

The doctor took a biscuit from the plate she held out, and said, 'Elsie.'

'He was, Douglas. You've said yourself.'

'Aye, well.' The doctor settled back into his chair and set his biscuit neatly on the saucer of his teacup. The curtains at the end wall of the sitting room were drawn well back this afternoon to let in the sunlight, which fell with a comforting warmth on my shoulders as I chose a biscuit myself, from my seat by the long row of glass-fronted bookcases.

'Daniel Defoe,' Dr Weir said, 'was doing what he thought was right. That's what motivates most spies.'

Elsie took her seat beside me, unconvinced. 'He was doing what he thought would save his skin, and line his pockets.'

The doctor's eyes twinkled briefly, as though his wife's stubborn dislike of Defoe struck him as something amusing. To me, he said, 'She won't even read his books.'

'No, I won't,' Elsie said, firm.

'Even though the man's been dead too long,' her husband pointed out, 'to profit from the royalties.' He smiled. 'Defoe,' he told me, 'was a stout supporter of King William, and no friend of the Jacobites. But he made the mistake, near the start of Queen Anne's reign, of publishing a satirical pamphlet that the queen didn't care for, and so he was arrested. He was bankrupt as well, at the time, so when the government Minister Robert Harley offered him an alternative to prison and the pillory, he leapt at it. And Harley was, of course, the queen's chief spymaster.'

I knew the name, from my own reading.

'Harley,' Dr Weir went on, 'was quick to see the benefits of having someone like Defoe to write his propaganda. And being a writer, Defoe was well-placed to do more for the government. Just before the Union, Harley sent him up to Edinburgh, to work in secret for the Union cause and to discredit those opposed to it. Defoe, as his cover, let dab he was writing a book on the Union and needed some help with his research. Not unlike what you yourself are doing, here in Cruden Bay.'

And, like myself, Defoe had found that people, by and large, were happy to sit down and tell a writer what they knew.

'They didn't think he was a spy,' said Dr Weir. 'But everything they told him found its way to Harley, down in London. And Defoe was good at learning things, observing, and manipulating. There's no doubt that he had an impact on the Union being passed.'

'A weasel,' Elsie said again, and set her teacup down with force.

I asked, 'Would he have ever been to Slains?'

'Defoe?' The doctor frowned. 'I wouldn't think so, no. He might have known what they were up to, and he doubtless would have met the Earl of Erroll, who was often down in Edinburgh, but I've not heard Defoe came up to Slains. But there were other spies. And not only in Scotland,' he told me. 'The English took a great interest in what went on at Saint-

Germain. They had a whole network of spies based in Paris, and some at Versailles, with their ears to the ground. And they even sent people right into Saint-Germain, when they could manage it. Young women, usually, who slept with men at court and carried back what news they could.'

'The tried and trusted method,' Elsie said, to me, her mood improving now that we'd got off the subject of Daniel Defoe.

Dr Weir was thinking. 'As for Slains…I'll have to do a bit of reading, see if I can't find a spy or two who might have ventured that far north.'

And with that settled, we moved on to talk of other things.

I stayed much longer than I'd meant to. By the time I left them it was dusk. The rooks were gathering again above the Castle Wood, great clouds of black birds wheeling round against the night-blue sky and cawing raucously. I quickened my steps. Up ahead I could see the warm lights of the Kilmarnock Arms spilling out through its windows and onto the sidewalk, and crossing the road I turned briskly down Main Street, my eyes on the dim looming shapes of the dunes rising up on the opposite side of the swift-rushing stream.

It was windy tonight. I could hear, farther off, the great roar of the waves as they rolled in to break on the beach and slip backward, collecting their strength to reshape and roll shoreward again in an endlessly punishing rhythm.

It had a hypnotic effect. When I started to climb the dark path up Ward Hill, my steps were all but automatic and my mind was filled with waking dreams. Not all of them were pleasant. There was something unseen on that path, not chasing me but waiting for me, and as I tried hard to fight the rising sense of panic gripping me, I suddenly stepped forward into nothingness.

It was like stepping off a kerb without expecting to. The ground was there, but lower than I'd thought that it would be, and when my foot came down it came down hard into a deep rut underneath the thickly tufted grass, and twisted so I lost my balance and began to slide.

There was no time to think. Pure instinct made me grab at anything to stop myself, and by the time I'd registered the fact that I had left the path and was now slipping dangerously down the steep side of the hill above the sea, my fall was stopped abruptly by a line of leaning temporary fencing that was strong enough at least to hold me while I tried to catch my breath.

From my ankle came a fiercely shooting pain that burnt like fire. In full awareness now, I looked up at the spot from which I'd fallen. What a stupid thing to do, I thought. The path would have been plain to see, despite the growing darkness. I had no excuse. Except...

Now that I thought of it, this hadn't been the first time that my judgement had been off. The only difference was that when I'd come close to stepping off the path before, there had been someone walking at my side to steer me back. Tonight, there hadn't been. I'd been alone, and lost in thought, and with no guide but my subconscious.

Distracted for a moment from my ankle's pain, I chanced a look down at the steep fall to the sea below me, and I wondered just what shape the shore had been, in 1708. Could it be possible my own steps were remembering a different path, along a stretch of land that had since fallen to the slow, eroding forces of the wind and sea?

As if replying to that thought, the wind blew colder, and reminded me I'd fallen in that place along the path that always made me feel uneasy. And when I saw the shadowed shape above me of somebody walking past along the path, my first response was not to feel relief, but apprehension.

I was glad to see the shadow stretch and shape itself to something more familiar, if a little unexpected. And I called to it as loudly as I could.

'Christ!' said Stuart Keith. He came down the hill like a sure-footed mountain goat, and in an instant was crouching beside me. 'What's happened?'

'I fell,' I said. 'It's nothing much, I've only hurt my ankle. But I need a little help.'

He frowned, and felt my ankle. 'Is it broken, do you think?'

I shook my head. 'It's only twisted. Maybe sprained.'

'Well, you'd best let a doctor decide that.'

'It isn't that serious. Honest,' I said, to his unconvinced face. 'I've broken my ankle before, and I know how that felt, and this doesn't feel anything like it.'

'You're sure?'

'Very sure. If you'll just help me up,' I said, holding my hand out.

'You're sure you can manage? Because I could carry you.'

'Great. Then we'd *both* end up over the edge.' With my jaw set, I said, 'I can climb, I'll just need you to help me.'

He did more than help me. He practically hauled me back up the long hillside and onto the path. Then, wrapping an arm round my shoulders, he supported my weight while I hobbled the rest of the way to the cottage.

'Here we are,' said Stuart, his own breathing laboured from holding me up. He waited for me to unlock the door, then helped me through it and steered me across into one of the armchairs.

'Thanks,' I said with feeling. 'I don't know what I'd have done, if you hadn't turned up.'

'Aye, well – rescuer of damsels in distress, that's me.' He flashed a smile more self-aware than Graham's. 'Keep that ankle up, now. I'll get something to put on it.'

All that I had in the small freezer part of my fridge was a bag of mixed vegetables, but that worked fine. And it did make my ankle feel better. I leant back in my chair and looked at Stuart. 'When did you get back, anyway?'

'Just now. I had thought of waiting till morning to look in on you. A good thing I didn't.'

The telephone rang.

'No,' he said, 'you stay sitting. I'll get it.'

The phone was a portable one, and I'd hoped he would just bring it over, but no – being Stuart, he answered it first. I was praying it wasn't my mother, or, worse still, my father, when Stuart said charmingly, 'No, she's just resting. Hang on a minute.' Crossing back, he handed me the phone.

I closed my eyes, prepared for anything. 'Hello?'

Jane's voice was dry. 'Shall I ring back another time?'

'No, of course not.'

'I just wondered. You sound…busy.'

'I—'

'You don't need to explain,' she swept away my explanation. 'I'm your agent, not your mother.'

Actually, I might have found it easier if it *had* been my mother on the phone, because my mother, while she did have her opinions, didn't pry, whereas Jane would never let this drop, no matter what she'd said, till she'd had all the details. Still, she'd known me long enough to not come at me all at once, with questions. 'I won't keep you long, at any rate. I only called to ask you up for lunch,' she said, 'on Saturday.'

I hesitated. Saturdays and Sundays were the days I spent with Graham, and I didn't like to lose them. But I valued, too, my time with Jane and Alan, and their baby, and surely by Saturday I would be able to walk. 'Yes, of course,' I said. 'I'd love to come.'

'Good. Will you need me to come fetch you in the car, or do you have a driver now?'

I didn't take the bait. 'I'll let you know.'

'Local man, is he?'

'Jane.'

'Right, I'll keep out of it. Let you get on with your evening.' I heard the conspirator's smile in her voice as she wished me good night and rang off.

I sighed, and set down the receiver. Stuart didn't notice. He was standing at the door, beneath the black electric meter, making some adjustment to it. Realising that I was off the phone, he turned and grinned. 'Don't look. You're nearly out of time on this. I'm fixing it.'

'Yes, well, your brother's done that once already, and your father's bound to figure out, someday, that I'm not paying what I should.'

He didn't seem concerned about his dad's suspicions. Something else I'd said had grabbed his interest. 'Graham's been here? When was that?'

I'd slipped up, and I knew it. 'Oh, a while ago,' I told him. 'He was helping with my book.' And then, before Stuart could think to ask anything else, I distracted his attention by leaning to push down my sock for a look at my ankle.

It worked. He said, 'Christ, look at that.'

It was swollen. The pain, though, now that I'd stopped

hobbling around, had dulled itself down to a steady throb, something I found easier to manage.

Stuart frowned. 'You're sure you won't have someone look at that?'

'I'll show it to Dr Weir tomorrow,' I promised. 'But trust me, it's only a sprain, if it's anything. Nothing that rest and some aspirin won't cure.'

His torn expression, I decided, wasn't just because I wouldn't see a doctor. More than likely it owed something to the fact that he'd have headed here to visit me tonight with a seduction scene in mind. But even Stuart, in the end, had too much chivalry to try it on with someone who'd been injured.

He brought me my aspirin and water to take it with, settled me into my chair with the phone at my side, and then smiled with the confidence of a commander who'd lost the day's battle but fully expected a victory the next time around. 'Get your rest, then,' he told me. 'I'll see you tomorrow.'

I had every intention of resting. I did. After Stuart had gone, I leant back in the chair and tried closing my eyes for a moment, but then the wind rose at the windows and rattled the glass and moaned low round the cottage, until the lamenting became a low murmur, like voices, and one voice from among them warned, 'The moment will be lost.'

So I knew the idea of resting was out. It was difficult, standing and making my shuffling way to the work table, but it would have been even more difficult to sit still when my characters called.

And I knew, at this point in the story, I wasn't the only one dealing with pain.

XI

Kirsty set the bowl of broth before Sophia. 'Ye must eat.'

Sophia had not managed anything at breakfast. She'd been grateful that the countess, with the earl her son, had gone to Dunottar, and had not seen her as she'd been this morning, pale and feeling ill.

She knew the reason for it. She had not been sure at first, but now it was August, and nearly three months had passed since her marriage to Moray, and there could be no other cause for this strange sickness that came on each morning and confined her to her bed. It had been so, she well remembered, with her sister Anna, when the bairn had started growing in her belly.

Kirsty knew, as well. Her cool hand smoothed Sophia's forehead. 'Ye'll not be so ill the whole time. It will pass.'

Sophia could not meet the sympathy in Kirsty's eyes. She turned her head. 'What will I do?'

'Can not ye tell her ladyship?'

'I promised I would not.'

Drily, Kirsty said, 'A few months more, and ye may find it difficult to keep that promise.'

'In a few months more, I may not have to.' Surely it could not be that much longer till the king would come, and Moray with him, and there would be no need then to hide their marriage.

Kirsty took the sense of that, and nodded. 'Let us hope that ye are right.' Again her hand passed cool across Sophia's forehead, and on inspiration she said, 'I will ask my sister if she knows of any potions that might help ye through this time.'

Sophia's hand moved in protection to her still-flat stomach. 'Potions?' She remembered Anna's agony. The evil, grinning woman with her bottles. 'I cannot take any medicines. I would not harm this bairn.' *His* bairn, she thought – born of his love for her. A part of him, inside her. She drew warmth at least from that.

'The bairn will not be harmed,' was Kirsty's promise. With a smile, she said, 'My sister's been through this more times than most, and all her bairns came full of life and yelling to the world. She'll know what ye should do. She'll help ye.'

It would not be soon enough, Sophia thought, as yet another wave of sickness caught her helpless in its roll, and made her turn her face, eyes closed, against the pillow.

Kirsty stood. 'I will send word to her, and see if she will come afore her ladyship returns.'

Before night, Kirsty's sister came, a calming presence with her understanding eyes and gentle ways. She brought Sophia dried herbs wrapped in cloth, to brew as tea. ''Twill ease the sickness greatly so that ye can feel yourself again and take a bit o' nourishment.'

It helped.

So much so that, next morning, she felt well enough to rise, and dress, and take her place at table. She was still the only person in the house, besides the servants, so there was no one to see the way she smoothed her hand across her stomach with new pride, protectively, before she sat. Her appetite was small but still she ate, and after eating sought a warmly sunlit corner of the library, to pass the morning reading.

She could draw some sense of shared communion, sitting here where Moray had so often sought escape from his forced inactivity at Slains, and feeling in her hands the smooth expensive leather bindings of the books he had so loved to read.

And one book, out of all of them, could draw her to a stronger feeling of connection to him, as though Moray's voice were speaking out the words. It was a newer volume, plainly bound, of Dryden's *King Arthur, or the British Worthy.* The pages were so slightly used she doubted whether anyone but Moray and herself had read the lines, and she was only sure that he had read them because in the letter he had left her – in that simple letter, with its sentiments so strong and sure that every night, on reading them, they banished all her worries – he had quoted from this very work of Dryden's, and the verse, writ in his own bold hand, stayed with her as though he himself had spoken it:

'Where'e'er I go, my Soul shall stay with thee:

'Tis but my Shadow that I take away;'

She read it over now, and touched the book's page with her fingers as though somehow that could bring him close. A few weeks more, she told herself. A few weeks more – a month, perhaps, and then the king would surely come.

The household spoke of nothing else. The visitors still came and went, in states of great excitement, and throughout the summer Slains had seemed as busy as a royal court itself, at times, the dinner table ringed with unknown faces, men who'd travelled miles to carry secret messages from nobles to the north, and from the Highlands.

The nobles dared not come themselves. A gathering of Jacobites would only draw Queen Anne's attention, and it was widely known the English Court had turned its ever-watchful eye toward the north, as might a hound that had caught some new scent upon the wind. This was no accident, according to the countess, who had made no false attempt to hide her own opinion of who was responsible. She'd counselled all who came to Slains that they should keep their words and actions guarded from the Duke of Hamilton. 'If he does seek to be a wolf within the fold,' she'd said, 'we would do well to let him carry on believing we are sheep.'

The earl had smiled at that, and told her, 'Mother, you are many things, but no man who has met you could consider you a sheep.'

Sophia privately agreed with him. The countess, who so many times had proved her strength of intellect, had this summer shown a strength of body that Sophia, for her youth, could not have matched. The older woman slept but little, rising early to her work of putting everything in order for the coming of the king – playing hostess to the many guests, and tending to her daunting correspondence. There was not a night, it seemed, but that the light within the chamber of the countess burnt long after all the others were extinguished.

And the pace at which she drove herself – a pace which might have left a man exhausted – had apparently done nothing but increase her sense of restlessness.

'For God's sake!' she'd exploded, only last week, when Sophia had been standing with her at the great bow window of the drawing room. 'What can they all be thinking of? They must come now. They *must*, or else the moment will be lost.'

And yet the sea beyond the window stayed dishearteningly empty. No new sails on the horizon, bringing word from Saint-Germain.

Sophia had, from habit, stood that morning upon waking at the window of her chamber, with her gaze turned eastward, hopefully, but she'd seen only sunlight on the water, hard and glittering, and after some few minutes that had pained her eyes so that she'd had to look away.

There would be no great news today, she thought, not with the countess and her son still on their visit with the Earl of Marischal at Dunottar. It was a day for rest, and solitary things. Sophia settled with the books, and read, and let the sunlight slanting through the window warm her downturned head, her shoulders, lulling her to drowsiness and then to the oblivion of sleep.

She woke to Kirsty's gentle shaking of her arm. 'Sophia, ye must waken.'

Sophia forced her heavy eyes to open. 'What time is it?'

'Past noon. Ye have a visitor.'

Sophia struggled upright in her chair, aware of Kirsty's urgency. 'Who is it?'

''Tis none other than His Grace the Duke of Hamilton, come all the way from Edinburgh by coach.'

At a loss, her mind still turning slowly after sleep, Sophia said, 'But he'll have come to see the countess and the earl, not me.'

'Aye, so he will, and Rory's riding now to Dunottar to fetch them home. But till they arrive, you're the only one in the house fit to receive him. Come, I'll help ye dress.'

She dressed in haste, and glanced with doubt into the looking-glass. Her face still showed the pallor of the sickness she'd just overcome, and even she could see, in her own eyes, that she was nervous.

She had no wish to face the Duke of Hamilton alone. *He knows too much*, so John had told her, *but he knows that he does not know all, and that, I fear, may drive him to new treachery.*

The countess, were she here, would be intelligent enough to see through any false advance that he might make. She would not let herself unwittingly be led into revealing any details that might harm the chances of the king, or injure those who served him. She would, in fact, if she were here, be more apt to manipulate the duke, than he would her.

But she was not here, and Sophia knew her own wits must this afternoon be sharper than they'd ever been. There was too much at stake. And not only for the king and those who followed him.

It was not of the king's life and his future she was thinking as her hands moved lightly down the bodice of her gown, as if to satisfy themselves the tiny life that beat within her was yet safe.

Kirsty, noticing the movement, said, 'It does not show. Ye need not fear the Duke will see.'

Sophia dropped her hands.

'But he'll see *that*,' said Kirsty, nodding at the heavy silver ring Sophia wore now always round her neck, upon a slender silver chain that could be easily concealed beneath her clothes. The chain had slipped now from the neckline of the gown, and Kirsty pointed out, 'It would be safer for ye not to wear it.'

She was right, Sophia knew. From Moray's tales about his childhood she knew well that his own father, who had given him that ring, had shared an intimate acquaintance with the family of the duke, and it was likely that the duke had from a young age seen that ring on Moray's father's hand. Sophia could not take the chance that he would see it now and recognise it, for she knew it would not take him long to reason out how she had come to have it in her keeping.

He must never learn that you are mine, warned Moray in her memory, and she slipped the chain off with reluctance. 'Here,' she said to Kirsty, handing her the ring.

'I'll guard it well.'

Sophia knew that. But she would have given much to feel the comfort of that ring against her heart to give her courage as she carefully descended to the drawing room to greet the Duke of Hamilton.

'Your Grace.' Was that her voice, she wondered, sounding so composed? 'You do us honour with your visit.'

He looked much the same as she remembered – the elegant clothes, and the curled black wig styled in the full height of fashion to fall past his shoulders. But she fancied the still-handsome features had hardened to something less pleasant in places, a self-serving mask that he wore to a purpose. His eyes, although languid, were watchful and noticing. In but the space of a breath they had taken her measure. The duke gave a bow. Raised her hand to his lips.

'Mistress Paterson. The honour is all mine, I can assure you.' His smile, as charming as before, was meant to put her at her ease. 'I must say, living here at Slains does appear to agree with you. You are more lovely even than I did remember.'

'You are kind.' Politely, she reclaimed her hand, and took a seat so he would do the same. She found it easier, to face him sitting down.

'I'm told the countess and her son are not at home?' His tone was casual, but underneath Sophia thought she sensed a probing pause that she was meant to fill. She filled it cautiously, her own voice light.

'They are expected back at any moment.' Then, to turn the

tables, she said, 'You will stay, I hope, until they do arrive? They would be, I know, most sorry to return and find they'd missed you, and would surely have not ventured from the house if we had known that you were coming.'

There, she thought. Let him explain his visit, and the reason he'd come all this way without first sending word. If what the countess thought was true, he'd likely come to spy on them, and gain his own intelligence on what was being done at Slains in preparation for the king's arrival. If that was so, Sophia thought, then he must now be thinking himself fortunate to find, in place of the more suspicious countess and the forceful young earl, a mere girl, on her own and – to his mind – a lamb to be easily led.

'Yes,' he said, 'I do regret I am come unannounced, but till today I did not know my business would compel me so far north. I thought only to pay my respects, I'll not trouble the family by staying. No doubt they've had enough guests, lately.'

She saw it for herself, that time – the briefest flash behind his smiling eyes, but still she saw it, and knew she had done right to treat him warily. 'No guests as gracious as yourself,' was how she stepped around the trap. And then she asked, as any young and guileless girl might ask, what news there was from Edinburgh, what gossip from the English court, and what the latest changes were in fashion.

Their conversation was a sort of dance, she thought, with complicated steps, but as the time wore on she grew to know the way of it, and when to step, and when to twirl, and when to simply stand and wait.

He led with skill, not asking questions outright but arranging his own statements so that she would follow on with some small bit of information, but she kept her own wits sharp and always countered with a seemingly ingenuous response that gave him nothing in the way of satisfaction.

She felt sure he did not know she was doing it deliberately – the duke was not the sort of man to credit someone like herself with that kind of ability – but still, throughout the afternoon his speech took on a faint edge of frustration, as a man might feel who tries to do a simple task and finds himself confounded.

Yet he did not leave, not even after four o'clock had come and they'd been brought the usual refreshments for that hour of wine and ale, and little cakes in place of bread today because there was a visitor. Sophia had thought, after that, the duke would surely take his leave and carry on his way to where he meant to spend the night, but he did not. He only settled deeper in his chair, and spoke at greater length, with greater charm, to make the dance steps still more intricate.

Sophia matched the effort with her own, but found it tiring. By the time she heard the sound of steps and voices from the entry hall that told her that the countess and her son had finally come, Sophia's mind was near exhaustion.

She was grateful when the countess, with her vibrant presence, swept into the drawing room. 'Your Grace, this is an unexpected pleasure.' From her easy smile one would have thought she meant it. 'I confess that I did scarce believe the servants when they told me you were here. Have you been waiting long?'

'I have been well attended,' he assured her. He had risen from his chair to greet her, and now gave a nod towards Sophia. 'Mistress Paterson and I have passed the time in conversation.'

The countess's own glance at Sophia betrayed none of the concern she must have felt at that revelation. 'Then I do not doubt that you have found her as delightful a companion as I do myself. Her presence in this house does daily bring me joy, especially since all my girls are married now, and gone from home.' Returning her attention to the duke, she said, 'You will stay the night?'

'Well...' He made a show of protestation.

'Yes, of course you will. 'Tis nearly dusk, you cannot venture out upon the road so late.'

The Earl of Erroll, coming through the doorway of the drawing room, agreed. 'We would not hear of it.' He gave the duke a hearty greeting, proving that his acting skills were equal to his mother's. 'It has been some time since you were last here. Come, let me show you the improvements we are making to the house.'

When the men had departed the countess sagged visibly, showing the strain of her hard ride from Dunottar. Turning to Sophia, she began to frame a question, but Sophia said, 'He came just after midday and has been with me for all this time. And as you did suspect, he seemed determined to confuse me into telling him the secrets of this house.'

The countess softened. 'Oh, my dear.'

'I told him nothing.' She was feeling more than tired, now. The sickness was returning, but she fought it as she used the chair's support to rise and stand before the countess. 'I was careful.'

'Oh, my dear,' the countess said again, but with a thread of warm approval in her voice. 'I am but sorry you were here alone to shoulder such a burden.'

'It was no great trouble.'

'Nonsense. It has wearied you.' The countess moved to help her. 'You are pale.'

''Tis but a headache.'

'Go and rest, then. You have earned it.' Once again Sophia felt that gentle touch upon her cheek, so like the memory of her mother's loving hand. The countess smiled. 'You have done well, Sophia. Very well. Now go and get some rest. The earl and I are equal to the duke's designs. We have him well in hand, and I would not for all the world have you fall ill because of such a man.' Her brief embrace was soothing. 'Up you go, and seek your chamber. I'll send Kirsty to attend you.'

So Sophia gladly went, and after that remembered little of the evening, which she passed in waves of sickness and of sleep. But in the morning, whether from the drink of herbs that Kirsty's sister had supplied or from some miracle, the sickness had departed, and the duke had gone as well, his dark coach setting off along the northern road before the sun was fully risen, and himself no wiser than he'd been before he'd come to Slains.

'It isn't broken.' Dr Weir's hands moved reassuringly across my swollen ankle. 'If you'd broken it, you'd feel it here' – he gently squeezed the place – 'not here. It's just a sprain.' He'd slipped easily into the role he'd retired from. He might have been wearing a white coat and stethoscope, questioning one of his surgical patients, not sitting here next to my fireplace and wearing a fisherman's sweater that still held the damp from the rain.

Reaching for a roll of wide elastic bandage, he glanced up from beneath his eyebrows. 'Stuart said you took a tumble off the path.'

Stuart evidently hadn't trusted me to keep my word and show my injured ankle to the doctor on my own, so he'd arranged this morning's house call. I suspected that his version of my accident, no doubt with ample mention of his own role in my rescue, would have gone a bit beyond the simple fact that I had fallen from the path, but, 'Yes, that's what I did.'

This time the upwards glance was curious. 'It's not a narrow path.'

I could think of no good reason not to tell him what I thought might be the truth. 'Well, I was daydreaming a bit, not really paying much attention, and I think that I was walking where I *thought* the path would be.' I met his eyes. 'Where I remembered it had been.'

'I see.' He took this in. 'How very interesting.' In silent thought he wrapped the bandage firmly round my ankle and sat back with the expression of a scientist considering a curious hypothesis. 'It's possible, of course. The hillside would have changed a good deal since that time, from the erosion of the wind and tides. It's possible the old path fell away.'

'And I fell with it.' With a rueful smile, I turned my ankle, testing it.

'Aye, well, you'll want to take care up at Slains, then, won't you? You'll do more than hurt your ankle if you lose your footing there.'

I looked beyond his shoulder to the window with its view of those red walls that clung so fiercely to the rocky cliffs, in shadow now that dark clouds had begun to mass above the sea to block the sun. 'I don't imagine I'll be up there in the next few days.'

He paused, then asked me, 'When you're up there, walking through the rooms, what does it feel like?'

It was tricky to explain. 'Like everyone just left the room as I walked in. I almost hear their steps, the swishing of their gowns, but I can never quite catch up with them.'

'I thought perhaps,' he said, 'you might see flashes of the past, there in the ruins.'

'No.' I looked a moment longer and then pulled my gaze away. 'The memories aren't at Slains, itself. They're locked in my subconscious, and they come out while I'm writing, though I'm not sure they *are* memories till I've had a chance to test them.' And I told him how his *Old Scots Navy* book had proved my Captain Gordon scenes were factual. 'I've decided not to read the book at all, I'm only using it to verify the details once I've written down a scene. But not everything is that easy to prove. I've just found out my heroine is pregnant, for example, so to prove she really was I'd have to find a record of the child's birth or baptism that lists Sophia as the mother. Records from so long ago don't always tell you what you need to know, if you can track them down at all. There are a lot of people in our family tree my dad can't find, and he's been working on the thing for years.'

'But you'd be at a slight advantage with Sophia Paterson,' he pointed out. 'You have a window on her life.'

'That's true. I know the dates of some events now, and the places where they happened, and my dad did find the proof of *those*.'

The mention of my father caught his interest. 'Did you tell him?'

'How I got the information? Yes. I didn't have much choice.'

'And what does he think about all of this?'

I didn't know for certain what my father thought. 'He said he'd keep an open mind.' My tone turned dry. 'I think he would have liked it better if I'd inherited the memory of Sophia's husband, David McClelland. Daddy still has lots of blanks he'd like to fill in on that side.'

The doctor watched me closely for a minute. 'I'd imagine that he's envious.'

'My father?'

'Aye. And so am I. Who wouldn't be? Most people dream of travelling through time.'

I knew that he was right. There'd been so many novels written round that premise, and so many movies made where people journeyed to the future, or the past, that it was clear to see the theme was an enduring one, a common human fantasy.

And one the doctor evidently shared. 'And when I think what it would mean to have the memory of an ancestor, to see what they had seen... I told you, did I not, that one of my own ancestors was captain of a ship? He sailed to China, once, and to Japan. I might have his love of the sea, but I don't have his actual memories.' His eyes grew wistful. 'And what memories they must have been – of storms at sea, and sailing round the Cape, and seeing China in the glory of its empire...who wouldn't wish for that?'

I had no answer to his question, but it lingered in my mind when he had gone, as did his mention of the sea and of the men who'd sought their fortune on its waves. The wind was rising at my window, and a winging band of low white cloud was closing on the castle. And in my imagination – or my memory – it began to take the shape of something else.

XII

Captain Gordon's ship had not been seen along the coast for so long that Sophia had begun to wonder what might have become of him. From time to time a dinner guest brought news of all the changes that were happening in Scotland and in England, from the Union of the nations, so she knew the Scottish navy had been feeling the effects of it as well, and she could only guess that Captain Gordon's orders had been altered so that he no longer sailed according to his former course.

She was surprised, then, when she woke one bright blue morning in the last days of October and looked out to see the now-familiar masts and rigging of his ship at anchor close below the cliffs.

He had not changed. His features were as handsome and his manners were as gallant as before. 'I swear, your Ladyship, each time I come to Slains young Mistress Paterson looks lovelier.'

He kissed her hand with warmth, and though Sophia did not welcome his attentions, she was nonetheless relieved to know that he, like all the others except Kirsty, had not noticed her condition. For in truth it did not show – she was but five months gone, her stomach still was flat, although it had begun to soften, and the fashion of her gowns was so forgiving that she knew it might be some time yet before she was found out. She felt quite healthy, with an energy that fired her from within and made her happy with the world. It was perhaps this radiance, she thought, that Captain Gordon had perceived.

He stayed to dinner, and when wine was poured he took his

glass in hand and raised it in a toast to young King James. 'God grant that he comes soon.'

The countess drank, and set her glass down, smiling. 'Were it up to God alone, I do not doubt but that the king would have been here already. But God passes His affairs into the hands of men, and there the trouble lies.'

'What says the Duke of Perth, your brother? He is there at Saint-Germain, and has the king's ear, does he not? What does he take to be the cause of their delay?'

'He tells me little in his letters, out of fear they will be read by other eyes than mine. But he is as impatient as the rest of us,' she said. 'I sense the problem does not lie at Saint-Germain, but at Versailles. The King of France does hold the purse-strings of this venture, after all, and the ships cannot set sail without his order.'

Captain Gordon said, 'In their defence, I must admit the winds of late have not been very favourable. Last month when setting out from Yarmouth we were damaged so severely in a gale that we were forced to put back altogether, and a few weeks afterwards, when coming into Leith, we found the winds so bad that it was not until some three days after we had dropped our anchor that I could be rowed ashore. Not that I minded, for in truth I had all but exhausted my store of tricks for delaying the voyage.'

The earl asked him, 'Why would you wish to do that?'

'Why, to give the French fleet a fair run at our coast. I had hoped they would have brought young James across before now, for there was a long time when my ship and I were being settled into our positions in this new united Royal Navy of Great Britain. Both Captain Hamilton and I appeared before the Navy Board the first few days in August, to receive our new commissions and the new names of our ships, there being English ships already named the *Royal William* and the *Royal Mary*. My ship is now the *Edinburgh*, while Captain Hamilton's is called the *Glascow*. After this our ships were both surveyed to judge how fit they were for service, which took time, and then both ships were ordered brought into a dry dock for refitting, so for all that time there was no ship assigned to cruise this northern coast. The king would have done well had he but seized that as his moment. But,' he said, and shrugged, 'for reasons that do pass my understanding, he did not, and I was after ordered northward. There was little I could do but make my progress slow, by means of varied misadventures. You'll have heard, no doubt, what did befall the *Edinburgh* at Leith?' He glanced around at their expectant faces. 'No? Then you have been deprived of a diverting tale. My crew,' he said, 'did mutiny.'

The countess raised her eyebrows in astonishment. '*Your* crew?'

'I know. 'Tis difficult to fathom, is it not, when I am so well loved by those I do command.' His smile held a good-natured conceit. 'I can assure you, it was not an easy thing to manage.' Slicing off a piece of beef, he speared it with his knife point. 'Several days before, I stirred a rumour round that we'd be bound for the West Indies after Leith. My men, who for the most part have been pressed to service, taken from their homes against their will, have little liking for the prospect of a passage to the Indies, with its dangers and its deprivations. By the time we'd reached the Road of Leith, they were fair fevered with anxiety. And so I went ashore, and stayed there some time on the pretext of my waiting on the Treasury to clear my old accounts, and sure enough, while I was gone, one hundred of my crewmen made good their escape in boats.' He grinned. 'It took two weeks for us to round them up and coax them back aboard. And in that time, of course, I could not sail.'

The countess could not quite achieve a look of disapproval. 'I do hope you did not punish them when they returned.'

'My men? No, all has been forgiven, and they've settled to their labours as before, with my advice to close their ears to idle rumours in the future.'

'Oh, Thomas,' said the countess, with an open smile now.

He gave a careless shrug. ''Tis not a tactic I am like to use again, at any rate. I can hardly hope to move my crew to mutiny a second time without it reflecting poorly on myself, and much as I do love my king, I have no strong desire to sacrifice my reputation for him.' But he said that lightly, and Sophia had a feeling that despite the show of self-importance, Captain Gordon stood prepared to sacrifice far more if he were asked. He carried on, 'No, I shall have to find some other means to keep these waters clear for him. It should not be so difficult. I've no reports of any ships to the northwards that want convoy, and no privateers have been seen on this coast for a long time, so we have no cause to make this cruise a lengthy one, nor keep close to the shore. No doubt I will be forced by the weather to stand off to sea a while,' was his straight-faced speculation, 'and the gales this far north can so damage a ship that, by the time we do reach England, enough small things may have suffered that we'll likely need repair. In fact, it's possible the *Edinburgh* may need enough attention to be put into a dry dock, and when that is done I would not be at all surprised to find some sudden business matter pressing me to ask for leave to spend some days in London. So with luck,' he finished off, 'the king may find his way unchallenged until Christmas.'

From the table's end, the earl asked, disbelieving, 'Can you do that?'

'I can try.'

The countess said, 'You must be careful.'

'I am careful.'

'You are good,' she told him. 'And I mean to see that young King James does know it.'

Gordon flashed a smile and shrugged. 'He can reward me when he comes,' he said, 'by making me an admiral.'

When the meal was over, he sat back and viewed his stomach with a pretence of dismay. 'Your cook does try to make me fat each time I come here.'

'It was not the cook,' the countess said, 'who made you take three helpings of the pudding.'

'Aye, you're right. Still, I'd be well advised to take a bit of exercise, else I may sink my ship when I return to her. I wonder,' he said casually, and looked along the table, 'if your lovely Mistress Paterson would join me for a turn around the gardens.'

With three heads turned to look at her, Sophia could not think of any graceful way to tell him no. She might have claimed a headache, but she'd not have been convincing since she'd been behaving normally the whole time of the meal. Besides, the countess was watching her now with a motherly interest. Sophia could not disappoint her by treating their favourite guest rudely. She nodded. 'Of course.'

It was cool in the garden. The walls blocked the bite of the wind off the sea, but the air held the chill breath of autumn. Those flowers that had not yet died had begun to fade, and everything had a more desolate feel. But a songbird, alone by the high wall, sat trilling his melody bravely, undaunted.

Sophia had not ventured out to the garden too often since

Moray had gone. She had come with the countess a few times, to walk and admire the colourful blooms of the summer, and once she had come out with Kirsty to help gather herbs. But she'd always been uncomfortably aware of Billy Wick, whether he was at work in the open or scuffling unseen in some weed-tangled corner. His dark-windowed stone bothy crouched like a loathsome great toad at the foot of the gardens against the high twisting trees edging the burn, and she could not look upon it without feeling in her heart a touch of dread, of something evil that was watching her, and waiting.

Billy Wick himself was in full view today, at work with shears among the branches of the lilac tree – the same tree she had stood beneath with Moray that last night, when it had showered her with petals and he'd kissed her...

'I must confess,' said Gordon, 'when I met you first, I did not know how you would fare at Slains. You seemed too quiet, and the countess is' – he paused, to find the word – 'a forceful woman.'

She was well aware he meant that as a compliment, but still she felt the need to rise a little to the countess's defence. 'She is a woman of intelligence and grace.'

'She is that, yes. And it is clear she has been teaching you the way of it. You've changed, these past few months.'

She could have told him that she had changed more than he could know, and that it had not been the countess's achievement, but she only said politely, 'For the better, I do hope.'

'Indeed.' He turned his head to smile down at her. He had not moved to offer her his arm, but walked beside her at his ease. 'You will forgive me if I say that you seemed yet a girl when you arrived, and now in this short time you have matured into a woman. 'Tis a stunning transformation.'

He was charming her deliberately, and might have said as much to any girl who struck his fancy, but Sophia had to steel herself to keep from laying one protective hand across her belly, as though fearing he could truly see the secret that had altered her. She told him, 'You do flatter me.'

'I tell the truth.'

Beyond his shoulder, Billy Wick was watching them in furtive silence, busy with his shears. And of a sudden it was more than she could bear to see him hacking at the lilac tree, to see the leafless branches fall to lie upon the barren ground, defiled. She looked to Gordon. 'Shall we try another path? The sun is in my eyes.'

'Of course.' He chose the path that ran between the roses, with their spent blooms scattered pale beneath the thorny shrubs. Reaching in his coat, he drew a flat and narrow parcel out and held it lightly in his hand. 'When I was in London, waiting for the *Edinburgh* to be refitted, I did chance to see these in the window of a shop. They made me think of you.'

He would have passed the parcel to her but she hesitated. 'Captain Gordon...'

'Please.' He stopped walking on the path and smiled his most persuasive smile. "Tis but a trifle.'

With reluctant hands, Sophia took the gift. The paper wrapping came away to show a pair of dainty gloves worked in white leather, with embroidered knots of gold. She held them dumbly, thinking back to when he'd last been here – when she had sat on Moray's gloves to hide them, in the drawing room; to hide the fact that she had just been wearing them.

He said, 'I do believe I told you that your hands deserved to have a softer covering than Mr Moray's gauntlets.'

She remembered. 'Yes, you did.' She felt the lovely gloves a moment longer in her hand, then held them out towards him. 'I cannot accept them. It would not be right.'

'How so?' He stood his ground, amused. This was a different sort of dance, Sophia realised, than the one that she'd been led through by the cunning Duke of Hamilton – the steps were more straightforward, but she still could not afford to put a foot wrong. Captain Gordon was a man whose handsome face and charm had doubtless gained him much, and he was clearly seeking now to add Sophia to his winnings.

She could choose to simply go along and play for time, till Moray could return...but she knew that would cost her conscience dearly. So she tried, without revealing all, to make him understand.

'You are a kind man, Captain, and your gift is very thoughtful, but I feel it has been offered with a certain understanding, and I would not so insult you by receiving an affection I cannot return.'

His eyebrow lifted slightly, as though it had never crossed his mind that he might be refused. Sophia thought, for one long minute, that she had offended him. But finally he reclaimed the gloves, and slowly said, 'I see.'

And she felt certain that he did see, from the way his gaze passed over her, returning with the faintest smile, conceding his defeat. 'Perhaps I was mistaken to presume you were in need of these. It seems that Mr Moray's gloves did fit you well enough.'

Her eyes betrayed her, gave him confirmation, and she knew it.

'So,' he said, quite softly. 'Does the countess know?'

Sophia shook her head. The sudden danger of his knowing struck her cold, and she looked up at him imploringly. 'You will not tell her?'

He was silent for so long she was not sure how he would answer. Then he gently tucked the fine embroidered gloves beneath his coat and brought his gaze to hers again with all his former gallantry. 'You have my word,' he promised her, and offering his arm said, 'Now, come walk me back. My ship and crew are waiting, and I do perceive that it is past the time I should be gone.'

It was the countess's reaction that Sophia dreaded most, but when the *Edinburgh* had once again sailed northward all the older woman said was, 'Captain Gordon is a charming man.'

Her head was bent with care above her needlework, her comment almost absent as though she were loathe to break her concentration. But Sophia felt the pause that followed, and she knew that she was meant to answer.

'Yes,' she said. 'A very charming man.'

'Were I younger, I myself would likely be in love with him. But such a man,' the countess said, 'is not for every woman.'

She glanced up at that, and in her smiling eyes Sophia read an understanding, a forgiveness. And although they never spoke of it directly, she was sure the countess somehow knew the core of what had passed between herself and Captain Gordon on the garden path, and that whatever hopes the countess might have had were laid to rest without regret, and would no more be mentioned.

I didn't need to look into the *Old Scots Navy* book to know that what I'd written was the truth, but I looked anyway. It was all there, as I had known it would be: the renaming of Captain Gordon's ship, the *Royal William,* to the *Edinburgh*;

his journey northwards in October, and the mutiny among his men at Leith.

And afterwards, it seemed he'd tried to keep his word to do whatever he could think of to make sure his ship would not be in the way of young King James and his invading Frenchmen, should they come.

'The ship,' he wrote in one report, 'has suffered much in the bad weather we had to the northward, and wants to be repaired.' And later, having requested and received an order to put the *Edinburgh* in a dry dock, he wrote in December to the Admiralty, 'All the docks here are full at present, and the master builder can't as yet determine when any of them can be cleared.' And later still, in January, reported that the ship had been examined by a master builder who had concluded the *Edinburgh* needed a great repair, or a rebuilding. 'There will be no necessity of my being here for some time,' Captain Gordon had concluded, 'therefore I desire you will please communicate this to his Royal Highness that I may have leave to come to town...'

Clever, I thought, as I closed the book. Risky, but clever. He'd kept the seas clear to the north, for his king.

But I had my suspicions the people at Slains should be worrying more about dangers that travelled by land.

XIII

November came, and brought a weary week of wind and storms, and one more unexpected guest. He came on horseback, blown across the threshold of the stables by a fiercely gusting north wind and a drenching sheet of rain, his cloak wet through and hanging heavily across his horse's steaming flanks. To Sophia, who'd been passing time by chatting with the soft-eyed mare and feeding kitchen scrapings to the mastiff, Hugo, this new stranger bursting in upon them seemed like something flung up by a force unnatural. He looked, to her eyes, darker than the devil, and as large.

As he dismounted she withdrew a step, her hand on Hugo's collar. It surprised her that the dog had not yet growled, nor even laid his ears back. She herself was measuring the distance to the door and wondering what her chances were of getting past the newcomer without his taking notice. He was standing with his back to her, and viewing him against the horse she saw that he was not as big a man as he had first appeared. In fact, he likely was not too much taller than herself – it was the cloak, with its great hood drawn up to shield his face, that had deceived her.

Merely wary now, she watched him while he tended to his horse, first lifting down the heavy saddle, then with clean straw rubbing dry the creature's heaving sides. No devil, thought Sophia, would have taken such great care. She looked again at Hugo standing calmly at her side and felt her fears recede, and then they vanished altogether when the man turned finally, pushing back the black hood of his cloak to show a lean and weathered face with pleasant features neatly bordered by a trim brown beard that here and there displayed the greying evidence of middle age. He wore no wig – his hair was greying, too, and worn drawn back and tied without a care for fashion.

'I'm sorry, did I frighten ye?' His voice was pleasant, and it held the cadence of a Highlander. 'Forgive me, lass. I took ye for a stableboy at first, there in the shadows. Is there one about?'

'A stableboy?' She did not know where Rory was, just then. She glanced around.

'Eh, well, I only need a blanket and a stall, and I can see to those myself.' Not far from where he stood he found an empty stall to suit his purpose, and when Rory did arrive a short time afterwards the horse was settled comfortably, the stranger having found a blanket on a nearby rail.

Rory's eyes held recognition. 'Colonel Graeme!'

'Aye,' the man acknowledged with surprise. 'I did not think to be remembered – it must be two years since my last visit here.'

The fact that Rory *had* remembered, and was moving round the man with obvious respect now, told Sophia that this Colonel Graeme was no common guest.

He was still thinking of his horse. 'He'll need a warm feed,' he told Rory, 'if ye have the means to manage it. We've ridden hard the day, and we were all the time in rain.'

Rory nodded, but his brief and silent glance seemed more concerned about the colonel, who was soaking wet himself and sure to suffer for it if he didn't soon get dry. 'I'll see him taken care of,' Rory said, about the horse. 'And Mistress Paterson can show ye to the house.'

'*Mistress* Paterson?' He looked at her with open interest, and Sophia could not help but smile. It was no fault of his that he'd assumed she was a servant, with her being here so freely in the stables, wearing one of her old gowns and with the mud upon her shoes. She let her hand fall from the mastiff's collar as she curtsied. 'Colonel. I'd be pleased to take you to the countess and the Earl of Erroll.'

He had laughing eyes that crinkled at the corners, and his smile showed beneath the greying beard. 'And it would please me, lass, to follow ye.'

She took him in the back way, through the stables and the storerooms to the corridor that ran along the courtyard. She'd been right about his height – his shoulders were not far above the level of her own, and he was built compactly, yet he had a presence and a strength about him and he had a soldier's walk, not swaggering but self-assured. It made her think of Moray. And like Moray, Colonel Graeme wore, beneath his cloak, a basic leather buffcoat over breeks and boots, his swordbelt slung across his shoulder with the ease of one who had long worn it.

'My memory is not what is was,' he told her, with a sideways glance, 'but am I right in thinking ye were not at Slains two years ago? Or were ye hiding with the horses then, as well?'

She liked his eyes, his face, his friendly manner. 'No, I was not here. I only came last spring.'

'Oh, aye?' He showed a keener interest. 'Was that afore or after Colonel Hooke was here, with his companion?'

They'd come around the courtyard now, and reached the steps that led upstairs, and she was grateful that she was ahead of him so that her face was hidden while her voice pretended ignorance. For though she liked this man, she could not easily forget the need for caution. Repeating, 'Colonel Hooke...,' she shook her head and told him, 'I regret I have no memory of the name.'

''Tis of no matter.'

As they reached the upper floor the earl stepped out into the passage from the library and narrowly missed colliding with them.

'Colonel Graeme!' Looking as surprised and pleased as

Rory had been earlier, the earl reached out to greet the colonel with a hearty handshake. 'Where in God's name have you sprung from?'

'I can tell ye that, your Lordship, when ye've offered me a dram.'

Sophia had not heard another man, except the Duke of Hamilton, be so familiar with the earl – the colonel said 'your Lordship' in a tone so much at ease that he might just as well have said 'my lad'. But from the earl's acceptance of it she assumed the two men shared a long acquaintance, and her sense of this was strengthened when the earl, with one hand clapped around the colonel's shoulder, steered him through the doorway of the drawing room, announcing, 'Mother, look at who has come.'

The countess came across, delighted. 'I heard no one at the door.'

'I came directly from the stables. Mistress Paterson was brave enough to guide me, though I look a proper rogue and we've not yet been introduced.'

The countess smiled. 'Then let me set that right. Sophia, this is Colonel Graeme. He is truthfully a rogue, as he admits, but one we welcome in our midst.' Turning to the colonel, she said, 'Patrick, this is Mistress Paterson, our kinswoman, who came this year to live with us.'

'An honour.' He did not bend low above her hand as was the current fashion; only took it in a firm and honest grasp and gave a formal nod that had the same effect.

The countess said, 'But you must come and sit beside the fire, or else you'll catch a fever standing in those wet clothes.'

'Och, I'm not so weak. It was my cloak that got the worst of it, the rest of me is dry enough.' He swung the sodden black cloak from his shoulders to prove it, and the countess took it from his hand and laid it on the fender.

'Nonetheless,' she said, and put her hand upon an armchair by the fireplace in a gesture that fell partway between invitation and command. The colonel gave way with a cavalier shrug, but he waited for the countess and Sophia to find their seats first before he took his own. The earl, who through all this had left the room a moment, now returned and pressed a glass half-filled with whisky in the colonel's hand.

'There,' he said, 'you have your drink. Now tell us what has brought you here. We thought you were in France.'

'I was. I landed to the north of here two days ago, and came to you as quickly as I could. I bring a message from your brother,' he said, looking to the countess and then past her, very briefly, to Sophia.

The countess told him, 'Mistress Paterson is family, and does know to keep a secret.'

'Aye, I gathered that much for myself.' Again his eyes laughed privately within the lean face. 'When I asked if she'd met Colonel Hooke, she near convinced me he had never been to Slains.'

Sophia blushed. 'I was not sure…'

'No, no, ye did the right thing, lass,' he said. 'Ye canna be too careful, in these times. It was my own fault, for forgetting ye did not ken who I was – I only meant to learn if ye had seen my nephew and could tell me how he looked, for though we both have been in France of late our paths seem not to cross.'

Sophia frowned in faint confusion. 'Colonel Hooke is your nephew?'

'No, lass.'

'He speaks of Mr Moray,' said the countess, and then answered in Sophia's place, 'Your nephew did look very well when he was here.'

The earl put in, 'He was not pleased with me, I think. With such a price upon his head, I could not let him venture out as he desired, to journey through the Highlands, so he had to stay the whole time here with us.'

'I see.' The colonel's glance touched on Sophia, giving her the feeling that he saw more than she would have wished. She felt relieved that she had already been blushing from her earlier embarrassment, so nobody could blame the heightened colour of her cheeks on this new talk of Moray, or on her reaction to the news that Colonel Graeme was his uncle.

'Still,' the countess said, 'he did not much complain, and seemed to keep himself well occupied. I found him very quiet.'

'Not like me, ye mean?' The colonel grinned. 'Aye, John does keep his thoughts and feelings to himself, for all he feels them deeply. He was like that as a lad, and in the years he's been a soldier he's grown harder in the habit of it.'

'Where is his regiment now fighting?' asked the earl. 'Are they in Flanders?'

And Sophia tried with downturned eyes to hide her own fierce interest in the answer.

'Aye, they are, but John's not with them. Hooke has kept him close, in Paris. They'll let no one who kens anything about the young king's plans stray far from Saint-Germain, these days, for fear the word may spread.'

The countess drily told him, 'They are fools if they believe that it is not already in the wind. Faith, it does seem from the reports we hear that half the court of Saint-Germain are Queen Anne's spies.'

'Aye, very likely. Which is doubtless why your brother thought to send his message using this' – he tapped his head – 'and not a pen and paper.'

'And what is his message?'

Through this last exchange Sophia had been listening with only half an ear, so great had been her feeling of relief to hear that Moray had not been these months in danger on the battlefield as she had feared, but safe somewhere in Paris. Not, she thought, that he'd be happy to be once again confined to what would seem, to him, a soft-barred prison, but at least she knew for certain he was well, and still alive.

No other news but that had seemed important. Only now she sensed the shift of expectation in the room, and brought her own attention back to what the colonel was about to say, because she realised suddenly it might be what they'd hoped to hear these many weeks.

It was.

'I'm sent to tell ye to expect a frigate out of Dunkirk that will soon arrive to signal all is set for the invasion to begin.'

The countess clapped her hands together like a girl. 'Oh, Patrick! When? How soon?'

'Your brother thinks the time is measured now in days, and that you should be ready. They'll be sending Charles Fleming as the messenger. Ye mind young Fleming?'

'Yes, I do remember him,' the countess said.

'A good man,' Colonel Graeme called him. 'He's to carry with him your instructions from the king, who will be following not long behind.'

Sophia's mind withdrew again, and let the others carry on their animated talk. She turned her head towards the great bow window and the sea beyond, and found in all that endless view of water nothing to contain her swelling happiness. *The time is measured now in days...* The words played like a melody repeating in a joyful round that drowned all other noises.

She was not aware of anybody seeking her attention till she felt the tiny nudge against her side. She shook her daydream off and looked round in apology, but nobody was there. The earl, the colonel and the countess were still sitting in their chairs as they had been before, in lively conversation. Again she felt that small sensation, not against her side this time but deeper in her belly, and she realised what it was. Her child was quickening.

This first faint contact with the life inside her left her filled with wonder. Even though she knew it was coincidence that it had happened now, for Kirsty's sister had been telling her for weeks now she might feel it any moment, still she could not help but let herself believe it was a sign of good to come, as if the child, too, was rejoicing at the news that Moray soon would be returned to them.

The countess started laughing at a comment Colonel Graeme had just made, and to Sophia's ears the outburst caught the spirit of her mood, and she laughed, too.

The colonel's lean face turned to hers, appreciative. 'Now, there's a bonny sound.'

'And one we have not often heard, of late,' the countess said, recovering her breath and looking fondly at Sophia. 'Patrick, I do see that we shall have to keep you with us yet awhile, for as you see we sorely need amusement.'

The colonel settled in his chair and smiled. 'I'm happy to supply it,' he assured her, 'while the whisky lasts.'

* * *

Jimmy, on my doorstep, held a covered dish in both hands like a Wise Man bearing precious gifts. 'I telt ma freens at the St Olaf Hotel aboot yer fa' doon Ward Hill, quinie, and they thocht ye micht need this.'

I stood aside to let him in. I still felt a little groggy from my writing, having surfaced at his knocking, and the darkness he stepped out of was my only way to judge the time. He'd clearly been up to the hotel himself – his eyes were shining happily and Scotch was on his breath, but it could not be all that late, or a gentleman like Jimmy Keith would not have even thought of coming round to call.

'Ye should be sittin doon,' he told me, nodding at my bandaged ankle, and he freed one hand to help me hobble to the nearest chair. A richly warm, brown-sugared smell was rising from the bowl he held.

'What is that, Jimmy?'

'Just a wee treat. Ye'll be needin a fork and a spoon,' he decided, and fetched them, then set the bowl down on the table beside me and took off the cover to show me a huge chunk of caramel-brown cake sweetly sinking in a pool of cream. 'That's sticky toffee poodin, and ye'll nivver taste better than fit they mak at the St Olaf Hotel.'

After the first heavy forkful I had to agree it was almost worth spraining my ankle for.

Jimmy shrugged my thanks aside. 'Nae bother. I was on ma wye up, onywye, tae empty oot yer meter.'

'Oh, I'm fine,' I told him, quickly. 'I've still got coins left.' I didn't especially want to get either of his sons into trouble, and I was pretty sure that, if he got a good look at the meter, he would know the needle wasn't resting where it ought to be. I was relieved when he accepted what I'd said without a comment and directed his attention to the Aga in the kitchen.

'And yer a'richt fer coal, are ye?' He had the door open, assessing the fire.

'Yes, thanks. Stuart stoked it up for me.'

'Oh aye, I see.' His tone was dry. 'He could nae build a fire worth a damn.' He took the poker, prodding round the coals until their new position suited him. 'Mind, it's rare ye'll see Stuie dee onything fer onybody but his ain sel. Ye've fairly inspired the loon.'

I was grateful I was eating, and I only had to mumble something noncommittal through a mouthful of pudding before the telephone began to ring, and rescued me. I hobbled over on my own to answer it this time, and Jimmy let me do it.

Graham's voice felt warm against my ear. 'Hello.'

'Hi.' Holding the receiver closer, I lowered my voice.

Behind me, Jimmy closed the Aga's door with a decided clang and stood. 'I'll jist fetch ye a bittie mair coal fae oot back,' he announced, and went whistling past.

Graham asked, 'Was that my father?'

'Yes.'

'You're being well looked after, then.'

'I am. He brought me sticky toffee pudding.'

'Good man. How's the ankle?'

'How did you hear about that?'

'I have sources. How is it?'

'Not bad. Dr Weir says I need to stay off it a couple of days.'

'Ah.'

'Why "ah"?'

'Because I had a proposition for you, but if you're supposed to rest...'

'It's just a sprain, it's not that bad.' I glanced around to make sure I was still alone. 'What kind of proposition?'

'Well, I thought that since my brother's home and looking after Dad, and since it's difficult for me to come to you with those two hanging round the cottage all the time...I thought that you might like to come to Aberdeen this weekend.'

It was my turn to say, 'Ah.'

'You could bring your computer,' he said, 'so you won't lose your writing time. I've got some marking of my own to do.'

'It's not that. It's just I promised to have lunch with Jane, my agent, up in Peterhead on Saturday.' I didn't tell him that Jane had, in essence, invited him, too. There was no way I'd even consider subjecting him this early on to Jane's scrutiny. She could be worse than my father when it came to grilling my boyfriends, and I didn't want Graham grilled. He was special.

'Nae bother,' he said. 'I could come and get you after lunch. We'd still have half the afternoon and evening, and all Sunday.'

Put like that, and with his voice so close against my ear, persuading me, I couldn't think of any reason not to tell him, 'All right, then. I'd love to.'

'Good.'

Jimmy, still whistling, was coming back. Raising my voice to a more normal tone, I said, 'OK, I'll phone you tomorrow. We'll work out the details.'

'I'll phone *you*,' he promised.

I rang off in my most businesslike fashion, so it caught me off guard when Jimmy asked, 'Wis that ma son?'

It was, I thought, a good thing he was looking at the coal hod he was filling, not my face. He didn't see me hold my breath. Head down, he remarked, 'He's a good-hearted loon, Stuart is, but he can be a nuisance.'

I exhaled, and relaxed. 'It wasn't Stuart.' Then, because I saw a useful purpose in it, I said, 'It was Jane, my agent. You remember Jane?'

'Aye. She's nae the sort o quine a man forgets.'

'I'm having lunch with her this Saturday in Peterhead,' I told him. Then, more casually, 'I might, in fact, stay over. Spend the weekend with her family.'

Jimmy thought that sounded like a good idea, and he said as much. 'Ye canna hide awa up here the hale time. Folk ging mad athoot a bittie company.'

I watched him tip the coal bag up and send the last bits rattling into the hod, and I thought how it must be for him, in his cottage alone. I remembered how Graham had told me his dad had been lost since his wife's death. He might have his sons and his group of friends at the St Olaf Hotel, but it wasn't the same thing as having a woman around all the time.

So when he'd finished with the coal and would have left me from politeness, I asked him if he'd make some tea, and then I asked him if he'd stay and have a cup, as well, and for the next two hours we sat and talked and laughed and played gin rummy with the deck of cards I used for playing solitaire.

Because, as Jimmy'd rightly said, it could be better sometimes having company than being on your own.

XIV

Colonel Graeme kept his word, and stayed.

Sophia reasoned that he stayed as much because he wanted to be there to see the frigate come to herald the beginning of the king's invasion, as because he liked the hospitality of

Slains, but either way she took great pleasure in his company. She came to envy Moray, that he had an uncle so engaging and as different from her Uncle John as daylight was from darkness. He talked more than his nephew, and was quicker to observe the humour in a daily happening, but he was enough like Moray that Sophia felt at ease with him and on familiar ground.

He brought a liveliness to Slains, for like his nephew he did not sit still long. If his body ceased its motion then his mind in turn grew restless and required diversion. He had them play at cards most evenings, learning all the new games now in favour at the French king's court and Saint-Germain. And on one rainy afternoon toward the week's end he began to teach Sophia how to play the game of chess.

He said, 'Ye've got the brain for it. Not many lasses do.'

She felt quite flattered by his confidence, but wished that she could share it. With a sinking heart she watched him set the pieces out upon the wooden board that he had laid between them on the little table in the library. There seemed so many figures, finely carved of wood with flaking paint of black or white – the castle towers, and the horses' heads, and bishops' mitres flanking two crowned pieces taller than the rest, their painted faces staring back at her with doubt.

'I do not have much luck at games,' Sophia said.

''Tis not a game of luck.' He set eight smaller figures in a row before the others. Sending her a reassuring glance, he said, 'It is a game of strategy. A battle, if ye will, between my men and yours. My wits, and yours.'

She smiled. 'Then yours will surely win.'

'Ye cannot start a battle, lass, by thinking ye will lose it. Now come, let me show ye how it's played.' He was a soldier, and he taught the movements from a soldier's viewpoint, starting with the forward lines. 'These wee men here, the pawns, they're not allowed to make decisions. They can only put one foot afore the other, marching in a straight line to the enemy, except when they attack. Then they follow the thrust of their sword arm, see, on the diagonal.' Moving his pawn against one of her own, he demonstrated. 'Now, the knights, at their backs, they can move that much quicker because they're on horseback, and bolder...'

And so piece by piece he revealed all the players and set them in play on the battlefield. Leading her through their first game, he took time with each turn to explain all her options, which moves she could make with which men, but he did not advise her. The choice was her own, and he either sat back in approval or with a good-natured grin captured the piece that she'd placed into jeopardy.

Sophia tried to learn from each mistake, and though the colonel won as she'd suspected that he would, she felt a sense of triumph that she'd given him some semblance of a battle. And her pride grew greater when the colonel said, 'Ye did uncommonly well, lass. Did I not say ye had the brain for it?'

'I like the game.'

'Aye, so I see.' He smiled at her. 'We've time for yet another afore supper, if ye like.'

Her skill improved with every day.

'She'll have you beaten, Colonel,' was the earl's opinion as he watched them idly from his reading chair one afternoon.

'Aye, ye might be right, at that.' With steepled fingers, Colonel Graeme eyed the board and whistled lightly through his teeth. He took his time. The piece he finally moved seemed, to Sophia, a mistake because it left a weakness in his ranks that she could then attack. But when she took advantage of the opening, she saw that the mistake had been her own, as Colonel Graeme slid his bishop silently across the board and told her, 'Check.'

She had not seen it coming, and she stared in disbelief now at the bishop sitting poised to take her king. To her dismayed expression, Colonel Graeme said, 'Ye have to watch the whole field, lass, and use your wits afore your weapons. When ye saw me move that knight, your first thought was to take the rook that I'd left unprotected, was it not? And so most soldiers who are new to battle think their first directive is to take the ground, to run against the enemy and do him damage where they can.'

'And is it not?'

He shook his head. 'Not always, no. In war, as in the game of chess, ye also must defend your king.' His smile was wise, forgiving of her youth and inexperience. 'No battle can be called a victory if the king is lost.'

Sophia gave a nod to show she understood, her frowning gaze directed at the board. She saw no move that she could make to bring her own king out of danger, yet she knew there must be one because the colonel had not told her 'checkmate', merely 'check'. Her stubborn concentration did not waver till the countess came in search of them.

The older woman's face was set in firm lines as she told her son, 'We have another visitor, and one who does not sit well in my favour. He has come to us with letters from the Earl of Marischal, but there is something in his aspect which I do not trust.'

The visitor was waiting at his leisure in the drawing room – an older man who looked to be past sixty years of age, though he was large in body with a heavy-featured face and hands that seemed to swallow up the earl's when they shook formally in greeting. He was taller than the earl, which made him well above six feet, and wore the costume of a Highlander, and would have been a fierce imposing figure had his face not held the weariness of one who had been beaten down by time.

'By God!' said Colonel Graeme, just now entering the room behind Sophia, 'Captain Ogilvie!'

The countess turned. 'You know each other?'

'Aye, we served in France together,' Colonel Graeme said, and crossed to greet the older man with pleasure. 'We do share a long acquaintance. How the devil are ye?'

Captain Ogilvie seemed equally as pleased to find a comrade and a fellow soldier in the house, and stood a little straighter as he answered, 'Well enough, though I've grown too old now to fight, and must seek my living elsewhere.' From his tone Sophia guessed the change of livelihood had been a bitter tonic for him, one that he'd found difficult to take. 'What of yourself? I would have thought ye'd be in Flanders.'

'Aye, well, I was given leave to come to Scotland on a family matter,' was the colonel's smooth excuse. 'But I'll be returning shortly.'

Standing to one side, the countess watched this unforeseen reunion with a guarded face that gave no hint of what she might be thinking. Sophia could not see herself what troubled the countess so much about Ogilvie. His eyes, to her, seemed kind enough when she was introduced to him.

The countess said, 'You must be tired, Captain, if you've ridden from the Earl of Marischal's this day. You must stay here at Slains until you are recovered from your travels.'

Ogilvie's bow was deep, and filled with open gratitude. 'You are too kind, your Ladyship.'

She smiled. 'Not at all. Come, let me call a man to show you to your room.'

When he'd left the room her smile vanished, and she turned to Colonel Graeme with an air of expectation. 'Patrick, tell me all you know about this man.'

The colonel told her bluntly, 'He's deserving of your trust.'

'And why is that?'

'Because he's withstood more than you or I have done, in service to the Stewarts. Twenty years ago he fought for old King James, and he was one of those brave Highlanders who charged the pass of Killicrankie with Dundee and broke the English lines. And when the tide then turned again, he joined that band of Highland men who chose to follow old King James to exile. A hundred and fifty of them there were, and they sacrificed all that they had to serve James, surviving on a common soldier's pay. There is an island in the Rhine yet called the Scotsmen's isle, because they charged it in the Highland way, by night and wading arm in arm through water to their shoulders, and they took that island from a stronger force. The king of France considers them a legend, as do all at Saint-Germain. But there are few of them surviving. When I first met Captain Ogilvie ten years ago, the hundred and fifty had dwindled to twenty. By now it must surely be less.'

The story appeared to have moved the young earl. 'I have heard of those Highland men, but I did not think to have one seek shelter beneath my own roof.' Coming forward he said to the colonel, 'Of course he is welcome.'

The countess said, 'Yes. Thank you, Patrick, for laying my worries to rest.'

But Sophia thought, watching her, that she still guarded her features with care, as though some of the doubts yet remained.

It was clear Colonel Graeme had none of his own. The next morning, as he sat down with Sophia to resume their interrupted game of chess, the door to the library opened and Ogilvie, seeing them already there and well occupied, apologised and started to withdraw, but Colonel Graeme would have none of it. 'Come in and join us, Captain.'

'If you're sure 'tis no intrusion.'

'None at all. Besides, it may improve our game to have an audience.'

Sophia doubted whether there was anything that would improve her game this morning, trapped as she still was, her king held helplessly in check. While Captain Ogilvie settled himself in a chair by the fire, she took the opportunity to study once again the way the pieces were positioned on the board, in hopes she'd chance upon the move that would release her king from peril.

Colonel Graeme watched her closely from across the table, making no attempt to hide his amusement. 'There is a way,' he told her, 'to get out of that.'

'You would not wish to tell me what it is?' She knew he wouldn't. He had never told her how to move or given her advice, but in the teaching of this game he had from time to time seen fit to help her train her sight along the proper line.

He did it now. 'It does involve your queen.'

'My queen...' She looked, but still she could not see it. And then, of a sudden, 'Oh,' she said, and made the move.

'See?' Colonel Graeme's smile seemed proud of her. 'I told ye. Now your king is safe. At least,' he told her, teasing, 'for the moment.'

Ogilvie looked on with partial interest, but Sophia knew he would not sit for long before the urge to tell a story overcame him. He had kept them fully entertained at last night's supper with his tales, for having lived so long he had amassed a wealth of stories, and the telling of them seemed to bring him pleasure. Neither did Sophia have any objection to hearing them. She found them fascinating, full of bold adventure – though she would have listened, truth be told, if they had all been dull, because her heart was not so hard she could deny a man like Ogilvie, whose days of grandeur and of glory were all now behind him, the chance to live those days again in memory, while he spoke.

'Aye,' said Ogilvie, relaxing back into his chair, ''Tis often in the power of the queen to save the king. Our young King Jamie owes much to his mother. He would not be living at all were it not for her bravery in taking him over the sea.'

Colonel Graeme seemed to also sense a story coming on, and did his part to encourage it. 'Aye, ye should tell this young lassie about all of that. She'd have been but a wee bairn herself, at the time.'

Ogilvie looked at Sophia, and seeing that she was receptive, said, 'Well, the young king – Prince of Wales he was then – was but half a year old. It was this time of year, the first days of December, and everything wild and windy and cold. Things were going poorly for the old king then. He was losing his hold on the kingdom. Most of his generals, and Marlborough with them, had left him, gone over to William of Orange, and his own daughter Anne had just secretly flown, too. That did him in badly. A raw wound, it was, that the daughter he loved would betray him. He lost a good part of his fight after that, and cared little what happened to him, but he cared a great deal for the queen and the wee Prince of Wales. He kent the lad would not be safe, for all the Whigs had whispered round the falsehood that wee James was not the queen's own son. The devil's lie, that was,' he said with feeling, 'and how the queen could bear it, having birthed him in a room stacked full with witnesses as all queens must endure, I—' He broke off, the strong emotion that had gripped him making further speech on that same subject difficult.

Sophia knew he'd meant to say he did not know. He did not know how Mary of Modena had withstood such slander, and Sophia did not know herself how any woman could. To carry a child and bring him to life, and then have him denied and rejected by those who knew otherwise…well, it was not to be thought of. Sophia resisted the now almost unthinking impulse to rest a hand on her own belly while Ogilvie, having recovered, went on, 'But the old king had made up his mind that the queen and the Prince of Wales were to be sent out of London and carried to France. There were but a handful let in on the secret.' The firelight cast shadows along his expressive face as he leant forward and brought them both into the secret as well. He went on with the story as surely as one who had been there: 'At supper, the night that the flight was to happen, the queen sat at table. Calm, she was. She played her part so well that none suspected. After she withdrew, she changed her fine gown for a plain common habit and took up the Prince in a bundle, as if she were only a servant and he were the clothes to be washed. She'd been given two trustworthy men for her guards, and she had her own women. By secret ways, all of them passed from the palace of Whitehall, and taking care not to be seen scurried into the carriage that waited to carry them down to the river.'

Sophia fought the urge to hold her own breath as she crept in her imagination through the watchful shadows with the queen. She bit her lip.

'The night was so dark,' Captain Ogilvie said, 'that they could barely see each other. And the crossing of the Thames in violent wind and rain was treacherous. But when they finally reached the other side, the coach and six that had been meant to meet them was not there. The queen was forced to shelter from the weather by a church wall, in a dangerous exposure, and so wait until her guardsman went to fetch the coach. They nearly were discovered. 'Twas but Providence protected them, as it did later on that wild night when they were almost stopped along the road to Gravesend. They escaped that too, but narrowly, and made it safely to the coast, where others joined them for the journey over sea to France. An awful voyage that was, too, but through it all the queen made no complaint. A rare, brave woman,' he proclaimed her, 'and 'tis by her courage we do have a king today, for if they had remained in England nothing would have saved them.'

Colonel Graeme, who, Sophia thought, would also have a memory of those troubled days of treachery, agreed. 'It is a stirring tale.'

'Aye, well, I had it straight from the Comte de Lauzon. He was there – he was one of the two men that guided Queen Mary that night out of Whitehall and over the river and down to Gravesend, and he went the whole journey to France with her, too. He saw all that did happen, and kept it stopped up in his memory, till one night I helped him unstop it with wine.'

Captain Ogilvie smiled, in remembrance. 'He told me other tales, as well, but few I'd want to tell a lass.' But he *did* think of one that was not too offensive, and settled himself deeper still in his chair while he told it.

Sophia half-listened, and smiled when she was meant to at the scandalous behaviour of the comte, but her own imagination had been captured so completely by the story he'd just told them of Queen Mary's flight from England into France, that hours later she was thinking of it still.

She stood a long time at the great bow window of the drawing room that afternoon and gazed upon the sea, and wondered how it would have felt to have been cast upon those rough and wintry waves, with no sure knowledge of what future lay ahead for the wee infant son you carried in your arms, and only fears about the safety of your husband in the land that you were leaving, and might never see again. How deep, she wondered, must have been the queen's despair?

She was not aware of anybody entering the room till Colonel Graeme spoke, behind her, in a calming tone that seemed to know her mood and sought to lighten it. 'I would not be surprised to see it snow before this day is out. Those clouds do have the look of it.'

Coming forward, he stood close beside her and let his gaze follow her own, saying nothing at all, only keeping her company.

Sophia looked a moment longer at the ice-grey swells that rose and fell beyond the window, then into the comfortable silence she said, without turning, 'My father always loved the sea.'

He glanced at her with eyes that were astute. 'And ye do not.'

'I do not trust it. It does seem a pleasant sight in summer, but it wears a different face, and one I do not like to look at, in December.'

He nodded. 'Aye,' he said, 'there is no sight so melancholy as the winter sea, for it does tell us we are truly at the ending of the year, and all its days are passed, its days of joy and sorrow that will never come again.' He turned to look at her, and smiled. 'But so the seasons turn, and so they must, by nature's own design. The fields must fall to fallow and the birds must stop their song awhile; the growing things must die and lie in silence under snow, just as the winter sea must wear its face of storms and death and sunken hopes, the face ye so dislike. 'Tis but the way of things, and when ye have grown older, lass, as I have, ye may even come to welcome it.'

'To welcome winter?'

'Aye.' He had not moved, and yet she felt his voice like an embrace, an arm of comfort round her shoulders. 'For if there was no winter, we could never hope for spring.' His eyes were warm on hers, and wise. 'The spring will come.' He paused, then in that same sure tone he said, 'And so will he.'

He meant the king, of course, Sophia told herself. He meant the king would come. And yet she thought she saw a fleeting something in his eyes before they slid away from hers again to make a new assessment of the snow clouds that were drifting ever closer to the shore, and in that instant she could not be sure he had not spoken to her, purposely, of someone else.

They never mentioned Moray. Having learnt his nephew had been well when he had been at Slains, the colonel seemed to be content to rest with that. He had not asked for any details of what Moray did, as though he deemed it not his business. They were very much alike, Sophia thought, these two men – bound by rules of honour that prevented them intruding into someone else's privacy, and made them guard their own.

It was as well, she thought, he did not know her private thoughts this moment. She was thinking of the desperate flight of Mary of Modena, of the fear and faith and hope that must have driven such a queen to brave a winter crossing with her baby son. And now that infant, grown to be a king, stood poised to cast his own spare fortunes on those same cold, unforgiving waves that seemed determined to divide the Stewarts from their hopes, and from their royal destiny.

She tried, as Colonel Graeme had advised, to see the promise in the winter sea, but she could not. The water, greenly grey and barren, stretched away to meet the shoreward rolling clouds whose darkness only spoke of coming storms.

In all the time since she had come to Slains and first learnt of the planned invasion to return the king, Sophia never once had paused to think the plan might fail. Until this moment.

From my window, I could see the breaking waves against the harbour wall. The wind was strong this morning, and the waves were coming high and fast and casting up an angry spray that made a hanging mist to all but hide the curve of snowbound beach. I couldn't see it clearly. Further out, the sea had turned a deeper colour in the shadow of the dark grey-bottomed clouds that were now gathering and blotting out the sun.

It wasn't difficult, while standing here, to feel the way Sophia must have felt. This winter sea was not so different from the one that I had pictured through her memory. Through her eyes.

Nor was it difficult to feel the shade of Colonel Graeme close beside my shoulder. I could feel them everywhere around me, now, the people who had lived at Slains that winter. They were with me all the time, and it was harder to detach myself, to pull away. They pulled me back.

Especially this morning. I had meant to take a break and get some badly needed sleep, but all I'd managed was to make a piece of toast, a cup of coffee. And I hadn't even finished that, and here the voices were again, beginning to get restless.

I could have closed them out, but at the window glass the wind rose to a wail and forced its way around the frame to swirl its cold around me and it breathed, 'Ye have no choice.'

And it was right.

XV

She'd thought to spend an hour in the stables with the horses, but she'd given up that plan when she had happened upon Kirsty standing close against the stable wall with Rory, their heads bent close in earnest conversation. Sophia would not for the world have interrupted such a private moment, so she stopped, and turned away before they saw her. Taking care to keep her footsteps soft so she would not distract the couple, she went round again the long way past the malthouse and the laundry.

It had snowed, as Colonel Graeme had predicted, and the branches of the sleeping trees that showed above the garden wall were frosted thick with white, and further down she saw the thin smoke twisting upwards from the chimneys of the bothy at the bottom of the garden. She had not set eyes on

Billy Wick since Captain Gordon's visit weeks ago, and she had no desire to meet him now, so it was with dismay that she caught sight of his hunched figure standing black against a snowy shrub whose crooked branches arched and reached towards the inland hills as though attempting to escape the fierce winds blowing off the bleak North Sea.

Sophia was about to seek escape herself, and carry on along the laundry wall and round the corner to the kitchen, when another movement from the garden made her pause, and look more closely. Billy Wick was not alone. A second man, much larger and well-wrapped against the cold, a thick wool plaid drawn cloak-like round his head and shoulders, had come now to stand beside the gardener. There was no mistaking who it was – the only question, thought Sophia, was what business Captain Ogilvie could have with Billy Wick.

Whatever it was, they took some few minutes about it; in that time her troubled frown grew still more troubled when the hands of both men moved and some unknown object passed between them.

It was only when the two men parted, disappearing from her view so that she could but guess that Captain Ogilvie was making his way back along the path towards the house, and might at any moment come upon her without notice, that she moved. Her steps were ankle-deep in snow but quick with purpose, and the hands that drew her cloak more tightly round her sought to warm the chill she felt within, as well as from without.

She found the colonel, as she'd hoped she'd find him, in the library. He smiled above the pages of his book as she came in. 'Have ye returned so soon? I would have thought ye'd had enough defeat for the one day.'

Ignoring the chess board, she asked, 'May I speak with you?'

He straightened as though something of her urgency had reached him. 'Aye, of course.'

'Not here,' she told him, knowing Ogilvie would soon be back and often chose this room himself to sit in. She needed someplace private, where they would not risk an interruption. As her fingers met the thick folds of her cloak, she asked on sudden inspiration, 'Will you walk with me?'

'What, now? Outside?'

She nodded.

With his eyebrow lifting on a note of resignation, Colonel Graeme took a last look at the warming fire and closed his book. 'Aye, lass. I'll come and walk with ye. Where to?'

The snow was not so deep along the cliff top, where the wind had blown it inland into low drifts that lay soft and melting from a long day in the sun. It was late afternoon, and shadows tangled thickly with each other on the ground beneath the snowy branches of the trees that edged the flowing stream. The scent of burning wood fires from the chimneys of the cottages smelt homely to Sophia, and the smoke that curled to whiten in the air above the wood appeared to mirror her own misting breath.

They walked between the cottages, and up the windy hill beyond, and down onto the wide fawn-coloured beach. The sand felt firm beneath her feet, not soft and shifting as it had been in the summer, and the dunes were dusted white with snow through which the tufted golden grass still rose to bow and bend before the wind that tossed the waves ashore.

In all that long, broad curve of sand there was no other person to be seen. No other person who could hear them. Yet

Sophia went on walking, looking not for privacy but inspiration.

All the while that they'd been on the path, she had been trying to decide how best to tell him that she thought his friend, the captain, might be more than he appeared. There were no easy words, she knew, for such a thing, and she might not have mentioned it at all if she had not had felt such a strongly warning sense that what was happening had happened once before. She set her mind, and chose to take that for her starting-place, and ventured, 'When your nephew was at Slains, he told me once of his adventures in the company of Simon Fraser.'

Colonel Graeme's eyes sought out her face with sudden interest. 'Did he, now? What did he tell ye of the matter?'

'That the king did send him here with Simon Fraser to enquire how many men might rise if there were a rebellion, and to meet with all the well-affected nobles in the Highlands and in Edinburgh.'

'It was the queen, King Jamie's mother Mary, who did send him, for she does esteem him highly. Did he tell ye that?'

She shook her head.

'Aye, well, he's not a lad to give himself much credit, but 'tis true. In fact, when Fraser did return to France without John it distressed the queen so greatly she said Fraser was a murderer, and did her best to see him thrown in prison. She's a very loyal woman is Queen Mary, and she'll not forget her favourites.'

She had not known that Moray was a favourite of the queen, and it gave her pride, but still she did not wish to be distracted from her purpose, and she would have moved to speak if Colonel Graeme had not said, 'The queen was wrong about the murder, mind. 'Twas only that Fraser had scuttled away like a rat without sending John word of his leaving, so John was left stranded in hiding some months afore he could find a safe passage to France for himself. I'd gone earlier, else I'd have been there to help, for the business was all in the wind then and he was in danger.'

Distracted again, she looked over and echoed, 'You'd gone earlier?'

'Aye,' he said, and then as if it were a well-known fact he added, 'I was here, too, sent with Fraser as John was, by orders from Saint-Germain. Did he not tell ye his uncle came with him?' The answer was plain on her face for he smiled and said, 'No, he'd not say. He's a close man with words, John. A rare one for keeping things secret.' He looked away, toward the rolling sea, and missed the change in her expression. 'Did he tell ye Simon Fraser was a traitor?'

'Yes.'

'A blow to John, that was, for he did hold the man in high regard. I had a sense of it myself when we came over. Something was not right with Fraser from the start. But John...' He paused, and gave a shrug. 'Well, John was younger then and counted Fraser as his friend. He found it very hard.'

Sophia said, 'All men, I think, would be surprised at such betrayal by a friend.'

He caught her tone and turned again as if to question it. 'Ye did not bring me all this way to speak of Fraser, lass. What's on your mind?'

She took a breath. 'I do suspect that Captain Ogilvie might be a spy.'

She'd feared that he might laugh, or even answer her with anger. He did neither; only asked her, 'Why is that?'

And so she told him what she'd seen, and what she thought she'd seen – the little packet that had passed from Captain Ogilvie to Billy Wick. 'I think that it may have been money.'

'Lass.' He gave her an indulgent sideways look.

'The gardener is an evil-minded man, and not well thought of by the other servants. He is not a man to trust. I could not think of any reason Captain Ogilvie might speak with him, except to gain some knowledge of the house and its affairs.' She kept her eyes upon the sand and said, 'I hope I'll not offend you, Colonel Graeme, if I say I find you much like Mr Moray, and I would not wish to see you suffer as he suffered at the hands of someone who does not deserve your friendship.'

There was no sound for a moment but the breaking of the waves against the frozen shore. And then the colonel asked her, 'Do ye worry for my welfare, lass?'

He sounded quite as moved by that as Moray had when he had made a similar discovery, all those months ago. That moment too, Sophia thought, had happened here, on this same beach, but then the blowing wind had been a warmer one and underneath a bluer sky the sea had seemed a place of hope and promise.

'There's no need,' said Colonel Graeme, kindly. 'And ye needn't worry about Ogilvie – he's not like Simon Fraser, and he's served the Stewart kings too long to turn a traitor now.'

She raised her head and saw from looking at his face that he'd dismissed her warning, but the small unquiet voice within her would not rest. 'But even so, you will be careful?'

'Aye, lass. For your sake, since it troubles ye so much, I will be careful.' But he said it in the same way that a naughty child might promise to be good, and there were crinkles at the corners of his eyes that let her know he did not think the matter serious. 'Now, was that the only thing ye had to tell me?'

From his tone she half-believed he had expected something more, but when she gave a nod he seemed to find that satisfactory.

'Well then, let's start back, for I've seen all I want of snow the day, and I can hear a dram of whisky calling from the fireside back at Slains.'

Though she was disappointed she had not convinced him about Ogilvie, she could not help but smile. 'You go,' she told him. 'I would stay a while, and walk along the beach.'

He looked along the sand without enthusiasm. 'If ye have a mind to stay, I'd best stay, too.'

'There is no need.' She tossed his own phrase back at him. 'I will be safe. There was a time when I did walk here nearly every day.'

'Oh, aye?' He seemed to smile, though she could not be sure. 'But ye did tell me that ye did not like the sea in winter.'

'And you told me, if I tried, that I might come to see its virtues.'

'So I did.' This time the smile was unmistakable. 'I'll leave ye to it, then, but see ye do not stay too long out in the cold.'

She gave her promise she would not, and watched him walk away along the sand, his shoulders set so much like Moray's that the likeness caught a little at her heart and made her pull her gaze away, then look again with misting eyes. She was half-glad when she was left alone.

She climbed the dunes and found the place where she and Moray had so often sat and talked, and though the ground was snowy now she sat with legs drawn up beneath her cloak and turned her gaze toward the sea.

It had been weeks since she had been here. In the summer she'd come often, for it was upon these sands that she most strongly felt the bond that yet connected her to Moray. She'd found comfort in the thought that every wave that rolled to shore had lately travelled from the coast of France to spread its foam upon the beach before her, and would then return with the inevitable rhythm of the tides to touch the land where Moray walked. That image, small but vivid, had sustained her through the length of days while she had looked toward the wide horizon for the first glimpse of a swift approaching sail.

But none had come, and when she'd sickened from the bairn within her belly she had not felt well enough to walk so far. Besides, the bairn itself had given her a new kind of connection to the husband who was absent from her arms, if not her heart, and she had not felt such a pressing need to walk among the memories on the shore.

But now she found them here, and waiting for her, and her eyes from habit turned to search the distant line where sea met sky, with apprehension this time more than hope, because she feared what might befall the herald ship from France if it arrived at Slains while Ogilvie was there.

For all that Colonel Graeme had not been convinced, and Ogilvie himself was such a harmless-seeming man, she could not cast aside her feelings of suspicion any more than she could keep from hearing in her mind again the words that Moray had once spoken to her here, among the dunes: *The devil kens the way to charm, when it does suit his purpose...*

It was more than what she'd seen that morning between Ogilvie and Billy Wick. Now that she'd turned her mind toward the possibility, it also struck her that although he'd been at Slains some days the countess had not warmed to him, but kept politely distant. And the instincts of the countess, thought Sophia, rated far above all others in the house.

She looked with doubt towards the cold horizon, and again she heard a voice – not Moray's but the colonel's, telling them: *The time is measured now in days.* And as the sun dropped lower into cloud she knew what she must do.

She did not wish to disappoint the colonel, or bring trouble on his shoulders, but if he would not believe her and take action, someone must. She would approach the countess, tell her what she'd seen, and let the older woman handle things as she saw fit.

Resolved, Sophia stood, and made her way down from the dunes and back along the beach, her steps imprinted in the drifted snow. She saw the footprints left by Colonel Graeme, and the fainter tracks of some small animal – a dog, she thought – reminding her that Moray had once told her not to venture out so far from Slains unless she brought the mastiff.

She could only smile as she remembered his concern, because the beach was so deserted, and the hill that she began to climb beyond the beach so barren, she saw nothing that could possibly endanger her. She'd walked this path a score of times since Moray had departed. She could walk it with her eyes closed, and she'd never had a mishap.

So it struck her strangely that when she was halfway up the hill, she felt a sudden crawling sense along her spine that made her hesitate, and turn to look behind.

Along the curve of beach the waves rolled in with perfect innocence. The dunes were soft with shadow, and deserted. Nothing moved besides the water and the wind along the shore that stirred the grasses. She relaxed. It had been only her imagination, hearing ghosts when none were there.

She smiled a little at her foolishness, and turned again to carry on along the uphill path...and walked straight into Billy Wick.

It seemed to her, as startled as she was, that he'd come out of nowhere, flung by blackest magic on that hill to block her way. He let her back away a step and did not move to hold her, but his smile was worse than any touch. 'And far would ye be going til, my quine, in such a hurry?'

He would feed on fear, she knew, and so she tried to hide her own, the only sign of it the clenching of her hands upon her gown. Chin raised, she told him calmly, 'Let me pass.'

'All in good time.'

No one could see them, where they stood. Not from the cottages, nor even from the high windows of Slains, because the hill's slope cut them off from view. And crying out would be a waste of breath. No one would hear the sound.

She fought her rising panic and tried hard to think. Going back towards the beach would gain her nothing – she could only try to force her way around him, and attempt to run. He might not be expecting that. Nor would he expect her to break round him on the seaward side of the steep path. He'd think that she would try the other way, the inland way, where drifted snow and tufts of coarse grass stretched off softly underfoot, instead of that one narrow strip of ground that broke so treacherously downward to the blackened rocks and icy sea below.

She took a breath, and took a chance.

She had been right. Her lunge toward the seaward side surprised him, and she gained a precious lead of seconds, and she might have even got the whole way round him had he not recovered, snapping round with snake-like speed to grasp her arm as she sped by. Her own momentum, stopped short by the sudden action, threw them both off balance, and Sophia landed hard upon the frozen ground, so hard she felt the impact in her teeth and saw lights bursting in her vision.

Billy Wick fell harder still on top of her and held her pinned, his face no longer smiling. They were lying full across the path now, and Sophia knew that though the gardener was a small man, he was strong, and she might not be able to find strength enough herself to fight him. 'Now, fit wye would ye dee that, quine? I only want the same thing as ye gied tae Mr Moray.'

Staring coldly up at him she said, 'You're mad.' But fear had taken full hold of her now, and Billy Wick could see it.

'Aye, ye'll gie it tae me gladly, quine, or else I'll have tae tell old Captain Ogilvie aboot the things ye said tae Mr Moray in ma garden on the nicht that he was leavin. Touching scene, it was.' His eyes held the hard satisfaction of a beast that knows its prey is caught, and means to toy with it. 'I fairly wept myself tae hear it. I've nae doot Captain Ogilvie would find it touching, too. He pays me siller fer such tales, and those he works fer have lang wantit tae have Moray in their hands.'

The wind blew sharply cold around Sophia's face, and in her ringing head she could hear Moray's voice repeating: *He must never learn that you are mine...*

He had been speaking of the duke, and not of Ogilvie, but she knew that the danger was the same, for Billy Wick had all but told her now that Ogilvie was in the pay of Queen Anne's court, and if they learnt that she was Moray's wife they would make use of her in any way they could to draw him out. She did not care for her own life – if they would threaten her alone she'd suffer it, for his sake. But it would not be her alone. There was the child. His child.

She felt Wick's searching hands upon her body and she shrank from them, and turned her face against the snowy ground with eyes tight shut.

'Ye see,' he said, his rank breath hot against her face, 'ye have nae choice.'

He shifted closer, pressing heavily upon her. And then suddenly he wasn't there at all. Some violent force had hauled him up and off her body in one movement.

'Oh, I think she does,' said Colonel Graeme's voice, as cold and dangerous as thinly frozen ice.

Sophia, scarcely able to believe it, let her eyes come open just enough to brave a look. She saw the colonel standing close behind the gardener, looking as he must have looked in battle, with his face no longer kind but deadly calm. He'd twisted Billy Wick's one arm back in a painful hold, and had his own arm wrapped around the gardener's neck. She saw in Wick's own eyes the fear that he had often fed upon from others as the colonel jerked Wick back again and brought his hard mouth close beside Wick's ear and said, 'I think she has a choice.'

And then Sophia saw the colonel's hand and arm, in one swift motion, sweep around and catch Wick's jaw, and from the sound that followed and the way the gardener slumped she knew his neck was broken. Colonel Graeme cast Wick's body to the side disdainfully. 'Now get ye to the devil,' he advised the corpse, and kicked it with his booted foot to send it tumbling over down the steep slope of the hillside to the rocks and sea below.

Stunned, Sophia watched him. She had never seen a man do murder. Not like this. This was, she thought, how Moray must himself be on the battlefield – he too must wear that calm face that had set aside its conscience, and his eyes would, like his uncle's, hold a fire she did not recognise. It shook her to observe the transformation.

She was staring at him, wordless, when the colonel's features altered once again. The soldier's face became the face she knew, and all the fury melted from his eyes as he bent down to her. Concerned, he asked her, 'Are ye hurt?'

She could not frame the words to answer, shaken still by Wick's attack, by what she had just witnessed. But she slowly shook her head. The pain of that small action made her wince.

The colonel placed a gentle hand beneath her, fingers warm against her hair, and then withdrew it. She could see his palm was wet with blood. Her blood.

'Christ.' He looked around and seemed to be deciding something, thinking quickly. Then he leant in close again. 'I need ye to be brave now for me, lass. We need to get ye home, and if I could I'd carry ye, but then the people that we pass would ken that ye've been hurt. There would be questions. Do ye follow what I'm saying?' Just to make sure that she understood, he spelt it out more plainly. 'No one saw this. No one kens Wick's dead. And when they find his body, if they do, they will believe he fell by accident. And Ogilvie,' he told her, 'will believe it, too.'

He held her gaze a moment, making sure she took his meaning, and she knew that he had overheard Wick's threat to her. For that at least, she thought, she could be grateful – Billy Wick had done what she could not. He'd given proof to Colonel Graeme by his words that Ogilvie, despite his years of service to King James, had come among them as a traitor and a spy.

She knew that Captain Ogilvie must never know the truth of what had happened on this hill, or he would know that he himself had been discovered.

Looking up at Colonel Graeme, she breathed deep and found her voice again to tell him, 'I can walk.'

He helped her stand, and held her steady on her feet, and with the hands that had so lately killed a man he gently drew the soft hood of her cloak up so it hid the blood upon her hair. 'Brave lass,' he called her, with a trace of pride, and placed her hand upon his arm. 'Go slowly now, and keep your head up. 'Tis not far to go.'

That was a lie, and well he knew it, for the walk was not a short one, but she managed it, and Ogilvie himself would not have known that she was injured, had he seen them coming up the path to Slains. She did not see him anywhere, but she could not be certain he was not against some window, looking out, and so she kept her head held high as Colonel Graeme had advised her, though the throbbing in it pained her and she felt at any moment she might faint.

The chills of shock had settled well upon her and her limbs were trembling, but the colonel's strong arm underneath her hand was a support. They had not far to go now, to the great front steps.

'How did you know?' she asked him, and he turned toward her, with an eyebrow lifting.

'What, that ye had need of help? I kent when I came back here and I saw the gardener setting out. I saw the way he marked that I was on my own, and I could see he had a mind for mischief. So I came,' he said, 'to fetch ye home.'

A few more paces, and he'd have accomplished that. She fought the rising blackness, and looked up at him in hopes that he could see beyond the pain that filled her eyes and know her gratitude. The words took effort. 'Colonel?'

'Aye, lass?'

'Thank you.'

For an answer Colonel Graeme brought his free hand over and for one brief moment squeezed her fingers where they lay upon his arm, but they had reached the entry now and no more could be said, for Captain Ogilvie himself was waiting just inside the door, to bid them welcome.

'Ye've been walking, so I see.'

'Aye,' Colonel Graeme answered smoothly, 'but I fear I've worn the wee lass out, and given her a headache from the cold.'

She forced a smile and took the cue. 'I can assure you, Colonel, it is nothing that a short rest will not remedy.'

'Och, there, ye see?' said Ogilvie. 'The lassies these days, Graeme, are a stronger breed than those we lost our hearts to.'

'Aye,' said Colonel Graeme. 'That they are.' His eyes were warm upon Sophia's. 'Take your rest, then. I've no doubt Captain Ogilvie can take your place for once across the chessboard.' And he raised an eyebrow once again to look a challenge at the older man and ask him lightly, 'Can I tempt ye to a game?'

And Captain Ogilvie, not knowing that the rules had changed, accepted.

'Right.' The colonel clapped a hand upon his old friend's shoulder, smiling. 'Let me see the lass upstairs and find her maid to tend her headache, first. And then the two of us,' he said, 'can play.'

* * *

Dr Weir was pleased. 'Well, that's much better.' He re-wrapped the bandage round my ankle, satisfied. 'Much better. You took my advice and stayed off it, I see.'

Something in the way he said that prompted me to ask, 'You didn't think I would?'

Behind the rounded spectacles his sage eyes briefly twinkled. 'Let's just say you strike me as the sort of lass who likes to pipe her own tune.'

I smiled, because no one had so neatly put their finger on that aspect of my character since my kindergarten teacher in her end-of-year report had written: 'Carrie listens to the ideas of other children, but likes her own ideas best'. I didn't share that with the doctor, only told him, 'Yes, well, every now and then I take advice. And it hasn't been hard to stay off it. The book has been keeping me busy.'

'That's good. Are you still needing details on spies? Because I did some reading, and found you a good one. You mind how we were talking about Harley?'

Robert Harley, Earl of Oxford and a man of power in the government of England, who was also Queen Anne's spymaster. I nodded.

Dr Weir said, 'I was reading up on Harley, with a mind to finding out a wee bit more about Defoe for you, and I came across some letters from *another* agent Harley sent to Scotland at the time, and who was actually at Slains.'

The feeling that was pricking at my shoulder blades was not unlike the feeling that I got when I sensed something sneaking up on me. And so it didn't come as a complete surprise when Dr Weir said, 'Ogilvie, his name was. Captain Ogilvie.' He reached inside his pocket and produced some folded notepaper. 'I copied out the letters...well, they're excerpts, really. Not much there. But still, I thought the name might be of use.'

I thanked him. Took the papers, and unfolded them to read the lines in silence. They began with an account of Captain Ogilvie's brief visits with the nobles of the north of Scotland and what he had learnt from them, then on to Slains, where the Countess of Erroll had received him with suspicion, and where luckily for Ogilvie there'd been a certain 'Colonel Graeme', of whom Ogilvie had written: 'He and I served formerly in France together, and we were long bed fellows.'

Dr Weir, watching my face while I read, asked, 'What is it?'

I lowered the papers. 'You've read these?'

'I have.'

With a faint smile I rose to my feet and crossed over to sort through the short stack of new printed pages beside my computer. Picking up the last three chapters I had written, I turned back and held them out in invitation. 'Then,' I told the doctor, 'you should have a look at *these*.'

He did. And when he'd finished, he looked over at me, wordlessly.

'I know,' I said. 'That's what I mean by proof, though. When I wrote that, I had no idea that there even was a Captain Ogilvie, or Colonel Graeme. Characters just come to me like that sometimes. They just show up. In any other book I would have said that my subconscious had invented them to serve the plot. But in this book, it doesn't seem like I'm inventing anything. And now you give me this' – I held the copied letters up – 'and I have proof both men are real, and that they truly were at Slains.'

He was still taking it all in, I knew. 'Remarkable,' he said, and scanned my chapters for a second time. 'It's too bad

Captain Ogilvie makes no mention of your Sophia in his letters to Harley.'

'I doubt he would have thought she was important.'

Dr Weir's eyes twinkled knowingly again as he passed back my chapters. 'Then,' he said, 'he would have made a very grave mistake.'

XVI

The countess and the colonel were both sitting by Sophia's bed when she awoke. She heard them talking.

''Tis the safest course to take,' said Colonel Graeme, 'for ye cannot have him here when Fleming's ship arrives.'

'No, that would be disastrous.' In the soft light of the early morning no lines marked the fine face of the countess. She looked youthful, and determined. 'No, I do agree he must be led away. But Patrick, let some other person do it. Let my son take on that burden – he is willing, and we would not see you put yourself at risk.'

'Your son will be more needed here, with what is coming. And I doubt that Captain Ogilvie would follow him as he would me. We are old friends.' The words were edged with bitter cynicism. 'I do have his trust.'

The countess waited for a moment before saying, 'I am sorry.'

'So am I. He was the very best of men, once.'

'He must need the money badly.' It was very like the countess, thought Sophia, to have sympathy enough to seek excuses for a traitor. Colonel Graeme did not share her generosity.

'A man, when he has fallen on hard times, should seek his friends,' he said. 'Not sell them to his enemies.'

The countess could not argue that. She only said, 'Take care he does not sell you, too.'

'Och, not to worry. He'll not have the chance. I'll not be staying once I get him there. Ye ken yourself, your Ladyship, I'm canny as a fox, and there'll be holes enough in Edinburgh to hide me.'

On the bed, Sophia came to full awareness now and moved against the pillow, and that movement brought the heads of both the countess and the colonel round. She thought she read relief in both their faces.

'There,' the countess said. 'We've woken her. I warned you that we would. How do you feel, my dear?'

Sophia's head still hurt her, but the dizziness was gone, and though her body ached in places and her limbs felt stiff and bruised, she could not bring herself to make any complaint. 'I am well, thank you.'

A flash of admiration briefly lit the older woman's eyes. 'Brave girl.' She gave Sophia's arm a pat. 'I will let Kirsty know you are awake, so she can bring your morning draught.'

It was a measure of how highly she regarded Colonel Graeme that she left him in the room without a chaperone, although from how he sat, with booted ankles crossed upon the side rail of the bed, his lean frame firmly rooted in the rush-backed chair, Sophia doubted any force would have the power to shift him.

She looked at him and asked, 'The countess…did you tell her…?'

'Aye. She kens the whole of it.' His smile was faint behind the beard. 'I think if I'd not sent the gardener on his way already to the devil, she'd have had it done herself last night.'

'And Captain Ogilvie?'

'I've managed to persuade him to accompany me to Edinburgh. I've led him to believe there is some matter in the wind down there that does deserve his interest, and that he, as a supporter of King James, will want to witness. 'Twas like saying to a wolf there is a field of lambs yet further on, if ye've the wish to feast.'

'So you are leaving.' Having said the words out loud, she felt a sadness she could not express, and did not want to think of life at Slains without this man who had become to her a father and a friend.

He did not answer her, but only watched her face a moment, silently. And then he said, 'Sophia, there is something I would ask ye.' He had never called her by her Christian name, and from that fact she knew that what he meant to ask was serious. ''Tis none of my affair. But on that hill, when Wick was...' Breaking off, as though he did not think it was a gentlemanly thing to speak of Billy Wick's intentions, he said only, 'He made mention of my nephew. And of you.'

She met his gaze, and did not look away. 'He overheard us speaking in the garden.'

'Aye, I gathered that.' He paused, and sifted words to find the right ones. 'As I said, I've no right asking, but I wondered...'

'You were wondering what Mr Wick had overheard that night that could so interest Captain Ogilvie?'

Apparently relieved by her directness, he said, 'Aye, that was the size of it.'

Sophia raised a hand to feel the slender chain around her

neck. Slowly drawing out the ring from where it lay concealed beneath her bodice, she held it up to show him. There was no need to say anything, to make an explanation. It was plain from Colonel Graeme's own reaction that the sight of Moray's ring around her neck told him enough.

His smile was slow. 'I must confess, I did suspect ye would have caught his eye. We're not so different, John and I, and were I his age I'd have done no less than try to win ye for myself. But it does please me, lass, to see he did conduct himself with honour. Will ye marry?'

'I did marry him by handfast, soon before he did return to France.' She closed her hand around the ring and felt its warmth. 'The countess does not know. John thought it best to keep the matter secret till he could return. But,' she went on, not wanting him to think that she'd betrayed his nephew's wishes, 'he did say that I might show his kin.'

'Well, I should hope so.' He pretended indignation with the small lift of an eyebrow, though his eyes and words were serious. 'Ye'll find there's not a one of us who would not walk through fire to keep ye safe for John, lass. Ye would only have to ask.'

Moray had told her so himself, but she was deeply touched to hear it said aloud by his own kinsman. 'You have walked through fire for me already, Colonel,' she said quietly.

'Aye, so I have. And so I would again,' he promised, 'even if ye did not wear that bit of silver round your neck.'

She knew he meant it. Sudden dampness pricked behind her eyes, and since he'd always praised her courage she would not have shown him weakness, so she bent her head and made a show of concentration on concealing Moray's ring again, lest other eyes should see it. But she did not trust her voice, and did not know the way to let the colonel know how fond she had become of him, and how much she would miss him when he'd gone.

He seemed to know without her saying, for he cleared his throat and stood. 'Now, come and send your Uncle Patrick on his way, lass, with a smile, if ye can manage it.'

She managed it, and though the smile was not her surest one, it served its purpose, for he took her hand in his and lightly raised it to his lips. 'I've no doubt I'll be seeing ye again afore too long.'

'I hope so.'

'Hope,' he told her, 'rarely enters into it. 'Tis action moves the world. If ye mind nothing else I've taught ye of the game of chess, mind that: ye cannot leave your men to stand unmoving on the board and hope to win. A soldier must first step upon the battlefield if he does mean to cross it.'

With her hand still lying in his own, she said, 'But I am not a soldier.'

'Are ye not?' He bent to kiss her forehead briefly, warm, then straightened and told her, 'Well, even a pawn plays a part in defending the king.'

Once again she could feel that same tug of emotion, the longing to thank him for all he had done. 'Colonel Graeme?'

'Aye, lass?'

But the words, as before, failed to come. 'Please be careful.'

'Och, no need to worry.' He gave her hand back to her, showing that flash of a smile that was so like his nephew's. 'I've lived all my years in the army surrounded by officers, lass, and I've learnt to look out for a knife in the back.'

From the doorway the countess said laughingly, 'Patrick! That is an impolitic statement to make.'

Unrepentant, he shrugged. ''Tis impolitic thinking that keeps me ahead of the devil, your Ladyship.' Casting a glance out the window, he noted the position of the sun above the sea and added, 'And if I am to stay so, I must be away.'

Sophia watched unhappily as he bade them farewell and left the room, and after he had gone she kept her face turned still towards the door a moment so the countess would not see her eyes.

The countess, having settled once again into her chair beside the bed, said, 'Colonel Graeme is a good man.'

'Yes.'

'He does remind me greatly of his nephew,' said the countess lightly. 'Do you not agree?'

Sophia nodded, cautious. 'They are very much alike, yes.'

For a moment there was silence, broken only by the rattle of the window in the wind, and by the ever-present rush of waves against the line of rocks below the tower. When the countess spoke again her voice was quiet, and the words were simple: 'Does he know?'

Sophia turned her head upon the pillow, her confusion so apparent that the countess softened even more and asked the question over in a phrasing that was plainer still: 'Does Mr Moray know that you are carrying his child?'

Sophia felt as though her heart had stopped. She'd been so careful that it seemed impossible the countess could have come to guess the truth. And then she realised, 'Kirsty told you.' In dismay, she would have looked away again had not the countess laid a hand upon her own.

'My dear child, no. No one did tell me. You forget I am myself a mother.' There was dryness in her tone. 'You must ask my own sons and daughters how they fared, when they did try to keep a secret from me.'

'How long have you known?' Sophia sagged against the pillows.

'Some few months now.'

'But you have said nothing.'

'No. I did trust that you would come to me, in time.'

Sophia cast her gaze down. 'I had hoped, you see, that John...that he...'

'He does not know?'

She shook her head, intending to explain and yet not knowing how to start.

The countess gave her hand a reassuring squeeze. 'My dear, you must not worry. Mr Moray is an honourable man.'

'He is much more than that.' Sophia raised her head and drew a breath. 'He is my husband.'

As the countess stared, surprised, Sophia drew the heavy silver ring upon its chain out for a second time and held it up as evidence. And once again it seemed her heart paused while awaiting the reaction of the woman whose opinion mattered more to her than almost any other's.

Moments passed. And when Sophia felt she could no longer bear the silent judgement any more, the countess said at last, 'I see there are some secrets, yet, that can escape my notice.' She was looking at Sophia's face as though she had not seen it before now. 'I would not have imagined you would think to marry without asking my permission.'

Guiltily, Sophia tried to think of an apology. She would have spoken, but the countess had not finished. Reaching out a hand, she brushed Sophia's hair back from her forehead, motherly. 'When you did come to Slains, I knew that you had suffered from those years within your uncle's house. It is a dreadful thing to rob a child of its innocence. 'Tis why I am so glad to see, whatever else he did to you, he did not kill your spirit, nor your independent mind.' She smiled. 'And if you would defy your wiser elders, you could do much worse than marry Mr Moray. In my younger days, I would myself have thought him quite a prize.'

It was Sophia's turn to stare, astonished, with no thought of how to make reply. She had expected punishment, and here she was receiving benediction.

'But,' the countess said, 'there is a place for independence, and a time when you must know enough to put it to one side.' Her tone was kindly, but decisive. 'It is no easy thing to birth a child. You are too young, my dear, to bear this burden by yourself.'

Sophia knew that there could be no arguing with those determined eyes. Nor was she in a mood to argue, for in truth the great relief she felt at knowing that the countess knew the whole of it at last had left her peaceful in her mind, with all her fears about the next few months already fading as though they had never been.

The child within her kicked with strength, as if to prove it had not suffered any harm from Wick's attack, and gathering some of that same strength to her own self, Sophia faced the countess. 'All I wish, now, is to keep my child from harm.'

'And so you will,' the countess promised. 'But you cannot do this on your own.' Her set expression made it clear she had been thinking on this long, and knew already what to do. 'You will need help.'

Chapter Sixteen

Jane set the pages to the side and said, 'Well?'

Looking up from my cake plate I asked her, 'Well what?'

'I'm intrigued, now. What happens?'

I admitted that I wasn't sure yet. 'But of course in those days you just couldn't have a baby on your own, with no one noticing. And since they'll be wanting to keep Sophia's marriage to Moray a secret, I think that the countess is going to send her away, somewhere safe.'

'And where would that be?'

'I don't know. I'll have to see.'

'But if the baby's due in...' She was silent for a moment, counting months. 'In March, then won't that mean Sophia's not at Slains for the invasion?'

'I don't know.' I licked the icing from my fork.

She shook her head. 'How *can* you write a book without a proper plan?'

'I've always done it like this.'

'Not exactly like this,' Jane corrected me, running her thumb down the side of the pages to straighten the stack. 'I've never seen you write a book this fast.'

'It must be the Scottish sea air. I'm inspired.'

I kept my tone carefully light. Jane only knew about the one episode of the castle floor plans, and she'd already put that down to overwork, and I had let her go on thinking that was all that it had been. It was a strange thing, but I found it much easier talking about what was happening to me with someone I barely knew, like Dr Weir, than with someone I felt closer to, like Jane. Or Graham. Maybe it just mattered more to me that they not think that I was crazy.

And I'd known Jane long enough to know there was no place for unexplainable phenomena within her ordered life.

She told me, 'If you're so inspired here, you ought to move to Scotland. Buy a little house. There's one the next street over, coming up for sale.'

Jane's husband Alan had been clearing dishes from the table where we'd eaten lunch, but now he felt the need to interject, 'She wouldn't want to live the next street over, Janie.'

'Why not?'

'Because you'd hardly make yourself invisible, would you? You'd be over there the whole time, nagging. "How's it going with the book?" and "When will it be finished?"'

'I would not.' Jane tried her level best to look indignant.

'Besides which, Carrie needs her privacy.'

'She'd have it.'

'Oh, aye?' Alan gave his wife a sideways glance. 'You want her to believe that, after all the grief you've given her this morning?'

'I only said she should have let us fetch her and not come by taxi.'

With a smile, I interjected, 'All that way. It's what, ten minutes?'

'That,' she said, 'is not the point.'

'The point is,' Alan said, 'you thought she'd bring a man.' To me, he added, 'That was why she made the cake. She'd never bother with a cake for only us.'

Jane couldn't quite manage to look truly offended with Alan. 'I wouldn't hold your breath waiting for another one if this is all the thanks I get.' Shifting position, she sent him the same sort of withering glance she might use on a bothersome publisher. 'Anyway, when I talked to Carrie last she said that she *might* bring a man.'

'I did?'

'You said you'd let me know.' She gave a shrug as though the wording didn't matter. 'It's the same thing. I just wanted to be welcoming, in case he came.'

Her husband rolled his eyes at me in silence, and I smiled. Jane missed the interchange, because at that same moment baby Jack, upstairs, let out a sudden wail to let us know he had awoken from his nap, and by the time he had been brought downstairs the focus of attention had been shifted on to him.

He was a lovely baby, bright and interested in everything, with Jane's blue eyes and reddish hair and happy, fearless nature. 'They're remarkable things, babies,' Jane told me. 'Such little things, and yet once they come into your life they just change it completely. Take over.'

Which led us back to talking of my character, Sophia, and of how her life would change once her child came.

'I don't know that I'm actually going to write a scene about the birth itself,' I said. 'It isn't something I've experienced.'

'You're wise.' Jane's voice was dry. 'Speaking for myself, I can't think anyone who *has* gone through it really wants to read about it.' Giving little Jack a hug, she said, 'The end result's all right, but I don't need reminding of the process, thank you all the same.'

I did convince her, though, to talk a little bit about it so I'd have the knowledge there in case I needed it. And by the time we'd finished talking it was nearly two o'clock, and time for me to leave.

I called another taxi, over Jane's objections.

'I can drive you,' was her protest, as she walked me to the door and watched me tuck the story pages back into my briefcase. It was an oversized case, built to carry my laptop computer and a couple of changes of clothes. Jane wouldn't have missed that, I knew, but I'd already thought up a good explanation.

It was tricky telling lies to Jane; she had such good antennae that you couldn't get much past her. I had always found it easier to start with something like the truth.

I said, 'But I'm not going home. I'm going down to Aberdeen. I need to do some research for the book. Depending on how long it takes to find what I'm after, I might just stay over and come back tomorrow.'

She seemed to accept that. She waited in the front hall with me till the taxi came, then said, 'Hang on a minute, will you?' and went back into the kitchen and returned with something in a plastic square container. 'Here, take this.'

'What is it?'

'It isn't for you. It's for him.'

'For whom?'

'You'll lose your taxi,' was her warning, as she ran me down the steps and to the waiting cab. She held the door and saw me safely settled in the back before she said, with innocence, 'You *did* say that he came from Aberdeen?'

She'd nailed me and she knew it, but I made a final sinking effort. 'Who?'

'The man who took you walking on the coast path. You did say he was a lecturer, in Aberdeen – in history, am I right?' Her smile was just this side of being smug. She nodded at the sealed container. 'See he gets his cake.'

And then she closed the door before I could react, and waved me off while I reflected on the great success she might have had if she had gone to work as a detective. Any criminal, I knew, would not have stood a chance, with Jane.

The Victorian end-of-terrace town house had been built, like most of Aberdeen, with granite. Not the red granite of Slains, but a granite of warm brownish grey that gave all of the houses along Graham's road a strong look of dependable permanence. A holly hedge lined the short walkway that led to the front steps. His blue-painted door had a polished brass knocker that bore not the head of a lion but that of the bard Robert Burns, but I didn't get to use it. When the taxi door had slammed behind me Angus had begun to bark, and by the time I'd reached the steps the front door had already opened.

Graham, looking as dependably permanent as the stone-built house itself in a well-worn black sweater and jeans, smiled a welcome. 'You found it all right, then?'

'No problem at all.'

He took the briefcase from my hand and looked a question at the plastic square container, which had sparked some new excited sniffing interest from the dog.

'It's cake,' I said. 'For you.'

'For me?'

'Don't ask.'

He didn't. Stepping back to let me in, he swung the door shut at our backs and bent to greet me with a kiss. It hit me with a sudden strangeness just how much I'd missed him – missed the comfort of his being there; his undemanding presence. And his touch.

He raised his head. 'Hello.'

'Hello.'

'Come in. I'll show you round.'

He'd only bought the house the year before, he told me, and it was in places still a work in progress. The front rooms, with their high bright windows and lovely corniced ceilings, sat half-empty and stripped of their wallpaper, waiting for paint. And upstairs only one of the bedrooms – his own – had been finished, in quiet greens, restful and masculine. The other upstairs rooms, besides the bath, were undecided. It was almost as if he was wearing the house like a new suit of clothes that still needed adjusting – too large in some places, confining in others. Except for downstairs, at the back of the house. There, it was all Graham. Everything fit.

He'd remodelled the kitchen, keeping its Victorian charm while allowing for modern functionality, and knocking out the back wall to add on a glass conservatory that allowed the sunlight to slant in across the wide plank floor. Stuart had said Graham could cook, and I got some sense of this myself from standing in his kitchen, seeing how he had his things arranged. Everything, from the checked tea towel drying on the oven door to the placement of pots and appliances gave the impression of regular, competent use.

And the way Angus flung himself down with a thump and

a sigh on the warm sunlit floor of the conservatory with its unpretentious furniture – a solid low-backed sofa and a faded chair with footstool and a stack of books beside it that rose high enough to almost be a table – told me this, too, was a favourite and familiar spot.

I could understand that. If this had been my house, I'd have found it hard to shift myself from here as well, with the sunshine and the view out to the tidy small back garden, where a wooden feeder hung from one bare tree branch for the birds. And there was warmth here from the kitchen, and the comfort of companionship, with Graham banging whistling round the cupboards while he put the kettle on and got the mugs and things for tea.

It surprised even me how seductive I found the whole set up; how easily my mind adapted to the thought of living here, with Graham. I hadn't lived with anyone since leaving home. I'd always liked my private space. But standing now and watching him, it struck me this was something I could stand and watch repeatedly. Forever.

It was not a feeling that I'd had before, and so I didn't know exactly what to do with it. This winter was becoming more and more a time of firsts for me.

'Good cake,' said Graham, testing it while waiting for the kettle. Holding the plastic container in one hand, he offered me the fork. 'D'ye want some?'

'No, thanks. I had two pieces at lunch.'

'And how did that go, your lunch?'

'Oh, I had a good time. I always do, with Jane. We talked about the book a lot.'

He glanced towards my briefcase, which he'd set beside the sofa. 'You did remember to bring your computer?'

'I didn't think you'd let me come otherwise.' When we'd talked on the phone he'd reminded me several times not to forget it.

'Aye, well, you can laugh, but you'll thank me when you're struck by sudden inspiration in the middle of the night, and need to work.'

'Yes, Dad.'

'I'm serious.'

'You think that I'll be struck by sudden inspiration, do you?'

Leaning on the worktop with his piece of cake in hand he flashed a faintly wicked smile and said, 'I mean to do my best.'

The room was strange. I didn't recognise the placement of the windows or the walls when I first woke, and there was little light to see by. For a moment I lay blinking in confusion, till I felt the solid warmth against my back and felt the rhythmic rise and fall of Graham's breathing and I knew then where I was.

I closed my eyes, contented, wanting nothing more than just to stay there, with his arm wrapped round me and his head so close behind mine on the pillow that his breath moved through my hair. I felt as I'd felt earlier, that moment in the kitchen when I'd watched him making tea – that I could live this scene repeatedly and never learn to tire of it.

But even as that drowsy realisation slumbered through my mind, another scene began to stir and shape itself and nudge me into wakefulness. I fought it, but it fought me back, and in the end I sighed, resigned, and gently lifting Graham's arm slipped shivering from the blankets, dressed, and went downstairs.

There was no sunlight now in the conservatory kitchen, but the moon cast shadows of its own across the floor where I had left my briefcase. I was cold. Hanging with the jackets on the coat pegs by the back door to the garden was a heavy navy rugby shirt with stripes of red and gold, faded and looking as though it had been through the wars. But it looked warm as well, and I shrugged myself into it, pushing the long sleeves right up to my elbows.

Angus, on the sofa, raised his head and gave his tail a thump of welcome as I crossed to sit beside him, then he rolled and held his four feet in the air so I could give his chest a scratch. I did, but absently, and Angus seemed to know what single-minded concentration looked like when he saw it, for he yawned and rolled again to curl himself against my side, his nose and one front paw tucked in the folds of Graham's rugby jersey, and he fell asleep as I began to write.

XVII

Sophia moved with care upon the bed so she would not disturb the baby's sleep. The feel of that small body nestled warm against her own was still an unexpected joy so sharply new it clutched her heart sometimes and stole her breath with wonder. It had been three weeks since the birth, and yet each time she looked upon her daughter's face the beauty of it blinded her to all else in the room. And she *was* beautiful, the baby named for Moray's sister and Sophia's: Anna. When the time came they would have her christened properly, as Anna Mary Moray, but for now the baby seemed content to be plain Anna, with her tiny perfect hands and feet, her soft brown hair, and eyes that were already changing colour to the green-grey of the winter sea.

Each time Sophia met those eyes she thought of Colonel Graeme standing next to her beside the great bow window of the drawing room at Slains, and saying one day she might come to see the promise of the sea in winter, and she thought perhaps he had been right, for in her daughter's infant eyes she saw the hope of new life breaking from the depths of this hard season that had held the world so long in frost and cold despair, a life that brought the word of coming spring.

For surely spring, Sophia thought, would reach them soonest here. They were far south of Slains, the countess having thought it best to send them where the baby could be born in safety, shielded from unwelcome eyes. She'd called upon the Malcolms, an obliging couple who had often served the Earls of Erroll and were loyal to the family. They lived modestly, close by the Firth of Edinburgh, that broad and busy tidal river leading from the open sea, and every day upon the road that passed the house Sophia heard the wheels of coaches passing by, and travellers on horseback heading to and from the royal town.

Her own slow journey south had been a hard one, coming down by coach with Kirsty in the days just after Christmas. Several times the wheels had foundered in the deeply rutted mud and stuck so fast that it had taken both the coachman and the footman hours to free them, and in one place they had tried to go around the mud and nearly overturned. Sophia, worried for the safety of the baby, had been glad to feel the strong kicks in her belly that had seemed to come in protest of the roughness of such treatment. She'd been gladder still to reach the Malcolm's house, and find both Mrs Malcolm and her husband kind and warm and welcoming.

They had asked no questions. To their neighbours, they'd explained she was a cousin from the north whose husband, called away by sudden business, had desired that she come there so she might be with family for the birthing of the child. Sophia did not know if this was how the countess had explained the situation to them, or if they had made the story up themselves. It did not matter. She was safe, and so was Anna, and when Moray came he'd find them here and waiting for him.

At her side the baby yawned and stirred and, sleeping still, pressed close in search of comfort, one hand flinging out and upward till the tiny fingers met the silver ring upon its chain around Sophia's neck, and clasped it with a fierce possessive grip. She liked to sleep like that, with one hand round the ring and one hand tightly clasped around Sophia's hair, as though she would hold both her parents close.

Sophia softly stroked her daughter's curls and watched her while she slept. She had not ceased to marvel at the fact that, while her love for Moray filled her heart as it had done before, her heart had somehow grown and changed its shape to hold this new love, too – this love that she had never felt, for someone who was more completely hers than anybody else had ever been.

She did not know how long she lay like that, in stillness, hearing nothing but the rapid and contented sound of Anna's breathing. But of a sudden she became aware a horse had stopped outside. She heard the restless dance of hooves, and then a knock against the outside door, and voices – Mr Malcolm's speaking with excitement, and another that she recognised.

Sophia gently lifted little Anna to her cradle, dressed in haste and crossed the room to waken Kirsty. 'Rory's come.'

The look in Kirsty's waking eyes was wonderful to see.

Sophia knew, when she came out and first saw Rory's face, that he had brought them happy news. Mr Malcolm was already fastening his cloak, his hat in hand, and making ready to be gone, no doubt to carry out whatever orders he had just been handed from the countess and the earl. And Mrs Malcolm, beaming, clasped her hands and turned towards Sophia. 'Oh, that I should live to see this day!'

Sophia looked at Rory. 'Has it then begun?'

'Aye. Mr Fleming has just come ashore to Slains, as Colonel Graeme said he would, with news the king does sail from Dunkirk, and will shortly be in Scotland.'

'He may be even now upon the seas,' said Mr Malcolm, as he pushed his hat down firmly on his wigged head. 'I must go and find him pilots who can meet his ships and guide them up the Firth.'

The Firth. Sophia's heart leapt with excitement at the thought the ships would pass so close by them.

It made good sense, of course, for young King James to find his way as quickly as was possible to Edinburgh and claim his throne, for few would there oppose him. From the talk she had been listening to these past months, Sophia knew the few troops that remained within the town were ill-equipped and likely to come over to the king by their own choice. And in the town's great castle lay an added prize: the 'Equivalent' money – the price of the nation, some called it – sent up by the English last summer as part of the terms of the Union. It would be such sweet irony if James could drive the English out of Scotland by using their own money to supply his Scottish forces.

More supplies, Sophia knew, would come from Angus, where a fleet of Dutch ships lately wrecked upon the coast sat full of cannon, powder, arms and more great sums of money. And the English army, most of which was still engaged in fighting on the continent, would be too weak, too unprepared, to offer opposition. By the time they'd reinforced themselves and started marching north, it would be over – James the VIII would be upon his throne in Edinburgh, and Scotland would once more be free.

Mr Malcolm took his hurried leave of them, and said to Rory, 'If ye carry any other letters for the people of these parts, my wife kens all our neighbours well, and can direct ye.'

Rory thanked him. 'But I have no other letters to deliver, only yours. And one for Mrs Milton, here.' He nodded at Sophia as he used the false name meant to guard her honour and identity while she was with the Malcolms.

Mr Malcolm, having no great interest at the moment in his guest's affairs, departed, and Sophia, holding back her hope, asked Rory, 'May I see the letter?'

'Aye. 'Tis from the countess.'

She had known it would not be from Moray, for he'd told her it would not be safe for him to write, but still she felt a twist of disappointment as she took the letter in her hand. She salved it with the knowledge that it would not be much longer now till Moray, as he'd promised, would be home. There would be no more separations.

She suddenly became aware of Kirsty, standing at her side in silent misery while Rory, his deliveries made, prepared to go. Sophia saw him glance at Kirsty once, and in that single look she glimpsed the force of his frustration and regret. For now, his duties lay at Slains and hers were here. They were divided, thought Sophia, as completely as herself and Moray.

Calling Rory as he turned to leave, Sophia said, 'When I have read this letter, I will wish to send the countess a reply. I pray you wait and carry it.'

He turned, a little slow in his acceptance of this unexpected gift.

She tried to look the part of the commanding lady. 'If, as you did say, you have done all that you were sent to do, it should not be too great an inconvenience to delay your journey home by such a small thing as an hour?' She felt a stir of hope from Kirsty, close beside her, and she saw a trace of gratitude chase briefly over Rory's stoic features.

'No,' he told her, 'it would not.'

'You must be hungry. Kirsty, will you show him to the kitchen?'

Kirsty's smile was broad. 'Aye, Mrs Milton.'

With them gone, and Mrs Malcolm having gone off to attend to preparations of her own, Sophia sat to read her letter.

It was written in the countess's clear hand, with care in case it should be intercepted by unfriendly hands. 'My dearest Mrs Milton,' it began, 'We are so pleased to hear that you have been delivered safely of a daughter. I am sure she brings you joy, and that you soon will come to wonder how you ever filled your days before she came. When you are able you must bring her north to visit us at Slains, for we would dearly love to see you both, although we would advise that you not venture it until our climate here has grown more favourable. I did this week receive a note from Mr Perkins,' she went on, and 'Mr Perkins' was, Sophia knew, the name the countess used in code when speaking of the Duke of Perth, her brother,

who was chancellor at the court of Saint-Germain. The Duke
of Perth wrote regularly to his sister, smuggling the letters over
sea by varied messengers to keep them from the prying eyes of
agents of Queen Anne. His news was mostly of the court
itself, but this time it appeared to be more personal. The
countess's own letter said, 'He writes that he did chance to
meet our friend the colonel and did play a pleasant game of
chess with him and found him very well indeed, and in good
spirits. And in that same house he met your husband, Mr
Milton, who was also well, and who did say that he intends
at any day to travel to the coast and seek his passage home in
company with Mr Johnstone.'

Here Sophia stopped, and read that passage for a second
time to make quite sure she'd read it right – for 'Mr
Johnstone', she knew, meant the king.

So it was real, then. Moray *would* be coming, and he would
be coming soon. Sophia sat to write her letter in reply, but she
could not at first compose it for her hands had started
trembling from no other cause than happiness – a happiness
so pure and strong she sought not to contain it but to share it,
so that when the trembling ceased she still wrote slowly,
knowing Kirsty and her Rory would make good use of the
extra moments she could give them. It was well beyond an
hour before she gave the letter into Rory's hand, and saw him
ride again towards the north, and Slains.

In the days that followed afterwards, Sophia kept a closer
watch upon the waters of the Firth, and woke each day in
expectation, with her ears tuned to the sounds of running
wheels and hoofbeats passing by the house along the road to
Edinburgh.

The very wind felt different in those days, as though the

smoke from some strange fire rode upon its currents, often scented yet unseen.

The baby fretted in her cradle and refused all comfort, while Sophia paced the chamber back and forth and back and forth until her slippers showed the wear. And still there was no word.

Then came the night when she heard cannon-fire.

Five shots, and silence. Nothing more.

When morning came she had not slept.

'What is it?' Kirsty asked her, waking.

But Sophia did not know. She only knew she felt a strangeness in the air this morning. 'Did you hear the cannon?'

'No.'

'Last night, upon the stroke of midnight.'

'You were dreaming,' Kirsty told her.

'No.' Sophia stopped her restless pacing by the window, gazing out across the grey mist that was melting with the sunrise, touched with bands of gold and red that shimmered like the blood of kings. 'It was no dream, I think.'

And she was right. For on the evening of the next day Mr Malcolm, who had been away from home for some few nights, returned in agitation.

'Fetch me bread and clothes!' he called. 'I must away.'

His wife, surprised, asked, 'Why? What is it? What has—?'

'Christ, woman, cease your talk and make ye haste, else ye may see me hang with all the rest of them.' And with that outburst Mr Malcolm sank despondent to the nearest chair and gripped his head with both his hands. He had not bothered taking off his heavy cloak, to which the salty dampness of the sea winds clung and channelled down in rivulets to drip upon the floorboards.

In worried silence Mrs Malcolm brought him wine, and haltingly his story came, in pieces, while Sophia stood and listened, though each word was like a stone cast up to shatter her own hopes.

It had begun so well, he said. Two days ago the first French ship, the *Proteus*, had sailed into the Firth, and he had met it two leagues in and gone on board with several pilots. There had been a storm at sea, the captain told him, and the *Proteus* had separated from the others, so they had expected they would find the other ships of the king's squadron there before them in the Firth. Their appearance had excited those on shore, and those who had put out in fishing boats to welcome them, but though they waited all that afternoon and evening no more ships arrived.

So at the break of day the *Proteus* had turned again and ridden on the ebbing tide towards the great mouth of the Firth, to see if she could find the other French ships and convey the pilots to them.

What the *Proteus* had found still bothered Mr Malcolm so much that it took him some moments to collect himself before he could continue.

The French, he said, had gathered at the entrance to the Firth the night before and dropped their anchors, and so lost their chance to enter in the river on a flowing tide. By dawn the tide had turned, and they could do no more than wait. 'And then the English came,' he said. 'Near thirty sail of them, and half of those had fifty guns or more.' He shook his head.

The *Proteus* had not been well-equipped for fighting. She'd been fitted for a transport ship, the best part of her guns removed to make room for supplies and troops. She could do little more than watch the battle.

Mr Malcolm showed a grudging admiration for the tactics of the French commander, who though trapped had turned his ships against the English as if he intended to attack. From his position on the *Proteus*, Mr Malcolm had seen the French throwing whatever they could over the sides in an effort to lighten the ships, and as the English had responded to the challenge by shouldering into their battle array, the French had swiftly turned and steered a course towards the north.

A few French ships were left behind, and one had been engaged so heavily by English men-of-war that it had battled all that day and passed the night pressed by its enemies. But King James's ship, at least, had escaped.

As had the *Proteus* which, having lowered Mr Malcolm to a waiting fishing boat, had steered its own course boldly out to sea, in hopes of drawing off a few more of the English in pursuit to give the king more time to find some safer harbour to the north.

Sophia said, 'So then the king is yet alive.' She could at least draw hope from that. For if, as Colonel Graeme had once said, no battle could be called a victory if the king were lost, then surely there could be no true defeat if the king lived.

'He lives,' said Mr Malcolm, 'and God grant he comes ashore, for my own life will be worth little till he does. Even now the English soldiers search for those of us who went on board the *Proteus*, and in the road of Leith they now do hold the crew and captain of a captured ship, and he that claimed it for his prize is blackest of them all, for he was once the king's own follower, and hearing of his deed today is like to break my Lady Erroll's heart, for she did hold him dear.'

Sophia frowned. 'Of whom, sir, do you speak?'

'Why, of the English captain – for I'll no more call him

Scottish – of the English rogue who did this day betray his friends by turning his own guns upon that same French ship that had so long been under siege, and forcing its surrender. I do speak,' he said, and spat the name, 'of Captain Thomas Gordon.'

She stepped back as though he'd struck her. 'I do not believe it.'

'Nor would I, had I not seen it with my own eyes.' His face grew bitter. 'I've seen many things this day that I would rather not have seen. But as ye say, the king does live.'

Sophia hugged her arms more tightly round herself and wished that she believed in God enough to pray that Moray, too, was still alive. But even if he was, she knew that he had passed beyond her prayers, to waters much more dangerous.

'Why did it fail?' I asked from curiosity, and Graham, who'd been lounging on the other sofa, marking papers, glanced across.

'What's that?'

'The invasion. Why didn't it work, do you think?'

'Ah.' He set down the paper and rested his head back in thought.

I had never been able to write, before now, with somebody else there in the room. It distracted me. Even my parents had learnt to stay clear. But this morning Graham had come downstairs while I was still deep in my trance and had settled in without my even knowing he was there. It wasn't until I'd gone three pages on and discovered that I was now drinking a fresh cup of coffee that I hadn't made, that I had looked over and seen him stretched out on the opposite sofa, his own cup of coffee forgotten beside him, head bent to his papers.

And then, having noted his presence, I'd simply gone back to my writing, back into the flow of it, lovely, unbroken. I'd never have thought it was possible. But here I was at the end of the scene, and here Graham was, still in the room with me, quietly comfortable, thinking of reasons why young King James hadn't succeeded in his first rebellion attempt in that spring of '08.

'The easy answer,' he began, 'is that it failed because the Stewarts never had much luck. I mean, from Mary, Queen of Scots on down, their history's not a happy one. They didn't lack for looks, or charm, but somehow they just never had it easy.'

'Most historians would say they brought that on themselves.'

His sidelong look was inwardly amused. 'Never trust a historian. Especially Protestant historians writing about Catholic kings. Most of history is only the tale of the winning side, anyway, and they've a motive for painting the other side black. No, the Stewarts weren't that bad. Take James, for example – old James, who was father to your King James. Most of the books that say he was a bad king and cruel and the rest of it, all that came down from one single account that was written by someone just passing on rumours years after the fact. If you read what was actually written by those who were with James, who saw what he did, they have nothing but good things to say of the man. But historians went with the rumours, and once it's been written in print, well, it's taken as gospel, and then it's a source for the research of future historians, so we keep copying lies and mistakes,' Graham said, with a shrug. 'That's why I tell my students to always get back to original documents. Don't trust the books.'

'So the Stewarts,' I steered him back round to the question, 'just had some bad luck.'

'That's one answer. And bloody bad timing.'

I frowned. 'But their timing was not all that bad in the '08. I mean, with the English off fighting in Flanders, and the Union making everyone up here feel mad enough to fight, and—'

'Oh, aye, you're right in that sense. Aye, of all the Jacobite rebellions, the '08 was the one that should have worked. They would have had to face the English fleet at any rate – you couldn't send some twenty-odd ships sailing out of Dunkirk without tipping off the English you were coming – but you're right, they did manage to get a bit of a jump on them, and on land they'd have met hardly any resistance at all. They nearly broke the Bank of England as it was, there was such panic when the word got out King James was coming. One more day and things would have been such a mess Queen Anne might have been forced to make a peace and name her brother as successor just to save her own position. But I didn't mean that sort of timing. I meant their *specific* timing. First,' he said, 'the young king catches measles just as they get set to leave Dunkirk. That sets them back a bit. And next they have a storm at sea. And then they miss their mark and end up miles off course, just off the coast up here, so that they have to turn around and lose a day in getting back to where they should be. Then, when they do make it to the Firth, they don't go in, but drop their anchors, wait the night and let the English catch them. History,' Graham said, 'is really just a series of "what if's". What if the French commander hadn't gone off course? He would have made the Firth a whole day earlier, far ahead of the English ships. What if that first ship that went up the Firth, the...I forget the name...'

'The *Proteus*?'

'Aye, the *Proteus*. Good memory. What if that ship hadn't got there first? The Scottish pilots all went out to board her, so there wasn't anybody left to guide the king's ship when it turned up later. If the pilots hadn't been already on the *Proteus*, the French commander might have tried to make it further up the Firth that first night when the tides were good, and not just dropped his anchor. He could have set the king and all his soldiers down in sight of Edinburgh before the English ships turned up next morning. Mind you,' Graham said, 'I'm not so sure the pilots would have made a difference.'

'Why is that?'

'Because I'm not so sure the French commander wasn't doing just what he'd been told to do.'

I caught his drift. 'You mean that it was *meant* to fail?'

'I wouldn't be at all surprised. The Jacobites had all along been asking for the Duke of Berwick to be in command of the invasion, but the French king gave them someone else. Berwick himself was furious, afterwards. Wrote nasty things in his memoirs about it, and said he'd have landed James safely on shore, and I don't doubt he would have. And not everybody thought the French ships went off course by accident. Your Colonel Hooke once told the story that he couldn't sleep that night, and went on deck, and saw that they were sailing just off Cruden Bay, far north of where they should have been. So he ran to tell the commander, who made a big show of being surprised, and said he'd correct the course at once, but later on Hooke saw that they were headed north again, and when he asked the helmsman he was told that was the order, so Hooke went to tell the king they'd been betrayed.'

'I don't remember reading that.'

'It's in Oliphant, I think. Oliphant's *Jacobite Lairds of Gask*. I'll look it up for you.'

There wasn't much to do with Hooke I hadn't read, but then there wasn't much of Hooke that had survived. Most of his writings were gone. After the rebellion failed, all sides had done a massive cover-up that would have put Watergate to shame, and most of Hooke's writings and notes were impounded. Only two small volumes had escaped the purge. What else he might have seen and known was lost to history.

My eyes must have begun to lose their focus because Graham smiled and rose and reached to take my empty coffee cup. 'I'll make some more. You don't look like you're done yet with your writing.'

I pulled myself back. 'No, I'm sorry. I don't have to, really, not if you were wanting to do something else.' I saw his mouth quirk and I hastened to add, 'What I meant was—'

'I know what you meant.' There was warmth in his eyes. 'Write your book. It's no bother. I've twenty more papers to mark, and I'll not get them done if you let me keep talking about the invasion. Besides, it's just talk. Just my theories. I can't say for sure why it failed, why the French made the choices they did. No one can,' he admitted. 'It's hard enough judging the motives of people who live in our own times, let alone the motives of those who've been dead three hundred years. They can't come back and tell us, can they?'

Handing him my coffee cup, I thanked him and sat back and gave the spaniel's floppy ears a scratch and counted myself lucky that he'd asked that question in a general sense, and hadn't been expecting me to answer.

XVIII

The harbour at Leith was a maze of great ships and small vessels, some anchored, others moving between and around them at various speeds and in varied directions, so that the oarsman seated opposite Sophia in the rowboat had to choose his course with care and change it often. This was Edinburgh's harbour and would at any time be crowded, but today the traffic was so thick it seemed that one could almost walk from oar to oar across the deep green water to the cheers of those who called to one another from their passing craft, in hearty voices made more boisterous with drink.

Sophia wrapped her hood more closely round her face and made an effort not to look beyond the oarsman to the crippled hulk of the French ship that rode nearby at anchor, marked with scars of heavy fighting, and its rigging all in tatters. She had seen it from the shore and been affected by it then, and it was worse to be this close and see the charred and jagged edges of the holes left by the cannon blasts, and know the men who had been standing where the holes now were would have been killed.

There were no scars that she could see upon the ship they were approaching. It rolled languidly upon the water like the great cat that it had been named for – the *Leopard* – and it seemed to overlook the harbour as a wild leopard might when resting from a recent hunt, self-satisfied, content to let the smaller prey pass by. Yet there was something predatory in its shadow as it fell across Sophia, and the scraping of the two hulls growled a warning as the oarsman brought the rowboat alongside. He reached to take hold of a hanging rope ladder and called to hail a crewman on the deck above.

'Here is a lady for your captain,' he said with a smirk that plainly showed what purpose he believed she'd come to serve.

She did not seek to change his mind – her own was set so fixedly she did not care what others thought. She landed steady on her feet upon the creaking deck, and bore the crewman's leering scrutiny with patience, only seeking to remind him when it seemed he had forgotten that the captain would be waiting for her.

She felt the stares as they passed by, and heard the voices of the other men call out and laugh and speak in rude suggestive language, but she took no more notice of them than she did of the ship itself, of the great rising masts and the knots of the rigging and wet canvas scent of the slumbering sails. She had wondered for so long just how it would feel to set foot on a ship and to walk on its decks, and now here she was walking upon one and none of her senses took note of the fact. She might have been walking the road of a town, and the steps to the door of the captain's cabin might have been but the steps to a house. All that mattered to Sophia was the man inside, and what she'd come to say to him.

The cabin had a bay of casement windows curving round its farther end, through which the afternoon's strong light poured in to warm the panelled walls and spill across the smooth edge of the desk at which the captain sat.

He had not looked up at the crewman's knock, he'd only said a curt 'Come in', and gone on looking at the spread of papers that so held his interest.

'Your visitor, sir,' said the crewman, and coughed, and discreetly withdrew.

And the captain raised his head then, faintly frowning, and seeing Sophia he stopped short as though he'd been struck.

'Captain Gordon,' she greeted him levelly.

Recovering himself, he rose and came across to take her hand and raise it to his lips, too much the gentleman to cast aside formalities in even such an unexpected circumstance. But clearly her appearance had surprised him, and he did not try to hide it. 'How the devil came you here?'

'It was not difficult,' she lied. She did not tell him the excuses she had made to Mrs Malcolm and to Kirsty of her need to come to town, nor of the earliness with which she had set out by hired coach, nor of the trouble it had caused her to negotiate her way around the busy port. 'I asked which ship was yours, and found a boatman who would carry me.'

'I meant how came you here to Leith? Why are you not at Slains?'

She drew her hand away from his. 'The countess thought a change of air might do me good. I have been staying some few weeks with friends of hers, not far from here.'

'Oh, aye? What friends would those be?'

Once Sophia might have told him, but not now. 'I do not think that you would know them.'

Captain Gordon fixed his gaze upon her face, and took her measure. Then he said, 'Come, let us sit.'

The cabin was a man's space, but was not without its luxuries. The chairs had been upholstered in a rich red fabric, and a silver tray upon a table gleamed beneath its strange assortment of small porcelain cups and dishes ringed around a central covered pot. 'You have good timing,' said the captain. 'Yesterday there'd not have been much I could offer you by way of a refreshment, but my cook today has done a bit of trading with a Dutch ship lately come from the East Indies that is forced to wait in harbour here, and chief among his prizes was a box of china tea, to the drinking of which he is trying to convert me.' Picking up the porcelain pot, he poured a clear brown liquid into one of the cups. 'I must confess I do prefer my whisky still, but I am told that drinking tea will be the coming fashion. Here,' he said, and handed her the cup. 'It is still hot, I think.'

She held the cup and looked toward the windows, through whose glass panes she could see the battered French ship framed as though it were a painting done in honour of the victory of the battle that had stained this same sea red with blood just days before. The drink was bitter on her tongue.

She said, 'I am surprised to find you on a new ship.'

'Aye, the *Edinburgh* did not survive the strain of my last voyage. You'll recall I had my doubts about its worthiness,' he said, and smiled in the manner of a man who means to share a private joke.

She felt a surge of anger at that smile, and could not keep it in. 'I do recall a great deal, Captain. Tell me, do you think King James will yet make you an admiral when he comes?' She flung the question at him, challenging, and pointed to the windows and the French ship. 'Do you think that he will honour you for that?'

He did not answer her, which only flamed her temper more.

'How could you? After all you told the countess and the earl, how could you do a thing like this? How could you so betray us?'

In a quiet tone he said, 'It was my duty.'

'Duty might demand you keep the English side, and even fire upon the French, but it does not excuse you everything. No other English ship but yours did take a prisoner, and *that*,' she said, 'I do not think was done because of duty.'

He was watching her with eyes she could not fathom. 'No,' he said at last. 'That was not done from duty.'

Rising from his chair he exhaled hard and turned away and crossed to stand before the windows, looking out. He did not speak for some few minutes, then he said, 'Were any man to ask me, I would tell him that I am more proud of what I did that day than I have been of any other thing I've done in all my life.'

There was a quality about his voice, a passion in his words, that made her anger start to fade. But still she did not understand.

Until he told her why.

A man in his position, he explained, had little chance to chart his own course in these times, but he had done what he could do. He'd kept the *Edinburgh* from being fit to sail and kept himself on land as long as he was able, in the hope the king would use that time to make good his return. The king had not, and in the end new orders came for Captain Gordon to assume a new command, and bring the *Leopard* north.

'And even captains,' he informed Sophia, 'must obey their orders.'

On arrival at the entrance to the Firth, he'd found the French ships already engaged and under fire. He'd kept the *Leopard* back as best he could, and had managed with seemingly clumsy manoeuvres to block some of his own side's fire against the fleeing *Proteus* to let it get away.

'But there was nothing to be done for them,' he said, gazing across at the ravaged French ship. 'No way to save the *Salisbury*. She was an English ship once, did you know? The French did capture her from us, in their turn, some while back. She's seen her share of war. And when the French commander wheeled his squadron round and headed north, she had the rearguard.'

She had done what she'd been asked to do, protecting the retreating squadron so the king might make good his escape, but she had done it at a sore cost to herself and her brave crew. They had not stood a chance.

The English ships had caught her up, and though two other French ships had turned back to try to help her, it had been no use. The battle had raged fiercely all that afternoon and evening till the other French ships too had finally slipped away and left the struggling *Salisbury* alone, to face her enemies as night fell.

In the darkness of the early morning she had struck her colours and the sight of that surrender had ignited something deep in Gordon that he couldn't quite explain, not even now. And it had stirred him into action.

'It occurred to me that while I could not rescue her, I might yet do some service to the men she carried. Better they should fall into my hands,' he said, 'than into those of men who had no sympathy for Jacobites.'

He'd roused his few most trusted crewmen and ordered them to get a boat at once into the water, with him in it, and they'd rowed like fury through the drifting smoke and charred debris, and beating out the other English ships nearby he'd climbed on board the *Salisbury* and claimed her as his prize.

The captain of the French ship had been gallant in defeat. An able-looking man, he had managed to conduct himself, in spite of his great weariness and bloodied clothes, with consummate politeness. 'It is kind of you to think of it,' he'd said when Gordon, having given proof that their allegiance was the same, had offered aid. 'There are some letters I would wish to send to France, to Paris, if that somehow could be managed.'

'I will see it done.'

'And one more thing. I have on board this ship a noble passenger, Lord Griffin…'

'Griffin! Is he yet alive?'

'He was but slightly wounded yesterday, and rests now with our surgeon, but I fear what may befall him when the English take him prisoner.'

The English, Gordon had agreed, would not be pleased to find the aged lord, who long ago had served the old King James and who had since been living at the court of Saint-Germain. 'What the devil were they thinking of? Why did they send Lord Griffin, at his age?'

'He sent himself,' had been the answer, with a Gallic shrug. 'He was not told about the young king's plans, and did not learn of them until we were about to put to sea, and then was so determined to be part of the adventure that he bought a horse and rode at once to Dunkirk, and secured himself a place on board my ship. He is a…how is it you say? A character. I would not like to see him come to harm.'

'Where is he now?'

'Come, I will take you.'

They had found the old man below decks, sitting calmly in the chaos of the wounded and the dead. Despite his bandaged head, he had looked fit and even cheerful, as though welcoming the prospect of adventure. He had listened to their plans politely, but had answered Gordon, 'Oh, you needn't bother with all that, my boy. I'll not be harmed.'

'My Lord, if the English do take a French nobleman, he will be treated with care, but if they come upon an English noble like yourself, then they will call your presence on this ship no less than treason, and will show you little mercy. They will have your head.'

Lord Griffin's eyes held all the patience of the aged speaking to the young. 'I am an old man, and I'll warrant that my bones will ache the same if I am sleeping in a palace or a prison. But,' he said, 'if it will give you peace, my boy, then I will come.'

He gave consent to being carried on a stretcher, so it would appear he was more gravely wounded and could be confined, upon the *Leopard*, to the surgeon's care. 'My surgeon,' Gordon said to both Lord Griffin and the French ship's captain, 'is a Jacobite, as I am, and will help to keep you hidden till we can arrange to move you somewhere safer.'

Someone jostled past Gordon and, stepping to the side, he bumped another wounded man who lay insensible upon the deck, his breaths so shallow there was barely any movement of the stinking, blood-soaked rags that bound his shoulder.

In that dim light the man's pale face was difficult to see, but Gordon saw all that he needed to. He did not look away, but in a tightened voice demanded, 'What did happen to this man?'

Lord Griffin gave the answer. 'He was wounded while saving the life of a young lad who had not the sense to get clear of a cannon-ball.' When Gordon did not move, Lord Griffin thought to add, 'The lad got out of it uninjured. I was there, I saw it all, though I confess it was that same shot brought the roof down on my head so I remember little else.'

He rubbed his neatly bandaged temple while the captain of the French ship looked more closely at the wounded man and said, 'I do not know his face, though by his uniform he looks to be an officer of one of the king's Irish brigades. We have several such men aboard the *Salisbury*.'

'My countrymen,' Lord Griffin said, 'will likely not be too pleased to find *them* here, either.'

'No.' The frown on Captain Gordon's face grew deeper. 'No, indeed they will not.' And he called for one more stretcher. 'I will take this man, as well.'

'But,' – this in protest from the French ship's captain – 'surely it will draw too much attention if you carry two such wounded men across on your small boat?'

Gordon's voice froze over. 'I remind you, sir, that "small boat" does obey my orders, as indeed your ship must now do also, and I'll thank you not to question my command.'

There was no more said about it until both the stretchers had been lowered to his boat and they were rowing back across towards the Leopard. Gordon's crewmen were all dutifully silent. Their allegiances lay squarely with his own, and he had no fears they would speak of what they'd seen, or heard. The wounded men upon the boat might well have been invisible.

The blanket on the stretcher of the still-unconscious officer began to slip and Gordon reached to draw it up and tuck it firmly underneath the man's uninjured arm. He turned to find Lord Griffin lying watching him.

'You know him.' It was not a question.

Gordon answered, 'Yes.'

'His voice did mark him as a Scot.' The aged eyes were curious. 'And I should think a young man who could fight so fiercely in his king's defence has done it once or twice before.'

'He has. And earned himself a price upon his head that would enrich the English soldier who did capture him.'

Lord Griffin nodded. 'Ah. Then it is well that you did reach your friend before them.'

Gordon turned again to study Moray's face. 'He would not count me as his friend.'

'But you admire him.'

Gordon thought on this a moment. 'He is dear to someone who is dear to me,' he said, 'and that itself does bind us to each other, whether either of us likes the fact.'

That said, he felt relief a short while later on the *Leopard*, when his surgeon gave assurances that Moray was not seriously wounded. Beneath the swinging lamps the surgeon leant in close to show the wounds. 'You see where something sharp has caught him right across this shoulder. Not a sword, but something rougher, like a splintered piece of wood. 'Twas that which caused the bleeding, but it is now fairly stopped, and should heal in time as neatly as this wound along his side will. Two more scars he'll hardly notice, when he wakes.'

Lord Griffin, who had turned aside the surgeon's offer of a hammock and was sitting in a chair against the sloping wall, glanced over and remarked, 'It does appear that someone tries to kill the lad with regularity.'

He too had seen, as Gordon had, the other scars that Moray bore upon his chest and arms to mark his years of being slashed and shot at on the battlefield. And hanging from his neck he wore a leather cord on which was strung a single pebble, small and black and smoothly worn, the purpose of which none of them could see.

Lord Griffin guessed it was a charm of some sort. 'Soldiers are a superstitious lot.'

'Well,' said the surgeon, 'he will have to do without it for a moment, while I dress and bind this shoulder.' But his movement to remove the stone and cord was stopped abruptly by a hand around his wrist.

A hoarse voice, barely recognisable, said, 'Leave that.'

Moray's eyes came slowly halfway open, with a waking man's awareness. He took stock of where he was, but did not loose his hold upon the surgeon's wrist until the latter said, 'You have been hurt. I need to dress the wound, sir, and this stone is in the way.'

A moment passed, then Moray's hand released its grip and moved instead to take the pebble on its cord and slide it over his own head with care before he gathered it into his palm and closed his fingers round it in a small act of possession. With his gaze fixed on the surgeon's face, he said, 'Your voice is English.'

'Yes, sir.'

Only Gordon saw the hand of Moray's wounded left arm move against his thigh as though he'd hoped to find his sword still there. 'What ship is this?'

Lord Griffin answered, 'You've no need to worry, my boy. We are on board the *Leopard*, and safe among friends.'

The sound of Lord Griffin's voice clearly caught Moray off guard and he turned his head sharply towards it, but Gordon was standing between them. The ship rolled and the lanterns swung and in the shifting bars of light and shadow Moray's gaze met Gordon's in a hard unspoken challenge. 'Among friends.' He did not sound convinced.

'Aye,' Gordon told him. 'For the moment. But I cannot keep you hidden here for long.' He aimed his next words at the surgeon. 'Do you think he will be well enough to leave by nightfall?'

Moray's face grew wary. 'Leave for where?'

'I mean to take advantage of the victory celebrations of this day. They will increase the great confusion of these waters,' Gordon said. 'With so many ships and vessels and so many drunken men it should be possible to get you both aboard the fishing-smack that waits prepared to carry you across to France.'

Lord Griffin said, 'And what then of the men who saw you bring aboard two prisoners this morning from the *Salisbury*? Will they believe we simply disappeared?'

His voice was dry, and his expression made it plain that while he did admire the plan he had his doubts about its chances for success.

'My crewmen saw me bring two wounded prisoners aboard,' was Gordon's answer. 'They will see me, on the morrow, hold a proper Christian burial at sea for those same prisoners who, sadly, were beyond our surgeon's aid. We sew the bodies into sheets, and none will know that there are ballast weights in place of men inside. They will be satisfied, and both of you will have escaped the English.'

'No, not both of us.' Lord Griffin shook his head. 'You simply cannot kill the both of us, my boy, they'll not believe it. And besides, what would that say about the skill of your poor surgeon?' With a smile he settled back, arms folded. 'No, you get the young lad off, and I myself will stand tomorrow at his burial and weep, and back your story with my own.'

Moray raised himself upon the table, to the protests of the surgeon who had not yet finished bandaging his shoulder. 'My Lord Griffin, if there is to be but one of us escaping, I insist—'

'Oh, save your breath, my boy. You are but young, you have your life ahead of you, and mine is near its end.' He said to Gordon, 'I have told you, there is nothing to be feared if I am taken. I have known Queen Anne since she was in her cradle, I was in her father's Guards. She will not see me come to harm.' He smiled again. 'Besides, the prospect of a room within the Tower from which I may look on London in my last years does not seem at all unpleasant.' And he paused, his words grown heavy with the weight of memory. 'I have been so long away from home.'

Moray had been stubborn in his arguments against Lord Griffin staying, but the Englishman had not relented, and in the end the matter had been settled only after Gordon had exploded, 'Christ, man, I may turn you in myself and claim the ransom if you do not let it lie.' And then, recovering his temper, he'd reminded Moray, 'You once told me it was not a soldier's place to ask who gave an order, but to follow it. Cannot you follow this one?' Low, he'd added, 'For her sake, if no one else's.'

Like combatants locked in equal battle both the men had held each other's gaze in silence for a moment. Slowly, Moray's hand had lifted and he had replaced the small black pebble on its cord about his neck, as though it were the only armour he had need of. And he'd given one brief nod.

Sophia stared at Captain Gordon as he stood, still with his back to her, against the curving bay of windows in the *Leopard*'s cabin. She had not said a word through all his tale, so tightly gripped had she been by her own emotions.

Gordon said, 'We got him off all right. With all the rum that flowed upon our decks that night my men were in no state to notice anything besides their own debauchery. He should by now be well into the crossing.'

Sophia knew that there was nothing she could say that

would be adequate, and yet she felt the need to tell him something. 'Captain Gordon...' But she faltered as he turned, and only asked, 'Do you still have Lord Griffin in your care?'

'No. He was taken by the soldiers just this morning. I can only pray that he was right to think the queen will show him mercy.'

Looking at his face, she felt ashamed that she had thought that such a man could turn a traitor. 'Captain Gordon,' she began again, 'I hope you can forgive me for—'

He raised a hand to cut short her apology. 'It is forgotten.' Glancing one more time across the harbour to the ruin of the *Salisbury*, he said, 'At any rate, you were quite right on one account.' His eyes came back to hold her own, intent. 'The things I did that night were not all done because of duty. They were done for you.'

She was silent for a moment in the face of that admission. It was hard to know a man could care so much for her that he would risk his whole profession, risk his life, while knowing that she did not, could not, answer his affection. In a quiet voice Sophia said, 'I am so sorry.' And they both knew she was speaking of much more than her unfounded accusations.

Captain Gordon, still the gentleman, released her with the words, 'You have no need to be.' He paused, then in a lighter voice remarked, 'In truth, I do admire your courage coming here to challenge me. I do not doubt you would have found the means to travel all the way from Slains, if you'd been called to do it.'

She smiled faintly at the charge. 'I might have done.'

'But I am glad that you are not now in the north.' He crossed to pour them each a glass of claret. 'And not only for the fact it has afforded me the pleasure of this visit, but because I fear the English will demand a heavy price for what has happened here.'

She drank, and tried to wash away the bitter taste of tea. 'The king escaped,' she said. 'It may be that his ships will take him north where they may find a better landing-place.'

'Perhaps.' His eyes were older than her own. 'But if he fails, there will be evil times ahead, and it will be as well for you,' he said, 'that you are not at Slains.'

Graham turned his head towards mine on the pillow, half-asleep. 'Lord who?'

'Lord Griffin. He was on the *Salisbury*, I think. An old man, English, who had been at Saint-Germain...'

'Oh, him.' He placed the name and rolled more fully over to his side so that his arm slid round my waist, a now familiar weight. I liked the way it felt, just as I liked the rumble of his voice against my neck. 'What did you want to know?'

'What happened to him after he was taken by the English? Was he ever tried for treason?'

'Aye, and sentenced for it.'

'So he was beheaded, then?' The penalty for treason in those times was inescapable. I didn't know why that small fact should bother me so much – I'd read reports of countless executions in the course of researching my novels, and I knew that it was just another end result of wars and royal intrigues. But I couldn't think of this one without seeing in my mind that old man sitting with his back against the *Leopard*'s slanting wall, and saying he would stay, that he would not be harmed, Queen Anne would never—

'No,' said Graham, cutting through my thoughts. 'They didn't kill him. There were some of Queen Anne's ministers who argued for it, but she wouldn't listen. Oh, she kept him captive, but she let him keep his head, and in the end he died of plain old age.'

That made me somewhat happier. I hoped he'd had his chance to have a view of London from his window, as he'd wanted. Certainly King James, I knew, had never seen *his* hopes fulfilled. His ships had been pursued along the northern coast until bad weather finally made them give up altogether and set back to open sea, and France. And those on shore, who'd waited for his coming for so long, had been left hanging in the wind to face those evil times that Captain Gordon had predicted.

'Graham?'

'Aye?'

'Was anybody else killed for their part in the rebellion?'

'Not that I recall.' His voice was very sleepy now, and had I known him less well I'd have half-suspected he was 'not recalling' with a purpose, in the hope that I'd stop asking questions.

'But the English rounded up the Jacobites and put them into prison.'

'Oh, aye. Most of the Jacobite nobles and gentry were thrown into prison, then taken in chains down to London. Paraded around for the mob.'

I was silent a moment, imagining this. Then I asked, 'Was the Earl of Erroll with them?'

Graham nodded, and even that effort seemed great for him because his voice had begun to grow thicker, less clear. 'Supposedly he got so out of temper as a captive that he pitched a bottle at the Earl of Marischal, and nearly took his head off.'

'Well, the Earl of Marischal must have deserved it, then.'

I felt Graham's mouth briefly curve on my skin. 'You're defending your own, are you?'

There was no way to explain that I knew the Earl of Erroll's character better than any historian could – that he wasn't a figure on paper to me, but a flesh-and-blood person held whole in my memory. All of them were. I remembered their faces. Their voices.

I was silent with my thoughts a moment. Then I ventured, 'Graham?'

In reply he nuzzled closer to my neck and made a muffled sound of enquiry.

'What happened to them when they got to London? I mean, I know they were eventually set free, but how?'

No answer came this time except the deep sound of his breathing. He had gone to sleep. I lay there for a while longer thinking in the dark with Graham's arm wrapped safe around me and the warmth of Angus sprawled across my feet, but in the end the question would not let me rest, and there was only one way that I knew to get a proper answer.

XIX

These days she was not often out of doors. Although two months had passed and spring had smoothed the sharper edges of the breezes from the sea, she kept inside with Mrs Malcolm and with Kirsty and the baby and she did not leave the house except on those rare days when her own restlessness consumed her and she felt that she must breathe the outside air or else go mad. Even then, she stayed as far as she could stay from the main road, mindful always of the fact that this was still a time of danger.

Mr Malcolm had not yet been heard from and they did not know how he had fared. At the beginning it had seemed that every day more men were taken and imprisoned, and from the single letter that the countess had been able to send down Sophia knew it was no better in the north. Indeed the only comfort in that letter had come from one small piece of news the countess had relayed, that she'd had in a message from the Duke of Perth, her brother, at the Court of Saint-Germain: 'Mr Perkins,' she had written to Sophia in her careful code, 'does tell me that he recently did call upon your husband Mr Milton and did find him well recovered of his illness, and impatient to be up again.' From which Sophia knew, to her relief, that Moray had managed to get safely back across the Channel, and was healing from his wounds.

That knowledge made it easier to cope with the uncertainty surrounding her, just as the sight of baby Anna sleeping in her cradle, small and vulnerable and trusting, gave Sophia every morning the resolve and strength of spirit to conduct herself with caution, so her child would be protected.

She would not, in fact, have been upon the road today at all if it were not for Mrs Malcolm's housemaid falling ill, so that somebody else must go to market if they were to have the food to keep them fed the next few days. Kirsty had offered, but as she had been recovering herself from that same illness and was weakened still, Sophia would not hear of it. Nor would she hear of Mrs Malcolm setting out for town, when Mrs Malcolm had already been accosted twice by soldiers who were searching for her husband.

'I'll go,' Sophia had announced. She'd started out before the dawn, and for some time she was the only one upon the road, which made her feel more free to take some pleasure in the coolness of the wind upon her face and in the spreading colours of the sunrise. It was early in the morning yet when she first reached the outskirts of the waking town of Edinburgh and houses started rising close about her, but there still was not much movement on the road.

So when she heard the sound of hooves and wheels approaching from behind she turned instinctively, not thinking of concealment, only curious to see who might be passing.

It was clearly someone of importance, for the coach itself was an expensive one, the coachman richly dressed and driving horses who were sleek and black and so disdainful that they did not even turn their eyes as they drew level with Sophia.

Inside the coach a sudden voice called out and bade the driver stop, and in a swirl of dust and dancing hooves the horses halted. At the window of the coach appeared a face Sophia knew.

'Why, Mistress Paterson!' said Mr Hall, with obvious surprise. 'Whatever are you doing here? Come in, my dear, come in – you should not be upon these streets alone.'

She had been worried, setting out, that she'd be recognised as being Mrs Milton, from the house of Mr Malcolm, and that somebody might question her on that account. It had not for a moment crossed her mind that she'd be recognised by anyone who knew her as herself. This was a complication she had not foreseen, and she was not sure how to manage it, but since there was no way she could refuse the priest without it stirring his suspicions, she had little choice but to reach up and take his hand and let him help her up the step into the coach.

Inside, she found that they were not alone.

'This,' the Duke of Hamilton remarked, in his smooth voice, 'is quite an unexpected pleasure.' Dressed in deep blue velvet, with a new expensive wig that fell in dark curls past his shoulders, he assessed Sophia from the seat directly opposite.

The coach's rich interior seemed suddenly too close for her, and lowering her face to fight the feeling of uneasiness, she greeted him, 'Your Grace.'

'Where are you walking to this morning?'

'Nowhere in particular. I had a mind to look about the market.'

She could feel his eyes upon her in the pause before he said to Mr Hall, 'The market, then,' and Mr Hall in turn leant out to call up to the coachman to drive on.

The duke said, nonchalant, 'I did not know the countess was in Edinburgh.'

Sophia, well aware that she was out of practice with his dance of words, stepped carefully. 'My Lady Erroll is at Slains, your Grace.'

'You are not here alone, I trust?'

'I am with friends.' Before he could ask more, she raised her gaze in total innocence and said, 'I cannot tell you how relieved I am to see that you are well, your Grace. We heard that you were taken by the English, and have feared the worst.'

She saw his hesitation, and felt confident that he would not be able to resist the urge to make himself look grander by the tale of his adventures. She was right.

His nod was gracious. 'I am touched by your concern, my

dear. In truth, I deemed it an honour to be taken, and only wished I could have been here with my well-affected countrymen to stand in chains beside them in the king's good cause.'

Sophia knew he did not mean a word of it. She knew that he had seen to it that he had been at his estates in Lancashire when young King James had tried to land in Scotland. From the countess's own pen Sophia had received the tale of how a messenger had reached the duke with news the king was coming, and in time for him to turn back and be part of the adventure, but how he, with sly excuses that his turning back might give the English warning, had continued on to Lancashire, from where he could await the outcome, poised to either take young James's part, should the invasion be successful, or to claim his distance from it, should the English side prevail.

It had given Sophia at least some satisfaction when she'd heard the English had imprisoned him as well, regardless. Though it now appeared he'd managed, with his usual duplicity, to orchestrate his own release. How many other lives, she wondered, had he been content to sell to pay the price of his?

She could not keep from asking, when he'd finished telling in dramatic style the tale of his arrest and journey down to London, 'Did you see the other nobles there? How does it go for them?'

He looked at her with vague surprise. 'My dear, have you not heard? They are all freed. Save of course for the Stirlingshire gentry, but I could do nothing to argue their case – they had taken to arms, you see, actually risen in force, and the English could not be persuaded to let them escape being tried, but I trust they will come through it fairly.'

Mr Hall, leaning over, explained to Sophia, 'The duke did kindly take it on himself to argue for the release of his fellow prisoners, and the English were not equal to his arguments.'

Sophia took this news with mingled gratitude and deep distrust. However glad she might be that the Earl of Erroll and the others were now free and would be coming home, she could not help but think the duke would not have done such an enormous thing unless he stood to profit by it somehow. And her own sense told her still that he was not upon their side.

The coach drew rattling to a stop upon the cobbles of a crowded street, with people pressing round and voices shouting and a thousand jumbled smells upon the air. 'Here is the market,' said the duke.

Sophia, in her eagerness to leave that plush, confining space and get clear of the duke's unsettling scrutiny, leant forward with such sharpness that the chain around her neck slid from its pins and tumbled from her bodice, and the silver ring gleamed for an instant in the light before she quickly caught it in her hand and slipped it back again.

She was not quick enough.

She knew, when she glanced over at the duke, that he had seen it. And although his face to any other eyes might have appeared unchanged, she saw the subtle difference in it; heard the altered interest in his voice when he remarked, 'I do have business to attend, but I will send my coachman back so that when you are finished here you may return in safety to the place where you are staying with your…friends.' The emphasis on that last word was not for her to hear, but still she heard it, notwithstanding, and it made her blood run cold.

Sophia tried to keep her own face bright, to make her voice sound normal. 'That is kind of you, your Grace, but I am being met and will be in good company, so there will be no need.'

His gaze was narrowed now, and fixed on her in thought. 'My dear Miss Paterson, I do insist. I cannot bear to think of you, in company or otherwise, upon these streets without a fitting escort. Here, Mr Hall will walk with you and see you do not come to harm.'

He had her, and he knew it. She could tell it from his smile as he sat watching Mr Hall get out and hand Sophia down onto the cobbled street. The duke's eyes in the dimness of the coach were like the eyes of some sleek predatory creature that had trapped its prey and could afford to wait before returning to devour it. 'Your servant, Mistress Paterson,' he said, and with a slight nod of his head he gave his driver orders to go on.

'Well,' Mr Hall said, looking round in expectation as the black coach clattered off into the growing crowd. 'What was it in particular that you desired to buy?'

Sophia's thoughts were racing far beyond her efforts to collect them, and it took her half a minute to reply. The market place was ringed with tall tenements whose upper storeys projected to more closely crowd the already close space and cast shadows across the rough cobbles. And over their roofs she could see the stern outline of Edinburgh castle set high on its hill like a sentry, and seeming to watch all that happened below. She could not see, at first, any route of escape.

Then her searching eyes fell on a small stand not too far away, set near a narrow gap between the buildings, and she forced a smile. 'I should be glad to have a close look at those ribbons.'

'As you wish.'

She'd always thought the priest a good man, and because of that she felt a bit ashamed of what she had to do, but there was simply no escaping it. She could not risk remaining here until the duke returned – she did not know what he intended.

She thought of Moray's parting words about the duke: 'Ye must be careful, lass,' he'd warned her. 'He must never learn that you are mine.'

Too late, she thought. Too late.

The duke's reaction to his glimpse of Moray's ring had left her little room to doubt that he had recognised it, and knew all too well to whom that ring belonged.

But she was not about to let him learn about the child.

She'd reached the stand now where the spools of ribbon, lace and silk were all arrayed in bright display. Sophia took a moment to examine one, and then another, then in what appeared an accident she knocked three spools of ribbon so they tumbled from the stand and spilt their rolling trails of colour on the stones and caused confusion in the steps of people passing.

'Oh!' she cried, pretending great dismay, and begged forgiveness.

''Tis a trifle,' Mr Hall assured her, bending to assist the ribbon-seller in retrieving all the tangled rolls. 'Do not distress yourself, we soon shall have things right again.'

Sophia waited through two more unsteady breaths, until she saw that everyone around was well embroiled in the mess, and then she turned and slipped into the shadowed gap between the houses and began to run as fast as she was able.

The alley was tight-walled and smelt of refuse, but to her relief it brought her out into a steeply downhill street that seemed deserted, and from there she made her way through twisting lanes and narrow wynds till she came at last upon a churchyard with a high stone wall and gate, and taking shelter there she pressed herself into as small a form as possible behind the leaning stones, among the shadows.

She did not dare to attempt the road in daylight, for she knew that once she left the town's last limits she would be exposed and vulnerable. The duke, on being told that she had run away, would surely seek her on that road before all others. Better she should wait for dark, and hope by then he'd think that she was either well away or safely hidden in the town.

It was the longest afternoon and evening she had ever spent. Her head ached, and the hunger raked like claws against her insides, and her thirst was something terrible, and every footfall on the street outside the little churchyard made her heart begin to race again in panic.

But at length the shadows deepened, and the noises in the streets grew more infrequent, and she took a breath for courage, straightened out her stiffened limbs, and cautiously set off again.

She did not afterwards remember much about the journey back along the open road, except that it was long and dark and filled with terror and imaginings, and by the time she finally reached the Malcolm's house she'd nearly reached the limit of her strength.

But she had some small portion of it yet to spare. Her entrance caused much turmoil in the house as Kirsty and their hostess met her at the door with questions and concern, but she brushed all of it aside and would not sit in spite of all their urgings.

Struggling to catch her breath, she fixed her gaze on Kirsty's. 'Has anybody been here?'

Kirsty answered, 'No,' but in a tone of apprehension. 'What has happened?'

'We must go.' Sophia looked to Mrs Malcolm. 'Can you find us horses, or a coach, at this late hour?'

'I can but try.'

'And Anna...' Turning worried eyes toward the closed door to the bedchamber, Sophia said to Kirsty, 'We must wrap her well, the night is not a warm one.'

'Sophia,' Kirsty tried again, more firmly. 'What has happened?'

But there was no way to answer that in Mrs Malcolm's presence without giving more away than would be wise. She only said, 'We are not safe here any longer.'

'But—'

'We are not safe,' Sophia said again, and with her eyes implored her friend to silence.

It was best, she knew, if Mrs Malcolm did not know the details of their journey, for then no one else could force her to divulge that information. Sophia did not know herself how she and Kirsty would be able with the baby to endure the hard trip north to Slains – she only knew that they must somehow manage it, for Anna's sake.

They must return to Slains, and to the countess. She alone, Sophia thought, would know what they should do.

It had started to snow.

It was only the last feeble blast of the winter before it conceded defeat to the spring, but the wind cut like ice through the front of my jacket till Graham moved closer in front of me, blocking the cold while he took my lapels in his strong hands and folded them together with the care of someone dressing a small child to ward off chills. His eyes smiled faintly when they touched upon the bold stripe of his old rugby jersey underneath my coat.

'You'd best not let my brother see you in that shirt.'

I hadn't thought of that. 'You're sure you don't mind me stealing it?'

'You've given it more use this weekend than it's had in years. And anyway, the colour suits you.' As another swirl of snowflakes blew between us he leant closer still and gathered me against him, with his chin resting comfortably close to my temple.

It felt strange to be so openly affectionate in public, standing out here on the bus station platform with other people only steps away from us. I was used to keeping how we felt about each other secret, but in Aberdeen I'd finally had a taste of how things could be. How they would be. And I liked it.

Graham sensed my subtle change in mood and bent his head to ask me, 'What?'

'Nothing. It's just...I had a really good time this weekend.'

'You don't have to go.'

It was, I thought, a bit like being tempted in the desert by the devil. But I resisted. 'Everyone expects me back today, that's what I told them, and I don't want to worry your father.' Drawing back enough to tilt my head so I could see his face, I pointed out, 'It's not like you can call him up and tell him where I am, now is it?'

Graham grinned. 'My dad's not such a Puritan.'

'Even so.' I glanced at the clock on the platform. 'The bus is late.'

'Nae bother.'

'You don't have to wait, you know. I mean, it's very noble of you, standing out here with me in the snow, but—'

'And whose fault is that? You should have let me drive you back.'

'You should have let me take a cab,' I said. 'I can afford it.'

'Aye, I know you can. But no true Scot would let his woman waste her thirty pounds to take a taxi when the bus can get her there for five.'

He was only teasing, of course, and taking the bus had been as much my idea as his – there was a comforting anonymity about riding a bus, and I liked to watch the people sitting round me. But I found his choice of words amusing. 'So I'm your woman, am I?'

'Aye.' I felt the circle of his arms grow firmer and the look he angled down at me was warm. 'You were mine from the moment I met you.'

It was hard not to feel the effect of those words even though they were ones I had written myself, in the scene where Sophia and Moray had said their farewells. 'You've been reading my book.'

'I have not.' He looked quizzical. 'Why?'

'Well, because what you just said – my hero says almost exactly the same thing.'

'Your hero...oh, hell,' Graham said. 'I forgot. No, it's still here.' He felt in his coat's inside pocket and took out a long business envelope. 'That's what I've found on the Morays, so far. It's not much, just the pedigree chart for the family with births, deaths and marriages, if that's of use to you.'

Taking it, I told him, 'Thank you.'

'I'm not sure I want to be John Moray anymore.' It was a half-hearted complaint. 'He—'

'No,' I said. 'Don't tell me.'

With reluctance I bent down to put the envelope inside my briefcase, clicking shut the flap. I didn't want to hear what had become of Moray, even though I knew that I would learn the truth in time, and no doubt sooner than I wanted to.

<h1 style="text-align:center">XX</h1>

The summer came and briefly shone its splendour before fading like the twisting leaves upon the trees that dropped and died and left the world to face the bitter frozen winds of winter, till the spring crept out reluctantly and warmed again to summer days that withered in their turn. And in that time there came no word of new resolve from Saint-Germain to bring the king again across the water.

Still there came each month with regularity a letter from the Duke of Perth to reassure his sister that their plans were not reduced to talk and argument. The messengers yet came and went between the Scottish nobles and the French king at Versailles, and as for young King James, he seemed more determined than ever to keep himself ready for war, having lately declared his intention to lead a charge himself upon the battlefields of Flanders. 'Although,' the Duke of Perth had written in his latest letter at the end of August, 'some do think it possible that peace may come before he gets the chance.'

Sophia would have welcomed peace. The young king's disappointment mattered less to her than did the fact that Moray was now back in Flanders fighting with his regiment, and every day the war stretched on she worried for his safety.

All the comfort that she had now came in dreams, when she could hear again his voice and feel his touch, and not two weeks ago she'd woken in the dead of night convinced he'd been beside her in the bed. She'd felt the warmth of him.

She'd felt it even when the moon had pushed its way clear of the grasping clouds to shine its light upon the sheets and show her there was nothing there.

Next morning Kirsty, upon seeing that Sophia had not slept well, had announced, 'Ye want an hour with your wee Anna.' And that very afternoon Sophia had gone down to find the drawing room alive with Kirsty's sister and the children, and with Anna's brown curls blending with the other dancing heads so well that nobody observing them would have had cause to think that she was not of that same family.

In fact Anna herself knew no differently, having been placed in their cottage just days after she and Sophia had come back to Slains more than a year ago. That had been the countess's solution, and it had so far kept Anna safe, for no one had discovered yet that she was Moray's child, and no one would, with Kirsty's sister standing guardian. ''Tis the benefit of living such an isolated life,' she'd told Sophia, with a smile. 'My neighbours are so used to seeing me produce a new bairn every year that none would even question she was mine.'

'Yes, but your husband...'

'Would do anything the countess asked, and gladly.' With a hand upon Sophia's arm, she'd said, 'You must not worry. We will keep her safe with us, I promise, till your husband does return.'

And Kirsty's sister had been sure to hold that promise, so that little Anna grew each month in laughter and in happiness and saw Sophia often, though from caution she had not been taught to call Sophia 'mama'.

There would be time enough for that, Sophia knew. And though she would have given much to have her daughter with her every day, she weighed her own needs lightly against Anna's, and was grateful beyond measure that her child was so well cared for.

She saw little of herself in Anna's features or her character – the eyes, the hair, the energy, were Moray's, and it gave Sophia joy to see his nature reproduced with such perfection every time she looked at her daughter.

That brief visit in the drawing room had raised her spirits instantly, as Kirsty had intended.

Just as now, these two weeks later, as she sat in her accustomed place among the dunes and watched the children play with Kirsty's sister on the wave-washed curve of beach, Sophia's darker thoughts ran from her as if they had been no more than shadows to be chased off by the brightness of the early autumn sunlight and the sound of Anna's laughter.

The little girl was happily at play with the great mastiff Hugo, who had cast aside his fierce façade to show his own true gentleness, his jaws clamped softly round the stick that Anna had held out to him.

Sophia was so focused on that tiny tug of war she nearly didn't hear the brush of skirts across the grass as Kirsty climbed the dunes to join her. ''Tis not a fair contest,' said Kirsty. 'The dog is too strong for her.'

Sophia smiled, still watching. 'But she will best him, regardless.'

'Aye, I do not doubt it. I do not doubt she can do anything,' said Kirsty. 'Not after seeing with my own eyes how she had my Rory galloping on all fours round the cottage playing horses, and him having sworn he had nae time nor liking for bairns.'

'Perhaps his views are changed,' Sophia said, 'and he does seek to make a family of his own, and settle to that life that you so long for.'

'Rory? Never.'

'There is no such thing as never,' said Sophia, as a sudden shriek of laughter turned her head again toward the shore, where Anna had succeeded in recovering the stick from Hugo's mouth and had begun to run. She'd walked with confidence at ten months and having had several months' practice since then ran easily on tiny feet that touched so lightly on the glistening sand they left no mark behind. Sophia thought of Moray walking barefoot on this beach and looking like a lad himself, and something he had told her on that day seemed fitting for the moment, so she said it over now for Kirsty, in a quiet voice: 'You cannot ever say which way this world will take you.'

The sand felt cool beneath her hands. She cupped a handful of it, sifting it with absent fingers while her eyes, from habit, searched the far horizon for a sail, but there was nothing to be seen in all that wide expanse of blue except the faint and fleeting lines of white along the breaking waves against the rocks that marked the far end of the beach.

Kirsty watched in silent sympathy. 'Perhaps there will be news today from France. The countess did receive a letter.'

'Did she? When?'

'As I was coming out.'

'Another message from His Grace the Duke of Hamilton, no doubt.' Sophia's voice was dry. The duke had written often to the countess since the spring. He had at first expressed his great concern about Sophia's welfare after Mr Hall had lost her in the marketplace, and he'd wondered if he might perhaps have details of her lodgings there in Edinburgh so that he could himself pay her a visit and ensure that she was well. The countess, reading that first letter, had remarked, 'He will be disappointed, surely, to discover you are back with us at Slains, for though his influence is great within the town he dare not challenge us in our own home. The worst that he can do now is to wait, and watch, and hope we will betray the king's designs.'

And so the letters of the Duke, professing friendship, filled with loyal sentiments towards the king, had started to arrive, and each one left the countess out of temper for an hour or more.

'This did not come from Edinburgh,' said Kirsty. 'It was carried by a fisherman, the same man who last month did bring the letter from the Duke of Perth at Saint-Germain, and anyway the countess seemed quite happy to receive it.'

'That is good,' Sophia said. 'The countess likes to get a letter from her brother. It will cheer her.'

She was lightened by the thought, and went on sifting sand within her hands while watching Kirsty's sister and the children. Hugo had retrieved the stick now and the game was on again, the gentle tug of war with peals of laughter rising happily above the rushing rhythm of the waves.

And then the game became a chase and Kirsty, filled with too much energy herself to sit in one place long, slipped running down the dunes and joined the children. And Sophia, left alone, could only think of how contented her heart felt at this one moment, and she raised her face towards the sun and closed her eyes.

When next she opened them, there seemed to be no change. There should, she later thought, have been at least a cloud to block the sun and send its shadow chasing darkly out across the brilliant sea – but there was nothing.

Only the countess, coming down the path to join them on the beach.

The countess was so rarely out this way that in all truthfulness Sophia could not bring to mind the last time it had happened, but she still thought little of it till the countess reached the bottom of the hill and stopped a moment, standing strangely still against the blowing grass. And then Sophia saw her take a breath and set her shoulders and continue on as though the sand between them had grown wider and was difficult to cross.

The countess did not try to climb the dune when she had reached it, but stood several steps below Sophia looking upward, and her face was like the faces of the women who so long ago had come to tell Sophia that her father and her mother would no more be coming home.

She felt the shadow touch her then, although she could not see it, and inside her a great hollowness consumed all other feeling. But because she did not wish to hear the answer to her question she said nothing.

'Oh, my dear,' the countess said, 'I bring sad news of Mr Moray.'

And Sophia knew what it would be, and knew she ought to spare the older woman all the pain of its delivery, but in the sudden numbness that had settled on her, words were somehow far beyond her reach. She dug her fingers in the sand and tried to focus on the feeling as the countess slowly carried on, as though she felt the pain of it herself.

'He has been killed.'

Sophia still did not reply.

'I am so very sorry,' said the countess.

There was sunlight in Sophia's eyes. It seemed so strange, that there should still be sunlight. 'How?'

'There was a battle,' said the countess, 'at a place called Malplaquet. A dreadful battle, so my brother tells me in his letter.'

'Malplaquet.' It was not real, she thought. A distant place, an unfamiliar name that tasted strangely on her tongue. Not real.

She heard the countess talking but she could not understand the words, nor did she try. It was enough to sit there, sifting sand and gazing out towards the line where sea met sky and where it seemed at any moment she might see the first white flutter of a fast approaching sail.

The waves kept coming in their soft way up the beach and slipping backwards, and the gulls above still hung upon the wind and wheeled and called to one another in shrill voices that were lost amid the laughter of the children playing at the water's edge.

Then Anna's laughter rose above the others and in that one instant something tore Sophia from inside and crumpled her like paper in a careless hand. She fought against it; fought the brimming pressure of her tears until her mouth began to tremble with the effort, but it was no use. Her vision blurred until she could no longer see the far horizon, nor the countess standing closer by in sympathy, and she could no more stop the first small tear that spilt across than she could stop the final bit of sand that slipped between her fingers and would not be held.

And so she let it go.

* * *

I didn't want to look. I didn't want to, but I knew I had no choice. The envelope of papers was still sitting where I'd left it on the corner of my desk, as far as possible from where I sat to write. It had been sitting there all day since I'd come back from Aberdeen. I'd only taken it out of my briefcase in the first place because I'd been missing Graham after our weekend and I had found it comforting to look up now and then and see the bold and certain letters of his handwriting spell out my name across the narrow envelope.

I hadn't changed out of his rugby jersey, either. The long sleeve slipped over my hand as I reached across my desk. I pushed the folds back to my elbow, took the envelope in hand, and drew the papers out in one determined motion, as though I were ripping off a bandage.

It was not, in actual fact, a pedigree chart, as Graham had called it. A pedigree chart would have started with one name and worked its way backward through just the direct line. What Graham had found was more useful, in my view. It was what my father would call a 'Descendants Chart', beginning with the earliest known ancestor and travelling forward, like the charts of English kings and queens found in the front of history books, showing the wide web of family relationships, the children of each union and who married whom and when each person died.

The Morays of Abercairney had been a busy bunch, and it had taken several pages to trace their line up to the point of John's birth. He was easy to find, in the section that listed his brother – the 12th Laird – his sisters Amelia and Anna, and two other brothers. I narrowed my focus to his name alone.

Written down, it was painfully brief. Just the year, and the note: *Died of wounds...*

There was no specific mention of the battle, but I was long past questioning my memories by now and I knew without doubting that Moray had fallen at Malplaquet. That name might have meant little enough to Sophia, but I knew it well. I still remembered reading Churchill's vivid description of that battle in his volumes of biography of his own ancestor, the Duke of Marlborough. I couldn't recall the exact numbers killed in that one day of fighting, but I knew that all of Europe had been shocked and sickened by the slaughter. Marlborough himself, a seasoned warrior, had been so deeply affected by the loss of life at Malplaquet that, according to Churchill, he had been forever altered. It would take another hundred years before that death toll would be reached upon a battlefield again.

John Moray had been only one more dead among the thousands, and Sophia only one among the wives who'd been made widows, and six months ago I might have read the papers I was reading now and noted down the facts with the detachment of a researcher, and thought no more about it.

But I couldn't do that now. I closed the papers on their folds and laid them carefully aside. The blank computer screen was waiting for my next word, but I couldn't do that either, not just yet. And so I rose and went to put the kettle on to make some coffee.

It was no longer night but early morning, and the winter sun was rising with reluctance. Through my windows I could see the dull light spreading grey like mist above the soggy-looking landscape, and the rolling lines of white that marked the edges of the waves along the empty curve of beach.

In my mind I almost saw the lonely figure of Sophia

standing on the shore, her bright hair hidden by her shawl, her saddened eyes still gazing seaward.

Even when the kettle whistled keenly to the boil and made me turn my gaze away, I saw those eyes, and knew they'd never give me peace until I'd finished with the story.

XXI

Sophia faced her pale reflection in the looking-glass while Kirsty made her choice among the new gowns that had lately been delivered by direction of the countess. There were three of them, of finest fabric, and their cost must surely have been felt by even such a woman as the countess, who had already put herself to such expense for the adventure of the king that, should he not come soon, the family's debts might bring this noble house to ruin. But the countess had not listened to Sophia's protestations. 'I am overdue in tending to your wardrobe,' she had said. 'I should have done this when you first arrived. A pearl, though it may gleam within the plainness of the oyster, shows its beauty best when viewed against a velvet case.' She'd smiled, and touched Sophia's cheek with tenderness, a mother's touch. 'And I would have the world observe, my dear, how brightly you can shine.'

The gown that Kirsty chose was soft dove grey, a fragile thing of silk that slipped lightly over a petticoat trimmed with silver lace. Frilled lace showed delicately at the deeply rounded neckline and the hem, and fringed the full sleeves that were fastened up with buttons at Sophia's elbows.

A velvet case indeed, she thought – but looking in the glass she did not think herself a pearl.

These last two months had left her thinner, hollow-eyed and wan. She could not dress in proper mourning clothes nor grieve her loss in public, but that loss was written plainly on her face, and even those within the household who knew nothing of the truth knew nonetheless that there was something sadly wrong with Mistress Paterson.

That had, in some ways, worked to her advantage. When the word had got about that she was leaving, many thought it was because she'd fallen ill and had been forced to seek a kinder climate than the wild northeast.

'You'll stay till Christmas, surely?' Kirsty had implored her, but Sophia had replied that she could not.

''Tis best to be away before the snow,' had been her explanation. Easier than saying that she could not bear the prospect of a holiday so based on hope and joy when she had neither.

'Anyway,' she'd said to Kirsty, 'you will have enough to occupy your time, I think, now that Rory has at last come to his senses.'

Kirsty had blushed.

'When will you wed? Is it decided?'

'In the spring. The earl has given Rory leave to take a cottage by the burn. It is a small place and will need repair, but Rory feels by spring it will be ready.'

'So you will have your cottage after all,' Sophia had said, and smiled above the pain that she was feeling at the knowledge she must leave behind her best and truest friend. 'I am so happy for you, truly.'

Kirsty, too, had seemed to find it difficult to keep her own emotions on a level. Now and then they'd broken through. 'I wish you could be here to see the wedding.'

Sophia had assured her, 'I will hear of it. I do not doubt the countess will be writing to me often. And,' she'd promised, 'I will send the finest gift that I can find in all of Kirkcudbright.'

Kirsty, setting her own sadness to one side a moment, had looked closely at her. 'Are ye still decided to return there, after all that you did suffer in that place?'

'I did not suffer in Kirkcudbright.' She had not thought at first to travel to the west, but when the countess had begun to search among her friends and kinsmen for a place that might be suitable, the matter had been taken from her hands by the great Duchess of Gordon, who although a Jacobite, was known and well-respected by the western Presbyterians. The perfect place was found, within a house of perfect sympathy, and somehow to Sophia it had seemed a just arrangement that her life should come full circle to the place where it began. She had memories of that town and of its harbour, where her father had once walked with her and held her up to see the ships. She'd said to Kirsty, 'Any suffering I did was in my uncle's house and to the north of there, not in Kirkcudbright.'

'But it is so far away.'

That knowledge hung between them now as Kirsty moved behind Sophia in the mirror and remarked, in tones that strove for brightness, 'Ye'd best hope the maids who travel with you have the sort of fingers that can manage all these buttons.'

'Will there be maids?' asked Sophia.

'Aye. The countess has arranged a proper entourage, so where you go the people will be thinking 'tis the queen herself that passes. There,' she said, and fastened off the final button, and it seemed to strike the both of them that this would be the final time that they would stand like this together in Sophia's chamber, where so often they had laughed and talked and shared their solemn confidences.

Turning from the mirror Kirsty bent her head and said, 'I must ready your clothes, they'll be coming to fetch them.'

The older gowns looked drab against the new but Kirsty set them out with care and smoothed the wrinkles from the fabric, and her fingers seemed particularly gentle on the one Sophia had most often worn, a plain and over-mended gown that once had been deep violet but had faded to a paler shade of lavender. Sophia, watching, thought of all the times she'd worn that gown, and all the memories that it carried. She had worn it on the first day she had ridden out with Moray with his gauntlet gloves upon her hands, the day that she'd first seen him flash that quick sure smile that now was burnt forever on her mind and would not leave her.

'Would you like to keep that one?' she asked, and Kirsty in surprise looked up.

'I thought it was your favourite.'

'Who better then to have it but my dearest friend? Mayhap when I am gone it will help keep me in your thoughts.'

Kirsty bit her lip, and in a voice that wavered promised her, 'You will be there without it. Every time I look at—' Then she stopped, as though she did not want to probe a wound that might be painful, and with downcast eyes she laid the gown aside and finished simply, 'Thank you. I will treasure it.'

Sophia blinked her own eyes fiercely, fighting for composure. 'One more thing,' she said, and reaching over, drew from deep within the heap of clothes the lace-edged holland nightgown with its fine embroidered vines and sprays of flowers intertwined.

'I'll not take that,' said Kirsty, firm. 'It was a gift.'

'I know.' Sophia passed her hand across the bodice, felt its softness and remembered that same feeling on her skin; remembered Moray's eyes upon her when she'd worn it on their wedding night. ''Tis not for you that I would leave it,' said Sophia slowly. ''Tis for Anna.'

Then, because she could not face the look in Kirsty's eyes directly, she looked down and smoothed the lovely nightgown and began to fold it carefully, with hands that shook but slightly. 'I have nothing else to leave her that is mine. It is my hope that she will never learn the truth, that she will always think your sister is her mother, but we cannot always know...' She lost her voice a moment; struggled to recover it, and carried on more quietly, 'We cannot always know what lies ahead. And if she ever does discover who she truly is, then for the world I would not have her thinking that she was not born of love, or that I did not hold her dear.'

'Sophia...'

'And if nothing else, when she has reached an age where she can marry, you may give it to her then, just as you gave it once to me, and she can value it for that alone.' The nightgown, neatly folded, seemed like nothing in Sophia's hands. She held it out to Kirsty. 'Please.'

A moment passed. Then Kirsty slowly reached to take the offering. 'For Anna, then.' And as her fingers closed around the nightgown something seemed to break in Kirsty, as though she'd kept silent for too long. 'How can you bear to leave,' she asked, 'and her not knowing who you are?'

'Because I love her.' It was simple. 'And I would not spoil her happiness. She has been raised within your sister's house, and to her mind the other children are her sisters and her brothers, and your sister's husband is the only father she has known.' That had hurt more than all the rest of it, because she felt that Moray had been robbed of more than just his life, but of his rights, to know his child and be remembered. But in the end she knew that scarcely mattered, as her own pain did not matter when she weighed it in the balance of their daughter's future. Trying to make Kirsty understand, she said, 'She has a family here, and is content. What could I give her that would equal that?'

'I do not doubt that Mr Moray's family, if they knew of her, would give her much.'

Sophia had considered that. She'd thought of Moray's ring, still on its chain around her neck, and of his saying she had but to ask his family for assistance, and they'd help her. And she'd thought of Colonel Graeme and his promise there was none of Moray's kin who would not walk through fire to see her safe. No doubt that promise would extend to Moray's child, as well – especially a child who looked so like him that it called his memory close.

But in the end Sophia had not chosen to reveal herself, nor ask for any help from Abercairney. It was true that in the lap of Moray's family Anna might have had the benefit of higher social standing, but, 'I will not take her from the only family she has known,' she said to Kirsty now, 'and have her live with strangers.'

'They would be her kin.'

Sophia answered quietly, 'That does not mean that she will be well treated. Do not forget that I was also raised by kin.'

And that reminder brought another silence settling down upon them both.

'Besides,' Sophia said, attempting brightness, 'I shall worry less about her knowing she is here. Should something happen to your sister there will be the countess and yourself who both would love and care for Anna as if she were your own child.'

'Aye,' said Kirsty, blinking fiercely, 'so we would.'

'It would be selfish of me, taking her from that to face a future that at best would be uncertain, with a mother and no father.'

'But you are young, like me,' said Kirsty. 'You may meet another man, and marry, and then Anna—'

'No.' Sophia's voice was soft, but very sure. She felt the solid and unyielding warmth of Moray's ring against her skin, above her heart, as she replied, 'No, I will never find another man I wish to marry.'

Kirsty clearly did not want to see her friend lose hope. 'Ye told me once that there was no such thing as never.'

She remembered. But the moment when she'd said that seemed so long ago, and now she knew it had not been the truth; that there were some things that could never be put right once they'd been ruined. Moray's ship would never come, and she would never wake again to feel his touch or hear him speak her name, and nothing could restore to her the life his love had promised her.

It was all gone. All gone, she thought. But still, she summoned up a smile to show to Kirsty, for she would not have this parting with her friend be any sadder than it had to be.

And there were other partings yet to come.

An hour later, in the library, she waited for the worst of them. There was no sun today to spread its warmth across the fabric of the chairs and cheer the room. The window glass was pebbled with the remnants of the freezing rain that had all night been flung against it by a wind from the northeast, and though that rain had stopped, the wind still wailed and tried its strength against the walls, its breath so cold that there was little that the small fire on the hearth could do to counter it.

Before the fire, the wooden chess board with its small carved armies waited patiently upon its table, but looking at it only called to mind the fact that they had had no word of Colonel Graeme yet, from France, and did not know if he was numbered in the wounded or the dead of Malplaquet. His quick grin crossed her memory and she turned from it, her back towards the chess board as she trailed her hand instead along the gilded leather bindings of the nearest bookshelf, searching out of habit for the book that she had sought out more than any other these past years – the newer volume, plainly bound, of Dryden's *King Arthur, or the British Worthy.* The pages that had once been lightly used now showed the marks of frequent reading, for this book had always managed to bring Moray close, somehow, despite the miles between them.

It still did. She felt the same connection when she held it that she'd felt before, and when she chose a random page and read the lines they spoke to her as strongly and as surely as they'd always done, although they did not speak this time of love but of defeat, a subject fitting to her mood:

'Furle up our Colours, and Unbrace our Drums;
Dislodge betimes, and quit this fatal Coast.'

She heard the door behind her softly open and then close again, and heard the slow distinctive rustle of the gown across the floor that marked the countess's approach. Sophia, looking down still at the open book, remarked, 'I have so often read this play I ought to know its lines as well as any actor, yet I still find phrases here that do surprise me.'

Drawing close, the countess asked, 'Which play is that?' and read the title, and her eyebrow lifted slightly. 'I suspect, my dear, that you may be the only person in this house who has attempted reading that at all. If it amuses you, then take it with you as my gift.'

Had it been any other book she might have raised a protest, but she wanted it so badly for herself she merely closed her hands around it and said thank you.

'Not at all. You must take several, now I think of it.' The countess scanned the shelves with newfound purpose. 'The Duchess of Gordon does assure me she has lodged you with the very best of families in Kirkcudbright, but notwithstanding that, my dear, they are still Cameronians, devoutly Presbyterian, and likely will have little use for pleasures such as reading. No, you must take some books from here, else you'll have nothing there to read but dry religious tracts.' She chose some volumes, took them down and stacked them near the chess board. 'I shall have these added to your box. Here, let me have the Dryden, too.' She stretched her hand to take it from Sophia, who released it with reluctance, but with heartfelt thanks.

'You are too kind.'

'Did you imagine I would send you all that way with nothing?' Looking down herself, the countess made a show of straightening the edges of the books as though that small act mattered greatly. 'I presume that you are yet resolved to go? I would not have you think you cannot change your mind. 'Tis not too late.'

Sophia tried to smile. 'I doubt the servants who have laboured these past days to make arrangements for my leaving would be pleased were I to change my mind.'

'There are none here who wish to see you leave. The servants would be overjoyed to see you stay at Slains.' She met Sophia's eyes. 'And so would I.'

'I wish I could.' Sophia felt the stir of sadness. 'But there are too many memories here, of him.'

'I understand.' The countess always seemed so strong that sometimes it was easy to forget that she had also lost a husband, not so long ago, and knew what it was like to live with memories. 'There may yet come a time when you do count them as a comfort.' And her eyes were very gentle on Sophia's downturned face. 'It does get easier, in time.'

Sophia knew it did. She knew from having lost her parents and her sister that the sharpness of her grieving would be blunted by the passing years, and yet she also knew that losing Moray had cut deeper than the others put together. His death had left her feeling more alone than she had ever felt before, and she herself might well grow old and die before enough years passed to dull the pain she carried now inside her.

There were footsteps in the corridor; a soft knock at the door.

'Do you feel strong enough to do this?' asked the countess, and Sophia bit her lip and shook her head before she answered, 'But I must.'

'My dear, you need not if it brings you too much pain. The child is not yet two years old, and being such a young age is not likely to remember.'

It was, Sophia thought, the very argument she'd made to Moray when he'd told her of his infant nephew, whom he'd never had the chance to meet. She understood his answer, now. Deliberately, she raised her head and in a quiet voice replied, 'I will remember *her*.'

The countess studied her a moment with concern, then gave a nod and crossed to let in Kirsty's sister, leading Anna by the hand.

The little girl was finely dressed as though for church, with ribbons in her hair. She did not venture far into the room, but stood and held fast to the skirts of Kirsty's sister, who looked over at Sophia in apology. 'She did not sleep well last night, she was troubled by her teeth. I fear she's out of sorts, the day.'

Sophia's smile was brief, and understanding. 'We are none of us as cheerful as we should be.'

'I will leave her here alone with you a moment if you wish it, but—'

'There is no need.' Sophia shook her head. 'It is enough that I should see her. Come, and sit with me.'

They sat where she'd so often sat with Colonel Graeme by the fire, the chess men lined up tidily across the board between them. Anna seemed to find them fascinating. Kirsty's sister would have kept the little girl from touching, but the countess, who'd stayed standing by the mantelpiece, insisted that the child could do no harm. 'The men are made of wood, and cannot easily be broken.'

Not like real soldiers, thought Sophia with a pang of sudden sorrow. Moray would not ever see his daughter's face, nor see those small, fair features form the image of his own as Anna, with her father's focused concentration, lifted knights and bishops from the board by turns and held them in her little hands.

Sophia watched in silence. She had spent the past days planning this farewell, rehearsing what she meant to do and say, but now that it had come the words seemed out of place.

How did you tell a child who did not know you were her mother that you loved her, and that leaving her was all at once the bravest and the worst thing you had done in all your life, and that you'd miss her more than she would ever know?

And what, Sophia asked herself, would be the point? She knew within her own heart that the countess had been right, that Anna's mind was yet too young to hold this memory; that as surely as the wind and waves would shift the sands till next year's coastline bore no imprint of the one the year before, so too the passing days would reshape Anna's mind until Sophia was forgotten.

Which was only as it should be, she decided, biting down upon her lip to stop its sudden trembling.

Reaching out, she stroked the softness of her daughter's hair, and lightly coughed to clear her voice. 'You have such lovely curls,' she said to Anna. 'Will you give me one?'

She did not doubt the answer; Anna always had been quick to share. And sure enough, the child gave an unhesitating nod and stepped in closer while Sophia chose one ringlet from beneath the mass of curls and gently snipped it with her sewing scissors. 'There,' she said, and would have straightened, but the little girl reached up herself to wind her tiny fingers in Sophia's hair, in imitation.

And that one small touch, so unexpected, made Sophia close her eyes against the sharpness of emotion.

She felt, in that brief instant, as she'd felt when it had only been herself and Anna newly born, and lying in the bed at Mrs Malcolm's, with the wonder of her daughter sleeping warm against her body and the feeling of those baby fingers clutching both her hair and Moray's silver ring...and suddenly she felt she could not bear it, what she knew she had to do.

It was not fair. Not fair. She wanted Anna back, to be her own again. Her own and no one else's. And she would have sold her soul at any price to turn time back and make it possible, but time would not be turned. And as the pain of that reality tore through her like a knife, she heard her daughter's voice say, 'Mama?' and the blade drove deeper still, because Sophia knew the word had not been meant for her.

She breathed, and swallowed hard, and when her eyes came open there was nothing but their shining brightness to betray her weakening.

Anna said a second time to Kirsty's sister, 'Mama?', and the other woman asked, her own voice curiously husky, 'Do ye want to have a lock of Mistress Paterson's, to keep?'

Sophia said, 'My curls are not as nice as yours,' but Anna tugged with firm insistence, so Sophia raised the scissors to her own hair and cut off a piece from where those baby fingers had so often clung in sleep.

'Aye,' said Kirsty's sister, when the child turned round to show her prize. 'It is a bonny gift, and one ye'll want to treasure. Let me borrow this wee ribbon and we'll cut it into two, and then ye both can bind your curls to keep them better.' Over Anna's head her eyes sought out Sophia's. 'I will send ye more.'

Sophia's fingers trembled so they could not tie the ribbon, but she folded it together with the curl into her handkerchief. 'The one is all I need.'

The other woman's eyes were helpless in their sympathy. 'If there is anything at all...'

'Just keep her safe.'

And Kirsty's sister gave a nod, as though she could not speak herself. And in the silence of the room both women, and the countess too, looked down at Anna, who in childish oblivion had once again begun to move the pieces on the chess board.

With an almost steady smile, Sophia asked, 'Which one do you like best, then, Anna? Which one is your favourite?'

She had expected that the little girl would choose a knight – the horses' heads had held her interest longest – or a castle tower, but the child, after some consideration, chose a different piece and showed it on her outstretched hand: a single, fallen pawn.

Sophia thought of Colonel Graeme, when he'd taught her how to play the game, explaining of the pawns: 'These wee men here, they're not allowed to make decisions. They can only put one foot afore the other...'

Looking down, she saw the pieces of the chess set scattered anyhow across the board and lying on their sides like soldiers felled in battle, and she saw that in their midst one piece still stood: the black-haired king.

She looked again at Anna's pawn and blinked to keep the tears back, but her smile held. 'Yes, that one is my favourite, too.'

And careless of propriety, she bent to wrap her arms round Anna one last time and hold her close, and make a final memory of the scent of her, the feel of her, the softness of the brush of curls against her cheek, so she'd have that at least to keep her company through all the hollow years to come. Then quickly – for the little girl, confused, had started drawing back – Sophia kissed the top of Anna's head and loosed her hold. 'It is all right, my darling, you can go.'

Anna stood her ground a moment longer staring upwards as though somehow she suspected more was going on than she could understand. Her solemn face and watchful eyes were so like Moray's at that instant that Sophia felt a painful twist of memory, like a hand that tugged against her heart and stopped it in mid-beat. She drew a shaking breath, determined, and her heart resumed its rhythm once again.

As all things must.

Still Anna stood and watched in silence, and Sophia tried to smile again but could not manage it, nor raise her voice much higher than a whisper. 'Go,' she gently urged the child. 'Go to your mother.'

And she did not cry. Not then. Not even when the little girl was led away, with one last backward look that would forever haunt Sophia's dreams. She did not cry. She only rose and went to stand before the window, where the cold wind off the sea was blasting hard against the glass and wailing still that it could not come in, while last night's rain yet clung hard to the panes like frozen tears.

The countess did not speak, nor leave her place beside the mantelpiece.

'So, you see,' Sophia said, 'my heart is held forever by this place. I cannot leave but that the greatest part of me remains where Anna is.'

'It would be so no matter how you left her,' said the countess. 'I have said goodbye to my own daughters, one by one.' Her voice was softly wise. 'And now to you.'

Sophia turned at that, and saw the sadness in the older woman's smile.

The countess said, 'I can assure you it is never such an easy thing to wish a child farewell.'

Beneath that quiet gaze Sophia felt her chin begin to tremble once again, and as the room became a blur she stumbled forward to the countess's embrace.

'My dear.' The countess held her close and stroked her hair as if she were as small as Anna, and in greater need of comfort. 'I do promise that you will survive this. Faith, my own heart is so scattered round the country now, I marvel that it has the strength each day to keep me standing. But it does,' she said, and drawing in a steady breath she pulled back just enough to raise a hand to wipe Sophia's tears. 'It does. And so will yours.'

'How can you be so sure?'

'Because it is a heart, and knows no better.' With her own eyes moist, the countess smoothed the hair back from Sophia's cheek. 'But leave whatever part of it you will with us at Slains, and I will care for it,' she said. 'And by God's grace I may yet live to see the day it draws you home.'

Chapter Seventeen

'No, *no*,' said Jane. 'You simply can *not* end the book like that. It's much too sad.'

To emphasise her point, she thumped the final pages of the manuscript down on the dark wood table of our booth in the Kilmarnock Arms, and made our lunch plates rattle.

'But that's how it really happened.'

'I don't care.' There was no stopping Jane once she got going, and I was glad there was no one but us in the Lounge Bar this afternoon. The lunch hour itself had been busy, seeing it was Saturday, but now the other tables had been cleared and there was only us. The girl who'd served us had retreated round the corner to the Public Bar, but even that seemed quiet, and to judge by all the footsteps passing by us on the sidewalk most of Cruden Bay today was out of doors. The breeze was chilly, but the sun was shining cheerfully for all that it was worth, so that from where I sat beside the window facing on the street, it looked like spring.

'It's bad enough,' said Jane, 'you had to go and kill the poor girl's husband – and I won't forgive you soon for that one either – but to make her leave her *child*.' She shook her head in disbelief.

'But Jane—'

'It isn't right,' she said. 'A mother wouldn't do a thing like that.'

'Oh, I don't know.' I thought I understood Sophia's reasons, even if I wasn't a mother myself, but my explanations fell on deaf ears. Jane was in no mood to hear them.

'Anyway,' she said, 'it's far too sad. You'll have to change it.'

'But I can't.'

'Of course you can. Bring Moray back from France, or Flanders, or wherever.'

'But he died.' I held the sheets I'd got from Graham out to show her. 'See? Right there, page three. John Moray, died of wounds.'

She took the papers from my hand and looked them over, unconvinced.

'They're all there,' I assured her. 'Look, there's Moray, and his sisters, and his mother's brother Patrick Graeme. I can't change what happens to real people, Jane. I can't change history.'

'Well, Sophia isn't history,' argued Jane. 'She isn't real, she's just a character, your own creation. Surely you can find some way to let her have a happy ending.' Standing firm, she pushed the pages back towards me on the table. 'You can try, at least. Your deadline's not for weeks yet. Speaking of which,' she went on, switching gears as she picked up her coffee cup, 'what shall I tell them you're working on next, when they ask me? I know you were thinking of Italy somewhere, but I don't remember the details.'

My own coffee had long since grown cold in the cup, but I lifted it anyway and drank so I'd have an excuse not to look at Jane directly. 'Actually,' I said, 'I've been thinking I might stay in Scotland awhile.'

'Oh, yes?' All her antennae were up, I could feel it.

'I have this new idea for a novel about one of the earlier kings of Scotland, James I. He ruled in the early fifteenth century and had a fascinating life, full of adventures, and he was murdered in this wonderfully treacherous way – there's a long Victorian poem about it, called "The King's Tragedy". Anyhow, I thought I might tell the whole tale through the eyes of his wife—'

'Was she murdered, as well?' Jane asked drily.

'No.'

'Glad to hear it. I thought this might be a new trend in your books, killing off all the likeable characters.' Over the rim of her own cup she gave me a moment's appraisal. 'It sounds like a good story, though. The publishers will like it. Scotland sells.'

'Yes, so you said.'

'And I'd be thrilled, of course, to have you living here. Assuming you'd be staying on in Cruden Bay.' She slipped that in as casually as some old angler stringing bait onto a hook.

'I like my cottage.'

'Yes, I know you do. I only thought your research might be easier if you were living near a university that had a decent library.' The hook danced closer still. 'Like Aberdeen.'

I didn't bite. I was, in fact, about to make some noncommittal comment when a knock against the window at my shoulder interrupted. On the sidewalk Stuart grinned and winked and motioned he was coming round.

Jane raised an eyebrow. 'Friend of yours?'

'My landlord's son.'

'Oh, really?' It was clear from her expression what conclusion she had leapt to, and the devil in me didn't rush to set her straight. Especially since Stuart, when he came into the Lounge Bar, wasn't on his own. Behind him, Graham shrugged his jacket off and met my gaze with warm indulgence, keeping to his brother's shadow while I made the introductions.

Everybody shifted round the circle of the booth as Stuart slid himself in next to me and slung an arm possessively along the window ledge behind. 'I think we talked once on the phone,' he said to Jane, and looking down at me explained, 'the night you hurt your ankle, you remember?'

'That was you?' Jane thought she had him pegged securely now, and barely glanced at Graham as he settled himself quietly across from her.

He knew what I was doing. I could read the faint amusement in his eyes as he took in the situation – Stuart leaning close against me, Jane positioning herself to cross-examine from my other side. He stretched one leg until his foot touched mine and left it there, a minor contact, yet for me the only one that mattered.

'So,' said Stuart, 'what are you two up to?'

Meaning Jane and me. I said, 'Jane was just telling me she hates the ending of my book.'

Jane looked at Stuart. 'Have you read it?'

'No, not yet. Is this it, here?' He turned the pages on the table round. 'I didn't know you'd finished it.'

'She hasn't,' Jane put in, and I knew better than to argue. 'It's too sad. You'll have to help me to convince her that the ending should be happy.'

'I can try.' He grinned, and shifted even closer to me as the waitress, seeing there were more of us, came by to clear our plates and see if anybody wanted drinks.

The two men ordered pints, I took a refill on my coffee, but Jane raised a hand. 'Oh no, I can't. I must get back. I promised Alan I'd be home by three. My husband,' she explained to Stuart, gathering her things before she rose and told him, 'Good to finally meet you.'

'Likewise.'

'And your brother. Graham, was it?' Reaching over to shake hands across the table, she asked, 'Did you like your cake?'

I hadn't seen that coming, and I held my breath, but Graham neatly caught the pitch and tossed it back again, his grey eyes laughing in his otherwise unaltered face. 'Aye, very much.'

'I'm glad.' She turned to hit me full force with the triumph of her smile. 'I'll ring you later, Carrie.'

I had no doubt that she would.

'Nice woman,' Stuart commented, when she had gone. Her reference to the cake had sailed right past him, it appeared, or he'd dismissed it as an unimportant detail since it wasn't about him. He drummed his fingers absently on top of my stacked pages. 'Why did she want me to convince you that the ending should be happier? How sad can it be?'

'I killed the hero.'

'Ah.'

'And I made the heroine give up her only child and go away.'

'Aye, well,' said Stuart, 'that'll do it.' Swigging back a mouthful of his pint, he said, 'So let the hero live.'

'I can't. He's an actual person from history, he dies when he dies, I can't change that.'

'So end the book before he dies.'

A simple answer. And it would have solved a lot of problems, I admitted. Only life was rarely simple.

I was vividly reminded of that fact an hour later when we three left the Kilmarnock Arms and started walking down toward the harbour. Stuart wasn't drunk, exactly, but the pints had left him happy and relaxed, and as we walked he put his arm around my shoulders and there wasn't any nice way to get rid of it. Graham, walking half a step behind us, didn't seem to mind.

Nor did he seem to mind when Stuart said he'd walk me to my cottage.

'No, you go,' said Graham. 'I'll look in on Dad.' His hand clasped briefly at my arm, a reassuring touch. 'I'll see you after.'

Stuart went on talking to me cheerfully as we trudged up the slushy path together, and when I had put my key into the cottage door he came right in behind me, stamping water off his feet and in the middle of an anecdote. 'And then I said to him, I said—'

He broke off so abruptly that it made me look behind.

He was still standing just inside the door, eyes focused on the table where I wrote. Well, not the table, but the chair in front. And not the chair exactly, but the shirt slung on the back of it: a well-worn rugby jersey, navy blue with stripes of gold and red.

He swung his gaze to mine. I was relieved I couldn't see real disappointment in it, just a rueful realisation, and acceptance. 'It's not me,' he asked me, 'is it? It was never me.'

I answered him with honesty. 'I'm sorry.'

'No, it's all right,' he said, lifting up one hand. He turned to go. 'If you'll excuse me, I'll be off to beat my brother senseless.'

'Stuart.'

'Not to worry, I'll leave all his vital parts in working order.'

'Stuart.'

Halfway out the door he stopped. Looked back, good-natured. 'Actually, the worst part is, I haven't got an argument to offer. Even *I* know that you chose the better man.'

And then he smiled, and let the door swing closed behind him, and I heard him trudging off along the path.

'Did I not tell you?' Graham asked me. He was setting up his next move on the chess board that I'd found in a back cupboard of the cottage. It was not quite in the same league as the one my characters had played on in the library at Slains – not all the pieces had survived, and we were using Liquorice Allsorts for my bishop and his rook – but when I set it on the small round table in between the armchairs near my fireplace, it made a close facsimile.

I looked at Graham. 'So he'll be all right, then?'

'Stuie? Aye. He's away to Peterhead tonight to search the pubs for your replacement. He'll be fine.'

He'd moved his knight, and I was forced to take a moment to consider my response. I wasn't the world's best chess player, and I tried to clear my mind, in hopes some buried memory – Colonel Graeme's teachings, maybe – might come down the line to steer my hand.

Graham waited. 'I've been thinking of your problem with the book.'

'Oh, yes?'

'You say that after Moray dies, his widow has to leave their child as well?'

'That's right.'

'There's no way she can keep it? When my dad lost Mum, the only thing that kept him going was the fact he still had Stuart and myself. A grieving person's like a person treading in deep water – if they've nothing to hold on to, they lose hope. They slide right under.'

I agreed. 'But for my heroine, it isn't quite that easy.' I explained the situation while I made my move.

He wasn't swayed. 'I'd take the child anyway.'

'Well, you're a man. Men think differently. And a woman on her own in the early eighteenth century wouldn't have had an easy time of it, raising a child.'

He pondered this while studying the chess board, then he moved his queen to take my liquorice allsort bishop, which he lifted from the board and ate, still thinking.

'And just what,' I asked him drily, 'do you plan to do when my pawn makes it to the other side, and I ask for my bishop back?'

Graham gave a cocky grin, and speaking thickly through the candy said, 'Your pawn'll never get there. You're in check.'

I was, at that. He'd done it neatly, and at first glance I could see no way to move my king to safety, but he hadn't told me 'checkmate', so I knew it wasn't hopeless, that there had to be a way...

'The thing to do,' he said, 'is give her someone else.'

It took a moment till I realised Graham was still thinking of my book, and how to make the ending happy.

'Give her someone else to love,' he said. 'Another man.'

'She doesn't want another man.'

It was the truth, I thought. The minute that I spoke the words, I knew it was the truth. And yet Sophia had, within a year, agreed to marry my own ancestor. I couldn't help but wonder why.

Perhaps, I thought, the answer to my problem with the ending didn't lie at Slains. My vision cleared. I made a minor move upon the chess board, and a pawn stepped up to shield my king and clear my other bishop. 'Checkmate.'

Graham, leaning forward, made a quick inspection of the pieces. 'How the devil did you do that?'

In all honesty, I didn't know. But I *was* sure of one thing: like Sophia, I would have to make the journey to Kirkcudbright, for the ending to my story waited there.

Chapter Eighteen

There was no station at Kirkcudbright, so I took the train to Dumfries, which was close. I didn't know what I expected, when I stepped down to the platform. An epiphany, I guess – a sort of wakening of memory now that I was in the landscape where Sophia had been born and raised. But there was nothing. Just the pretty little station with its curving track and platform and the sunshine sparkling down through the glass roof that stretched above me.

The weather was thawing in earnest, and the breeze was almost mild against my face as I stepped back to let another woman pass me, her wheeled suitcase rumbling purposefully across the paving bricks.

'Carrie!'

I shifted the weight of my own case and took a look round. I'd never actually met Ross McClelland, but over the years I'd formed a mental picture of him, making him in my own mind an older version of my father, someone I'd recognise, seeing as we had all sprung from the same stock. The man who came forward to greet me was nothing like what I'd imagined he'd be. He was big and tall and ruddy-faced, with thick wavy hair and a beard that, though grey, still showed black round the edges. I wouldn't have known him for family.

He'd recognised *me*, though.

'Oh, aye, my wife buys all your books,' he said. 'You look just like your photo on the jacket flap. Is this all you brought?'

'Yes. How is your wife?' I asked him, as he took my suitcase from my hand and led me out towards the parking area.

'A wee bit better. It's her gout, you see. She has attacks of it so fierce these days she finds it hard to move, but she's been out of bed this morning and her sister's come to sit with her awhile, so that's all right.'

I hadn't taken Ross up on his offer of a place to stay. I'd known that he *would* offer when I phoned him up last Sunday, but I'd also known his wife had not been well, and that they didn't need the added burden of a house guest – especially one who would be staying up till all hours writing, wandering round when everybody else was fast asleep, and lying late in bed. So I had booked myself a room at a hotel, and although Ross had raised a protest, I had sensed he was relieved.

Just as I sensed now, from the way that he was chatting to me while he put my suitcase in the car and saw me safely buckled in, that he was pleased to have the chance to leave his nursemaid duties for a day, and spend a bit of time with someone else who shared his love of genealogy.

He'd promised me a proper tour, and that was what I got.

It was a lovely drive from Dumfries, down through countryside that rolled with hills of green and darker forests, and the trees in places arching overhead to make the road seem like a tunnel. There were sheep, and curiously banded black-and white Galloway cattle, and when we made our first stop at a little country kirkyard we were greeted by a lively burst of birdsong.

'There you are,' said Ross, and pointed to a small and tilting headstone. 'That's your Anna Mary Paterson.'

I knelt to take a closer look. The stone was crusted thick with lichen, and the passing years had worn the words away till they were barely there at all.

Ross said, 'It was a bit of luck, my finding that. You don't find many stones that age, and those you do find often are past reading.'

He was right, I knew. But still, I had a feeling that I might have found this grave myself, if I had tried. The kirkyard faintly stirred my memory. Standing up again, I looked across the fields and saw a dark place near the distant trees that made me feel as cold as if I'd stepped into a shadow. 'Did there used to be a house once, over there?'

Ross couldn't tell me, but I felt sure that if I ever had the luck to come across an old map of this area, I'd find a cottage sitting on that spot – John Drummond's cottage. It was fitting, in my mind, that time had claimed those stones as well, and left no mark behind of all the evil that had happened there.

I touched Sophia's sister's headstone gently, and felt closure.

Our next stop was a field as well. 'See over there?' asked Ross, and pointed to a level place along the river shore. 'Your ancestor and mine, old Hugh MacLellan, had a farm there. That was where his sons were born and where he died, before they both were sent across to live in Ireland among the Ulster Scots.'

I knew the story. David John McClelland – when and why they'd changed the spelling of the name, we didn't know – had gone to Ireland with his brother William, and we'd lost their trails until they'd both returned to marry wives in Scotland. William had found his wife first, and in what must have been a disappointment to the Scottish settlers in Ireland, had stayed on in Kirkcudbright. Not for long, though. He had died a young man, leaving only one son to survive him and to carry on the family line that Ross became a part of.

'Would you like to see the house that William lived in, after he came back from Ireland?'

It wasn't my branch of the family tree, but Ross seemed so pleased to have me there for company that I said yes, of course I would, and so we drove the short way down into Kirkcudbright.

It was one of the prettiest places I'd been to, its houses built shoulder to shoulder and painted soft yellow and grey, pink and blue – some whitewashed, some left plain of red stone or of dark stone, with their neatly painted window frames and tidy iron railings and the chimneys with their little rows of chimney pots.

The High Street was unusual in that it was an L-shape and, though I could see a few shops and commercial establishments, it seemed to otherwise be almost all residential.

'Aye, it's always been like that,' said Ross. He drove us past the ancient Tollbooth with its pointed high roof tower, round the corner where the narrow street grew narrower from all the cars parked end to end along it, and he found a space to park his car among them, and we both got out.

The house in question was a stone-built, square-walled building huddled close against its neighbours, with a bright green-painted door and windows that were open to the warming air of spring.

Ross looked it over. 'Now, I can't be certain, mind you, but from letters that I've found describing where his house was situated, this is where I think he lived. A shame you didn't come here last year, I'd have taken you inside – it was a bed and breakfast then. But it's been bought up by a lad from Glasgow. Artist. Lots of artists live here now.'

I stopped. A breeze blew past, and something stirred. Enough to make me take my camera out, and snap off a few pictures of the street, the door, the windows...that far window, in particular. I said, to Ross, 'I'm guessing David McClelland was here, too, at one time.'

'Aye, it's possible.'

It was a little more than that, I thought. And it was one of my regrets that, in the moment before Ross resumed our tour, I didn't just step up and knock at that green door and ask the artist lad from Glasgow for a tour of his front rooms, and of the room in the far corner where the window seemed to watch me like a gently knowing eye.

I was restless that night.

I had wanted to treat Ross to supper, to thank him for taking me round, but he'd cheerfully waved off my offer. 'No, no, there's no need for that. The wife's sister will be watching the door as it is, I've been gone so long. But,' he'd said, 'it was a pleasure, my dear, to have met you.'

Our handshake had easily turned to a hug.

'Oh,' he'd said, drawing back so he could search his coat pockets, 'I nearly forgot. I was meaning to give you a catalogue.'

'Catalogue?'

'Aye, for the auction. I've sent one last week to your father, but I thought you might like to have one yourself. It's the New York McClellands,' he'd said. 'Tom and Clare.'

'Oh, yes.' Tom was my Dad's distant cousin, and traced his line back, as did we, to Sophia and David. Somehow or other his side of the family had managed to gain possession of most of the family's historical keepsakes – our family Bible being the only notable exception – and Tom and his wife had a habit of blithely disposing of things to help fund their extravagant lifestyle, which left my dad fuming since often we didn't find out until after the sale.

I'd looked at the catalogue cover to see what the date of the auction was – next Friday – and Ross had said, 'Oh aye, I got that away in the post to your father as soon as I opened the envelope. Tom's done this so many times now I've had to get one step ahead of him, so I set up an arrangement,' he'd said, 'with the auction house. Any time they take in something to do with McClellands, they send me their catalogues.'

'Clever.' I'd smiled. 'I'm surprised Tom and Clare still have things left to sell. I'd have thought they'd cleared everything out by now.'

'Oh, there's not much this time. Only a table or two and some jewellery. But still, I thought you and your father would like to at least see the pictures.'

I'd thanked him, and tucked it away in my bag.

After supper, I'd gone for a walk and had sat for an hour on a bench at the back of the Greyfriars Church by the harbour. It wasn't the kind of a harbour I'd thought it would be, after all that I'd read in the history books. Centuries ago the great Scottish patriot William Wallace had supposedly sailed from here after his failure at Falkirk, fleeing to the safety of the continent, and his arch-nemesis, the English King Edward I, had once landed his fleet of some sixty-odd ships in Kirkcudbright, so in my own mind I had pictured a harbour like those of the towns on the coast, but this hadn't been like that. There had been little more than the river itself, with a wall at its edge where the boats could be moored. And at low tide those boats would be sitting on mudbanks, and anything larger would have to wait out in the river's deep middle, at anchor.

But still, when I'd squinted, I hadn't had trouble imagining ships sailing past, coming in from the sea to seek shelter and unload their cargoes. The town would have changed since that time. The power plant off to my right and the bridge arching over the bend in the river would not have been there, but when I'd filtered out all that, I'd felt I might be seeing what Sophia would have seen had she been sitting in that spot beneath the trees three hundred years ago, and looking out across the River Dee. The farther shore was still and peaceful, with its green hills rising gently through the deeper green of woods above a white farm and a small boat sailing past upon the tide.

I hadn't been so certain of the church behind me – Ross had told me it had been rebuilt at some time in the eighteenth century, and was not the original – but I'd been sure the castle that stood even taller behind *that* was something that Sophia would have known. MacLellan's Castle, named for my own family, though we hadn't yet established any link on paper between our McClellands and the man who'd built the castle. It had suffered, as had Slains, the great indignity of having had its roof removed, and so had fallen into ruin. Even so, considering MacLellan's Castle's roof had been removed almost two hundred years before the one at Slains, it had seemed to be bearing up wonderfully well.

Ross had shown me around it as part of our tour, and we'd walked round the outside on tidy gravel pathways edged by neatly clipped sections of lawn and new-flowering borders so that he could show me the armorial engravings chiselled over the front doorway. I confess I'd paid little attention except to the fact that the arms had been those of the laird and his second wife, with whom he'd apparently been very happy, and that had started me thinking about second marriages.

And that, I knew, was at the core of my problem.

I needed Sophia to marry again as she'd done in real life, but I couldn't see how she'd be happy with anyone other than John, and my fear was that once I got into the writing, I'd find that she *hadn't* been happy – that she'd only married my ancestor for the security, or to get out of Kirkcudbright, or for some other practical reason. And once I had written the scene, I'd be stuck with it. I couldn't change what had actually happened, not even to satisfy Jane's desire for a happy ending.

It wouldn't ring true.

That was why I was restlessly pacing my room now, unable to focus enough to just sit down and write.

I'd never had writer's block, but sometimes when I was approaching a scene that I didn't want to deal with I had trouble getting on with it, and pairing Sophia with David McClelland would be, in some ways, even harder than killing off Moray. My subconscious sensed what was coming and shrank from the task, finding any excuse not to work.

A part of me wanted to just pull the plug on my laptop and go straight to bed and forget the whole thing, and I might have, except at that moment Sophia's voice started to form in my mind, her words faint but insistent.

She'd said them before, when she'd spoken to Kirsty before leaving Slains. And though, when she had said them, she'd been speaking of her childhood, I believed that in this room, here in this place, her words meant more than that. I felt them like a nudge at my shoulder, encouraging me to go on.

I did not suffer in Kirkcudbright, she reminded me.

And what else could I do, I thought, but take her at her word?

XXII

After the first month Sophia had stopped trying to keep track of days, they were so much alike – all filled with prayer and quiet work and sober conversation. Only Sundays stood out from the rest, for she had found them quite exhausting when she'd first arrived among the Presbyterians: up early and to prayers, and then to kirk at ten, and briefly home to eat a meagre meal of bread and egg before returning to the kirk at two, and sitting through the sermons all the afternoon, by which time she was far too tired to enjoy the supper that was served at night, or take full part in all the evening prayers and singing that were yet to follow before she could take herself upstairs to bed.

The Countess of Erroll, while a woman of devotion, had kept Sundays in the manner of a true Episcopalian – a morning service followed by a midday meal that made the table groan and had left everyone quite lazy and content to spend the leavings of the day in happy idleness.

It was on Sundays that Sophia missed her life at Slains the most, and though the people of this house where she was living now – the Kerrs – had been most kind to her, and welcoming, she felt a certain sadness on a Sunday. Although she tried to hide it, her feelings must have showed upon her face as she sat now among the family while they ate their cold noon meal, for Mrs Kerr had long been watching her and finally said, 'Sophia, I do fear that you must find us very dreary, after living in the north. I have been told the Earl of Erroll and his mother keep a lively house.'

Sophia liked Mrs Kerr, a soft-faced woman younger by some ten years than her husband. Mr Kerr, a man of mild temperament and pleasant manners, had a sombre air about him that had not yet fully claimed his wife, so she was more inclined to smile. Not like her husband's mother, Mrs Kerr the elder, who although she had displayed at times a cutting wit, still turned a disapproving face toward the world in general.

The older woman said, not looking up, 'I should imagine Mistress Paterson, like any decent woman, would be relishing the quiet after suffering the company of such a house as Slains.'

Her son said, 'Mother.'

'Do not "Mother" me, my lad. You know full well what my opinion is of all this foolish talk of bringing back the king, and what I think of those who entertain the notion, and that does include yourself,' she told him, with a sidelong glance that put him in his place. 'You mark my words, he may now promise us that he'll not interfere in our religion, but the instant he sets foot on Scottish soil you'll hear him pipe a different tune. He is a papist, and you cannot trust a papist.'

Mr Kerr remarked that he would sooner trust a papist than an Englishman.

'On your head be it, then,' his mother said, and turning in

her seat she asked Sophia, 'What is your opinion, Mistress Paterson?'

But Sophia had been living here three months, and knew enough to step around the trap. 'I am afraid I have not met that many papists. And no Englishmen at all.'

The elder Mrs Kerr could not contain a quirking of her mouth that spoilt her dour expression for an instant. 'Aye, well then you have been fortunate.' Her study of Sophia held new interest. 'Tell me, how is it you came to be at Slains? The Duchess of Gordon has told us your family did come from this place, and that you had been brought up not far from Kirkcudbright. What took you so far from your home?'

'I am kin to the Countess of Erroll.' She said it with pride, and for all of her weariness sat a bit straighter. 'I went there at her invitation.'

'I see. And what made you come back?'

There it was, that sharp twist at her heart that was now so familiar she'd learnt to breathe through it. She spoke the lie lightly, 'I thought I had stayed long enough in the north.'

Mr Kerr nodded. 'I seem to remember the Duchess of Gordon did say you were keen to come back to the place of your birth.'

Young Mrs Kerr was thinking. 'Is the duchess not a papist?'

'The Duchess of Gordon,' her mother-in-law said firmly, 'is a woman quite above the common mark, who at her heart I am convinced is Presbyterian.'

Sophia had heard much about the duchess since she'd come here. Colonel Hooke, as she recalled, had spoken much about his correspondence with the duchess, who despite her Catholic faith had gained the trust and high regard of the great chieftains of the Western Shires, those fervent

Presbyterians who had been just as outraged by the Union as the Jacobites, and who had sought to join their forces in a fight to guard the Scottish crown against the English. From her Edinburgh home she served as a go-between, fully aware she was narrowly watched by the agents of Queen Anne and by the less visible spies of the Duke of Hamilton.

The duke, Sophia had learnt, was distrusted as much by the Presbyterians as by the Jacobites, since it was he who had stopped them from rising in protest of the Union when it might have done some good. She'd also been told he had sent a private envoy once to tell the western chieftains they would better serve themselves by giving him the crown in place of James, since he alone could guard their interests. But they would not undertake such treason, and had earned the duke's fierce enmity.

The rumour was he regularly turned his eye toward the west, and that his spies yet walked among the people of this shire, but he would dare not make a move here, with the people so against him. Sophia knew that, in Kirkcudbright, she was safe. And anyway, with Moray dead, she'd be of little value to the duke.

Mr Kerr, at the head of the table, was slicing the meat for the next course when young Mrs Kerr changed the subject.

'Did you see the widow McClelland in kirk? She has put off her mourning.'

Her husband shrugged. 'Aye, well 'tis almost a year now.'

His wife replied, 'I should not doubt that it has more to do with the arrival of her husband's brother. *He* was not in kirk this morning.'

Mr Kerr remarked he would not know the man to see him. 'I am told he is not well.'

Sophia knew that Mr Kerr was trying not to let the conversation dwindle into gossip, but it was no use. His wife had that peculiar light of interest in her eyes that people got when they were speaking of the actions of another.

'I did hear that he was well enough to tell old Mrs Robinson to mind her own affairs.'

The elder Mrs Kerr said, 'Oh aye? When was this?'

'Two days ago, or three, I am not certain. But I have been told that Mrs Robinson did call upon the widow McClelland, to tell her that keeping a man in her house, kin or no, was inviting a scandal.'

'Oh aye.' The older woman sniffed. ''Twas likely envy, for I cannot call to mind that Mrs Robinson did ever keep a man in her own house besides her husband, and he was not much to sing about.'

Sophia smiled privately as Mr Kerr said, 'Mother!' and the older woman waved him off and carried on, 'So Mr McClelland...what name does he go by?'

''Tis David, I think,' said young Mrs Kerr.

'So then David McClelland was not pleased to have such advice?'

'Not at all.' And the young woman smiled as well. 'I am told he has neither the amiable looks nor the soft-spoken ways of his brother. He told Mrs Robinson straight out that those who saw sin in his sister-in-law must carry sin in their own hearts, to colour their view.'

The older woman's mouth twitched. 'Did he, indeed?'

'Aye. And then he suggested she be on her way.'

'That will make him no friends,' was the dour Mrs Kerr's observation. 'Still, I must say for my own part this does make me view him favourably. I do prefer a person who defends a woman's honour over one who seeks to stain it. But,' she said, 'if you should have the chance this afternoon, you might wish to tell the young widow McClelland more gently to look to appearances, for she is not wise to put her mourning off so soon. A wife should mourn her husband properly.'

Sophia felt another stab of sorrow near her heart. The food left on her plate had lost all its appeal, and had no taste. She tried to eat it, but the effort was so slight that even Mr Kerr took note.

'Why, Mistress Paterson, are you not well?'

She raised a hand to shield her eyes. 'I have a dreadful headache. Do forgive me,' she excused herself, and grateful for the chance to leave the table made her way upstairs.

She was not made to go to kirk that afternoon. She heard the others leaving while she lay upon her bed, dry-eyed, and mourned the only way she could, in private. But that too was interrupted by a knocking at her door.

Sophia answered, dull, 'Come in.'

The maid who entered was, though young, as unlike Kirsty in her manner as could be – head down and timid and not wanting to be spoken to. There was no question here of making friends among the servants, they kept closely to themselves. Sophia often longed for Kirsty's laughter, and their walks and talks and confidences. Kirsty would have cheered her now, and drawn the curtains wide to let the light in, but the maid here only stood inside the door and said, 'Beg pardon, Mistress, but there's someone come to see you.'

Sophia did not look around. 'Do give them my apologies. I am not well.' It would most likely only be some prying neighbour who had seen that she was not in kirk, and wished to know the reason why. She'd had her share of visitors these past months, all curious to view this new young stranger in their midst who'd lived so openly with Jacobites. Like the young widow McClelland, Sophia had been offered much advice as to how to conduct herself, and she had listened and smiled and endured. But today she was not in the mood for it.

Still the maid hovered. 'I told him so, Mistress, but he seemed quite sure you'd be wanting to see him. He said he was kin.'

Sophia rolled over at that, for she could not think who...? 'Did he give you his name?'

'He did not.'

With a frown, she rose slowly and smoothed out her gown. As she went down the stairs she could hear someone moving around in the front room, the leisurely steps of a man wearing boots. Either he – or more likely the maid – had been careful to leave the door standing fully open to the entry hall, mindful of the fact that there was no one in the house to serve as chaperone, but because he had crossed to stand before the mantelpiece she did not see him until she had stepped into the room.

He had his back to her, head angled slightly while he took a close look at the paintings done in miniature that hung upon the wall, his stance and manner so like Moray's that the memory tugged again a little painfully before Sophia caught herself and realised who it was. She gave a happy cry of recognition, and as Colonel Graeme turned she gave no thought to what was proper, only rushed across the room into his hard embrace.

There was no need to say the words, to speak aloud of sorrow or of sympathy. It passed between them anyway, in silence, as she pressed her face against his shoulder. 'I did fear you had been killed,' she whispered.

'Lass.' The single word held roughness, as though he were deeply touched by her concern. 'Did I not tell ye I would keep my head well down?' He held her tightly for a moment, and then pushed her back so he could have a look at her. 'The maid said ye were ill.'

Sophia looked back at the doorway, and the quiet maid still standing there, and knowing that whatever happened in this room would be told to the Kerrs, Sophia gathered her emotions into something like composure. 'It is all right, you may go,' she told the maid. 'This is my uncle, come from Perthshire.'

With a nod, the maid retreated, and Sophia turned again to look at Colonel Graeme's face, and found him smiling.

'Neatly done,' he said, 'although ye might have thought to have her bring a dram for me afore she went. I've had no whisky yet the day, and it has been a long hard road from Perthshire.'

'Did you really come from there?'

He shook his head. 'I took passage over from Brest, lass, and sailed into Kirkcudbright harbour on Saturday last.'

'You have been here a week?' She could scarcely believe it.

'I'd have come to see ye sooner, but I had a bout of sickness on board ship, and it was lingering, and I'd no wish to pass it on to you. And anyway, it's been the devil's task to get ye on your own. I thought it an uncommon bit of luck to see the others trooping off to kirk without ye, so I told myself 'twas time I paid a call.'

She could not fully take it in, that he was truly here. She sat, and motioned him to do the same, and said, 'I had a letter from the countess not three days ago, and she did make no mention of your coming.'

'Aye, well,' he said, and took a chair close by, 'she likely was not told. Few people ken I am in Scotland.'

'But how then did you know I was not at Slains, but in Kirkcudbright?'

He spoke low, as she had spoken, in a voice not meant to leave the room. ''Twas not the countess, lass, who telt me where to find ye. 'Twas the queen herself, at Saint-Germain.'

'The queen?' She shook her head, confused. 'But—'

'It would seem a wee bird once did sing to her that you were John's own lass, and since he'd always had her favour she did take a special interest in your welfare. She brought you to Kirkcudbright.'

'No.' It sounded too incredible. 'The Duchess of Gordon did find me this place.'

'Aye. And who has the ear of the Duchess of Gordon?' He eyed her with patience. 'When you set your mind to leaving Slains, the countess wrote her brother and her brother telt the queen, and it was she who asked the duchess if she'd find a home to suit ye here.' He watched while she absorbed this, then went on, 'So when the word got round the king had plans to send me here as well, the queen was quick to tell me where ye were.'

She felt at sea again. 'The king has sent you here?'

'Oh aye.' He settled back at that, although he did not raise his voice. 'By his own order.'

'To what purpose?'

'I am here to guard a spy.'

'A spy.' She did not like the word. 'Like Captain Ogilvie?'

'No, lass. This man does risk himself for our own cause and

has a right to my protection, and a need of it besides, for even though the Presbyterians do claim to take King Jamie's part, they would not think so kindly of a fellow Presbyterian who now has turned a Jacobite and seeks to move among them as a spy.'

Sophia thought of the expression in the elder Mrs Kerr's eyes when she'd spoken of King James, and knew that many others here were of a like mind. 'So you are sent to keep him safe?'

'Aye, for the time that he is here, afore he goes across to Ireland, to Ulster, for 'tis there King Jamie wishes to have eyes and ears and voices that can turn men to his cause. I'll not be needed there. But we must wait awhile afore he makes the crossing, for the sickness that did strike me on the ship from France did strike him harder, and he's not yet well enough to travel.'

Something made a faint connection in Sophia's memory – something Mr Kerr had said this very day while they'd been sitting at the midday meal, about a man who had but lately come to live here in Kirkcudbright, and who was not well. 'This spy of yours,' she asked the colonel, curious, 'would his name be McClelland?'

She could tell from his reaction that it was. 'And how the devil would ye come to think of that?'

'The people of this house do take an interest in their neighbours. And your Mr McClelland, by choosing to stay with his sister-in-law, has been giving them much to discuss. I am told he defended her honour most ably, in spite of his illness.'

The colonel half smiled. 'Aye, he would. She's a sweet lass, and was good enough to take him in despite the fact they had not met afore this and she barely has the means to keep her own self and her wee son fed and clothed. Who was it attacking her honour?'

'An elderly woman of rigid opinions.'

'Aye well, he'd have measured his words, then. But illness or no, I don't doubt he'd cross swords with a man who spoke ill of the lassie.' He glanced at her sideways, assessing. 'You'll not yet have met him.'

'No.'

'Then let me tell ye a bit about David McClelland. He came from Kirkcudbright, or near to it anyway, he and his brother, but when they were wee lads their father took ill and died, and they were sent into Ireland, where they had kin. David's brother, being older, was apprenticed to a cooper and became one in his own right, and returned here several years ago. But David,' said the colonel, 'had a different sort of soul, and had a yearning for adventure, so he took up with the Royal Irish Regiment and went to fight in Flanders. That's the other side from us, ye ken. I likely faced him once or twice myself across a battlefield.'

Sophia had gone silent, looking down at her linked fingers while she thought. She asked him quietly, 'Was he at Malplaquet?'

'He was.' She felt his eyes upon her face. 'But no man who did fight at Malplaquet came out the same as he went in, and David McClelland was changed by that day more than most men.'

She gave a small nod. She had heard many tales of that battle these past months, and many accounts had been printed and widely discussed in the drawing rooms here, so she knew it had been an unthinkably bloody and brutal encounter beyond even what the most hardened old soldier could bring to his mind. While she might bear resentment that David McClelland had fought on the opposite side, against Moray, she knew any man who had lived through that day was deserving of sympathy.

Colonel Graeme carried on, 'He was too badly wounded in the battle to continue with his regiment, and after that he came to serve King Jamie, and has served him with a loyalty that none would dare to question.'

She was mindful of the earlier betrayals that had touched both him and Moray. 'You are certain that he does deserve your trust?'

'Aye, lass. As certain as my life.' He was still watching her. 'I'd like for ye to meet him. Will ye come with me?'

'What, now?' She glanced instinctively toward the open doorway to the entry hall. 'It would not be so wise for me to leave the house when everyone believes I have a headache.'

With a crinkle at the corners of his eyes he said, 'Ye've done things in the past that were not wise, and have survived them. Come, 'twill be two hours yet till your good hosts are home from kirk, and ye can tell the servants that ye have a mind to go out walking with your uncle, which is no more than the truth.' She knew that look, the one that dared her to accept his challenge, knowing that she would. 'My mother always said a walk in open air was the best way to cure the headache. Tell them that.'

'All right. I will.' Her chin went up with something of her old defiance, and he gave a nod.

'Good lass.'

Outside, she drew the loose hood of her cloak up so it all but hid her face, though there was no one in the High Street to observe them. There was nothing but the quiet of a Sunday afternoon with everybody gone to kirk, including, most likely, the widow McClelland. She asked, 'Does David McClelland have no other kin in Kirkcudbright?'

'No, not anymore. Nor in Ireland, for all his kin there have died off.'

'He's alone, then.' She knew what that felt like. She thought to herself that it must have been hard coming back to this place after being so wounded in war, to be ill and surrounded by strangers.

The colonel was reading her thoughts. 'You're much alike, the two of ye. 'Twill do ye good to meet.' They'd reached the turning of the High Street where the old stone mercat cross stood lonely in the empty marketplace.

Sophia said, 'Perhaps he will not wish to have a visitor.'

Colonel Graeme felt more sure that he would welcome the diversion. 'He is not a man to lie so long abed. It fouls his temper. And as fascinating as I am myself, I do suspect he's borne enough of my own company these past weeks.'

She smiled at that, and then fell into sober thought once more. 'Is he recovered of his wounds?'

The colonel shrugged. 'He has a limp that he will carry all his life, for he did nearly lose his leg. And he was shot below his heart, which left his lungs so weakened that the illness we encountered on the ship did strike him badly. But in all, he was most fortunate. So many in those woods of Malplaquet did not survive.' And then he too fell silent.

They did not have far to walk before they reached the house – a stone-built, square-walled building huddled close against its neighbours, with its windows standing open to the warming air of spring.

'He may be sleeping,' warned the colonel as they entered, so Sophia kept behind him as he knocked upon the door to the front room. There was a brief word of reply, which she could barely hear, and then the colonel swung the door full open, motioning that she should step inside.

The room was dim, the curtains only partly drawn as though the daylight was not wanted here.

The man they'd come to see was up and standing at the window with his back to them, so that Sophia only saw his squared stance and his shoulders and the brown hair fastened back above the collar of his shirt. He wore no coat, just breeks and boots, and in the fine white shirt he stood there still and pale and like a ghost, the only thing of light in that dull room.

He spoke again, not looking round, his voice grown hoarser from the illness. 'Did ye see her? Was she well?'

'She will be now,' the colonel gently said, and stepping back retreated to the entry hall and closed the door behind him.

Sophia could not move from where she stood. Could not believe it.

Then he turned, a ghost no longer, but a breathing man. A living man, whose shadowed eyes grew brighter in the grip of hard emotion as he left the window and in two strides crossed to fold her in his arms, his touch as careful as it had been on their wedding night, as fierce as it had been at their last parting.

Still she could not move or speak, not even when he took her face in both his hands and brushed away her tears and drew a ragged breath himself, and in a voice she had not thought to hear again he said, 'I told ye I'd come back to ye.'

And then his mouth came down on hers and for a long time after that there were no words at all.

XXIII

The village of Malplaquet stood at the border of Flanders and France, with deep woods to the north and the south. On September 11th, the morning of battle, the French had been firmly dug into those woods and were waiting for first light, and for the attack of the massed Allied forces – the English and Germans and Dutch fighting now with the great Duke of Marlborough.

Dawn had come, and brought a dense mist rolling from the fields into the wood to make grey phantoms of the men who crouched there, waiting, weary from a lack of rations and a night of little sleep. The Allied armies used that mist to hide their movements; when it cleared they started firing, and a short while after that they gave the signal and began the fight in earnest, throwing everything they had against the wood.

It seemed to Moray there were four of them for every one of his own men. The air hung thick with smoke and screams and cannon-fire, the edges of the wood were set ablaze by the artillery, and men on both sides fell beneath the fury of the guns and flashing swords.

He fell himself at midday. The cut across his leg came first, and brought him to his knees so that he scarcely felt the pistol shot that tore him near his heart and knocked him down to lie in leaves and mud among the dying and the dead. He could not move. The pain within his chest was so consuming he could only breathe by concentrating, and although he willed his arms to find the strength to lift him, drag him, anything, they would not answer.

He could hear the sounds of struggle moving past him, leaving him behind – the clash of men and steel, the raw-voiced yells and rush of feet and sound of branches splintering, and further off the thunder on the ground that shook the forest as the cavalry advance of countless horses and their sabre-wielding riders started down upon the battlefield beyond.

And some time after that there came a silence that to Moray was more horrible than any sound of war, because it was not truly silence. In the dimness of the shattered wood, where smoke yet rolled across the trampled undergrowth and mingled with the smells of fire and blood, he heard the moans and anguished praying of the fallen. Some men prayed for life and some for death, in languages as varied as their uniforms – the Dutch and Germans and the Scots and French and English tangled side by side, for all men looked alike when they were dying.

To his left there lay a boy who had been dead before he fell and was released from fear and suffering, but on the ground to Moray's right a soldier in the colours of the Royal Irish regiment was trying now without success to roll upon his side, his grey face sweating with the effort.

Moray told him, low, 'Keep still.'

The words burnt fire within his chest, but somehow he found strength to roll his head to meet the stranger's wide, uncomprehending eyes.

'Keep still,' he said again. 'Ye'll bleed to death, and no one will be coming yet awhile.'

He saw the man's eyes calm, and gain their sense again. A man his own age, and a soldier like himself, for all that they were enemies. It was a trick of fate, thought Moray looking at their uniforms, that they had faced each other on opposing sides – his own brigade was Irish also, though it served the

French king and King James, and not Queen Anne.

The stranger lay his head back with a sigh. ''Twas useless trying, anyway. I've no more feeling in my legs. Are they yet there?'

Impassive, Moray angled his own gaze towards the bloodsoaked ground beneath the other's boots, and answered, 'Aye.''

The man's eyes closed a moment, either from the pain or in relief, and then he opened them again as if determined not to drift. 'You are a Scotsman, like myself. Why do you fight for France?'

There was a pause. Moray was not inclined to talk, but he himself could feel the deadly lure of drowsiness, and knew the conversation would help keep him conscious. Help him stay alive. He said, 'I fight for James.'

'For James.'

'Aye.'

'I have never met a Jacobite. I thought you all had horns.' The smile was faint, as though it hurt him, and he coughed. 'Where do you come from then, in Scotland?'

'Perthshire.'

'I am come from Ulster now, but I was born in Scotland, near Kirkcudbright in the Western Shires.'

A breeze had swept by Moray like the memory of a touch. He said, 'My wife is of the Western Shires.' He had not spoken yet to any person of his marriage, but from the glimpse he'd had of this man's wounds he knew that little harm could come of speaking now.

The other soldier in surprise asked, 'Is she Presbyterian?'

And Moray was not certain how Sophia would herself have met that question, she who claimed to have no faith yet prayed when no one else was watching, so he simply said, 'She is my wife.'

'I have no wife.' The other man was drifting once again. He shook himself and said, 'My brother did. He was a cooper in Kirkcudbright, and he has a widow and a son who live there still, though he himself did die before the summer. He was all the kin that I had left. If I die here, there will be none to mourn me.'

'There will be your nephew.'

'I have never met my nephew, nor his mother.' And the smile this time was sad enough that Moray felt a stirring of compassion for the man, enough to make him keep the other talking in the hope that it might somehow ease his suffering, if nothing more.

And so the two had lain there through the afternoon and on into the evening, holding death at bay by telling tales to one another of their boyhood days, and of their lives as soldiers, and though Moray had more often listened than he'd talked, he still had done his part. But in the end, as he'd already known, it was no use.

By nightfall there was no one left but him to face the darkness, and the screams that marked the killing and the plunder of the wounded by the soldiers yet alive. He lay as dead and felt the cold creep through him as he fought a battle with delirium. At times he thought he must be truly dead, and then he'd draw a deeper breath so that the pain would tell him otherwise. And once he closed his eyes and for that moment he was back again at Slains, beside Sophia, lying warm against her body in the bed. It was so real he felt her breathing, and he tried to hold her closer but the darkness pulled him back again, and shivering he woke.

Someone was coming.

He could hear the stealthy movement of their legs against the underbrush, and instantly he closed his eyes and made his breaths as shallow as he could. The steps went past him. Stopped. Returned.

And then somebody knelt and placed a hand against his throat.

A voice called out, 'This man is yet alive!'

A voice he recognised, and with it came a light so bright that Moray knew he must be dead. His eyes came open cautiously. The woods were still in darkness, but a torch was being held nearby, and by its light he clearly saw the man who bent above him, dark eyes clouded with concern.

The young king's face was pale and weary, and his own arm had been bandaged, but the pain that showed upon his features was not for himself. He leant in closer.

'Colonel Moray, can you hear me?'

It was just a dream, thought Moray, so he answered, 'Aye, Your Majesty.'

And smiling went to sleep.

He was aware of being carried, and a softer brightness and the taste of something bitter, and of gentle hands that cleaned his wounds and not-so-gentle hands that bound them, while he floated with the pain.

He woke to voices.

Or at least, he thought he woke, though when he heard the voices he was not so certain, for the first belonged to Colonel Graeme, who should not have been there. 'Aye, I'll see to it, Your Majesty.'

And the king, who could not possibly have been there, said,

'My mother will not soon forgive me if he were to die.'

'He will not die. He's half a Graeme, and we're not such easy men to kill.' A pause, and then, 'Your arm does bleed.'

'The devil take my arm!' There was a sound of movement, and when next the young king spoke his voice was changed, as though he'd turned away. 'Have not you seen the field? The woods? What is my arm compared to that? Compared to what this man has suffered for my family?'

Very quietly the colonel said, 'He'd suffer it again, and more, Your Majesty.'

'I will not have it. Not from him, nor anyone. No crown is worth what I have witnessed here at Malplaquet. What is a crown?' His words were harsh. 'A bit of metal set with stone, and by what right should I command a man to give his life that I may wear it?'

'By the right God gave ye when he made ye king.' The colonel said that calmly, stating fact. 'There's not a true Scot standing would not do whatever ye did ask, and for no other reason than ye are our king, and we do love ye for it. And 'tis not ourselves alone. I have been told your health was drunk afore the battle in the English camps as well, and they did take pride in your conduct on the battlefield the same as we did. Ye did lead the charge a dozen times upon that field, and I can promise ye, Your Majesty, there's none among your men would say ye had not earned the right to wear that crown.'

There was silence for a moment. Then more movement, as though both men had come closer to the bed.

The king remarked, 'If he does live, he will not fight again.'

'He'll find another way to serve ye.'

Moray heard no more than that, for he was sliding back into the darkness. When he surfaced next the pain within his chest was agony. He had to clench his teeth to keep from crying out.

'There, lad,' said Colonel Graeme, close beside him. Moray felt a cup pressed to his lips. He drank. The brandy burnt, but helped to take his focus from the effort of his breathing. He lay back again, and looked around the room. He did not know where they had taken him – it looked to be a private house or cottage, plainly furnished, with bare walls and floors and curtains of white lace that let the daylight through to touch the wooden chair where Colonel Graeme had been sitting with his feet propped on the bed – the dent still showed upon the blankets. Moray's gaze, disoriented, fell upon the red coat that was hanging from that chair, and he inhaled enough air to speak. 'Not mine.'

'What's that?' His uncle looked round, saw the coat, and turned back with a soothing nod. 'Oh aye, I ken it's not yours, lad. We took it off the soldier lying next to ye and used it as a blanket when we brought ye from the woods. Ye felt like ice, and that poor laddie had no further need of it.'

He knew that coat. Knew every button on it, he had looked at it so long. 'He was' – he drew in breath to force the words – 'a Scot. McClelland.'

'Fighting for the wrong side, from his coat. That's Royal Irish.' Colonel Graeme raised the brandy cup again, his wise eyes knowing. 'Fell to talking, did ye? Well, 'tis sometimes what does happen, though I'm fair surprised he had the wit to talk. Ye saw his legs?' And glancing down, he read the answer in his nephew's eyes. 'What did ye speak of?'

'Life. His life. He came from' – Christ, it hurt to talk – 'Kirkcudbright.'

'Oh, aye?' Colonel Graeme's tone held interest as he

glanced again at Moray's face. 'When I was last at Slains, I met a lass who came from near Kirkcudbright. Bonny lassie, so she was. Ye might have met her?'

Only Moray's eyes moved, locking silently upon his uncle's face as Colonel Graeme said, 'I took it on myself to teach her chess, while I was there. She did fair well at it, her only weakness being she did seek to guard her soldiers in the same way she did guard her king, and did not like to see them taken.' He was smiling faintly at the memory as he offered up the brandy one more time and said, 'Had I a lass like that, the very thought of her would make me fight to stay among the living.'

Moray meant to make reply, but he was drifting with the pain again and though he did not want to close his eyes he could not help it.

When he opened them the next time he at first thought he was dreaming that first day again, for there were both his uncle and the king in conversation by the window, with their backs toward the bed.

'Aye, he is much better now, Your Majesty,' said Colonel Graeme with a nod. 'I do believe we've brought him through the worst of it.'

The king was glad to hear it, and he said so. 'I do leave for Saint-Germain within the hour, and it will please me to have some good news to carry to my mother.'

Moray's voice was weaker than he wanted it, but when he called across to them they heard it, all the same. 'Your Majesty.'

The young king turned, and Moray saw it really was the king. 'Well, Colonel Moray,' he said, crossing to the bed. 'Are you in need of something?'

Speech still hurt him, but he braved it. 'Nothing but my sword.'

'You will not need that yet awhile.'

And Colonel Graeme came behind to put the point more bluntly. 'Lad, your leg was badly wounded and it never will come right again. Ye'll no more be a soldier.'

And he knew it. Though his mind might yet resist the truth, his body could not hide it. 'There are other ways to serve.' He winced as, rolling slightly to his side, he looked beyond his uncle to the king. 'I've not yet lost my eyes and ears, and both are yours if ye see fit to send me back where I can use them.'

The king looked down at Moray, and his youthful face belied the steady wisdom in his eyes. 'I thank you for your offer, Colonel, but till I am safely back in Scotland I cannot allow you to return there, with so great a price upon your head.'

'I do not speak of Scotland.' Moray winced again and had to wait a moment for the stabbing pain within his chest to pass, before he could go on. 'The man who fell beside me was an Ulsterman. We talked. I do remember all his stories, all the details of his life. He has no kin.' He fixed his gaze upon the king. 'I could become him for a time. Move among the Scots in Ulster. Let ye ken their thoughts and plans.'

He saw the thought take hold. The Irish were important to King James's cause, and knowing how the Irish Protestants were thinking would be valuable. The king said slowly, 'You would do this?'

'Aye. If it will help to speed ye home to Scotland.'

Colonel Graeme interrupted. 'Think, lad. Think, for this is not a move that should be lightly made. If ye would take this path, then none can learn ye are yet living. Till the king's return, lad, all your kin and all who love ye must believe John Moray died in that infernal wood, and that is what your mother and your brothers and your sisters will be told.' His grey eyes serious, he added, 'And your lass.'

The pain wrapped still more tightly round him, and it came not only from his wounds this time but from a deeper place within his chest, so each breath burnt. 'It is for her sake I would do this. So that we may one day be together.'

The king looked down in sympathy. 'I did not know you had a woman.'

Colonel Graeme, noticing that Moray had begun to fight against the darkness and was past the point of answering, looked down as well and asked permission of the pain-filled eyes before he turned towards the king and said, correcting him, 'He has a wife.'

The light within the room had altered with the passing of the afternoon, and it no longer reached the bed on which they lay. Sophia touched the black stone on its cord that rested now against the pulse of Moray's throat.

'Ye kept me safe.' His eyes were steady on her face. 'The thought of ye did keep me safe and living, these past months, just as my uncle said it would.'

She did not want to think about the past few months. She nestled close to him. 'Your uncle also said that it was by the queen's design that I was brought here to Kirkcudbright.'

'Aye. A great romantic, is Queen Mary. I was made to understand that when she learnt I had a wife, she thought it only right that I should have ye with me when I went to Ireland, although I do confess I see my uncle's hand in this, as well. He thought it very hard of me to leave you for so long alone.'

Sophia closed her eyes a moment, trying to decide how best to tell him. 'I was not alone.'

It was no easy thing to speak of Anna, but she did it, and he listened to her silently, and held her while she cried. And when she'd finished, he stayed silent for a moment longer, looking down at Anna's small curl tied with ribbon lying soft within his calloused hand.

Sophia asked, 'Can you forgive me?'

Moray closed his hand around the curl and brought his arm around Sophia, holding her so tightly that no force could have divided them. ''Tis I who should be asking that of you.' His voice was rough against her hair. 'Ye have done nothing, lass, that needs to be forgiven.' Then he kissed her very tenderly and eased his hold, and opened up his hand to look again at that dark curl that was the colour of his own.

Sophia watched him, and she sensed the struggle in his heart as reason sought to overcome the pain of knowing his own child might never know his face, that she must live so far away from him. So far from his protection.

'We could send for her,' Sophia said. 'Now that you are returned and are alive, she could come with us...'

'No.' The word was quiet, but she knew from hearing it how heavily it cost him. 'No, ye did right to leave her where she was. There will be danger still, in Ireland.' Regretfully, he closed his hand upon the little curl of hair, then found a smile and trailed his knuckles softly down Sophia's cheek. 'I have no right to take ye with me either, but it seems I've grown to be a selfish man and cannot let ye go.'

She lay warm in his embrace. 'You will not have to.'

'Well, I will for this first while,' he conceded, 'else the fine upstanding people of your house may be offended.'

She'd forgotten them; forgotten that the Kerrs would soon be home from kirk to find she was not there. 'But John—'

He took her face in both his hands and stopped her protest with a kiss of promise. 'Wait a few days more, and then I will be well enough to come and pay a call, and I can court ye then in public.' In his eyes she saw a glint of his old humour, gently teasing. 'Will ye wed me for a second time, or have ye had a chance to see the folly of your choice?'

And it was she this time who kissed him in her turn so that he would not doubt her answer. And she felt his smile against her lips, and in that moment she believed she understood at last what Colonel Graeme had been saying on that day when they had stood together at the great bow window of the drawing room at Slains, and gazed together at the winter sea. For now she knew he had been right – the fields might fall to fallow and the birds might stop their song awhile; the growing things might die and lie in silence under snow, while through it all the cold sea wore its face of storms and death and sunken hopes...and yet unseen beneath the waves a warmer current ran that, in its time, would bring the spring.

It might be that the king would come, and it might be that he would not. It scarcely mattered to her now, for she had Moray back. He'd promised he'd return to her, and so he had. He'd promised her that one day she would stand upon a ship's deck, and she knew that she would do that too, and he would be beside her. And wherever that ship took them, and however far it carried them from Scotland and from Slains, she would be bound to both by memory.

She would see in dreams the dark red castle walls that rose so proudly from the cliffs, and hear the roaring of the sea below her tower chamber, and Kirsty's bright voice calling in the morning to awaken her. She'd feel the warming sunlight spilling through the windows of the corner sewing room where she had sat so often with the countess, and the closer warmth of horses dozing upright in their stalls while Hugo kept his faithful watch beside the stable door.

She would no more forget these things than Slains itself would lose its memory of herself and Moray, for she knew that they had left their imprint there as well, and left it deep enough that one day Anna, walking on the beach, might hear the windborne echo of their laughter from the dunes, and glimpse their shadows on the shore, and wonder at the lovers who had left such ghosts behind. She would know little else except that they'd been happy. And in truth, Sophia thought, there would be nothing else to know.

Whatever might become of them, she knew that there was nothing that could rob them of that happiness. For they had lived their winter, and the spring had finally come.

Chapter Nineteen

It was cold, but in the shelter of the dunes there was no wind, and for an hour I sat and watched the sunrise. It was beautiful – the first small glint of gold that split the dark clouds to the east above the water, growing steadily until the sky caught fire and flamed to brilliance for a breathless moment.

From here on the beach I could not see the walls of Slains, but I imagined them. I roofed the castle in my mind and gave it life again, and saw a couple strolling far off on the pathways of the garden, and the countess coming down the steps to greet her latest visitors who'd just arrived on horseback, riding hard to bring the hopeful word from France.

And if I turned my head I saw the phantom of a running sail against the grey horizon, as I'd seen so often in my childhood from a different shore. And now I understood why I had seen it, and why even now I felt the strange pull of the sea that drew me like an outstretched hand and called me back when I had been too long away.

My father had been right: the sea was in my blood, and had been put there by Sophia's thoughts, her memories, all that she had sent to travel down through time to me. I felt the bond between us as I sat and watched the sunrise fade to morning light above the sea that seemed now to be casting off its winter face, the long waves rolling in to dance more lightly on the sand.

I sometimes felt a sadness when I'd reached the ending of a book, and had to bid the characters goodbye. But I could find no sadness in this story's end, and I knew Jane would find none either, and be pleased with it, as I was. And that sense of pleasure stayed with me as, finally giving in to the demands of my half-frozen body, I got up and slowly walked across the beach and up the path to where my cottage waited on the hill.

It had looked glad to see me yesterday when I'd arrived back from Kirkcudbright, and I felt the same sense now of welcome when I came in through the door to find the Aga warmly burning and the papers spilling over on the table where I'd spent the long night writing. Though I knew I'd soon be moving down to Aberdeen to Graham's house – *our* house, he had corrected me – I'd still arranged with Jimmy for the cottage to be here for us to use when we came down weekends. I'd come to think of it as mine, and while I would have gone with Graham anywhere, just as Sophia went to follow Moray, I felt comfort in the knowledge that I didn't have to lose my views of Slains and of the sea.

And Graham seemed to understand my feelings, even though he didn't know the reason for them, and he maybe never would. I hadn't yet decided if I'd tell him what had happened to me here, for I felt certain if I did he'd only laugh and kiss my face and call me crazy.

Bad enough I'd have to tell my father that we might not be

McClellands after all, but Morays. It was too early in the morning yet to place a call to Canada, he'd still be fast asleep, but I would have to do it sometime. He would read it in the book when it came out and be suspicious, and although it wasn't something I could prove I knew him well enough to know that once he'd got his mind around the possibility, he'd do his best to find his own proof. He had always loved a challenge, had my father. He'd be hunting through the records of the Royal Irish Regiment, and tracking down descendants of the male line of the Abercairney Morays to compare their DNA with his.

I smiled faintly as I filled the kettle for my morning coffee, thinking that if nothing else, my father might uncover some new relatives a little less eccentric than the ones we had – Ross McClelland exempted, of course. I was keeping Ross, no matter what.

He'd seen me to the station yesterday, and sent me off with homemade fudge that I'd forgotten until now. Remembering, I rummaged in my suitcase, which was sitting where I'd dropped it just inside the door when I'd come in. I found the bag that held the fudge, and as I tugged it out the little auction catalogue that Ross had given me came with it, so I took it, too. I hadn't had a chance to read it yet, to see what heirlooms our New York McClellands would be selling off this time. Nothing too terrible, obviously, or else my father would have called me to complain about it.

Waiting while my kettle boiled, I took a bite of fudge and turned the pages of the catalogue. There wasn't much. A table and a mirror, and two miniature portraits of McClellands from a different family tree branch than our own, and some assorted jewellery: rings, a necklace of pink pearls, a brooch...

I paused, and felt a chill chase up my spine as though a sudden wind had struck between my shoulder blades and lifted all the hair along my neck. Forgetting both the kettle and the fudge, I moved to lean against the counter for support as I looked closely at the picture of the brooch.

It was a simple thing – a small but heavy square of silver with a red stone at its centre.

No, I thought. Not possible. But there it was. Beneath the photograph, a brief description of the item stated that, in the opinion of the jeweller who'd appraised it, this appeared to be an old ring that had been made over as a brooch, most likely in the later Georgian period.

I traced the outline, plain and square, of Moray's ring, and thought of all the times that I had seen it in my mind while I'd been writing, all the times I'd almost felt its weight against my own chest, all the times I'd wondered what had happened to it.

Now I knew.

She'd kept it, and the years had sent it travelling down through the family until no one could remember where it came from, who had worn it, what it meant. It might have passed out of our family altogether and been sold to strangers, if I had not come to Slains.

But I had come. The sea, the shore, the castle walls had called to me, and I had come.

I touched the picture of the brooch with fingers that shook slightly, because Moray's ring, too, had a voice – a quiet but insistent voice that called to me across a wider sea, and when I heard it there was no doubt left within my mind what I was meant to do.

* * *

Graham was still up and reading when I came to bed. He'd put on one of the small electric heaters to take the chill out of the room, but it was no match for the storm winds blowing strongly off the sea, so strongly that I'd spent the evening worrying the phone lines would go down and I would miss my scheduled call from New York City. But I hadn't.

Graham looked up from his book as I came in the room. 'Did ye get it?'

But he knew the answer from my smile as I climbed shivering beneath the covers. 'Yes.' I didn't bother saying what I'd paid for it, because it didn't matter. I had known when I'd arranged to bid by telephone tonight at auction that I wasn't going to stop until I got the brooch. The ring. And in the end there hadn't been that many people bidding for it, only two besides myself, and they had lacked my private motivation. To them, it had been nothing more than jewellery, but to me it was a piece of Moray and Sophia that I could hold in my hand, and keep with me for always, to remember them.

'What's that you're reading?' I asked Graham, and he turned the cover round to show me.

'Dryden's plays. The one that you had marked,' he said. 'The Merlin one. Where did you dig this up?'

'Dr Weir loaned it to me.' I'd been at Dr Weir's for tea two days ago, and seen the book of Dryden on his shelf – a modern volume, not an old one, but I'd asked about it anyway, and he had known the play I meant.

'Except it was renamed,' he'd said. 'Yes, this is what you're after, here. *Merlin, or the British Enchanter.*'

Why Dryden had changed the play's title from Arthur to

Merlin I couldn't imagine, but it *was* the same play. I'd read
the lines with the warm sense of recognition that I felt when
picking up a favourite novel.

Graham said, 'I'm nearly at the end. King Arthur's just been
reunited with his Emmeline.' He quoted smoothly from the
page: '"At length, at length, I have thee in my Arms; Tho' our
Malevolent Stars have struggled hard, And held us long
asunder". Sounds like us,' he said, and setting down the book
he switched the lamp off, rolling over while I snuggled close
against him in the dark.

It sounded more like someone else, to me. I smiled. 'We
didn't have any malevolent stars.'

'Well, maybe not, no. Only Stuie.'

He was drifting, I could hear it in his voice. He always fell
asleep as easily as some great lazing cat, he only had to close
his eyes and moments later he'd be gone, while my own mind
kept on whirring round with scattered thoughts and images.

I felt his breathing slow against my neck, the heavy warmth
of him behind me like a shield to block the fierceness of the
storm that even now seemed bent on shaking its way through
the windows of the cottage. I was lying there and thinking
when I heard the click. At first I didn't realise what had
happened, till I saw the glow of the electric heater dying. 'Oh,
no. The power's out. The storm—'

'It's not the storm,' said Graham. 'Just the meter. It was low
this afternoon, I meant to fix it for you. Sorry.'

'Well, I'll fix it now.'

But Graham held more tightly to me. 'Let it be,' he
mumbled, low, against my shoulder. 'We'll be warm enough.'

My eyes closed and I started drifting, too. Until I realised
what he'd said.

I was awake again, and staring. 'Graham?'

But he was already sleeping deeply, and he didn't hear.

It might be just coincidence, I thought, that he had twice now used the same words that I'd written in my book, the words that Moray had once spoken to Sophia. And Moray only looked like him because I'd made him look like him...I *had* made Moray look like Graham, hadn't I? It couldn't be that Moray had in fact had eyes the colour of the winter sea, the same as Graham's eyes, and Graham's mother's eyes...

My mother's family goes a long way back here, he had told me.

And an image crossed my own mind of a little girl with darkly curling hair who long ago had run with outstretched arms along the beach. A girl who had grown up here and presumably had married and had children of her own. Had anybody ever traced the line of Graham's family tree, I wondered? And if I tried to myself, would I find it included a fisherman's family who'd lived in a cottage just north of the Bullers of Buchan?

That, too, seemed impossible. Too like a novel itself to be true. But still I saw that little girl at play along the shore. The wind rose swirling at my window with a voice that was familiar and again I heard Sophia saying, as I'd heard her say my first day in this cottage, that her heart was held forever by this place. And I could hear the countess answering, 'But leave whatever part of it you will with us at Slains, and I will care for it. And by God's grace I may yet live to see the day it draws you home.'

As I lay listening to Graham's steady breathing in the darkness, I could almost feel that tiny missing fragment of Sophia's heart rejoin my own and make it whole. Behind me,

Graham shifted as though he had felt it, too. And then his arm came round me, solid, safe, and drew me firmly back against the shelter of his chest, and I felt peace, and turned my face against the pillow, and I slept.

About the Characters

Any work of historical fiction relies on real people. With very few exceptions – little Anna, and the servants at Slains, and Sophia – the characters from the eighteenth-century story are real, and their actions are bound by the limits of what truly happened.

Not that finding out what truly happened in the '08 is an easy thing. All sides, for their own purposes, tried hard to cover up the truth, and even what was written by the people who lived through it can't be trusted. I'm indebted to John S Gibson's masterfully succinct history of events surrounding the invasion, *Playing the Scottish Card: The Franco-Jacobite Invasion of 1708*, the book that first inspired me to write about the period, and to Colonel Nathaniel Hooke's wonderfully detailed memoir of the incident, published in 1760 as *The Secret History of Colonel Hooke's Negotiations in Scotland, in Favour of the Pretender*. I was fortunate enough to find an original copy of Hooke's account that not only became one of the treasures of my home library, but also proved invaluable in sorting out the movements of my characters.

I've tried, wherever possible, to seek out the best evidence – the letters and the transcripts of the time. If an account was written down of what was said between two people, then I've had them say the same thing in my book. If Captain Gordon's ship was in Leith harbour on a certain day, I've put him there. I've used this rule with even minor characters: Mr Hall's* visits to Slains on behalf of the Duke of Hamilton are a matter of fact, as is Mr Malcolm's part in the invasion, and his going into hiding when it failed.

That said, I *have* taken a couple of liberties. For all the research I've done on John Moray, I don't know for certain that he was at Malplaquet. But since the only reference to his death that I have found fits with the date of Malplaquet, and since it helped my plot to have him there, I put him on that battlefield, where in the woods the Royal Irish Regiment in fact did meet and fight the Irish Regiment that fought for France and James.

And while it's also a recorded fact that Captain Gordon captured the *Salisbury* during the invasion, and that he was the only British captain in the fight to claim a French ship as his prize, there's also little doubt that Gordon was a Jacobite. And since no one but Gordon knows exactly why he took that ship, I gave him an excuse that seemed to fit the man as I had come to know him.

His Jacobite loyalties lasted the rest of his life. When Queen Anne died in 1714 and the first Hanoverian king, George I, was brought over to sit on the British throne, Gordon refused to take the oath of allegiance, and as a result was dismissed. He promptly accepted a commission in the Russian navy of Tsar Peter the Great, where he served with distinction and rose to be an admiral and the Governor of Kronstadt.

*In *Playing the Scottish Card*, Gibson states 'Mr Hall' was a codename for one Father Carnegy.

Throughout his time in Russia he continued to promote the Jacobite cause, and kept up a correspondence with King James and his supporters. When he died in the spring of 1741, a wealthy and respected man, his obituary in *The Gentleman's Magazine* stated he had always been 'a true Friend to his Countrymen.'

The Duke of Hamilton was not to be so fortunate. By 1711 his ambition was beginning to bear fruit – he'd been raised to the British peerage by Queen Anne, and had just been appointed ambassador to France. But before he could travel to Paris to take up his post, his longstanding dispute with a rival, Lord Mohun, flared into a duel. The two men met at dawn in Hyde Park, London, one November morning. Both men drew their swords, and in the fight that followed both were killed. The incident caused quite a scandal in its day, and the details of what really happened and why have been debated ever since. In death, as in life, he defies all attempts at an easy analysis.

As for Moray's uncle, Colonel Patrick Graeme, it is not difficult to trace his early life in Scotland, when he served as Captain of the Edinburgh Town Guard before his conscience made him take up arms for old King James and follow James to France in exile. But I haven't yet discovered how he spent his later years, after the failed invasion in '08. However, since I'm sure his nature would have kept him near the action, I am hopeful that I'll someday come across a letter or a document that shines a light on his adventures in that time before his death in August, 1720.

More light, too, is needed on Anne Drummond, Countess of Erroll, who becomes all but invisible in the years following the '08 – no easy task for a woman of such forceful character.

Her son Charles, 13th Earl of Erroll, continued to fight for the rights of his countrymen after the Union which he had so passionately opposed. Though his position as Lord High Constable of Scotland meant he was expected to take part in the coronation of George I, he refused to attend the ceremony. He died not long after, in 1717, at the age of 40, unmarried and childless, the last male of his line. His title passed to his sister Mary who, like all the Countesses of Erroll, was a woman of great courage and a fierce supporter of the Stewart cause.

Nathaniel Hooke, who had put so much time and effort into bringing about the invasion of 1708, was deeply disappointed by its failure, and highly critical of the French commander who had led it. Though he had a long and successful career in the diplomatic service of France, he returned to his memories of the '08 in his later years, and with the help of his nephew began compiling his various papers and journals relating to the adventure. He died in 1738, before the task was completed, and when his son attempted to sell the papers two years later an officer of the French court arrived instead to confiscate them. Those papers that were taken were presumably destroyed, and lost to history. But two packets of documents in Hooke's nephew's handwriting had escaped the attention of the French official, who luckily for us had no idea they contained Hooke's own account of his negotiations for the planned invasion.

Of such small unexpected accidents is history made.

And no one was the victim of more accidents than young James Stewart – by his birthright James VIII of Scotland and III of England. There is some reason to suspect that his half-sister Queen Anne was indeed giving serious thought to naming James her heir, and in the last years of her reign there appears to have been a great deal of behind-the-scenes negotiating going on. In the midst of this, the war of the Spanish succession was ended by the Treaty of Utrecht, which among its terms demanded that Louis XIV expel James from France. James went willingly, moving his court to Lorraine where he promptly gave all of his Protestant servants the freedom to worship in their own faith, something he hadn't been able to do when his court had been bound by French laws.

But James was still a Catholic, and when Queen Anne died in 1714 it was the Protestant contender, George I, who won the crown.

The reply was another Jacobite rising in 1715, and although this time James did manage to land safely in Scotland, just north of Slains at Peterhead, the golden opportunity of 1708 had passed. The western Presbyterians who had been so prepared in the '08 to rise for James this time opposed him. The rebellion failed. James retreated to Lorraine, but King Louis XIV had died and without the old king to console and support him James found his French neighbours unwelcoming, so he moved his court again, at first to Avignon, and finally Rome.

Two more attempts to gain his throne involving the help of the Swedes and the Spanish came to nothing, and even James's marriage in 1719 to the Princess Maria Clementina proved less than successful. After six years, she left him and retired to a convent, though not before she gave him sons. The elder of these, Charles Edward, grew to be that 'Bonnie Prince' whose handsome face and charming ways would rouse the Scottish Jacobites to take up arms again and march beside him twenty-five years later...but that is another story, and too sad to tell.

I much prefer to think of James VIII and III in his old age in Rome, perhaps half-dozing in the sunshine of a warm Italian afternoon, and dreaming of the northern coast of Scotland and the proud red walls of Slains as he'd once seen them from the sea, and of the crown that must have, for that moment, seemed so nearly within reach.

A Note of Thanks

When doing my research, like most writers, I must depend on the kindness of strangers, and in Cruden Bay I was spoilt by kindness. So many people, from the shopkeepers to people I passed on the street, gave me friendly advice and assistance, that even if I'd learnt their names I doubt I'd have the space to list them here!

I'm grateful above all to Joyce, Stuart and Alison Warrander of the St Olaf Hotel, where I stayed, who made sure that my room (No. 4) had a view of both Slains and the sea, so that I could imagine what Carrie was seeing. The Warranders and their staff were incredibly helpful to me, as were their regulars in the hotel's public bar, who cheerfully answered my questions and even suggested the perfect place for me to put Carrie's cottage.

My thanks also to all the drivers of Elaine's Taxis who ferried me around, and to Elaine herself who took good care of me and even switched the meter off one afternoon to help me hunt down some of my elusive settings.

I'm also grateful to the landlord and staff of the Kilmarnock Arms, and to local historian and fellow author Mrs Margaret Aitken and her husband and daughter, who were kind enough to have me in to tea and share their knowledge of the history of the area.

I'm indebted to both Brenda Murray and Rhoda Buchan of the Cruden Bay Library, who searched out articles and books for me and found me details I could not have found without their help.

I've tried to repay all this kindness by getting my facts right. I hope I've succeeded, and that you'll forgive me if I've slipped up anywhere.

Finally, I owe thanks to Jane, for her years of encouragement, and to her family, for welcoming me to Glendoick.